MW01135331

TWISTED
THREADS

Kaylin McFarren

THREADS SERIES—Book #4
Distributed by:
Creative Edge Publishing LLC
8440 NE Alderwood Road, Suite A
Portland, OR 97220

Copyright October 2017 by Linda Yoshida
Cover Artist: Amanda Tomo Yoshida
Editor: Jodi Henley

ISBN-10: 1975921356
ISBN-13: 9781975921354
Library of Congress Control Number: 2017914918
CreateSpace Independent Publishing Platform
North Charleston, South Carolina

Praise for Kaylin McFarren's Threads Series

Severed Threads—Book #1

With plenty at stake—erotic chemistry, dastardly villains, a lost relic, an unusual setting, and a touch of the supernatural—this indie novel could stand on any romance publisher's shelf. The full package of thrills and romance.

—*Kirkus Reviews*

Crisp writing and sparkling dialogue that will hold the interest of any reader who enjoys a good mystery story that's well told.
—Mark Garber, president, *Portland Tribune & Community Newspapers*

I highly recommend this story for people who enjoy romance and suspense. Kaylin McFarren will not let you down! I look forward to future stories in this series.

—Paige Lovitt, Reader Views, *Chicago Sun Times*

Buried Threads—Book #2

The many levels of this story will engross readers into the world of the Japanese syndicate, a Buddhist monk, and the American couple, while they quickly read to a satisfying conclusion, absorbing the culture the story is set in along the way.

—*San Francisco Book Review*

Buried Threads, an erotic thriller, combines the action and adventure found in a Clive Cussler novel, the plotting and romance of Danielle Steel's books, and the erotic energy and supernatural elements of a work by Shayla Black.

—Lee Gooden, *Foreword Review/Clarion Reviews*

More than a murder mystery, [*Buried Threads*] mingles a treasure hunt, an international race against time, a dark prophecy, Japanese culture, erotic encounters, and a clever killer's modus operandi into a story that just won't quit.

—Diane Donovan, *Midwest Book Review*

Banished Threads—Book #3

As with *Severed Threads* and *Buried Threads*, book three closes on a cliffhanger—one that indubitably will keep readers on edge. Well written and absolutely enthralling, *Banished Threads* is a wonderful addition to McFarren's award-winning series!

—Anita Lock, *Pacific Book Review*

This intricate escapade is as carnal as it is cerebral. If you're into vivacious prose and bodice-heaving melodrama, this just may be your cup of tea.

—Joe Kilgore, *The US Review of Books*

Family secrets, engaging characters, the heat of romance, and a standout suspense plot with a twisty, surprise ending make *Banished Threads* a must-read addition to McFarren's popular Threads series.

—*Chanticleer Book Reviews*

Twisted Threads—Book #4

A sexy mystery that brings the timeless themes of murder, revenge and family loyalty to the high seas. A great series for fans of romantic suspense.

—Bella Wright, *BestThrillers.com*

Kaylin McFarren has written a novel with a mix of intrigue, romance and action, resulting in a story for readers wanting adventure and love all in one exhilarating book.

—Ella Vincent, *Pacific Book Review*

Followers of McFarren's Threads series will be thrilled, and readers of this divertingly different, first-class murder mystery will be too.

—Angela Fox, Publisher, *Clackamas Review/Oregon City News*

The layers of deliciousness never end, and the seamless writing that incorporates multiple genres into one engrossing story truly provides non-stop action and entertainment for all tastes!

—Sheri Hoyte, *Reader Views*

An intelligent crime thriller infused with thwarted love and desperate desires, *Twisted Threads* makes a worthy new companion to McFarren's earlier creations—*Severed Threads, Buried Thread,* and *Banished Threads.*

—Barbara Bamberger Scott, Editor, *A Women's Write*

A tantalizing glimpse into a secret world of desire. Dive deep into the layers of this intoxicating blend of twisted pleasure and intricate mystery. Edgy, fierce, and undeniably stimulating.

— Alicia Tomelloso, *San Francisco Book Review*

CONTENTS

The Death Ship

A silent being filled with hate
Crossed oceans in a bitter state.
Spied a scourge in Everglades port,
Contrived a plan—the wicked sort.
The only way to find relief?
Destroy the vicious, heartless thief.

Justice was served at dinnertime,
With no one near to see the crime.
The dour man lurched, his fate was sealed,
Disposed at sea—his death concealed.
Though retribution was a need,
It came by way of evil deed.

The absent beast was soon dismissed,
Except by the recidivist.
Questions were asked, no clues were chased,
His bags were gone—his name erased.
The nefarious soul remained consumed,
The ship sailed on, routine resumed.

Revenge the price for freedom bought,
Arrived in time to stir the plot.
Two doors slammed shut, a blade dropped fast,
Shipmates stood by—their mouths aghast.

A headless corpse bled on the floor,
While villains planned to kill once more.

The ship's crew masked their growing fears,
As mounting deaths slowed moving gears.
From steel-lined lift to ocean deep,
Lives were lost—yet few would weep.
For who could love a blackguard's heart,
Except a heinous counterpart.

The sullen riders sought to blame,
All trapped inside a villain's game.
Was there a demon on this craft?
Starboard, port, bow—or on the aft?
The ship of fools sailed aimlessly,
While hooded death steered 'cross the sea.

—Kaylin McFarren

AUTHOR'S NOTE

The first thing that dawned on me after reviewing my completed manuscript for *Twisted Threads* was how truly twisted it is when compared to traditional modern literature. While thousands of novels on store shelves ooze with poetic phrases, chest-thumping warriors, and earth-shattering revelations, this book was written purely as a form of entertainment—a mind-bending thrill ride, taking readers on a journey they've never experienced before. In other words, while being pulled into the story, there's no way of knowing where the next rise will occur, how many twists will happen, or how far the drops will go.

The characters within my stories are credible, compelling, maligning, three-dimensional beings who are about as flawed, troubled, and contradictory as the written word allows. This makes for some wonderful conflicts, humorous interactions, dubious villains, and eccentric heroines while testing the boundaries of reality. In addition, my favorite practice when writing a novel is to see how many story lines I'm capable of weaving together in order to create the fabric of an interesting, complex drama. In the process of developing a series of subplots, it has become a huge undertaking to fill every hole created while producing a well-balanced, frolicking adventure. But the greatest challenge in writing a series in this manner is drawing on the story lines of the secondary stringers—those minor characters who have remarkable tales to share but have been, thus far, limited to cameo roles in the ever-evolving Threads series and are now being given a voice to be reckoned with and, I hope, remembered. —Kaylin

For the women in our family who make my life whole and brighten the world with their smiles: Kristina McMorris, Erika Yoshida and Amanda Yoshida. You are and always will be my greatest accomplishment!

For my amazing friends: Jody and Terry Smoke, Michelle Guthrie, Judi Swift, Madi Deotsch, Staci Sigala, Tami Arashiro and Chuck Sigmon –who look after me, offer endless support, make me laugh, overlook my failings, and provide great shoulders to cry on. Life would be empty without you.

And, of course, for my dear husband Junki, who has taught me the true meaning of affection, hope and happiness…and how to be patient when all else fails. I'll love you forever, my darling.

We cannot change the cards
we are dealt,
just how we play the hand.

—Randy Pausch

PROLOGUE

The watcher boarded a cruise ship in Fort Lauderdale, Florida, with a full stomach and renewed appetite for vengeance. Strength and confidence had been gained over the last year, not by murdering wrongdoers or controlling them, but by using their weaknesses against them and reveling in their self-destruction. All of this was done by secretly encouraging the overindulgence of tantalizing depravities, giving credence to rumors of their wickedness. Whether it was drugs, prostitution, or sexual perversion, there would always be a price to pay and a contributing factor to ensure their speedy demise.

The interest in power for the sake of power did not exist for the watcher, unlike the doctors who had sought to control every aspect, every action...every thought. But the interest in winning the game remained, because by winning, the possibility of eliminating old enemies was reinforced. Their extermination would provide the opportunity to wipe the smirch from one's name—from the poor, oppressed being who dwelled deep inside, longing for vindication.

This had become the watcher's passion, almost a monomania. Pessimism had taken hold in recent years, however, and the watcher had scorned to hesitate at means. Ends only were vital. Sloughing off the zest for vengeance upon former enemies had become an unavoidable necessity. Work for the sake of survival, constant physical activity, the grinding necessity for normality—these were the chief things that kept the watcher occupied.

If fate delivered as the London travel agency had promised, however, the villains would take the bait for a free Caribbean vacation, complete with an upgraded suite, onboard vouchers, and enticing shore excursions. It was the fourth and final attempt to draw them into the watcher's playing field, away from the safety of electronic gates, security guards, and nosy neighbors on their nightly walks with their nasty barking dogs. Every hard-earned dollar would be worth the aches and pains endured if the greedy, self-serving bastards stepped onto this ship with the rest of the arriving passengers. Then nothing would stop the watcher from delivering long-overdue justice.

Not even the captain.

1

KILLING TIME

Blood streamed down the side of Akira Sato's face at an alarming rate, mixing bright red against the white porcelain tub. As the showerhead splayed hot water over her body, she watched it with strange fascination, circling and disappearing through tiny holes in the drain. She picked up a white washcloth and mindlessly scrubbed against her narrow waist until her skin turned bright pink. Then she lowered the coarse cloth and rubbed longer than usual at the triangle of black hair between her legs and upper thighs, stopping only when it became painful. At least on the outside she felt cleaner, but inside was a different matter.

The consequences of her actions could not be remedied, nor could they be wiped away. Yet despite her resolve for this justified killing, she remained lost in a sea of hopelessness—incapable of seeing a way out.

Then why are you still here? Pick up your sword and end it now. The words echoed in her mind, taunting and teasing. She didn't care about anything—or anyone. Why should she? Mitsui had insisted all ties be cut with the people she had once loved, including the Buddhist monk she might have married.

She poured a generous amount of shampoo into the palm of her hand and lathered her long black hair, gingerly touching the wound her victim had inflicted. The gash in her scalp would disappear in due time, just like her other scars. But the bloody slaughter in the living room had left a horrible mess and would need to be addressed before she left the house.

After thoroughly rinsing her hair, she worked on her face with the bar of lavender soap, removing the black eyeliner, blue eye shadow, and whorish red lipstick she had applied for Kurosaki's benefit. It wasn't fair by any means, but there was no going back to the naive *geiko* she had been. With eight deaths to atone for in her afterlife, she was cursed in both worlds and simply waiting to die at the hands of another assassin. She squeezed her eyes shut and pressed her back against the cold white tile, hugging herself as water washed away her tears.

She heard a muffled sound in the next room and turned off the water. After easing the shower door open, she strained her ears and heard nothing, but her instincts told her otherwise. She stepped onto the bamboo grate covering the stone floor and grabbed the katana sword resting against the wall. The sound of someone rapidly approaching increased her heart rate. Her right hand shook involuntarily, yet she managed to remain calm. The bathroom door flew open suddenly, exposing two members of Kurosaki's gang.

The first man stared at her, snarling. "You murder a man in his home and have the nerve to use his shower? What kind of monster are you?" He reached for her arm while the second man stood back watching—his coal-black eyes piercing her skull.

"The worst kind," Akira spat. She drew her sword with lightning speed, beheading the first one with a one-handed horizontal cut. Blood sprayed over the mirror above the sink. She dropped her sheath and held the sword in front of her with both hands. The second man's face paled, and his jaw slacked. He remained motionless for endless seconds before charging at Akira with a knife stretched out before him. With one swift movement, she raised her sword above her head and brought it down hard and fast across his neck. She pulled the blade back, sending blood spraying across her face.

Another body fell to the floor.

Akira could feel sweat gathering at the base of her spine. She wiped her eyes with her forearm to clear her vision. Tears threatened to break loose and destroy the fortification she'd built.

The voice was back in her head, moving her forward. Keeping her from crumpling into a pitiful mess. *Don't be a fool. Finish the job you were sent here to do.*

She found two capsules in the outside pocket of her bag and popped them into her mouth. It took nearly a minute for the numbing effects to take hold. Then she set to work dragging bodies from the house and dropping them into the pit she had found in the woods. When she was finished, she stepped into the shower to wash the dirt and blood off a second time. After cleaning the bathroom floor and walls and scrubbing the living room thoroughly, she dumped all the evidence into the pit outside and set everything ablaze with a match and a bottle of Château Guiraud. Her only salvation rested in the fact that Kurosaki's nearest neighbor lived too far away to witness the gruesome scene and strange smell filling the air.

A cool breeze touched her skin. *Too* cool. She looked down at herself and was instantly reminded of her nudity, which she had forgotten with the work she'd undertaken. A nervous laugh escaped her lips, and once more she found herself questioning her sanity.

2

NEW ASSIGNMENT

Gravel crunched under the tires of a rapidly approaching car, sending Akira scurrying to the house. She secured the door behind her and pulled on her clothes. Then she peered through the glass panel in the entry. With her sheathed sword at her side, she waited for an intruder to take shape. Seconds ticked by as the dust settled. Then the car door opened. Black boots appeared below a pair of faded black jeans. They were topped with a red T-shirt, half covered with wavy black hair. A huge wave of relief washed over Akira when she spied a face. It was Yuki Ota—Mitsui's daughter-in-law—coming here to assist with the aftermath of her mission. However, as usual, her timing was way off.

Anger smoldered in Akira's heart. She opened the door and called out, "What took you so long?"

Yuki shrugged a shoulder. "I had some important matters to take care of tonight."

Akira tossed her head haughtily. "More important than helping me?"

Yuki curled her full lips in disdain. "Have you already forgotten? I protected you from Mitsui-san when no one else would."

Of course, Yuki was right. If not for her intervention, the gang lord's men would have made short work of Akira after discovering the threat she had made on Mitsui's life. But reaffirming that knowledge didn't wipe away the extreme measures she'd taken to hide her murders.

"Maybe you should have left me to die."

"Stop feeling sorry for yourself," Yuki snapped. "At least you don't have to kiss up to Mitsui-san."

Akira handed her a baggie containing "tokens" from her last job—personal items to confirm the deaths of the men in the burn pile. Yuki turned it over, studying the silver lapel pin and gold chain necklace Akira had lifted from Kurosaki's men before dragging them outside. "Oh, almost forgot this." She gave her the silver dollar Kurosaki had been rolling with his knuckles. "It's interesting what people place value in."

Yuki studied it for a few seconds before tucking it into the back pocket of her jeans. Then she slid into the driver's seat of her black Lexus and waited. Akira climbed in the passenger side and slammed the car door behind her, anxious to disappear.

"I have great news for you," Yuki told her as she turned over the engine.

Anger trickled away and left her head throbbing. She touched her scalp again. It was tender, and she noticed a trace of blood on her fingertips. "Let me guess. Mitsui-san's leaving Japan for good, and I never have to see him again."

Yuki laughed. "Sometimes I wish that too." She tied her unruly hair in a knot and secured it with a red lacquered chopstick. Then she grabbed the steering wheel and stepped on the gas, sending gravel flying.

"So what kind of news do you have?" Akira watched Yuki's profile, testing her patience.

"He wants you to take down another murderer. A British gallery owner cruising in the Caribbean."

Akira huffed. "And you consider that great news?"

Yuki glanced at her. "Take care of this job, and your obligation to Mitsui-san ends. He's given permission for you to start your life over anywhere you choose. Just as long as it's not in Japan."

Akira took a deep breath and rubbed her palms on her skirt. Where would she go? What would she do? Like most girls in Japan, her dreams of being famous began at a young age. She studied harder and longer than all the maikos in her family home, excelling in music, dance, social graces, and international languages. As the seasons changed in Gion, she matured in her abilities and ultimately earned the respect of everyone around her. Yet she lived a sheltered life as a geiko—always being told where to go, what to do, what to say. After being forced by Mitsui-san to leave her profession, she never considered what freedom would mean—away from his control and the only home she had known.

Yuki turned to her. "I assume that's what you were hoping for."

Akira nodded. The scooped collar on Yuki's red shirt revealed the three gold stars tattooed on her neck, matching the ones on Akira's hip. They were a constant reminder of their commitment to the Zakura-kai, Japan's notorious yakuza family. They were a ruthless, barbaric crew who considered compassion a weakness and failure the best reason to die. After spending six months in their company perfecting her techniques, Akira was no better than the rest of them—just a little less obvious.

As the landscape sped by, her delayed reaction took hold. She jiggled her leg up and down, chewed a ragged nail, and checked the time. The pills she had taken to dull her reality were wearing off quickly, leaving fragments of a surreal nightmare in her brain.

"Damn it, relax," Yuki told her. "You've got nothing to worry about." She motioned her head toward the rear seat. "Everything you need is in the black binder: background information, photographs, travel documents, and an altered passport. You have ten days for this job—more than enough time. Do it right, and you'll be rewarded for your loyalty. Mess up or kill yourself, and Oka-san will die."

Akira stared at the dashboard, gnawing on her bottom lip. She hated the thought of killing another human being, but risking the life of the woman who had raised her was simply out of the question. And according to Mitsui-san, suicide wasn't an option. "Are you going with me this time?" Akira asked. "Is that the plan?"

Yuki smirked. "What's wrong, little geisha? Don't think you can handle the job yourself?"

Akira frowned. "I think something may have escaped your attention. How am I supposed to deal with the crew and tourists on the ship? If someone should see me..."

"Like I told you, you've got nothing to worry about. There's been more than five thousand deaths on passenger ships, and the majority of them are still unsolved. No one will suspect the involvement of a pretty, young tourist, especially with her father on board."

Akira's voice faltered. "My...my father? What do you mean? He died years ago."

Although Yuki's smile was sardonic, her eyes held a glint of humor. "Your *new* father: Takashi Hamada. Mitsui-san chose him because he has the right look. He studied in Los Angeles and speaks perfect English. He's also a Zakura-kai cleaner and will make sure nothing goes wrong."

Akira stared straight ahead, her mind swimming in doubt.

As they approached an intersection, Yuki slowed the car to a stop and took the opportunity to provide more information. "Two months ago, Mitsui-san's sister was found dead at the bottom of a swimming pool. The Mexican authorities in Cabo San Lucas ruled it an accidental drowning, but her best friend and the men sent to retrieve her are convinced that an English couple was involved. Apparently, they got into a heated argument with Keiko over two reserved lounge chairs, of all things. The pool manager relocated their belongings and did his best to calm everyone down. But early the next morning, a gardener found Keiko facedown in the pool."

Akira narrowed her eyes. "Why would anyone kill someone over deck furniture? I mean...isn't it possible that Keiko accidentally fell into the pool and drowned? It's not like it hasn't happened before..."

"It doesn't matter what you think, Akira. It's Mitsui-san's decision. But just so you know, a bartender was strangled in a neighboring town. It was the same place where Paul Lyons's wife was refused service and asked to leave." Yuki increased speed as she veered off toward the freeway. "I've been told that if you can't figure out which member of the Lyons family was involved, then you need to take them both out."

A married couple? Are you kidding? Akira had disposed of more men than she cared to remember, but she'd never considered the possibility of killing a woman—let alone a foreigner. She glanced at Yuki, knowing this was the same ambitious archaeologist who had been dismissed from a drilling project in Mexico after attempting to sell artifacts on the Internet. The same woman who had castrated a lover for failing to please her. The same schemer who had a long history of blackmailing businessmen with illicit photos and had been shipped off to Thailand by Mitsui-san after stealing diamonds from a hidden tomb in the Sea of Japan. And now she was sitting here insisting on the assassination of a British couple whose greatest mistake could turn out to be arguing with the wrong person at the wrong time. Yuki wasn't just a sociopath; she was a murderous, conniving bitch who had no feelings or empathy for anyone.

Akira released a deep, resentful sigh. There was no possible way she could do this. Not without being absolutely sure of their guilt.

Chilled air blew in through the car window, whipping her long ebony hair across her face. She dismissed it and stared off into the distance, allowing herself to be hypnotized by the green landscape unfurling beyond the sedan's shiny black hood. The car jittered when Yuki turned the wheel a second too late trying to avoid a dead rabbit. It was just a small bump, but Akira shivered and pushed her hand into the cleft between the seat cushions. She touched something fragile and withdrew a crushed red rose—like a boutonniere a man might have worn.

Yuki huffed. "It was already dead...and anyway, there are zillions of rabbits in the world." Her voice had an artificial huskiness, undoubtedly acquired from the tough characters she kept company with in the seedy nightclub below her apartment.

Akira whispered, "Stupid things." She squared her shoulders and sat up straight. "Where are we, anyway?"

"Just below Onekama." Yuki jammed the car's cigarette lighter in with her thumb. "Get me a smoke, huh?"

Akira pulled a large tan purse from the back seat and fished around for a cigarette.

Yuki cleared her throat. "You're important to our family, Akira. Our boss is depending on you to do this right. Understand?"

"Completely." Akira poked a cigarette between the woman's lips.

Yuki smoothed her hair again. "He won't forgive a screwup, not even by you."

"Yeah, I get it."

Akira's thigh muscles cramped. Her temples throbbed. Something was terribly wrong with this scenario. She could feel it in her bones.

Yuki lit her cigarette and replaced the lighter before adding, "Then we're all set, right?"

"Well, I don't...think so. I just wondered, you know? About using a phony passport. I mean, it's not something I would have ever considered trying. Not unless I was planning to spend a million years in jail."

Yuki half shrugged. "It's not phony...just altered." She took a long pull on her cigarette and blew a stream of smoke to the side before flipping it out the window. "Tastes like crap."

"So whose is it? The passport, I mean."

"It belonged to my cousin." Yuki pushed the cigarette lighter in again and nodded toward her purse. "You mind?"

Akira tore the cellophane off a fresh pack of Winstons and tapped the box the way Yuki sometimes did. Then she passed the cigarette over and asked in a casual way, "What's her name?"

Yuki lit up and replaced the lighter. "Amato. Akira Amato. Thanks to Mitsui-san, you have something in common. A beautiful name."

Akira almost laughed out loud. After being forced to join his band of assassins, Mitsui-san had erased her birth name along with her lifelong career. Even if Yuki thought otherwise, there was nothing attractive about it. "So what about her photograph?" Akira asked. "Do we look anything alike?"

"Close enough. Jesus, what is this? The Spanish Inquisition?"

Akira wasn't about to back down. "Does she know?"

"Know what?"

"That I'm using her passport."

"She knows. Now get over it."

Interesting. Akira couldn't help wondering if the woman was deceased. "Do you ever see her?"

Yuki knocked the ash off her cigarette and leaned forward to stub it out in the ashtray with jerky, angry motions. "Not anymore. She moved to another city."

"Which one?"

"It was three months ago. I don't remember. Give me a break, OK?"

Twenty seconds passed before Akira said softly, "I wonder what she does for a living."

"She's a doctor," Yuki answered in a tight little voice. "Some kind of specialist."

"Really? Doesn't she need her passport to travel?"

Yuki stared straight ahead. "Not anymore."

Akira squeezed her lips together, burying her next question.

"I just want to remind you there's no room for mistakes...not like the ones you made today."

That's when the truth finally registered—the reason why Yuki had gone to great lengths to research death rates on cruise ships. The reason why a cleaner had been chosen as Akira's traveling companion. When the job was done and the ship reached its final destination, she would be punished for mishandling Kurosaki's death and delivered a final blow for attempting to kill Mitsui-san.

Akira studied Yuki's stern profile. Despite her villainous past and treacherous ways, she wasn't responsible for the geiko's current situation. She was simply a messenger sent here by Mitsui-san. His son had died years earlier, but she would always be his daughter-in-law and a loyal member of the notorious Zakura-kai gang.

A tear rolled down Akira's cheek, but she wasn't crying. Not really. It was merely pent-up frustrations threatening to reveal her true feelings. She caught it with a whisk of her tongue and ate it. She had to stay strong and self-assured. No matter how dire her situation might be, she could never allow her guard to drop, especially in front of Yuki Ota.

A plan began to form in the back of her brain, and she welcomed the silence in the car. After boarding the ship in Florida, Akira would need an ally: an attractive, unassuming man with a weakness for women. Her sex appeal and feminine wiles would come in handy for securing his trust and devotion and for assisting in her timely escape.

Don't forget about the money you put away, she reminded herself. "I won't," she murmured aloud.

Yuki eyed her suspiciously. "Won't what?"

"Forget it." She dropped the dead flower out the window. Then she sat back in her seat, anxiously watching the landscape race by.

3

CRUISE BLUES

It was just a ship—a small caravel from a Danish island in the Baltic Sea that had found its way to Port Everglades, a bustling seaport near Fort Lauderdale. As far as Devon Lyons could tell, there was nothing special about the full-rigged vessel aside from her catchy name—the *Merry Mermaid*. Devon, Uncle Paul, and his second wife, Sara, were her short-term passengers, along with twenty-two easily impressed tourists that had made the short walk from the ocean liner's gangway to the end of Pier One. The deckhand assigned to their tour provided more information than anyone needed to know, including the fact that the crew had accepted the ship's name and hadn't talked about changing it for even one second. The 3,600-passenger cruise liner on which their group had been traveling wasn't quite so lucky. It had been named the *Soaring Eagle* and later the *Starfish* by the cruise line that had acquired her. In Devon's mind, the demotion in stature was almost as demeaning as the Caribbean vacation he'd been forced to take to please his uncle. Nothing about this trip would make up for the time lost between him and his uncle or the two weeks he'd taken off from his job on the *Stargazer.*

The deckhand cleared his throat, capturing the group's attention. "Much like the passengers who travel aboard," he said, "the birth name of a ship isn't just a name. It's their essence, their personality, their honor...you see. *Merry Mermaid* is more than just a play on the creator's own name. It means that this ship will go anywhere merrily, cheerfully carrying its crew through even the darkest and most dangerous corners of the world."

"Underway!" a voice called out from behind them.

"Aye, Captain," a bare-chested mate returned. The sails bellowed as the wind caught hold and moved the ship through the harbor.

Despite men running about and all the bustling activity on board, the deckhand proceeded with his history lesson. "This ship has seen straw hats through a handful of adventures and challenging environments. It survived the bitter cold of Banks Island in the Arctic and the tropical heat of Micronesia. It braved the Horn of Africa and the Gulf of Aden to herald its passengers safely to Yemen and Somalia, respectively. It dodged marine ships and stray cannonballs and crossed stormy seas. There have been times when her days were numbered, but the crew rebuilt this beauty with love and timber, and somehow it's found the strength to voyage onward. Even after everything this ship's gone through, it continues to show its spirit to everyone she meets."

"Look to the sea!" the captain shouted.

The shaggy-haired deckhand smiled. "When Compton rested his head against her side, this ship soothed him and kept away his nightmares. She wrapped Dobby and Mace in her warm embrace, protecting them from harm. And when Calico Jack sat on her figurehead, the smiling mermaid...she was the happiest and most loved of all."

Sara Lyons removed her straw hat from her auburn-dyed hair and tucked it under her arm. "After this silly tour, let's get a cold drink at the bar. This heat is insufferable."

"What about you, Devon?" Paul asked. "Do you want to join us?"

A pair of blond cuties in their early twenties stood next to the ship's rail, dressed in crop tops and micromini shorts. When their eyes met Devon's, the pair giggled like silly schoolgirls. "I'll wait here if you don't mind," he said. "Spent four months on the *Stargazer's* lower deck, and the scenery is definitely better here."

Paul's light-hazel eyes traced his nephew's line of vision. "Now, if I were only twenty years younger..." His smile widened.

"And single," Sara added, punching him in the arm.

"Hey, take it easy. I'm not as tough as I used to be."

"Ah, that's right. You're dying next month—right after your fifty-fifth birthday. You might recall that I passed that landmark ten years ago, and just look how fit I am."

Paul rubbed his arm. "Yeah, I noticed." His bottom lip took a sudden dip. "Bloody hell. Is that Peter Bradshaw? It's bad enough that he's on our ship. Does he have to join us on every excursion too?"

Upon seeing them, the steely-haired doctor waved his companion off and headed in their direction. Just as he was prone to do, he jumped at the chance to be the center of attention. "Good afternoon, fellow shipmates. I understand we're adding two Japanese passengers today. They flew all the way from Tokyo to meet up with us. Now that's a *long* trip. Can't imagine what possessed them to come here."

Sara nodded. "Indeed, it is. I've never met a true Oriental... other than the gardeners at Sissinghurst Castle. They do such wonderful work there, you know. I've been thinking of hiring a few of them myself. Our grounds could use a nice sprucing up after the terrible downpour we had."

Devon mentally shook his head. "I believe Orientals are rugs, not people, Aunt Sara."

She flashed a broad smile. "Yes, of course, dear. I tend to forget that."

Bradshaw stroked his gray beard meditatively. "I read that the national police are cracking down on gangs in Japan and are investigating anyone doing business with them, which should prove interesting, since the same gangsters own a good portion of the television stations."

Paul scrunched his nose. "What are you yapping about now, Peter? Are you saying we have hoodlums joining us?"

Bradshaw laughed. "I certainly hope not. I came across an article on the Internet this morning and just found it worth mentioning. You know, it does pay to be informed with all the craziness going on in the world. If not for my medical practice, I would travel considerably more and find ways to escape reality as much as possible."

Paul grumbled under his breath. "You're kidding, right? Every time I look, you're never more than five feet away."

A man decked out in white slacks and a blue blazer moved closer, allowing room for other passengers to pass by. He wore a white baseball cap that shaded his long Roman nose and had a gray-trimmed goatee, resembling both Sean Connery and Burt Reynolds. He was accompanied by a petite redhead who Devon assumed was his wife. Although her eyes seemed to be assessing him.

"Did I hear correctly?" the man directed at Bradshaw. "Are you a physician?"

"No," Paul answered for him. "This man hypnotizes vulnerable woman and fleeces them for every dime he can get."

Bradshaw twisted the gold ruby ring on his right hand and shook his head, feigning his disappointment.

"I can't believe you said that, Paul." The color deepened in Sara's thin, oval face, with its prominent curved nose and dull brown eyes. "Your rudeness is embarrassing."

Paul looked at Devon and smiled. "Am I embarrassing you?"

Devon shrugged a shoulder. "Not me." For some unknown reason, the two men were combatant whenever an audience was present. But having them on the same cruise added a degree of amusement to the otherwise mundane trip.

Sara huffed. "Unbelievable." She shifted her attention toward the stranger in their midst and shook the storm from her thin arched brows with a dead smile—undoubtedly the best piece of serenity she could put on for public wear. "I want to assure you that Dr. Bradshaw is an upstanding British citizen and a world-renowned psychotherapist. He's helped hundreds of patients in Europe, including me." She pursed her lips and looked at Peter. "Please don't pay him no mind. As you're well aware, Paul just likes to tease."

Bradshaw's stern mouth shaped into a twisted smile. "I know," he murmured. "It's how he amuses himself."

The stocky stranger stepped forward. "It's a real honor to meet you, sir," he said, extending his hand. "The name's Benjamin Hoffman, and this is my...fiancée, Vivian Ward." The middle-aged woman standing beside him had an oval face too, high in the cheekbones, the color of pink roses. Her dancing brows reminded Devon of an eager enthusiast, waiting for the chance to express her views on any given subject.

"It seems we share a country as well as a profession," Hoffman added. "I assume you're attending the medical conference onboard the ship. There's no better forum for psychiatrists, psychologists, and health-care professionals than a relaxing cruise filled with keynote speakers, presentations, great food, and a wide range of entertainment. Don't you agree?"

Bradshaw's gray, heavy-lidded eyes twinkled under their bushy brows. "I sat through two panel discussions yesterday and attended a workshop this morning. Nothing to write home about, except the hospital director I met during the briefing. She was born in Russia, took up modeling, speaks five languages, and is a remarkable intellect. I'm sure you'd enjoy meeting her as well."

There was a snap in Sara's voice when she said, "I've had dealings with quite a few Russians. Personally, I have found them to be rather arrogant and even insufferable at times. The fact that any man would find that woman attractive surprises me."

Vivian's mouth sagged. She seemed to be as shocked as Devon was by Sara's outrageous remark. During the five days he'd spent traveling with his uncle and aunt, he had discovered Sara's tendency to sort and organize everyone into tidy categories based on her exaggerated beliefs. Arguing with her or trying to sway her opinion had proved pointless, as Vivian would soon discover.

"Excuse me," the deckhand called out. "If you would like to join me downstairs, I'll direct you to the cabins where the crew stays during our voyages. The woodworking is quite remarkable and reflects the age of our ship. You can also peek into our galley and the captain's quarters. Right this way, everyone."

"Well, it seems we're off again," Hoffman said. "Perhaps we can share a table tonight? I would greatly appreciate your advice, Dr. Bradshaw. It concerns a rather difficult case I'm currently working on, and I—"

"Oh, I've had a few of those. It never hurts to get a second opinion. What about you, Sara? Will you and your delightful husband be joining us this evening?"

Paul smirked. "We've already made plans."

"Oh, that's right," Sara added. "French cuisine at the chef's table tonight."

Bradshaw's face brightened. "Really? I'm scheduled to dine there as well."

Paul disregarded the couple in their midst in light of his growing anger. "Why shouldn't that surprise me? There are more than twenty restaurants on our ship, and yet somehow you manage to join us every friggin' night. By the way, did I mention that my favorite nephew will be there? He's been working out every morning in the gym and would love the opportunity to flex his muscles."

Sara squeezed Paul's forearm. "I believe he's your *only* nephew, darling…and he's not a brute." She looked at Devon. "Are you, dear?"

Devon was caught in the middle and just wanted to get away. "Not that I know of."

Sara smiled. "See?"

Devon leaned in and whispered to his uncle, "Try not to do any damage while you're downstairs."

Paul angled a look. "Who, me?"

"Yeah, you."

Sara took her husband by the hand and towed him toward the departing tour group. However, Vivian Ward elected to stay put. "I'll be here when you get back," she told Hoffman. As soon as everyone was out of sight, she turned to Devon. "So I understand you're from California…"

He wasn't a fan of idle chatter, believing nothing useful came of it. But there were no immediate escape routes, and Vivian had made it impossible to ignore her. "Yes. I've been away from home for six weeks now," Devon told her. "I'm looking forward to getting back."

"If you don't mind my saying so, you don't seem like the cruise type, Mr. Lyons. What made you decide to come along?"

Devon reckoned that the woman he'd been forced to babysit had a legitimate reason to be curious. Aside from the cute girls he had spotted and the dozen thirty-something passengers he'd encountered during the past twenty-four hours, everyone on the trip could be labeled a senior citizen or middle-aged doctor. "My uncle asked me to come along," he volunteered. "We had issues when I was young, so I came here to make amends. And how bout you?"

"I'm here at Ben's request. He was supposed to take my sister on this trip last year, but she was killed by a drunk driver. I came along to help spread her ashes in Jamaica. She loved it there and was looking forward to returning."

Oh, Christ. What could he say? "I'm so sorry, Vivian."

"The fiancée thing is strictly for decorum," she added. "You see, the fare was rather expensive, so we elected to share a suite. Normally, I would never have agreed. But under the circumstances…"

"Oh, sure. Makes perfect sense," Devon said. Although it really didn't. But who was he to judge? At thirty years of age, his accomplishments, or lack thereof, included defying his father, scaring off his mother, crashing a race car, participating in a Ponzi scheme, having an affair with a mobster's sister, and barely surviving his own death. His assets and future plans depended on his sister's skill in finding long-lost treasures and her generosity in sharing what she had found. Until this voyage ended and his bags were packed, he had no choice but to assume the role of a referee in his uncle and aunt's melodrama.

"So I understand you're single." Vivian smiled. "Do you have a girlfriend at home, Devon?"

Was this fifty-year-old woman hitting on him? Devon couldn't help but smile back. In a weird sort of way, it was flattering. With her curly red hair and trim physique, she might have been attractive in her younger years. But the creases on her upper lip and at the corner of her eyes were telltale signs of her age and hard to ignore. "Not at the moment," he answered.

Devon took a quick glance around the ship. A bartender was wiping down a makeshift bar a short distance away and had no customers waiting. "I could sure use a drink right now. How 'bout you, Vivian?"

She linked her arm through his and towed him toward the row of bottles and filled ice bucket. "I was hoping you would ask. Grey Goose with two olives," she told the bartender. She proceeded to tell Devon about her new phone app, her Maltese puppy, and her new cocktail dress that cost more than $400, while throwing back one martini after the other. It never occurred to him that she had a drinking problem or that she would be looping an arm around his waist to keep from falling over when her brother-in-law returned with the rest of the touring passengers.

The embarrassing scene had everyone believing Devon was responsible for Vivian's condition and not the innocent bystander he professed to be. As he stood by watching the sociable woman wobble across the gangplank and nearly fall over, it was hard to disagree. After all, he was the one paying for the drinks and downing them with equal enthusiasm, just like he did every night in hotel bars and cocktail lounges. It was the best sedative known to man—the only way to forget.

4

DEPARTURE

A limousine driver stood outside the Fort Lauderdale baggage claim area with a white sign in his hands reading *Hamada*. It took a moment for Akira to remember that she was traveling under the dubious surname. Her male companion, who correctly bore the title, was a leathery-skinned man of medium height with slicked-back gray hair and coal-black eyes that looked soft and muted in the light of day. However, his stocky frame and thick biceps gave the impression that he could snap someone's neck with very little effort. He was wearing a charcoal linen jacket with a white pin-striped shirt underneath, slightly frayed at the edges. He also wore black jeans and a black cord necklace that was wrapped twice around his neck, with a bronze key hanging from it that stirred her curiosity. She had considered asking about its purpose while traveling from Japan and waiting for connecting flights. But Takashi Hamada's quiet demeanor alluded to his need for privacy and her obligation not to pry. It also became clear that enjoying the tropical scenery or any aspect of their trip would be considered a waste of time until

Keiko Mitsui's murderer was eliminated and their assignment was deemed complete.

After waving the driver over, Takashi pointed at their luggage and spoke in a deep, emotionless voice. "Just two. I'll keep this one with me." He set his black bag between them on the seat and put on his reflective sunglasses. Then he sat back and stared out the window, emitting negative energy.

No words were exchanged by anyone as they sped along the highway toward their final destination, adding to the heat in the car. Upon arriving at the cruise terminal, the limo driver opened the right rear door, and Takashi was the first to exit. The driver extended his soft hand to Akira in a kind gesture and closed the door behind her.

"Have a nice cruise," he said.

She nodded politely but chose not to answer, not with Takashi standing nearby. He palmed a tip to the driver and grabbed his brown duffel bag. Then he left Akira to follow behind with her rolling black suitcase in typical Japanese fashion. They showed their travel documents, one after the other, and crossed the gangplank leading to their assigned ship. Their bags were taken by one of the crew members, and they were presented glasses of shimmering champagne. The bubbles spiraled up in the flutes and burst as if trying to escape. As she accepted the drink, Akira felt a sudden longing to get away and also escape. But Takashi's presence made it impossible.

"When you're ready, check in at the registration desk," the cruise director told her. "They'll take care of you and your father and show you to your cabin. If you have any questions while you're there, don't hesitate to ask."

Akira lowered her chin and said softly, "Thank you."

"Of course. That's why we're here," he said, "to make your trip as enjoyable as possible."

To Akira, the tall, chiseled-faced man seemed perfectly cast as the cruise director. He kept his hands clasped behind his back and his shoulders squared in a rigid pose like an officer in the military. The fine lines etched at the corners of his dark-blue eyes deepened with his broad smile.

"This is our first cruise," Takashi volunteered. "It's very exciting for both of us." He displayed his perfect white teeth and kept a hand on Akira's back, reminding her who was in charge.

"Welcome aboard," the director said. "My name is Michael Donley. Don't hesitate to let me know if there's anything you need."

While making her way to their room, Akira realized she'd never seen such opulence, such luxury, oozing from every corner of a ship. Fine art and sculptures dotted the lobby, and the staircase and chandelier reminded her of the luxury liners she had only seen in movies. According to the information packet she'd been given, there were fourteen decks on the ship, ten of which were allotted to passengers. There were also two coffee bars, a champagne bar, sports bar, terrace bar, dance club, nightclub, six lounges, two theaters, one casino, four pools, two spas, a rock-climbing wall, a gymnasium, and two game rooms for kids. When it came to restaurants, Akira lost count at fifteen. She passed by the Asian dining room on her way to the elevator, and the exuberance of the staff and abundance of food on display left her speechless.

While Takashi stood beside her, Akira used the card key and was instantly struck by how much the spacious cabin reminded her of the expensive hotel room in Kyoto she had shared two years ago with her *danna,* Kenji—a man who had paid for the right to be her contracted sponsor. As promised, the suite was outfitted with every amenity for the ten-day cruise. Takashi stepped in front of her and announced that she would take the

24

master bedroom located on the lower level of the suite. He would take the guest bedroom on the upper level, which included an additional bathroom and large exterior windows. Before their arrival, Akira had been nervous about sharing a room with a man she barely knew. But Takashi was quick to inform her that he would be spending most of his time familiarizing himself with the ship and would do whatever was necessary to maintain the father-daughter illusion.

While she unpacked, he left the room with a spare key in hand, still dressed in his jeans and linen jacket. A British gentleman arrived soon after, outfitted in a white shirt, black bow tie, and vest. He introduced himself as Bradley and explained that he would be serving as their butler throughout their journey and would be handling their dinner reservations and afternoon tea service. He also showed her how the wall plugs and lighting system in the rooms were activated by inserting a card key into the plastic box mounted on the wall in the entry.

Another knock at the door sounded and resulted in the appearance of Felicia, a middle-aged, dark-skinned maid who patiently waited for confirmation from Akira that her accommodations were to her liking. Her slender assistant stepped out from behind her and left a stack of white towels on the rack above the shower before returning to her station. Akira extended her thanks, but the dutiful, timid woman didn't respond. She kept her eyes fastened on the beige carpeting under their feet, reminding the geiko of the class separations she'd experienced in Japan.

After everyone had left the room, Akira changed into a short black skirt, sleeveless white blouse, and black strappy sandals. She buried her anxieties before setting off to explore the ship, feeling like a young, inquisitive child. The spa offered an incredible array of services; the fully equipped gym, with fitness classes and a personal trainer, had her gasping for air. Near the top deck, she entered the ship's culinary center and discovered that passengers had the opportunity to learn gourmet cooking while working side by side with master chefs. The library offered a wide variety of books, stretching out over one hundred meters, with deep leather seats where guests could delve into the latest bestsellers. Adjacent to the library was a coffee bar with floor-to-ceiling windows providing panoramic views as baristas served the finest espressos, cappuccinos, pastries, and homemade cookies.

She ventured outside and found the top deck replete with patio furniture, a large swimming pool, and an unbelievably handsome man with exquisitely drawn features. He was stretched out on a lounge chair enjoying a frothy beer in a chilled mug. His light-brown, almost red hair was squared off in the back and long in the front, and his cheeks were clean-shaven and gave rise to nicely sculpted bones, which melded into a square jaw and chiseled chin. She estimated him to be in his late twenties and assumed he was a rich playboy who spent his spare time sunbathing and bodybuilding—enjoying his life without a care in the world.

Akira smiled, wondering what it would be like to feel that way...for just one day.

A waitress with spiky blond hair was serving guests on the deck and approached her with an empty tray. "Gorgeous, huh?"

"Excuse me?" Akira's vision trailed from the woman's round face to the thin scar on her neck.

"The hunk over there," the waitress pointed out with a nod. "The one with the cute dimples and killer eyes. I've been enjoying him for hours—along with half the women on this ship."

Embarrassment warmed Akira's face. *Were all Americans this forward?*

"That's Devon Lyons…from California. He shares interest in a treasure-hunting business and is the hottest thing I've seen all year." Her lips curled into a smile. "I sure wouldn't mind jumping his bones."

Akira was startled into reluctant laughter. It was the first time she'd heard the remark, although she assumed it was nothing new. As she stood watching, another cocktail waitress approached Devon and asked about his drink. Then she walked away smiling.

Amazing. There were thousands of men on this ship, and in less than twenty minutes, Akira had found the right one—a robust member of the Lyonses' family to act as her ally. With no photograph in his file to guide her, even Takashi would be impressed by her discovery.

She glanced down at her hand, still holding her room key, and attempted to divert the conversation. "Actually, I was wondering about the temperature in the pool."

"Oh, right. Silly me. It's a comfortable seventy-two degrees. Were you planning to change and go swimming? I can have a chair set up and bring you something cold to drink if you'd like."

Akira could feel Devon's eyes on her, and it wasn't a good place for them to be. At least not for the time being. "Perhaps later," she said. "I'm new on board and was just trying to get my bearings."

"Oh, right. Of course. We were told that you and your father would be arriving today. You must be exhausted. If you need anything at all, don't hesitate to let me know. I'll be here until nine o'clock tonight."

Akira made a mental note of the name on her badge. "Thank you, Adriane. I might take you up on your offer tomorrow." She watched the cocktail waitress approach another guest before stealing another look at Devon. He was leaning on his elbow,

listening to something the young woman beside him was saying—smiling and laughing on cue. Akira became keenly aware
of him occasionally glancing at her, increasing her discomfort.
She released a short breath before walking away in search of the
closest elevator.

After arriving at her cabin, she pulled the sliding glass
door open and stepped out onto the balcony with her files in
hand. The ship was still docked and not scheduled to leave for
several hours, giving her time to review information about the
Lyons family and to process her encounter with Devon. His bio
described him as selective when it came to romance. Apparently
he was drawn toward strong, powerful women but struggled with
maintaining relationships. He would be a tough one to win over
in the limited time she'd been given, especially with trust being
an issue. She decided the best way to earn it was by playing the
role of a shy, innocent, naïve soul—longing for his approval,
love, and protection. It would be something new for Devon—a
chance to show off his virility while staking his claim. As for the
rest of the family members, she came to the conclusion that they
would confide in her in due time, but only with Devon's help. It
would essentially be a game of chess, silently moving into a position of power before eliminating the right opponent.

Bradley knocked at the door and called out "good evening"
before entering the room. He uncorked a chilled bottle of champagne and poured a generous serving into a fluted glass before
setting it down on the patio table, along with a small plate of
crackers and assorted cheeses. After he left, she took advantage
of her free time to enjoy the refreshments she'd been given and
to focus on the key component to her plan: Devon Lyons. He was
the perfect man to assist her, provided he was receptive to her
advances and had fully recovered from his recent heartbreak.

She was finishing her last bite of cheese when the entry door suddenly opened. It was Takashi returning from his reconnaissance mission. His frown told her that he wasn't pleased with her behavior and was preparing to reprimand her, as he had done throughout their trip.

"Well, I hope you've been having a good time," he snapped. "I couldn't help noticing that you've been all over this ship. You didn't talk to anyone, did you?"

Akira considered lying, then realized the old man had probably seen her next to the pool. "A cocktail waitress asked me if I wanted a drink, and I refused it. She also identified Devon Lyons, who happened to be outside at the time. I didn't speak to him, knowing how you feel, but I'm sure he noticed me."

Takashi nodded. "Good, good. I've been scouting out the best way to meet his uncle. According to the concierge, he eats in a different restaurant every night with his wife, Sara. Tonight he's dining at the chef's table in the Aquarian restaurant. I was also informed that there was a last-minute cancellation, so I reserved a place for you. Find out everything you need to know about him and his companions without being conspicuous. You have twenty minutes to freshen up before dinner. I suggest you stop wasting time and get ready."

Akira disregarded his abruptness and unzipped her bag. She took out a black sequin cocktail dress and matching stilettos and laid them on the sofa. Then she turned back to Takashi. "Do you want me to bring you something to eat?"

"It's not necessary. I'll grab something later and meet you back here."

"How soon do you want this to happen?"

"We have ten days on this ship before reaching our final port. You need to blend in with the passengers and not draw any suspicion. I'll let you know when the time is right. Until then, you're simply a guest on board."

"Understood." Akira gnawed on the inside of her mouth, longing for this job to be done. Takashi was here on Mitsui-san's behalf, not hers. She needed to be careful not to upset or disappoint him—or she would be the first to go.

5

ENTICED

A beautiful Japanese woman with a flawless complexion, golden-bronze eyes, and long slender legs stepped through the door of the Aquarian restaurant. The mere sight of her lifted Devon's heart and sent it soaring. It was the same woman he had seen by the pool in a cute casual outfit, but now she was dressed to the nines in a shimmering cocktail dress, molding her shapely figure.

She walked toward him cautiously and extended her hand. "Hello. I'm Akira Hamada. I believe I'm joining your group tonight…" Her voice was like music, a beautiful song drowning out everything around him.

He took her hand in his. "I'm Devon Lyons. It's a pleasure to meet you."

"And you as well," she offered, bowing her head politely. Her long black hair was pinned up in a sleek fashion, exposing her toned arms, defined shoulders, and sensuous neck. She eyed him surreptitiously beneath her long dark lashes before sharing the most enchanting smile he'd ever seen.

"Akira...how lovely." Oh my God. Did he actually say that? The words came out before he could stop them.

She smiled again, acknowledging his compliment.

"I'm...glad you're here," he said. Another stupid line. What was wrong with him?

"There you are!" Paul's voice traveled from the restaurant entry. Devon realized he was still holding Akira's hand and quickly released it. "And who do we have here?" his uncle asked. Sara had followed him inside and was looking at her with curiosity, as if wondering what she was doing there.

The Asian beauty held out her right hand and fearlessly met Paul's eyes. "My name is Akira. I hope you don't mind my intrusion."

Paul took her hand, grinning. "Are you kidding? We're delighted to have you join us. The men on this ship are going to be climbing over one another to get to know you."

Akira's soft blush became more pronounced. "My father and I came on this cruise for relaxation, not romance."

Sara adjusted the layered pearl necklace filling her cleavage. "Well, I suppose it isn't for everyone." She gave her husband a malcontent look before making her way to the dining room table.

When Akira turned to watch Sara, Devon noticed that her cocktail dress was split clear to the hip, an unexpected but welcome surprise. He unbuttoned his beige silk shirt, unsure if it was the heat in the room or this stunning woman causing his body temperature to escalate.

"Do you want to sit next to this pretty young lady?" Paul asked him.

Devon wasn't sure what to say. He stepped up to the adjacent bar and picked up the cocktail list as his excuse for not sitting. "Maybe you could help me decipher this," he said to Akira. "Do you have any idea what Louis Roederer Cristal Brut is? It must be great stuff. They have it priced at four hundred dollars a bottle."

She smiled sweetly. "You're not a wine buff, I take it." She stated it as though it were a fact.

"Am I that obvious?" He grinned at her and was tempted by the almost irresistible desire to kiss her but immediately squelched the notion. "Dewar's on the rocks," he told the bartender. "How about you, Akira? Can I buy you a drink?"

The corners of her mouth dropped. "Oh no. I didn't bring my purse. I thought the drinks were free."

"They are…for the most part. I was just teasing."

"Oh, I see." A blush colored her cheeks once again, making him smile.

Both doctors arrived with Vivian Ward and slipped into their seats at the table. Akira and Devon joined them and began looking at the menu to determine what their prix fixe meal included. She seemed to be as confused as he was by the courses. However, before long, they were laughing and leaning close to each other as they looked over their choices.

Paul's voice reminded Devon that they weren't alone. "Seems we have quite a selection to pick from. What are you ordering, Akira?"

She rattled off her choices, and Paul used the opportunity to engage her in conversation. "So you're from Japan. Where's your father tonight? I'm surprised he's not dining with us."

"It was a long trip. He's resting this evening," she answered. Then she turned back to Devon and asked questions about his job and diving adventures. Paul didn't seem pleased at all, but Devon couldn't care less. He was enjoying Akira's company and the chance to expound on his favorite subject: treasure hunting.

The waiter arrived and proceeded to circle the table to record each of their selections. Paul was the last to order, and then Bradshaw stole the show.

"You should have seen him. I've never witnessed anyone so terrified of flying on a floatplane. Talk about white-knuckling it..."

Paul's frown deepened. Bradshaw was talking about him, and from the sound of the story, it wasn't an experience he could make light of.

Hoffman and Vivian Ward laughed as Bradshaw continued. "At one point, I thought maybe I should hold his hand to make him feel better but was afraid of the looks we might get." He guffawed, and the group at the far end of the table erupted again.

Akira leaned toward Paul and lowered her voice. "I never flew on a plane before coming here. I absolutely dread doing it again."

Sara came to his aid as well by detouring the subject. "Did anyone have a penguin made out of towels on their bed? Our cabin steward said he made it and that he's creating a new design every day."

This was the perfect diversion. Everyone started talking at once. Paul gave Sara a grateful look, and calm was restored for the time being.

"Let's take turns going around the table," Sara said. "I want to hear what kind of animal everyone had. I'll start. It was so adorable. Here, look. I took a picture." She passed around her phone.

"I had a wolf," Hoffman said. He passed the phone to the last two couples who'd joined them.

"I got a swan!" Vivian chimed in. "So did I," another woman added. Meanwhile, the men in their company sipped their drinks and smiled.

"What about you, Peter?" Sara asked. "What kind of creature do they take you for?"

"A crocodile. I've had a few dealings with folks who would have no problem comparing me to one." The doctor smiled mischievously at her, and Paul coughed loudly. Devon found himself wondering if jealousy was a contributing factor to their irrational exchanges.

An executive chef appeared in his white cooking jacket and introduced himself as Phillip Bering. He explained that dinner would include five courses, with wines highlighting various regions in France.

Sara's eyes were filled with glee. "I've been looking forward to this all day."

Just as promised, each dish arrived with paired wine, adding volume to the jovial exchanges in the room. When the meal finally ended, the chef returned and shook everyone's hand. He told them that he'd enjoyed cooking for them and to have a good day tomorrow. It was going to be a day at sea, which meant relaxing around the pool and a broad range of onboard activities. He also announced that a cocktail party would be taking place the next evening, and everyone at the table was excited to hear it.

"Peter, I'm hoping to have a moment to talk to you about my patient in Brighton." The serious tone in Hoffman's voice drew Devon's attention. "One moment she's as relaxed as any of us, talking about her trip to Vienna and new grandson in Los Angeles. Then she has a psychotic break, becoming belligerent and requiring heavy sedation. I performed psychotherapy on her for six months and found a trigger mechanism, but I can't seem to break the pattern. Would you mind swinging by my room for a nightcap? I brought notes with me from our sessions. Perhaps there's something I've overlooked. I'm really at my wits' end with this one."

Bradshaw nodded thoughtfully. "I experienced a similar condition while in Mexico. A Japanese woman was there on vacation with her friends and had an unfortunate episode. I offered my assistance to the attending physician, but since I had to leave the next day, I wasn't privy to her prognosis. However, in your case, I'm sure I can provide some helpful advice."

Devon glanced at Akira, who appeared to be captivated by their conversation. "Dr. Bradshaw, please excuse my interruption," she said, "but do you remember the woman's name...the one in Mexico?"

"I'm sorry. I don't recall. But if memory serves me, she did mention Kyoto. Such a lovely city, with beautiful gardens and temples. I understand you're from there as well."

Akira nodded. She glanced at Devon, but something seemed different to him. Did she know the woman Bradshaw was talking about?

"Well, I think that does it for me," Paul said, stretching. "It was nice meeting you, Akira. I hope you and your father enjoy your vacation."

She lowered her chin. "Thank you, sir. I should probably head off to bed myself."

Akira began to rise, and Devon reached for her hand, keeping her in place. "Good night, Uncle Paul. I'll make sure this lovely lady is returned to her cabin."

Everyone was standing, mumbling their goodbyes. Sara kissed Peter Bradshaw's cheek, and he hugged her in an open show of affection.

The look on Paul's face was stern, angry...defiant. "Maybe you should stay with him," he told Sara. He shook his head in disgust and stormed out of the room, with Sara trailing behind.

Devon looked at Akira, feeling slightly embarrassed. "My uncle seems to have a jealous streak when it comes to Sara. Tomorrow, they'll be laughing again...until they find something else to argue about."

The corners of Akira's lips lifted slightly, and his eyes locked on hers. His lips played with a smile as his mind considered stealing a kiss. He expected their conversation to go back to the playful banter they seemed to enjoy throughout dinner, but something was obviously wrong.

"I enjoyed your company very much tonight," she said, "but there's something I need to tell you. I'm terrible at relationships and famous for leaving. That's why I avoid romance altogether." She looked away as if suddenly shy. "While I'm here on this trip, I'm sure my father would prefer to keep it that way. So if I seem distant the next time you see me, please don't take offense. You're a great person, Devon, and I'm sure you'll find a wonderful young lady to—"

He held up his hand, silencing her. "I've already found her. I want to spend tomorrow with you, getting to know you better. Don't you want to spend time with me?" His heart was racing, anxious for the right answer.

She remained silent for an endless moment. Then she looked up and smiled. "Yes, of course I do. I'd love to see you again."

He glanced at his watch to confirm the time. "It's twelve thirty a.m. I need to get some rest, and I'm sure you do too. What time do you want to meet tomorrow?"

"I...I'm not sure."

"Well, I was up late last night playing poker in the casino, so I may sleep later than usual. I'll order breakfast tonight for nine a.m. and have it delivered to my room, 501. Do you want me to order for you as well?"

Akira angled her head ever so slightly. "In your room?"

"It's totally on the up-and-up, I swear. I'm actually sharing a suite with my aunt and uncle. So there's a good chance we won't be alone." Akira was slow to respond.

"What if I promise to keep my hands to myself?"

She smiled again. "OK. I'll join you there." She moved closer and kissed him on the cheek. "Get some sleep, Devon. There's no need to walk me back. I'll see you in the morning."

Before he could object, she left the restaurant, vanishing into the crowds.

6

CLOSE QUARTERS

Due to his overindulgence in alcohol the night before, Devon woke up at 8:00 a.m., an hour later than usual. He touched his cheek, recalling Akira's soft kiss and their plans to meet up later that morning. Other than a dull headache, he felt surprisingly good and was looking forward to a hardy breakfast with his new acquaintance. He put on a white T-shirt and denim cutoffs and walked out on the balcony, hoping the fresh air would clear his head.

"Good morning." Paul's voice drifted down to him from the upper-level balcony. "You're up early."

Devon looked up and smiled. "So are you."

"No matter what time I go to bed, I always wake up at the same time. But Sara's been up for hours, stressing over our missing waiter. Do you mind if I come down and join you?"

"I haven't showered yet. I just threw on some shorts." He didn't expect anyone else to be up this early.

"It's all right. No need to change. I'll bring down some coffee."

Paul descended the stairs with two steaming cups in his hands and joined Devon next to the railing. After handing him a cup, he launched into a story that left Devon scratching his head. "He normally arrives at six a.m. with her petit fours and Earl Grey tea, but he didn't show up this morning, and no one has seen hide nor hair of him."

"Well, Irish is a good-looking kid," Devon told him. It was the name Sara had given him based on his nationality. "He probably hooked up with some cute girl and fell asleep in her room. I'm sure he'll turn up soon enough."

"That's what I told Sara, but she isn't having any part of it. Seems she was rather short with him yesterday after her session with Bradshaw and wants to apologize for her outburst."

Devon blew the steam from his cup. "I'm sure there's a reasonable explanation. No one disappears from a cruise ship. Not unless they fall overboard. And if that was the case, I'm sure someone would have noticed."

"I completely agree with you there. But Sara insisted on contacting security. They're making a thorough search of the ship today and will probably question all his friends. I know it sounds heartless to say this, but as far as I'm concerned, that woman has more important matters to worry about than chasing after a waiter."

Devon arched a brow. "Such as?"

"Divorce, for one. I'm filing right after we return to England."

"Aw, come on. You can't be serious. The two of you have been together for over a decade. I've seen how you are together. Kissing and hugging...teasing each other. Just because you had a bad fight doesn't mean you should split up."

Paul wouldn't meet Devon's eyes. He seemed more comfortable talking to his chest. "I'm not proud of my past. In fact, I'm rather ashamed of it," he claimed. "Your sister was told not to share what I'm about to tell you. But after agreeing to come with us, you should know the truth."

Devon took a long sip of coffee. The last thing he wanted was to hear about someone else's problems, particularly his uncle's. The relationship between them had been strained for more years than either of them was willing to admit. But curiosity left him asking the next question.

"And what is that?"

Paul looked up. Devon noticed a sliver of terror behind his hazel eyes. Paul was scared of his wife—of what she might do. And yet it made absolutely no sense. Sara could be stubborn at times, even downright annoying. She wasn't meek or mild-mannered and could be overbearing with her preconceived notions. But she was hardly a threat.

"I signed a contract guaranteeing I'd stay married to her for ten years. At the time, I didn't know where my next meal was coming from or anything about her. And I sure the hell didn't know about…"—Paul hesitated before adding—"all her dead husbands."

Devon burst out laughing but tried to cover it with a cough. This was pure drama on his uncle's part—a ridiculous way to validate his displeasure with Sara. Yet in spite of his misgivings, Devon chose to play along. "Dead husbands? And just how many are we talking about?" His uncle went silent. "How many?" Devon repeated. "Five? Six?"

"Three. All of them died from heart attacks—before their contracts expired. I was willing to accept Sara's explanations about their health issues and stress-related jobs until I came across that damn jar of hers."

His uncle wasn't making this easy. "What jar?" Devon asked.

"The one I found in her bag. It's filled with all kinds of weird stuff. I didn't think much of it at first. But then I spotted an earring belonging to Gwen Gallagher, a woman I had an affair with six months ago. Her body was found at the bottom of a fifty-foot cliff." Paul rubbed his jaw. "I've tried to give Sara the benefit of the doubt; honestly I have. But I'm finding it hard to believe in coincidences. Particularly when they seem to be happening so frequently."

Devon leaned back against the railing and considered his words. For the last two weeks, there had been times when he'd been frustrated with Sara himself. He was damn certain she had been angry with him for a score of offenses and rightly so. But between the two of them, they had managed to defuse things and seemed to get along quite well. "There's got to be a thousand earrings that look the same," Devon told him. "How can you be certain it belonged to Gwen? Or that your wife was involved in her death?"

Paul frowned a little. "It was the way she reacted when I found the jar. She practically snarled and told me that I was being ridiculous. I honestly don't know what to believe or how to act around her anymore."

Devon chuckled. "I'm sorry, Uncle. I know it's not a laughing matter to you, but I can't say I blame her. After all, you're a mystery writer. Your imagination sells books."

Paul's eyes narrowed slightly, challenging Devon's words. "You wouldn't say that if you were there."

"Then why are you still with her? Why haven't you gone to the police?"

"She's extremely rich, Devon, and highly respected. No one in Bellwood would ever believe me. And besides, she threatened to replace me if I didn't come on this trip. I've already been in the hospital once."

"Oh yeah. I heard about that. Angina, wasn't it?"

"Well, I might not survive next time."

Devon gripped the back of his neck and let out a deep sigh. Obviously, there was no winning this argument.

"I'm telling you, one minute she's perfectly fine," Paul said, "charming, chatty, flirty, wanting to be around me as much as possible. The next, she goes off, shuts down completely, and talks to everyone except me. I give her the space she wants, and then two days later, it starts all over again."

"At least she keeps things interesting." Devon's lips quirked into a smile. "So clear something up for me, Uncle. If you hate Sara so much, then why were you upset when Bradshaw hugged her?"

Paul's brows drew together. "It's complicated. You'd never understand."

"Come on, enlighten me. I'd really like to know."

Paul sighed. "Peter is a bad influence. He puts strange ideas in her head and encourages her to act on her impulses. He's also got her believing that she can't live without his treatments—or him."

"I guess that explains why he's always around."

"Exactly."

The door opened, and Sara rushed inside looking flushed and upset. "They searched the entire ship, and Irish is nowhere to be found. I can't believe it! And now Peter is gone too, and no one is bothering to look for him. Bloody hell! What's happening on this ship?"

Devon's ears perked up. "Bradshaw is missing?"

"I knocked on his cabin door, and he didn't answer. The passenger next door to him is insisting he got off the ship last night. But I know for a fact it's not true."

"How so?" Devon asked.

"He would never leave me behind."

Paul shook his head and snorted. "Leave you?"

"Yes. I mean...he would have called or sent a note or something. He wouldn't just go off like that—with absolutely no explanation."

Paul smirked at Devon. "Like he did in Edinburgh."

"That was different," Sara said. "We went there as a group and had tickets to a play. His client in Southampton required his immediate attention."

"And you were worried for days on end," Paul reminded her.

"I don't care what you say. Something is terribly wrong. I can feel it!"

"Well, it seems to me that if no one's concerned on this ship, there's no reason for you to be."

Sara was silent, and then she broke down in tears. "How am I supposed to live without him?"

Paul slammed his fist into a table, nearly knocking a lamp over. "That does it! I'm leaving this ship as soon as it docks."

"You're impossible," Sara sobbed. Her face was white with rage. "I hate you!" She ran through the living room and up the stairs to their bedroom.

Devon laid a hand on Paul's shoulder. "I suggest you make amends. That is if you're hoping to wake up tomorrow."

Paul faced him, looking panicked and afraid. "You're absolutely right. I'd better see to her before something happens."

Devon smiled. "Relax, Uncle Paul. I was only kidding."

"Yes, of course. I'll catch up with you later." Paul rushed up the stairs and closed the bedroom door. From where Devon stood, he could hear their loud voices through the ceiling and found himself regretting his involvement. By all accounts, they were both batshit crazy, and so was he for being here.

7

NEWFOUND LOVE

Devon looked up at the white ceiling above his bed and chose to ignore thoughts of Sara and her band of deceased husbands. He blew them off, along with his uncle's strange accusations, believing it was too much sun or strange food or just too much time on the ship. Oddly, the silence in the room seemed louder than usual. He was alone for the first time in days, and the sound of it was almost deafening. For the next thirty minutes he busied himself showering, shaving, and pulling on a fresh pair of jeans, and by the time breakfast arrived, he was ready to see Akira. He directed the steward to bring the cart out onto the balcony, where a table with an umbrella and four chairs had been set. Although he had ordered extra food in case Paul and Sara decided to join them, he hoped to avoid any drama that might trickle down from upstairs.

"Good morning." Akira appeared in the doorway just as the steward was leaving. She was looking fresh and lovely in a yellow, strappy dress and tan open-toed sandals. Her long black hair cascaded down her back in a casual windblown hairstyle, giving her a youthful, carefree appearance. Devon held out a chair for her in the shadiest spot. Her skin was porcelain white, and he remembered from a book he read that Japanese women preferred to keep it that way.

"You're very sweet," she said, placing her hand on his arm.

Nobody had ever called him sweet before. Charming, handsome, and cavalier, but never sweet. The remark made him feel warm and fuzzy inside. He wanted to lean down and kiss her but instead stood there not saying or doing anything.

Akira smiled. "Speechless again?"

"Yeah, I'm afraid so." He grinned back at her. "You have a way of doing that to me."

Akira glanced at the shimmering sea. "It's lovely out here this morning." She leaned back and let the breeze flow through her hair.

"Yes, it's quite nice." God, she was beautiful. Devon couldn't resist eyeing her exposed cleavage. His body's response was immediate and intense. He had to force himself to look away.

"Like heaven...I imagine." She gazed at him, smiling. Then she picked up the white teapot and gracefully filled their cups with tea, as he imagined a geisha might do.

He sat down next to her and helped himself to the fruit and scones he had ordered. "So did you sleep well?" he asked, genuinely interested.

"Yes. I was exhausted from the trip. I'm not much of a drinker or a partyer, so I guess it caught up with me as well." She put her hand over his. "Actually, I would have preferred a light supper and strolling on the deck."

Paul's booming voice made Devon jump. "My goodness! You're up early, Akira. I thought you and your father would be resting. How nice to have you join us again." He laughed heartily and sat down at the table, but Sara was conspicuously missing. "So what's for breakfast?" He surveyed the offerings. "I guess I'm going to have to order my own food if I don't want to starve." In spite of his complaint, he helped himself to a heaping plate of fruit and scones. "Got any coffee?"

Devon reached down to the lower shelf on the cart to retrieve the pot and watched his uncle place his order on the phone. "Toast, jam, scrambled eggs, ham, and plenty of bacon." Paul covered the phone and asked Akira, "You sure you don't want something else?"

Akira giggled like a young girl. "I'm pacing myself. They serve a lot of food on this ship. I passed two dining rooms on the way here, and every plate was full."

"I know. It's great, isn't it? So what are your plans, Devon? There are all types of activities going on today." Paul smiled. If he was concerned about Sara and her missing doctor, he was doing a great job of hiding it. He launched into recommendations ranging from bingo and a scavenger hunt to shuffleboard and a rock-climbing wall. This led to a story about his first attempt at climbing a mountain and nearly dying when he was eighteen years old. Thankfully, it was cut short when the steward knocked and had to be let in by Devon. After placing Paul's phone order on the table, he removed two metal domes and waited for his approval.

"Good man," Paul said. "I knew I could count on you."

"Enjoy your meal, sir," the steward said before leaving the room.

Devon returned to his seat and refreshed Akira's tea. Then he watched her with interest as she politely talked about her homeland and interest in music and dance. He was surprised to discover that she had actually trained as a geisha in Kyoto and left her profession to spend time with her father.

Paul hemmed and hawed as he devoured his food. He finished off a third cup of coffee, then finally rose to leave. "Enjoy your day, you two. I have to get going. My walk starts in five minutes. I'm leaving Sara upstairs to mourn her dimwitted doctor." And with that, he was off.

Akira looked hopefully at Devon. "Do you like art?"

He grinned. "Well enough. But you're asking the wrong person. My uncle is an art dealer and has been in the business for years. You should see his home in England. The walls are covered with paintings. He and his wife live in this huge mansion with beautiful gardens, an indoor pool, and a horse stable. It's really quite the place."

"Sounds incredible."

"It is. But I think you had something else on your mind."

"You're right. I was hoping you'd like what I was planning."

Devon chuckled. He was sure he'd like it even if it weren't part of his crazy fantasy.

"I'm not sure how much you know about this ship," she continued, "but it's filled with original artworks. There are paintings and sculptures and decorative pieces lining the corridors and all the public areas."

"Yes, I noticed some of them yesterday. I was thinking about taking a better look at them today." Paintings were the last thing on his mind. He was only interested in spending time with her, and if that involved art, he was all for it.

"Our suite came with an iPad that is programmed with all the background information for taking a tour. It's like being on a floating museum. Don't you agree?"

"Absolutely. That sounds like a great idea."

"I guess the theme of the artwork on this ship is fairy tales and fantasy. It should be a lot of fun." She smiled again, and he couldn't help but do the same.

"If you don't mind, I'm going to grab a glass of water and take some aspirin before we go." He reached into his pocket and pulled out a packet with two white tablets in it.

"Do you have a headache?" She seemed genuinely concerned.

"Just a dull throbbing I can't seem to shake. I thought the fresh air and breakfast would help. I'm just grateful that it's not worse, considering how much wine I drank last night."

Akira put her hand on his arm. "I know a massage technique that works wonders. I used to be prone to tension headaches, and my adoptive mother showed me how to relieve them. I can try it on you if you'd like."

Devon swallowed hard. His mind betrayed him as soon as she said the word *massage*.

"It's just gentle rubbing to the cheeks, temples, and neck." She looked expectantly at him.

"It's worth a try."

She flashed him a warm smile and got up to stand behind him. "You stay seated and just relax. I'm going to start with your cheeks and slowly move to your jaw." She reached from behind and began gently applying pressure to his cheekbones with her fingers. Just as she had explained, she moved over his face, gently massaging his forehead and temples with little circular motions. Then she cupped his chin with her hands and used her thumbs against his jaw. Devon moaned as the feeling of her hands on him seemed to alleviate all the tension in his body.

"Now I'm going to work on your neck and ears." Akira applied pressure to the base of his neck with her fingers and thumbs. She leaned close to him, and he could feel her hot breath on his skin. "How does that feel, Devon?" she asked.

"Mmm...that's incredible." His voice was husky in his own ears.

"I'm glad."

Devon could almost feel her lips, and his body was threatening to betray him. He was now painfully aware of the fact that he had become aroused. She slowly eased her hands up on the sides of his neck, reaching his earlobes. Taking them between her forefingers and thumbs, she rubbed ever so gently. "Does that feel good?" She was leaning close to him again, and this time her lips brushed against his ear.

"Yes..." His brain could barely formulate a response.

Akira let go of his ears and began massaging his scalp and from his forehead to the nape of his neck. "Your hair is so soft and silky, Devon," she said. She kept massaging and running her fingers through his brown hair. He couldn't suppress another moan. His arousal was completely apparent, and she'd see it if she happened to look down.

"Akira..." His voice was a rasp. He wanted to tell her to stop, but it felt so damn good.

"How does your head feel?"

"Great."

She put her hands on his shoulders. "There's one more pressure point that I'm going to massage." She knelt down in front of him and began to massage his knees with her thumbs. He moved both hands over his lap to hide his arousal. Her position wasn't making things easier. He'd never been so embarrassed in his life.

If she noticed, she didn't say or do anything to acknowledge it. Instead, she finished her massage and then got up and ran her fingers through his hair again. "Better?"

"Yes. Thank you, Akira." Devon smiled weakly at her, still uncomfortably aware of his situation. He wasn't going to be able to get up for a while.

"I brought a toothbrush with me," she said. "Do you mind if I freshen up?"

"Not at all." He waited until she was in the bathroom and then got up and went into his room. There was no denying that he was taken with her and how inappropriately he had behaved after a few simple touches. He really needed to get himself under control. But it was easier said than done.

Akira was waiting for him when he returned to the living room. "All set?"

"Yep." He offered his arm, and she linked hers in his.

"I have the iPad in my purse. I think it will be best to start on the third deck and work our way up. This ship is huge, so we'll only be able to get through some of it today. I thought we'd look around for a while, and then maybe we could go on a tour of the galley this afternoon. I'd love to see how they prepare meals for such a large group of tourists. Is that all right with you?"

Devon chuckled. "Sounds like you have it all figured out. I defer to you." His eyes met hers, and they both smiled.

"Thank you." She squeezed his arm. "So let's get started." She directed them to the elevator, and they descended to the third floor. Then they turned right and began their tour.

It took them a couple of hours to cover the entire deck. They were completely engrossed in discussing each work of art while sharing little tidbits of personal information. Devon learned that Akira was a gifted musician, and she was surprised to discover that he was a former stockbroker and had earned a business degree at Stanford.

Akira leaned close. "So when did you get interested in diving?" She seemed fascinated by his extracurricular activities, and he was more than happy to share.

After expounding on his experiences for five minutes, he added, "Just before their trip to Japan, I got pulled into the business by my sister and brother-in-law. Which reminds me, with you being a geisha, you might know this remarkable woman they met. Her name was…uh, let me think of it." He was disappointed by his sudden loss of memory. He was usually so good with names, and the blank look on Akira's face left him struggling to get it right. "Maybe Marita. No…Mariko. Mariko Abe. That's it. Does that name sound familiar to you?"

She hesitated before answering. "No, I'm sorry. Mariko is a common name, and Japan is a very large place…at least when it comes to people. There are more than eight hundred geishas living in closed communities, and many of them have never met."

"Oh, I see. Anyway, my sister and brother-in-law own a company called Trident Ventures. They've developed quite a reputation for recovering rare treasures and hidden antiquities. They also caused quite a stir while traveling through your country."

A tiny crease formed between Akira's eyes. She seemed to be troubled or perhaps preoccupied by something he had said. Having had limited experience with Japanese women and absolutely none with geishas, Devon wondered if his remarks might have offended her in some way. "Are you all right?" he asked. "I get carried away sometimes. But I assure you that I have no problem taking directions. Just tell me to zip it, and I'll—"

She smiled. "No, Devon-san. I'm fine…honest. Just a bit more tired than I thought. Perhaps a little refreshment would help."

"I was thinking the same thing. Do you want me to find a shady spot on the deck? We could relax with a cold drink and get some fresh air."

Akira agreed. They made their way to the next deck and ordered iced teas. Then they found empty lounge chairs on the side of the ship. They sat and talked for nearly an hour, although Devon seemed to be doing most of the talking. It wasn't until he brought up his sister's wedding that he realized her married name had never been shared. Not that it made any difference. But he could have sworn Akira's brow dipped ever so slightly at the mention of Chase Cohen's name.

As their talk continued, she said she assumed Americans preferred using their first names but believed it proper to address elders by their surnames. Devon didn't see the problem in simply calling his uncle Paul, but then recalled from his experience with Japanese businessmen that formality was a sign of respect.

When it was time to move on, Akira rose first and then offered her hand to Devon. He gratefully accepted it, and she linked her arm in his again. They were just rounding the corner when Devon's uncle and aunt appeared, as if they'd been searching them out.

"So what are you two doing?" Sara asked.

"Akira and I are viewing the art on the ship," Devon said, smiling. "We were just taking a break. What about you? Where are you both headed?"

"Paul and I are investigating the safety features on this ship. We're getting a private tour later this afternoon."

"How commendable, Mrs. Lyons," Akira said, smiling sweetly.

"It's not for our benefit, dear. The tour involves a more urgent matter. You see, according to the Cruise Vessel Safety and Security Act, safety railings must be a minimum of forty-two inches high, and over one thousand security cameras are required to be in working order. If this ship passed a safety inspection like the cruise director said, foul play of any kind would be recorded. I want to know why the captain is refusing to acknowledge Peter's absence and why he isn't making any effort to find him."

Akira looked up at Devon. "I don't understand. Did something happen to Dr. Bradshaw?"

Paul groaned. "He jumped ship last night and ran off with a hospital director, only Sara refuses to believe it. I'm hoping our security tour will put her mind at ease and this whole matter to rest."

Sara huffed her disgust. "Paul detests Peter. If he fell overboard and was never seen again, my husband would be the happiest man alive."

"Oh good God, woman," Paul grumbled. "Are we going down this path again?"

"I'm sorry to interrupt," Akira said. "But if he truly fell overboard, I'm sure he would have been seen."

Devon laid his hand on hers. "It's probably best if we stay out of this."

Akira nodded.

"So are you ready to explore the ship again?" he asked.

"Yes." Akira turned to Sara. "I'm sure he'll turn up soon."

Sara held an intent, suspicious look, measuring everything about Akira. "Of course you'd say that. You seem to know everything."

Paul gave his wife a sharp look in response, as if he knew her thoughts and didn't approve. "Enough already. If you expect me to help you, then you need to behave yourself."

Sara looked away, pouting.

"We'll see you both later tonight," Paul said.

They parted ways, and, surprisingly, Akira avoided the subject of Bradshaw and dismissed Devon's aunt's rude behavior. Another hour passed during their self-guided tour before she suggested a break for lunch. They ate at one of the specialty restaurants, and both agreed that hamburgers and fries with an iced tea was the perfect meal. When their food finally arrived, Devon was thrilled to see pickles on his plate.

Akira smiled. "You're very easy to please, aren't you?"

"Well, I can't seem to get them at the diner back home."

"Really? Why not?" Akira looked puzzled.

"About a year ago, they were offering sweet gherkins on the menu, and I didn't know the difference between a regular pickle and the owner's homegrown specialty. He explained that pickles are the size of a corn dog, whereas gherkins are about the size of a Vienna sausage. So I changed my order from chili with gherkins on the side to a burger with dill pickles. By the guy's reaction, you would have thought I was a communist or something."

Akira laughed while Devon crunched triumphantly on his pickle.

When lunch was over, she directed them to the ship's galley, where the tour she had spoken of earlier was about to take place. There was a small group of people waiting, including Ben Hoffman and his roommate, Vivian Ward.

"Devon! Akira!" Vivian seemed thrilled to see them. "I'm surprised to see you here."

Devon snorted a laugh. He'd been enjoying his private time with Akira and had no interest in sharing her with anyone. Particularly these two. "So how was the napkin-folding class?" he asked.

Before Ben could answer, Vivian chimed in. "It was a lot of fun. We learned how to make a fan and a sail...and a bird of paradise."

Akira smiled. "They teach origami?"

"If you mean folding, indeed they do. There's something for everyone on this ship, including a bingo championship." She mentioned the cooking demonstration they'd signed up for, which was starting in five minutes.

Akira turned her attention to Hoffman. "I guess you must be terribly disappointed in Dr. Bradshaw. He was supposed to meet with you to discuss a patient's condition, wasn't he?"

"Oh, I never depend on doctors," he said. "Something urgent always comes up."

"Tell me about it," Vivian moaned. "I don't know why I agreed to come on this trip. Must have been blindsided by Ben's irresistible charm."

"Yep, that's me. Prince Benjamin Charming." Hoffman laughed. "We'd better get going. That is if you're still planning to make that Baked Alaska they're promoting."

"See you later," Vivian called out as they hurried away.

Devon noticed fine lines developing at the corners of Akira's eyes. Was she worried about something or just tired? "Ready to go back?" he asked. "The captain's reception starts at six forty-five p.m. in the Cabaret lounge. It's formal. You know, tuxedo attire. I'm not big on dressing up, but my uncle has insisted." He took her hand and brought it to his lips. "You don't mind joining us, do you? It would be incredibly boring if you said no."

Akira brushed loose hair away from her face. "I had a good time today, Devon. You were great company and very entertaining."

Devon was mortified and utterly disappointed. Somehow he'd blown it, but he wasn't sure how. "Sounds like a curse," he mumbled. "Guess I'm not your type after all."

Akira stood on her toes and kissed him on the cheek again. "You most definitely are. And you're sexy too—*very* sexy."

He gulped, and she smiled.

"Let me check with my father first," she said. "I'll let you know as soon as I can."

Devon looked down. He wanted her to go with him more than anything, but he needed to back off and abide by her decision. Loyalty and respect were essential elements in Japanese society—the key to a successful relationship. At least that's what he'd learned after witnessing his sister's turbulent romance with her hardheaded husband. If there were any hope of earning trust from this remarkable woman, Devon would need to reel her in slowly, like a prizewinning marlin.

Akira's eyes met his in a tender embrace. "By the way, when I touched your hair this morning, that wasn't part of the head massage. I did it because I couldn't resist."

Before he could gather his senses, she turned and left him standing there—speechless once again.

8

PLEASANTRIES

Devon had been called clever, an Adonis, lovable, and incredibly handsome by the women he kept company with but never sexy. Akira's compliment left him thinking about her for the rest of the day.

He wasn't sure what to make of Akira. He only knew that he couldn't wait to be in her presence again. This alluring, beguiling creature seemed to have cast a spell over him, and he was happy to be under her control.

After a final inspection in the mirror, Devon straightened his black bow tie and was as ready as he was going to be for the reception. He had attended dozens of parties during his stint as a stockbroker, but for some unknown reason, he hated formal affairs. Whether it was because of dressing up or being forced to interact with potential clients, he'd viewed cocktail parties and black-tie dinners as a complete waste of time and the people attending them as pretentious assholes.

Paul descended the stairs in the suite wearing a black Armani suit. "There you are, Devon," he said. "Looking good, son. The sea air seems to agree with you." He slapped Devon on the back in a fatherly fashion, then took a step back. "Or is it that Asian beauty you've been keeping company with?"

Devon was about to respond when the doorbell sounded. Paul swung the door wide open, and Akira magically appeared. She was dressed in a shimmery gold gown that had an ethereal quality to it. Her long black hair was swept to one side and fell in long spiraling curls over one shoulder. Her dramatic eye makeup, pink lipstick, and soft blush highlighted her gorgeous features. Devon was already taken with her natural beauty, but the cosmetics she wore made her stunning.

For the first time in Devon's recollection, Paul was almost speechless for a moment. "Would you look at her—have you seen anyone so beautiful?"

Devon had already locked eyes with Akira. "No, never. She's breathtaking," he half whispered. He approached her and extended his hand. She kept her eyes on him as he drew her hand to his lips and kissed it softly. She smiled, raising the temperature in the room ten degrees.

"You look so handsome, Devon," she said.

Paul cleared his throat, turning their eyes to him. "Sara isn't feeling well tonight. And I'm afraid Devon and I are sorry excuses for escorts. I hope you don't mind us distracting from your beauty." Paul laughed at his own cleverness, and Akira squeezed Devon's hand.

"I respectfully disagree, Mr. Lyons," she said. "I'm paired with the two most attractive men on the planet." She smiled at Paul, then locked eyes with Devon. He could feel his pounding heart threatening to burst through his chest. She hooked her arm in Paul's and continued to hold Devon's hand. Then she surprised him by linking their fingers. "Shall we?" she said.

As they made their way to the elevator, Paul turned to Akira. "So have you two been enjoying yourselves on this trip?"

She tightened her grip on Devon. "Yes, I believe we—"

"It's the best!" Devon cut in. "What about you and Sara? I thought she was feeling better...after hearing that Bradshaw was located."

"He's back?" Akira asked. "On board the ship?"

Devon leaned toward her. "Not quite yet. He's flying to Princess Cays to meet up with us. According to the purser, he missed the last call in Fort Lauderdale after hooking up with a Russian woman."

"Hooking up?"

Devon laughed. "They snuck off to a hotel last night, and he apparently lost track of time. She was a speaker at the conference and not a paid guest on the ship. So as it turned out, Sara's been worrying about nothing."

Paul sniffed. "Just try convincing her of that. She thinks the crew contrived an absurd story to keep her quiet."

"Oh, I see," Akira said. "What about the woman? Is she coming back with him?"

"No. Seems she had another engagement and made arrangements for a flight home tomorrow. So I guess it wasn't meant to be."

Devon smiled. "Well, that's not hard to imagine...after spending time with that guy."

"Maybe we should focus on something more interesting," Paul said. "You know, rumor has it that the ship's captain is a real heartthrob. According to Vivian Ward, women on the ship are swooning over him." He winked at Akira. "They're going to be incredibly jealous after discovering you had dinner with him."

They reached the fifth floor, and the elevator door opened. Before them stood a long line of people waiting to have their picture taken with the captain before attending his reception.

Paul turned around. "I think you should take a photo of just you and the captain, Akira. No need to have me and Devon in there breaking the lens." He guffawed.

"Absolutely not," she said. "I hate having my picture taken. So if I have to do it, then so do you."

Paul smiled. "She's gorgeous and hates being snapped. I'll never understand that." He rested an arm on her shoulder. "We'll do whatever you want, my dear."

The line moved faster than expected, and before long, they were meeting the captain. The rumors circulating about him had been right. The guy had dark, deep set eyes, a tawny face, and a chiseled jaw. His impressive uniform was wrapped around his toned physique.

"Well, hello there," the captain said to Akira. "Aren't you a looker? Captain Kevin Brice at your service." He took her hand and brought it to his lips. Then he smiled directly at Devon, leaving him bristling.

"So which one of these lucky men is joining you tonight?"

"Both of us," Devon informed him.

"It appears that you have two bodyguards this evening." Brice's smile widened as he watched Devon.

"That's right," Akira said. She linked her arm through Devon's and looked up smiling. "I'm well protected."

After taking their photos, they entered the reception area. Everyone on the ship was dressed to kill, but no one was more impressive than Akira. Waiters were working the room with trays of champagne and fancy hors d'oeuvres. There were two bars set up for hard liquor and assorted cocktails. Devon stopped before one and turned to his date. "Can I get you something?"

"Just a soda. I'm not a big drinker. I'll wait to have wine with dinner."

"What about champagne?"

"I'll have to pass." Akira smiled. "But it doesn't mean I'm not tempted."

Paul chuckled. "I knew they'd still be here." Benjamin Hoffman and his would-be fiancée stood next to a bar, anxiously waving Paul over. "You don't mind, do you?" Before either of them could answer, Paul hurried to join his new friends.

Devon's eyes dropped to Akira's full, luscious lips. He forced himself to keep from kissing her by focusing on a group of giggling women in the opposite corner. "What do you suppose they're laughing at?"

"Women can be catty. They look for any reason to poke fun at people they don't understand."

Devon quirked a brow. "Maybe they resent threatening women."

Akira looked down, shaking her head. "Certainly not me."

"Oh, I beg to differ." Devon caught the eye of the flirty blonde in the group. "Seems you've given them plenty of reason to worry. You're the brightest star in this place."

Akira lifted her chin. "You flatter me too much."

Devon's eyes traveled past her. "I guess I should thank your father for allowing you to come."

"My father?"

He motioned his head toward the double-door entry. "That's him, isn't it?" An imposing man in a navy-blue suit visually scanned the room before locking eyes on them. His permanent scowl and stocky physique reminded Devon of a Japanese mafia character he'd seen in an old Sean Connery movie.

Akira's eyes followed his gaze. "He's never been the social type. I'm actually surprised to see him here."

"Why do you suppose he came?"

"To make sure I arrived safely."

"I hope I'm not upsetting him by being here with you."

"Don't worry, Devon. He doesn't control my social life."

Her father strode toward them. "Mr. Lyons," he said, acknowledging his presence.

Devon stiffened his posture and bowed deeply in respect. "Mr. Hamada. It's a pleasure to meet you, sir."

The man grimaced and looked back at his daughter. "Watashi to issho ni kite kudasai."

Her eyes remained on Devon. "Iie. Daijoubu desu. Shisurei na koto ha arimasen."

"Devon, yaoi ni muchuu na bakamono. Anata no jikan wo matte imasu."

"You're being impolite, Father. I won't stay out late. Have a good night and enjoy your dinner." She held a steady gaze, and he stormed away, mumbling words under his breath.

Devon wasn't sure what to make of this strange exchange. However, hearing his name mentioned made it easy to assume he was the cause of their discord.

"So what was that about?" he asked.

Akira laid her hand on his forearm. "He figured out how much I like you."

"Really? You do?" Devon's heart leaped in his chest.

"Yes. Very much." She smiled and linked her arm in his. "Let's make the most of our evening together, shall we?"

He grinned. "If you insist." As if there was anything else he'd rather do.

She leaned forward and kissed him on the cheek again. "I promise you won't be disappointed." She gave him a rather naughty look.

Vivian Ward was smiling as she and Dr. Hoffman walked up to greet them. "You two look awfully cozy," she said.

The doctor moved close to Devon and half whispered, "I see napkin folding in your future."

"Not if I can help it."

Hoffman laughed.

"We were just discussing our plans for this evening," Akira said. "I'm looking forward to sitting at the captain's table. Did you get a chance to meet him, Vivian?"

"Yes. I was surprised by how handsome he is," she gushed. "Like a young Harrison Ford."

Hoffman's face took on a sour expression. "He's handsome; I'll give him that. But I don't care for his constant flirting."

Devon laughed. "Not your type, huh?"

Akira glanced at Devon. "I suppose he's good-looking in that movie star kind of way, but it barely registered with me. I'm more attracted to someone whose face says something about them. You know…a man with sculpted features, auburn hair, and beautiful hazel eyes. Personally, I find that much sexier."

All eyes were on Devon, adding heat to the room. Thankfully, the dinner bell rang, alerting everyone that it was time to proceed. Paul showed up, reiterating the announcement. "It's happening. Time to go, folks." He took Akira by the hand, leaving Devon trailing behind.

They arrived in the dining room and were escorted to a large table in the middle of the room where sixteen upholstered armchairs and corresponding wineglasses of every size awaited. The maître d' informed them that the ship's commander would be sitting at the head of the table and the staff captain would be seated at the opposite end. Name cards had been placed on the Cherrywood table next to fancy folded napkins and round gold chargers. It quickly became apparent that Akira would be seated next to Captain Brice and across the table from Devon. After a second round of introductions, Brice impressed everyone by memorizing the names of every woman at the table, but unfortunately, the same didn't apply to men. They were addressed as *sir, mister,* and *ahem* and basically avoided, which multiplied Devon's growing resentment.

"He's a real charmer, isn't he?" Vivian whispered to Devon.

Devon snorted a laugh. "He certainly thinks so."

The meal proceeded with the wine flowing like water and included five gourmet courses. Devon was surprised that the captain, when distracted from his flirtations, was actually interesting and knowledgeable on virtually any subject. He regaled them with fascinating stories and even invited them on a private tour of the bridge on their next day at sea.

When the captain wasn't talking, Paul kept the conversation flowing by discussing modern art and troubling politics. Vivian found an opportunity to rave about her onboard classes. And Akira smiled whenever she and Devon made eye contact, adding a new layer of excitement to the evening.

Dr. Hoffman had been seated beside Akira and, for the last twenty minutes, remained determined to command her attention. He finally gave up and turned back to Vivian. The meal ended, and the captain departed. Everyone rose to their feet and seemed anxious to return to the comfort of their rooms.

Devon took Akira's hand. "Do you want to walk with me on the upper deck? It's beautiful out tonight, and the sky is amazing." He brought her hand to his lips. "To tell you the truth, I don't want to end our time together. Not just yet."

Despite the late hour, Akira agreed and joined him outside, shivering a little.

"Are you cold?" he asked. Before she could answer, he removed his jacket and slipped it over her shoulders. He put his arm around her waist and pulled her closer to him as they continued their walk. They were engaged in easy conversation when Akira began to slow down a bit.

"Do you want to sit on one of the lounge chairs for a while?" Devon asked. "We can lean back and look at the stars."

"I'd like that," she said.

They found an oversize chair in a quiet spot and managed to squeeze into it together, with Akira lying partially on top of him. He couldn't get close enough, and his body had already begun to respond to her proximity. He gently caressed her cheek, and she sighed contentedly.

The vast, seemingly empty space above them was filled with glittering, diamond-like stars. Devon had never noticed how lovely the evening sky was before, not until he met Akira, that is. Each twinkling star seemed to be in its proper place, filling the expanse of the heavens. Shadowy, ribbonlike clouds were flowing around the full moon as it ruled over the glorious night.

"The moon is so beautiful," Akira half whispered.

Each crater on its bright face was visible. The moon, the stars, the streaming clouds—everything glowed with its own luminous light. Everything was perfect with this amazing woman in his arms.

"Devon?"

"Yes?"

She shifted her position, and he followed suit so that they were lying face-to-face. "Kiss me."

He leaned forward and pressed his lips gently against hers. They kissed slowly and tenderly with no tongues, just lips caressing lips. A radiating warmth spread throughout his body. It was obvious to him that there was an intense physical attraction between them that grew with each passing day. He wanted to make love to her here and now, but he would have been just as satisfied with holding her in his arms. There was something about this sweet simple kiss they were sharing that was arousing him in ways he never thought possible. He wanted to savor every minute of it for as long as it lasted.

"Devon?" Akira pulled back and smiled at him. "I haven't felt this happy in a very long time."

She traced his lips with her finger, and he sensed himself getting harder than he already was. He began questioning how much longer he could hold back with her. "Me neither."

He could hear a huskiness in his own voice. They lay silent for a few minutes without saying a word. Then Devon broke the silence. "I should get you back to your room. It's awfully late, and we could both use the rest. I have a feeling that neither one of us got much sleep last night."

Akira agreed. Devon helped her up from the lounge chair, and they headed back inside with his arm around her waist.

"The ship will be docking in the Bahamas tomorrow," she said. "Did you sign up for any shore excursions? I'm on an eight o'clock tour to see some ancient ruins and a pirate's keep...and maybe snorkel if time allows."

He grinned and pulled her closer. "I already signed up on the same tour. Guess we'll be spending the day together after all."

Akira's smile lit up her whole face. "I was hoping that we would, but I wasn't sure if you had made plans. Do you know what everyone else is doing?"

"I think Paul is going on a boat tour with Sara and a large group from the ship. He wanted me to come along, but I don't think he'll argue the fact when he finds out you're keeping me company." Devon wasn't so sure Akira's father would feel the same way. "Do you want to have breakfast with me tomorrow? We can have it delivered to my room or go to the international buffet together."

Akira smiled brightly. "If you don't mind, let's try the buffet."

He agreed, and they made plans to meet in the morning. After arriving at her suite, they stood outside in the hallway for a few minutes.

"I had the perfect evening, Akira," Devon said, "thanks to you." He leaned forward and gave her one last lingering kiss, and she responded by running her fingers through his hair. He couldn't suppress a moan.

"I thought you might like that."

He smiled wickedly at her. "Just for the record, the part of the headache massage where you knelt between my legs and rubbed my thighs…"

"Yes? What about it?" Akira asked innocently.

"I liked that part the best." He gave her a long, inviting look.

She giggled. "I know. I couldn't help noticing." And with that, she turned and used the key to her room. She stepped inside and smiled back at him. "I'll see you in the morning." Then she closed the door, leaving him in the hallway.

Devon just stood there staring after her. He couldn't have responded even if he'd wanted to.

9

PREMONITION

Blood was pooling and spreading across the wood floor at an alarming rate. Akira knelt in it, stuffing bath towels under the brown metal door. She couldn't stop the flow, no matter how hard she tried. It covered her legs, soaked her white nightgown, and seeped through cracks in the wall.

"Akira!" Takashi screamed her name from the other side of the door. "Help me!" He was trapped in the hallway, drowning in an ocean of blood. She grabbed a chair from the living room and braced it against the door, trying to save herself from the crushing tide. Standing on her toes, she peeked through the eyehole and watched as waves of red splashed against the door.

That's when she woke up and realized it was all a dream. A horrible, gut-wrenching nightmare. For a few seconds, she just lay there with her heart pounding in her chest as her eyes adjusted to the dim light in the room. She had a raging thirst and a dull ache in her temples. There was a half-empty water bottle on the nightstand that she'd placed there the night before. She reached for it and drained it dry. Then she let her head fall back on the oversize pillow.

It suddenly dawned on her that Takashi hadn't been waiting in his usual place on the beige tweed sofa when she returned hours earlier. She had assumed he was upstairs sulking after her refusal to follow his orders. Having heard his negative opinion of Devon, she had no interest in returning to her room or listening to anything he had to say. And it seemed pointless to remind him she was doing her job by building an alliance with passengers on the ship. How else would she get the information she needed concerning Paul and Sara Lyons's involvement in Keiko's death and details about Bradshaw's recent disappearance? Besides, Devon was proving to be a nice diversion and a great source for alleviating her pent-up stress. Especially after Juno Kurosaki's assault on her. However, it was going to be more difficult than she thought to leave Devon behind, knowing that she had used him to get closer to his aunt and uncle.

Akira smiled sardonically. The bashful, timid woman Devon Lyons had come to care for was in truth a wanton creature, coached and experienced in sexual gratification. No one, including this kind, caring man, could please her for more than a week, no matter how hard he might try. Kenji Ota had seen to that in a beautiful hotel room overlooking Kyoto, Japan. He used her body, twisted her mind, and made it virtually impossible for her to love another man, as Devon was soon to find out. But in the meantime, was it so wrong to enjoy his company and how different he made her feel? She felt younger, pure and innocent, as if everything in her life were new once again, as if she had been given a second chance at happiness—even if it wasn't true.

Akira swung her legs out of bed and stood up. She wrapped herself in the white terrycloth robe she had found in the closet and ventured into the living room, half expecting to see Takashi with his mug of steaming coffee flipping through a Japanese newspaper with a scowl on his face. But he was nowhere in sight. She climbed the stairs and knocked at his door before opening it to take a peek. The navy suit he had worn the night before was thrown across the foot of his bed. The covers had been turned down for the night, but it appeared that the bed hadn't been slept in.

She opened Takashi's closet and noticed a few empty hangers—most likely from the clothes he had changed into before leaving the suite. In the corner, behind his black suitcase, was the carefully wrapped katana he had received permission to bring on board. According to the documents he carried with him, the sword was being delivered to a collector in England who had purchased it as a rare antique. Even though it had actually been brought there for Akira's use.

In Takashi's absence, she took the opportunity to collect it for safekeeping. She didn't want to visit his room again if it became necessary to retrieve it.

She returned downstairs and was preparing to change her clothes when a knock at the door snagged her attention. She scanned the living room before leaning the sword against the wall. Upon opening the door, she was surprised to see the housekeeper and her silent assistant waiting outside.

"Do you need extra towels, miss?" Felicia asked.

"No...I'm fine. Thank you." Akira's eyes bypassed the housekeeper and landed on the shy woman stationed next to the rolling cart. She was the same woman she had passed at various times while touring the ship. The petite brunette was surprisingly attractive and fit for her age, which Akira estimated to be near sixty. She had soft brown eyes that refused to connect and a sweet, unreadable expression.

"What's your name?" Akira asked her. While tracking her targets, the geisha had discovered that silent observers like this woman were great witnesses, often possessing a storehouse of information.

"This is Clare Richards," Felicia answered. "She's not able to speak. But she's one of the hardest-working employees we've ever had." Felicia patted her assistant on the shoulder, then smiled at Akira. "Was there anything else you needed?"

"Dr. Bradshaw boarded the ship two days ago and had been missing for a while. I understand he's back now but was just wondering if either one of you had heard anything? You know… about why he was gone."

Clare shook her head.

"It doesn't appear so, Miss Hamada," Felicia said. "People disembark for various reasons, and we're often not aware until it comes time to clean their rooms. In fact, an elderly gentleman with a sprained ankle flew home yesterday, and a new passenger is arriving tomorrow. It's rather difficult to keep track of everyone with so many guests on board."

"I completely understand," Akira said. "It's really not my place to ask. But I would like to leave a note for the doctor. Do you happen to know which room he's staying in?"

"No, I'm sorry, miss. You would have to contact the reception desk for that information."

"Oh yes, of course. By the way, have you seen my father anywhere? He seems to have wandered off as well."

Both women shook their heads.

"Well, if you happen to see him, would you please tell him that I'm concerned?"

"Yes, I will, Miss Hamada," Felicia said. "But you needn't worry. He'll be back soon."

Akira watched the door slowly close. She thought about Clare's speech impediment and found it rather intriguing. But what was even more interesting was the flash of recognition in her eyes when Bradshaw's name was mentioned.

10

INFATUATION

Devon had no problem understanding his physical attraction to Akira—with her being the most beautiful creature he'd ever seen. But his need to just be with her was something strangely unknown. It wasn't blind obsession like he had experienced with other women, not even mindless lust like he had shared with the infamous Selena Pollero. More than three years ago, after his terminal relationship with Selena had ended, he'd shut down completely. Yet here he was again, opening his heart up to a woman he barely knew.

Akira had made her interest very clear with her touches, soft kisses, and sexual innuendos. He was the one who kept doubting himself and his willingness to commit. But even if she hadn't wanted a physical relationship, he would have accepted it and been perfectly happy to spend time with her. His connection to her had nothing to do with sexual desire. It was far deeper.

He left the entry door to the suite slightly ajar and went out onto the balcony to enjoy the morning air. He knew Akira would be arriving at any moment for breakfast and their outing, and just the idea of seeing her made the day a little brighter.

Akira stepped inside to greet him. "Good morning."

"Good morning, beautiful."

She crossed the room and kissed his lips softly. He put his arm around her and pulled her closer, deepening the kiss. When they finally separated, Akira's cheeks were flushed, and his heart was racing.

Akira smiled. "I'm starving. What about you?"

"Famished. Let's go before I collapse." He took her hand, and they left the room to search for the buffet. It took a while to reach the other side of the ship, but Devon didn't notice. They discovered a dozen things to talk about and an equal number of shared interests. After arriving in the Window Café, they joined the short line that had already formed and picked out their favorites. Then they found a seat on the heated deck and ordered two cappuccinos from an assisting waiter.

They talked about food, the scheduled tour, and Akira's father wandering off. In Devon's mind, her devotion to him was the cause of Devon and Akira's problems although she refused to believe it. She claimed she couldn't care less about his approval or lack thereof, which seemed out of character for a woman who'd been trained to please men most of her life.

"If a geisha signs a contract with a sponsor," Devon quizzed, "does she become his lifelong mistress?"

Akira finished her mimosa and set her glass down. Then she rested her elbow on the table and her chin on her fisted hand. "*Memoirs of a Geisha* was a fictional book and Hollywood movie. Geishas in Kyoto are referred to as geikos and are professional entertainers skilled in the art of illusion. They provide a glimpse into the past and share elements of our culture that would otherwise be lost." She sat back and sighed deeply. "I hope I didn't make a mistake by being honest with you. I'm not ashamed of my past. The fact is, I'm rather proud of it. But you need to understand, Devon, it's not who I choose to be anymore."

She hadn't answered his question, but for obvious reasons, he didn't care. "I think you know how I feel about you." He hesitated before adding, "I just want you to know that I'm not interested in having a fling. That's not me, and I don't think it's you. Whatever we have between us, it's not something I take lightly." His honesty left him feeling exposed, vulnerable, and incredibly foolish.

Akira squeezed his hand. "I know you're not like that, and neither am I." She smiled shyly at him, and then she leaned close and lowered her voice. "But I might be tempted to go all the way—if that's what you want."

"Maybe you shouldn't have told me that, Akira." His voice deepened. "Now I have the upper hand." He leaned forward until they were almost within kissing distance.

Her lips curled up in a smile. "We'll see about that."

He laughed in return. Who was he kidding? She had him eating out of her hand, and he was doing so willingly.

"Shall we get going?" she asked.

Devon had his arm around Akira as they made their way back to his room, smiling and laughing all the way. When they stepped inside, Paul looked up from his coffee cup and newspaper.

"So there you are," he said.

Devon removed his arm from Akira's shoulders. "Akira and I had breakfast together at the buffet. We're on the same tour today."

"That's great. I would have felt bad forcing you to stay with us. Especially with Sara in one of her moods. The cruise director refused to refund our fees even though Sara is suffering from a migraine. Turns out you have to cancel the day before your tour and have until eleven p.m. to do so. It's her own fault for waiting so long to call."

"Is Dr. Bradshaw planning to go?" Akira asked.

"According to Sara, he slipped a note under our door and was planning to bail today. I'm sure his refusal to talk to her isn't helping, but it's sure a nice break for me."

Devon studied his uncle's face. "Is he still treating her?"

"Yes. But unless there's something urgent, she's on her own for a few hours."

Akira's eyes moved from Devon to Paul. "Is there anything I can do to help?"

"That's very kind for you to ask, but Dr. Bradshaw is the only person Sara trusts with her health. If you don't mind, just look after my nephew today. I'm sure she'll be better by the time you get back."

Akira nodded. "Yes, of course. I'm going to go finish getting ready. I'll be back in ten minutes."

Devon agreed and watched her walk away with a perpetual smile on his face. Before he could enter his bedroom, Paul stopped him in his tracks. "Can I speak to you for a minute?" He put his arm around Devon's shoulders and urged him to sit down. "Between you and me, that girl is too trusting and dependent for my liking. She's apt to get hurt if someone doesn't look after her, which is why I'm glad you've chosen to do so. But I strongly suggest you be careful, son. Her father has been skulking about…popping in and out of rooms. He seems to be spending a lot of time at the Internet café researching people on this ship. I get the distinct impression he's not someone you'd want to cross."

"I'll be with Akira the whole time, Uncle Paul. I'm not going to let anything happen to her."

"Well, I certainly hope not."

"There's no need for you to worry. We're all grown-ups here."

"I agree. Just watch your back, OK?"

Devon smiled. "Right." He took his leave and returned to his room to finish getting ready. When he was done, he walked back into the living room and found Akira waiting for him with a bright orange bag draped over one shoulder.

"Looks like you're all set," Paul said. "Have fun on your outing."

They stepped out into the corridor, and Devon stopped Akira. "Did your father say anything about me?"

Akira flushed slightly. "He commented on how much time we spend together."

"He did?"

"I told him that I like you a lot and that I was planning to be with you as much as I could." She looked at him shyly. "Is that all right?"

Devon let out a deep breath. "I basically told my uncle the same thing."

She rose up on her toes and kissed him on the right cheek.

"Tell me what you want, Akira." He needed to hear her say it.

"You, Devon. I want you." She kissed him again in a way that made it impossible for him to doubt it.

He grinned foolishly at her. "And I want you to have whatever you want."

She giggled. "Then we're in agreement. Now let's get going." Akira led them to the tenders, and they boarded to make their way to Princess Cays. Although it was a little bumpy, it didn't seem to bother either of them. They disembarked, boarded their bus, and seated themselves toward the back.

Once they were settled, Devon grinned at her. "May I ask what you have in that bag?"

She laughed. "Sunscreen, a hat, a blouse to cover my arms, water bottles for me and you, a small towel, and practical shoes."

"You're better prepared than I am. I forgot about sunscreen."

"No problem. I was planning to share with you. In fact, I think we should put some on now before the tour starts. I can help you with your face. It's hard to do without a mirror."

Devon agreed, and Akira applied some lotion to her hand and then began rubbing it into his skin, starting with his forehead and working down to his cheeks and chin. He couldn't stop thinking about the headache massage and how much he liked being touched by her.

"Mmm...that felt good." He gave her a naughty grin. "My turn." She squeezed lotion into his hand and raised her face to him. She wasn't wearing any makeup—only her natural beauty, which continued to amaze him. He applied the sunscreen slowly and sensually, tracing every contour with his fingers. "Did that feel good?" he whispered in her ear.

"Yes," she murmured.

"Glad to hear it. I'd be happy to apply more wherever you'd like it." His hot breath blew against her skin.

"I may take you up on your offer...if I decide to go swimming."

Devon couldn't get the thought of running his hands all over her body out of his head. He leaned in close and told her, "You don't play fair."

She giggled. "I know. You don't mind, do you?" She caressed his cheek.

"No, not at all."

The tour guide interrupted them, explaining how the tour would work. Then he launched into a talk about the culture in the region and continued until they reached their destination. "Much of the island's architecture and way of life were influenced by Loyalist settlers in the late 1700s," he explained. "There were miles of glistening pink-and-white-sand beaches, serene colonial villages, and rolling acres of pineapple plantations." At that point, they exited the bus and began a short walk out to an old ruin. Akira opened the umbrella she had brought and insisted that Devon borrow her straw hat to cover his head. He hesitated but eventually agreed. She took a photo of him alone and then got another tour member to take a picture of them together.

Devon could just imagine the ribbing he'd suffer if his uncle got wind of him wearing her hat. "Do not, under penalty of death, share these photos with anyone."

Akira reluctantly agreed, and he settled back in step with her. When they arrived at the site, Devon was awed by its breathtaking beauty. The stone ruins were sitting on a sandy cliff overlooking the Caribbean Sea, and the views were spectacular. The visit alone would have been worth the trip. But there was more to come. The tour guide gave them an entertaining and informative explanation of the history of each of the structures. They were allotted two hours, and Devon and Akira set out on their own to explore their surroundings. After finding the perfect spot to enjoy the ocean view, they sat down and opened the bottles of water Akira had wisely packed.

Her eyes met his. "This is very romantic, don't you think?"

"Yes, it is." He put his arm around her and kissed her cheek. They sat there silently for a few minutes until Devon spoke. "It's taken me a long time to trust again. And to tell you the truth, it's because of you that I believe in the possibility of love."

Akira blushed and looked away.

"Women have always been a mystery to me. I guess my ineptness comes from my mother abandoning our family when I was eight years old." Devon took a deep breath, closed his eyes, and lowered his voice. "It was a traumatizing, hurtful time in my life. I grew up blaming myself and everyone around me and made some bad choices along the way."

Akira put her hand over his, opening his eyes. "I'm sorry you've had such a hard life, Devon. It must have been very difficult for you and your sister to grow up without a mother."

"I guess it was at times. My father wasn't very good at being an only parent, and the mistakes I made damaged our relationship. I'm not proud of who I became, not after risking and losing so much. I'm just glad that my sister turned out so well. She was always there...determined to keep me on the right track. I don't know how I would have survived this long without her."

"I'm sure you've helped her in many ways too and are stronger than you know."

"You're very sweet. That's one of the many things I like about you." He smiled, and her cheeks reddened. "And you blush at compliments. It's very endearing." She looked away, and he grinned. For once, he had her at a disadvantage and wasn't the one left speechless. "So tell me about your father, Akira. I'm sure he isn't happy about me monopolizing your time."

"He doesn't control who I am or whom I love, Devon. I told him that we spent the day together yesterday and that I thought you were extremely attractive. He figured it out from there."

"You actually said that? About me being attractive?" Devon forgot his uncle's warning. Going slow wasn't in his vocabulary and would never be his style.

"I guess I needed to share that with someone." She smiled at him.

Shit. He wanted her in the worst possible way. "I suppose we need to get back to the bus." Devon glanced at his watch, but the time didn't register.

"Yes, you're right. Unless you want to be stranded here alone with me." Akira looked at him hopefully.

Devon laughed. "I'd be more than tempted if I didn't have your father to answer to."

Akira looked down. "He wouldn't be pleased about my absence. I'm sure of that."

Devon got up and helped Akira to her feet. They walked slowly back to the bus, enjoying the last views of beautiful scenery.

As they approached the bus, a cruise ship photographer snapped their photo. Akira looked surprised and slightly upset. "Why did he do that?" she asked.

"They take photos on different tours and sell them back to you as mementos of your trip. You can buy them in the photo shop after they display them for purchase. That's why they took our photo on the way into the captain's reception and as we got on and off the ship."

Akira's brow furrowed. "Will my father be able to see it? The picture of us together?"

"If he visits the camera shop. Is that a problem?"

Her lips took on a dour expression. "No. Of course not. I was just curious."

"We can look for it together and buy it or destroy it before anyone sees it, if that's what you want."

"Actually, I would like to keep it...but only for me. For a reminder of our wonderful day together."

Devon chuckled. "Whatever makes you happy, Akira."

They got on the bus for the hour ride back to town, and she turned to him. "Do you have a tropical-print shirt you can wear to dinner tonight?"

He gave her an "are you serious?" look. "I think you already know the answer."

It seemed that Akira found his answer amusing. "I didn't think so. Tonight's dinner has a tropical theme. According to the schedule I received in our suite, they want us all to wear tropical clothing." She bit her lip to suppress her laugh. "I can help you find a shirt to wear in one of the shops here, if you don't mind skipping lunch."

Devon groaned but didn't argue. By the time they got back to the dock, they were both exhausted, and Devon realized the pain from an injury in his lower back had returned.

"Are you OK?" Akira was obviously concerned about him.

"I'm fine. Got a slight ache in my back, but nothing a little rest can't fix."

Akira bit her lower lip. "I know a massage technique that might help."

Devon couldn't hide his interest, nor could he tear his eyes away from her lips. He swallowed hard. "Hmm...considering how well the massage worked last time, I might give it a try."

Akira smiled seductively at him. "I thought you might be interested."

Devon laughed. "Am I that transparent?"

She giggled. "Yes, you are. But all kidding aside, I think a massage will help. Do you promise to take it seriously?"

"Yes, baby. I'll be good." He hoped he would be able to keep his word. His reaction to the last massage had been pretty intense and embarrassing.

"You'll need to lie down. I think your bed is the best spot for this."

He swallowed hard. She wasn't going to make this easy for him. "As you wish."

They walked across the ramp leading to the ship and presented their identification cards for scanning. Devon was surprised to see Captain Brice taking part in the security detail and noticed the broad smile on his face when Akira came into view.

"Well, hello there, Miss Hamada. Did you have a nice day?"

"Yes, I did. Thank you."

"Glad to hear it. Looks like you found your black purse too. It's a good thing, because we don't like to reissue boarding cards and room keys. I'm sure you can understand why."

Akira glanced at Devon. "I'm sorry, but I don't recall having a conversation with you about my purse. Exactly when did this happen?"

The captain chuckled. "With so many beautiful women on this ship, I have a hard time keeping track."

Devon snorted a laugh. "Yeah, right."

The captain disregarded Devon and addressed Akira. "Will I see you at dinner?"

"I'm not sure what our plans are. But it's possible."

"Well, if you'd like to dine in the Neptune Café tonight, I'm sure I can arrange for a seat at my table..."

"Good evening, Captain," Devon said.

He reached for Akira's arm and steered her toward the elevator. When they arrived on his floor, he walked past several members of the housekeeping staff, and Akira nodded to them.

"That man has a thing for you," he told her, opening the door to his suite.

She angled a look. "You think so, huh?"

"Without a doubt."

"Along with five hundred other women." Akira smiled. "So, Devon...do you wear boxer shorts?"

"Yeah, why?" He gulped at the thought of where this was leading.

"They're less constricting than a bathing suit. You don't mind my asking, do you?"

"No, of course not." He stood there frozen again.

Akira smiled. "Then take off your pants and lie facedown on the bed. When I'm finished, you'll feel much better. I promise."

Devon didn't doubt it for a moment—only feared it would make him feel *too* good. He removed his pants and lay down on the mattress as instructed. Akira applied pressure to his shoulders and worked her way down to his hips. Her touch was firm but gentle, and the pain in his spine began to ease at her touch. "You're amazing," he told her. "Where did you learn how to do this?"

"It's an acupressure technique I learned from a Chinese physician. It works on different muscle groups." She continued the massage for fifteen minutes, and Devon relaxed, thankful that his body was cooperating. "How's your back now? Any better?"

"It's perfect. I can't believe that I feel this good. Especially after tweaking it on the *Stargazer*. Traveling on a yacht sounds like a picnic, but it comes with a lot of hard work."

Devon rolled over, and Akira sat beside him on the bed. She ran her fingers through his hair and traced his lips with her fingers in the most erotic fashion. His body reacted immediately. He was lying faceup in his underwear, and she was sitting here touching him. Driving him absolutely crazy.

She leaned forward to kiss him, but this time the kiss wasn't just on the lips. Her open mouth met his, and their tongues caressed each other in a way that spoke volumes about their need to physically express what they were feeling. Akira entangled her fingers in his hair, and Devon ran his hands down her back. He was fully aroused, and there was no hiding it in his current state of undress. "Akira…"

She nibbled his earlobe and planted soft kisses on his jaw, trailing them down to his throat. "I feel the same way. I wouldn't be here with you if I didn't."

Devon's arousal intensified. He was sure the head of his cock was peeking out of the flap in his boxers, and there was nothing he could do to hide it. He moaned as waves of desire passed through him. She looked up, met his gaze, and kissed him once more on the lips. Then she began to rise from the bed.

"It's getting late. My father will be waiting, and I still need to get ready for dinner."

Devon covered himself with his hand and stared at her in disbelief.

"I had the perfect day," she said, smiling. "I'm looking forward to being with you tonight."

The way she said it made it impossible for him to doubt her meaning and to stop obsessing over her.

11

CLUELESS

Akira's plan to win Devon over was working just as she had hoped. Before long, she could ask him anything, and he would gladly comply. However, she couldn't help wondering what he knew about Keiko's death. Her directive from Yuki Ota was to take Paul and Sara out, if she couldn't determine who was responsible. However, Devon could hold the key to the mystery of who was truly guilty—without even knowing it. Meanwhile, it was becoming increasingly difficult to separate her emotions while playing the part of a naïve Juliet. She couldn't stop thinking about Devon's incredible body and imagining him making love to her. He filled her dreams at night and was in her thoughts throughout every waking hour. It would be the saddest day in her life when the cruise ended and they were forced to part ways. But unfortunately, there was no getting around it.

Akira stepped into the closest elevator with the intention of returning to her room and discovered there had been some excitement while they were gone. According to the gossip flowing among the passengers, a cocktail waitress by the name of

Adriane had slid beneath the water in the hot tub after throwing back two beers. Two men from the bar called their friends over to take a closer look, and a member of the waitstaff had to tell them to pull her body out. But what was even more disturbing was learning that the nurse who had obtained a defibrillator from the medical office had failed to resuscitate Adriane because she thought it was unsafe to use it on a wet body.

As Akira listened, one of the passengers in the elevator remarked that the incident and set of circumstances were extremely peculiar. "That woman was in her underwear. I don't think she was drunk at all. But no one's going to know for sure until the autopsy report comes back. And by then, everyone will be off the ship."

Akira stayed on the elevator until it reached the ninth floor. She wanted to investigate further but was blocked from entering the pool area by crew members. Instinctively, she looked up at the balcony above the pool and hot tub through an enclosed promenade. Her eyes locked on Sara Lyons, who was standing in the crowd that had gathered along the tenth-floor railing. Sara was watching the covered body being lifted onto a gurney and rolled away and had the strangest look on her face. While the rest of the passengers covered their mouths and stared aghast at the disturbing scene, she seemed to be enjoying the drama unfolding below.

A gentleman in a white uniform tapped Akira on the shoulder. "I'm sorry, miss. We need to have you move along now."

"What happened?" she asked, wanting to hear the story firsthand.

"It was an unfortunate accident. Nothing for you to be concerned about."

A woman behind her asked, "What about the dinner party?"

"It will proceed as planned, ma'am," the man answered. "Please try to enjoy the rest of your trip." He watched her leave before addressing questions from other passengers.

Akira walked up to the elevator and waited. A young man in a tennis outfit joined her with an eager look in his eyes. "I couldn't help noticing that you were talking to that security officer. I just thought maybe you'd like to know the truth."

Akira nodded.

"Adriane messed up her shoulder in a car accident five years ago," he said, talking so fast she could barely keep up. "She got hooked on meds and swore she was clean but obviously lied. No one walks into a hot tub and drowns after downing two brews. Not unless they're fucked up."

The elevator opened. Akira stepped in and held the door, but the man continued down the hallway, shaking his head. She arrived at her suite and found Takashi sitting in a lounge chair on the balcony, staring out at the rolling sea.

He turned when he heard her approach. "A rescue attempt was made by the Coast Guard today. Turns out a waiter was found floating facedown. According to the captain, there were some embarrassing photos of him posted on the Internet."

Akira was puzzled by the new development, and yet something was certain: they must have been nasty to send him over the edge like that. "I think he was the guy who was supposed to take care of our table. He stormed off after Bradshaw insulted him."

"Hmm...interesting timing."

Akira nodded. "Did you hear about the cocktail waitress downstairs?"

"Yeah, just a few minutes ago. Right after I heard a woman scream. Either our murderer is on a rampage, or there's something wrong with the drinking water."

"Well, I can guarantee Paul Lyons wasn't involved," Akira said. "I've been observing his behavior, and I don't think he's our murderer. However, his wife is a real possibility. She watched that woman's body being carried away, and you would have thought it was the highlight of her day. I'm still planning to spend time with all of them tonight, but I could really use your help. If Bradshaw leaves the dining room for any reason, can you follow him to see where he goes?"

Takashi nodded and silently stared at her as if assessing her actions. "There's something else I need to share," he finally said. "While searching the Internet, I came across a news bulletin. It turns out a Russian hospital director was mugged and killed last night. If I remember correctly, didn't you say Bradshaw was staying at a hotel with her?"

Akira nodded. "Interesting. Do you think it's a coincidence?"

Takashi picked up his cup from the table. "No, I don't. And there's more. It seems a few years ago, a crewmember and passengers were attacked by islanders in Saint Thomas. One of the crew was shot and killed, but that's not all. A passenger vanished during the night and was never found. Both incidents were investigated and prosecuted by local authorities to prevent national publicity. But what's even more interesting is the captain was severely reprimanded and demoted. It took five years for him to earn his position back with the cruise line involved." Takashi took a long sip from his cup.

Akira shrugged a shoulder. "And the point of all this is?"

"It was Brice. He goes into self-protect mode when people die on this ship. One more incident, and he will lose his job forever."

Akira couldn't imagine Brice cut off from the sea. From what little she knew of him, the captain would find it impossible to survive without the respect he demanded or the admiration of his crew. She shook her head in disbelief. "This ship is the perfect place to commit murder."

"I'm not so sure about that. But it seems likely that the captain is going to dismiss anything that would involve bringing the FBI aboard. Which might turn out to be good for us."

"Well, if Bradshaw *is* our murderer, there's a good chance Sara is his accomplice. And if that's the case, she's a better actress than I am."

Takashi nodded. "We need to bring this to an end as soon as possible."

"I agree. Tonight I'll be watching for any reactions when I bring up the topic of Mexico. If Bradshaw dodges the subject again, then there's good reason to believe he was involved. I just need to be sure before I kill him."

12

ADORATION

Devon had been aroused almost beyond the point of no return for the second time that day. It was embarrassing and slightly unnerving, especially at his age. He needed to have better control over himself. But when it came to Akira, his body seemed to have a mind of its own. He found himself responding to her whenever she was near, and it was thrilling and disconcerting to him at the same time.

He glanced in the mirror as he buttoned up the tropical shirt she had chosen for him and almost didn't recognize himself. He looked relaxed and happy, and it was all thanks to her. After he finished getting ready, he went out onto the balcony. The ship had departed from the Bahamas ten minutes earlier than scheduled, and they were once again at sea.

Devon heard a knock at the door and Akira's voice outside in the hallway. Upon opening the door, his heart skipped a beat. He knew she was strikingly beautiful—had known that all along—but tonight when she walked into the room, it was as if he were seeing her for the first time. Her face was a vision, and her body had him riveted. Although he'd seen her in a short dress before, he couldn't tear his eyes away from her long, shapely, bare legs. He followed them up to where they disappeared under the hem of her dress—her very short, tight-fitting dress. His mind played with the idea of running his hands up the inside of her thighs and under her skirt. When he looked up to meet her eyes, he couldn't help feeling guilty and a little warm around the collar.

Akira moved close to him and whispered in his ear, "Do you like what you see?" She was a temptress in every sense of the word.

"Yes." He grinned sheepishly.

"It's OK, Devon. I like the way you look at me."

He put his arm around her, and she ran her fingers through his hair. He bent down and kissed her lips. The tropical air closed in around them. What he wouldn't give to skip dinner and just drag her back into his room to continue where they had left off earlier.

Akira looked up at him with a mischievous grin on her face. "Do you like my dress?"

Why was she asking? He had made it pretty clear just how much he liked it. Well, at least the length of it anyway. He pulled back from her to take a better look at the lavender creation. Then he looked down at his shirt, and the reason suddenly dawned on him. "Akira?"

"Yes, Devon?" She was laughing.

He wanted to look stern but couldn't help laughing himself. "Baby, you're going to pay for this."

Akira reached for his hand and squeezed it. "I didn't realize your shirt had the same print as my dress when we bought it. I honestly thought they were similar and would be fun to wear together." She covered her mouth, stifling a giggle. "I'm afraid it's funnier than it should be."

Now Devon really wanted to drag her back into his room. "I'm glad you're so amused."

"We look like a perfectly matched pair."

He ran his finger across her jaw and down her throat. "Like I said, you're going to pay big-time for this."

She smiled coyly. "I'm looking forward to it."

This was going to be a long night as far as Devon was concerned. He couldn't wait to get her alone again. Only this time, she wouldn't be walking away. At least not for a few hours.

He wrapped his arms around her, and she pressed against him, depleting his waning endurance.

"Devon!" Paul's voice jolted him. They separated at the sound of his voice. "Oh, there you are." He walked toward them and stopped a short distance away.

"Mr. Lyons, what happened to you?" Akira asked. "Your face is so badly burned. Didn't you use any sunscreen?" She stepped up to him and touched his cheek. "This doesn't look good at all."

"I'm fine, Akira. Just a little too much sun today. I'll be fine by tomorrow." Paul was bright red, and Akira had reason to be concerned. "Don't worry about me, you two. I've already seen the ship's doctor, and he gave me a salve."

Akira looked slightly relieved. "OK. Just make sure you use it. You'd better stay out of the sun for a few days too." She was like a little mother hen, and Devon found it endearing.

"Enough about me," Paul said, obviously trying to change the subject. "Did you have a good day, Devon? How were the ruins?"

"We had a great time." Devon smiled at Akira as he spoke, and she smiled back.

Paul cleared his throat. "Excellent. I'm delighted that everything worked out so well." He studied Devon's shirt for a moment and then burst out laughing. "After hearing your negative remarks about the commercialization of the Pacific Islands, I never thought I'd see you in a factory-made Hawaiian shirt."

"Yeah, I know," Devon answered drily. "And I see that you managed to find the perfect shirt to suit you." He crinkled his nose at the ridiculously gaudy design. It was covered with blue, red, green, orange, and yellow parrots and macaws. Oddly, he was relieved by the subtle pattern on his own shirt.

Akira giggled and mouthed the words "be kind" to him.

Devon gave her an incredulous look. He was glad Paul hadn't pointed out their matching attire but half expected it to come during dinner. "So where's Sara?" he asked.

"Adding the finishing touches to her dress. She had a long session with Bradshaw today, which is making her a bit late for dinner. She wants us to proceed and will catch up with us downstairs."

"Then let's go," Devon said.

The three of them made their way to the dining room and discovered five available seats at a shared table. Akira and Devon sat between Dr. Hoffman and Vivian, while Paul sat across from them and next to an empty seat.

"Hi, Akira…Devon…Paul," Vivian said. "We were just talking about the tropical theme. It's so fun to see what everyone's wearing."

Sara entered the room with Akira's father and greeted them with a thin smile. Her eyes moved from Akira to Devon, and he knew full well what was coming next. "Oh…my…God," she squealed.

Akira squeezed Devon's hand.

"Do you two have on matching outfits?" she asked.

"Aren't they adorable?" Vivian said. "They look like an old married couple."

Everyone stared at them but no one more intensely than Mr. Hamada. Devon wanted to crawl under the table and hide, but Akira simply smiled. "It was purely coincidence," she pointed out. "We had a good laugh about it ourselves."

Sara crinkled her nose. "Coincidence, you say. It seems you've found a unique way to fit into our family, Akira. I'd say that's quite remarkable indeed."

Devon could hear Paul laughing one minute and choking on his drink the next. The sarcasm in Sara's words was hard to miss, but he became easily distracted by Akira's hand on his thigh and her father's stern, unwavering expression.

"I promise to make it up to you," she whispered in his ear.

He barely registered what she said, as his whole body was tuned in to the location of her hand. Thankfully, Vivian proceeded to analyze everyone's choice of clothing in the room, allowing the attention to veer away from them. Most of the women were wearing sundresses with green vines, bamboo, and colorful flowers. And the men's shirts were a complete eyesore. Even Dr. Hoffman's shirt was tacky and obscene. It was covered with every species of tropical fish known to man and was as audaciously ornate as Paul's. In contrast, Mr. Hamada wore a white cotton shirt subtly embossed with palm trees.

Dr. Bradshaw arrived and scoped the table for an empty spot. Even though Paul's face indicated his disapproval, the man boosted a gold Chiavari chair from the corner and dropped it beside Sara, forcing everyone at the table to squeeze closer together.

Paul grunted. "I thought you had other plans tonight. What are you doing here?"

"Had a last-minute cancellation. It's good to see you too, Paul."

A waiter arrived with an assortment of tropical drinks on his tray, and Paul chose a pink concoction. While everyone picked their favorites, he jumped at the opportunity to ridicule Bradshaw. "Well, it seems the designer of your whale shirt found the perfect specimen to wear it."

Devon chuckled, and Sara reminded Paul to behave himself.

Bradshaw glanced in Akira's direction. "Do you have an extra napkin over there? We seem to be missing one at this table."

Paul pursed his lips. "We had the right number before you arrived."

Devon erupted in laughter, while Sara scowled, demonstrating her disapproval. Vivian spun the conversation around, bringing the attention back to Devon and Akira. "You two are so cute. I searched for matching outfits for weeks, but I couldn't find any. I can't believe you found them without even trying."

Akira was stroking Devon's thigh now, and he was too distracted to respond to anything. Her hand moved close to his crotch, and his breath caught. He grabbed her wrist to hold it still and smiled at Mr. Hamada. "I don't know about the rest of you, but I'm famished."

Akira's lips curled. "So am I."

Everyone focused on their menus, and the waiter returned to explain the five course selections. Devon elected to try sea bass prepared in miso, and Akira followed suit. She agreed with him that it was nice to try something different.

Dinner continued, and Vivian asked about their shore excursion. Akira's eyes were radiant with the glow of excitement as she described the pirate's keep, the exquisite scenery, and the pineapple plantation. The whole time, Devon could feel Mr. Hamada's eyes on him. It seemed he was aware of the depth of Devon's feelings for his daughter, leaving him shifting in his seat.

Then something changed. There was a shift in the air that couldn't be seen, only felt. Devon wondered if he was the only one sensing it, but then he noticed the serious look on Akira's face. She leaned forward, turning toward Dr. Bradshaw. "I understand they have a natural hot springs in Mexico. Was the heat as warm there as it is here?"

Sara set her glass down hard on the table. There was a tinge of red in her cheeks. "Why do we keep coming back to this? Are you planning a trip to Mexico or something?"

Paul's hand was on his wife's arm. "Sara...stop it. Akira was just asking a question."

Sara lowered her eyes. "You're right. That was unkind. of me. I'm sorry, Akira." She turned to her husband. "I would just like to enjoy this trip and not think about that one. Do you mind?"

"No, of course not," he grumbled. "There wasn't anything thrilling about it anyway."

Bradshaw was quick to stick his nose in. "Well, I happen to agree on that count." He made a lame attempt at a joke. Paul didn't laugh. He didn't even smile. He continued to scowl but said no words. "Some of us were invited to join this cruise," Bradshaw persisted. "So why don't we make the best of our time together?"

Paul shot the doctor a dirty look, opening himself up for further ridicule.

When dinner was over, Mr. Hamada politely excused himself, and Devon breathed a sigh of relief. He had no idea how he was going to win this man over or if it was even possible.

Everyone else at the table was anxious to see the magician performing that evening, despite the fact that Devon was hesitant. He didn't care for the acts on board and considered them pretty cheesy. But Akira said it would be fun, especially since the magician was a comic as well. The fact that she wanted to go—along with the smile on her face—was enough to change his mind.

They arrived at the theater and surprisingly found a section with enough seats for all of them. Paul made a point of sitting next to Devon, and Peter Bradshaw plopped down in a chair next to Sara at the end of the row.

"I have a feeling that my uncle is here to chaperone us tonight," Devon whispered to Akira.

She looked over at Paul. "He's awfully quiet. Is he all right?"

Devon glanced at his uncle, still red from his overexposure. "Are you OK?"

Paul seemed to perk up at the sound of Devon's voice. "I'm fine, son. I'm just tired from a full day of snorkeling. Tomorrow we have a day at sea. I'll catch up on my rest then." He studied Devon's face. "What about you? It seems that Akira kept you on your toes today."

Akira chuckled. "Actually we seem to be in perfect sync with each other. I've never enjoyed anyone's company as much as Devon's," she assured him.

"Good to know. I'm glad you're both having such a great time."

Devon swallowed hard. He badly wanted to kiss her and disappear from Paul's piercing gaze. Luckily, the magic show began and diverted his uncle's attention. As it turned out, the magician was more of a comedian than anything and had the crowd laughing in no time. Paul seemed to have gained his second wind, as his big hearty laugh filled the auditorium. Evidently there was some advantage to being so vocal, since he was picked along with two other audience members to join the entertainer on the stage. Akira clapped enthusiastically with the rest of the audience and then rested her hand on Devon's thigh. Meanwhile, he concentrated on only two things: how much he wanted to place his hand on her bare thigh and how much he wanted the show to end so they could be alone together.

Paul proved to be the perfect choice for the magician's act. His reactions had the crowd in stitches, and they gave him a standing ovation when the routine ended, leaving Sara glowing with pride. When the show was over, Paul tried to convince everyone to join him in the casino. He told them it was his lucky night but didn't seem to mind when Devon begged off. After wishing them a good night, he headed off to gamble with their tablemates, which surprisingly included Sara. She was a pro at blackjack, according to her boasting, and Bradshaw was preparing to root her on.

Devon put his arm around Akira's waist. "Finally. I was starting to think that my uncle wasn't going to let us out of his sight."

Akira watched everybody leave, wearing a hard-to-read expression. "I don't think he approves of me."

"Really? I'm sure that's not the case. He was glaring at me all night. It's about my past mistakes, not you, honey."

"Which reminds me," she said. "About that picture that was taken…"

"Let's go find the photo gallery to see if it's on display. It's only one deck below us."

They wove their way through the crowd and made their way to the elevator. After arriving on the lower level, they pressed through a group of passengers and arrived at the photo gallery. There were countless photos covering the walls, and Devon had no idea where to begin.

"It looks like they're arranged by day, event, and location," Akira told him. "Our photo should be at the far end."

They pressed through the crowd and started searching. After a few seconds, Akira announced, "Got it!" She pulled the image from the wall and held it before Devon. "We can purchase it or pass it through the shredder. What do you think?"

Devon's first instinct was to shred it simply because he hated candid shots. But when he looked at the photo and saw how adorable Akira looked, he wanted to keep the photograph and stare at it all night long. "Do you want a copy?" he asked.

She surprised him with her answer. "Yes. I love how you look, Devon."

He smiled. "Then we'll purchase two copies. One for each of us." He charged the purchase to his suite, and they made their way out of the shop. But Akira halted before reaching the elevator.

"You need to buy a bathing suit."

"What?" Devon wasn't expecting this. "But I already have one."

"You're going to need a new one for what I have in mind for tomorrow…and later this week. I'm sure we can find one in the boutique."

He followed after her until she arrived at the duty-free shop. It didn't take long for her to help him find trunks that weren't too offensive. They settled on a brown pair with a gold Mayan pattern on them. Devon put his arm around her waist and pulled her close to him. He lowered his voice so no one else could hear. "Just promise me one thing before I buy these."

"Anything," she said.

"Just tell me you don't own a bathing suit that matches this one."

She bit the corner of her lower lip and smiled. "Nope."

"Thank you. Now let's get out of here." They found their way out of the shopping arcade to a less congested area of the ship. Akira took Devon by the hand and led him to a quiet spot on the outside deck. She turned to face him and smiled. He drew her into his arms and held her tight. They kissed each other tenderly for endless minutes, leaving him breathless.

"I've been wanting to do this all night." Devon stroked her cheek and looked into her stunning eyes.

"Me too," Akira said. "It's so beautiful tonight, Devon. Why don't we go back to your suite? We can enjoy looking out at the water and at the stars from your balcony. With everyone at the casino and my father secured for the night, we'll have more privacy there."

Devon's heart skipped a beat. He had wanted to be alone with her ever since they parted that afternoon. "Your wish is my command." He took her hand in his and kissed it. "Come with me, my lady."

She followed him back to the suite and into his room, and for some strange reason, he grew a little nervous being alone with her. To his relief, she suggested going out on the balcony to enjoy the evening air.

"Let's lie down on the lounge chair like we did last night," she said. She took his hand and urged him back onto the chair cushions. He didn't hesitate. Not for a moment.

Last night, Akira wore a long gown that covered most of her body, but tonight her short dress exposed more of her skin. His eyes landed on her bare legs. He felt an uncontrollable urge to run his hand up her thigh, and it took all of his willpower not to do it. He didn't want to rush their time together but didn't know how long he could resist. She seemed to want a demonstration of his affections as much as he wanted to deliver it.

She pressed her body against him, causing a moan to escape his lips. He moved his hands down to cup her butt and pulled her in close. She let out a whimper, and he thought for sure he would lose it. She pressed her lips against his and deepened the kiss. Then she wrapped her right leg over his hip, forcing her dress to slide up even higher.

Devon could see her black panties and could no longer control his desire to touch her. He placed his hand on her bare inner thigh and slowly ran it up her leg until he was just shy of her center. Akira reared back. He stroked her through the fabric of her panties and found himself completely aroused. When he felt the wet fabric, his cock became further engorged. She was moving against him, exciting him beyond anything he could imagine. He cupped her panties with his hand, and she rubbed against him, begging for more.

Devon broke their kiss and met her gaze. Her eyes were dark with desire. She bent in to continue their kiss, and he pulled her panties to the side so he could touch her naked flesh. She let out a little cry as he gently teased her clitoris. She moaned and pushed back against him. The pressure of his strokes increased, and her urgent need grew.

"Take them off," she urged. He removed her panties while she whispered in his ear, "I want you, Devon. I want you sooo bad."

His cock was throbbing…longing to enter her. "OK, baby. I hear you." He increased the pressure of his strokes, rubbing her clitoris in little circles. She opened her legs wider to him, and he continued to cajole her until she was arching against him, begging for a climax. He wanted desperately to put his mouth on her and bring her over the edge. But then, as if in response to his thoughts, her body began to shudder, and she cried out as waves of release washed over her. Her body collapsed next to him. He pressed his hand over her mound as her body recovered from its arousal.

Akira clung to him, and all the while, his cock begged for the same release. He pulled her closer to him and kissed the top of her head. "Did that feel good?"

"So good," she murmured. "Thank you." She reached down and stroked his cock through the fabric of his pants. It seemed that she wanted him to experience the same pleasure.

"Oh, baby..." Devon wanted to slow the action down and enjoy every moment.

Akira kissed him and reached down to undo his belt. "I want to touch you," she whispered. "Only you."

He looked into her eyes, and her mouth captured his again. Her tongue circled round and round, taunting and teasing. He reached down and helped her remove his pants, and his cock sprang into action. She wrapped her hand around it, causing Devon to moan.

"Take it easy. I'm almost there," he told her. She began to stroke him faster than he expected. "That's so good, baby. So good..." He barely choked out the last words before his whole body jerked. His seed spurted out of him and then continued to pour. More than he imagined possible.

Devon relaxed with Akira lying on top of him. She kissed him, and he pushed her hair out of her face to look into her eyes. "Thank you, honey." He paused. "I didn't intend for that to happen between us so quickly." For some reason, he needed to apologize. Being out of action had left him unprepared to satisfy the likes of this woman. If this relationship were to continue and develop as he hoped, he would need to temper his libido to the level he'd once been capable of reaching.

"I'm not sorry I did it," she told him. "It felt right—so incredibly right." She grinned at him, and he smiled back.

"There's no denying that." He closed his eyes, and when he opened them again, she was staring down at him. "I'm just worried that I might do the wrong thing," he told her. "I never want to do anything that would make you unhappy."

Akira stroked his cheek. "That's not going to happen." She kissed him tenderly and smiled. "You didn't seem worried just now."

"That's because my body was in control, not my brain." He grinned sheepishly at her, and she giggled again.

Devon realized it was time to broach a topic that had been on his mind all night. "I told you a lot of personal things about myself, Akira. I was just wondering if there's anything about yourself that you'd like to share with me. Like...is there anyone in your life besides me? Is there someone you dream about? Have you ever been deeply in love?"

She pressed her finger to his lips. "No to the first two questions, but I think you knew that." She looked at him thoughtfully and seemed to be contemplating her next answer. "As to your last question, I met someone while I was in Japan. It was a special arrangement, like an engagement in the Western culture. He died a few years ago, but now I've moved on in my life."

"I'm sorry, honey." Devon felt bad for any pain she might have suffered, but he was happy that she hadn't married this young man. She wouldn't be with him right now if she had.

Akira appeared to be deep in thought. "The future we talked about wasn't meant to be."

"Did he teach you how to make love?" He felt a twinge of jealousy at the idea of another man touching her.

Akira blushed. "Yes, but I never realized how incredible it could be until I met you." She gave him a seductive look that made his pulse race. Then she kissed him on the mouth and laid her head on his shoulder. "Devon?"

"What is it, baby?" He stroked her hair again.

"I never want to forget what this feels like. Not ever." She gave him a slow smile, and he couldn't help but smile in return. "You make me so happy."

"You make me happy too, Akira." Yes, happiness was one of the things she made him feel. But it was something more—so much more.

"Can I ask you a question?" She looked deep into his eyes, making him melt.

"Of course. What is it you want to know?"

"It's about Sara and Dr. Bradshaw. Have you heard them say anything about their trip to Mexico? I wouldn't ask this, but the woman who died while they were there was a good friend to my family."

"I'm so sorry, Akira. I wish I had something to tell you. My aunt never shares anything with me...at least nothing of value. But I can ask her if she knows anything about your friend, if you'd like."

Akira shook her head. "No, that's not necessary. It just seems like a lot of people have been dying lately. It's difficult to let go."

"I know. It's real sad to me too, especially after what happened to the crew members on this ship. I guess there are more messed-up people in this world than I thought."

Akira offered him a weak smile. "You're definitely right about that."

13

INTRODUCTION

When Devon awoke the next morning, the sun was already high in the sky. He walked out onto the balcony and looked out at the turquoise ocean, transparent as glass.

Akira approached him from behind and wrapped her arms around his waist. "Good morning, handsome," she said. "The butler let me in."

He was amazed by the feeling of contentment her touch generated. For the first time in his life, he had found something real—something deeper and far more intense than lust.

Was this love?

Devon covered her arms with his and lingered in her embrace, relishing the warmth of her body against his back. "Good morning, beautiful. Did you sleep well?"

"Uh-huh. And you?"

He released his hold and turned to face her. "As well as can be expected." He stroked her cheek and smiled, choosing to withhold the wicked thoughts in his mind. For several minutes, they stood side by side on the balcony, gazing at the view.

"It's so peaceful here," she said. "I hate to even speak."

Devon kissed her on the forehead. "Is there something you want to say?"

Her lips curled in a smile. "I'm starving."

Devon laughed. "Would you like to try the dining room? I'm sure we can wrangle a quiet table for two at this hour."

Akira agreed.

They strolled along the promenade deck and reentered the ship to make their way to breakfast. The maître d' seated them at a table for two by a window. There were only a handful of other couples scattered about, allowing them the privacy they hoped for.

Devon surveyed the menu. "So are we going to be healthy today, or have we decided to throw caution to the wind and indulge our every desire?"

"I think we should indulge ourselves." The way she said it got Devon's attention. He was sure she wasn't talking about break-fast. A day ago, he would have been taken aback and rendered speechless. But today he could laugh.

"I'm not sure how to respond to that."

She grinned at him, leaving him longing to pull her onto his lap and kiss her. Fortunately, their waiter arrived before that could happen.

Devon ordered a strawberry waffle with extra whipped cream and watched Akira while she ordered blueberry pancakes. "So what do we have in mind for today?" he asked, suspecting she had something already planned.

"Seems you have me all figured out." Akira giggled. "The captain is giving us a private tour of the bridge at eleven a.m., which should be interesting. Then I thought we could explore Jamaica with a ride down the Rio Bueno. The tour includes snor-keling in Bengal Bay, a visit to Montego Bay, and a walk through the haunted halls of the great house."

He looked at her expectantly. "Sounds like you have a lot planned. You sure there's enough time in the day?"

"Absolutely. But there's something I'd like to do before that."

She had a guilty look on her face, leaving Devon hesitant to ask, "Like what?"

"A lesson."

Devon groaned. "Don't tell me you want to attend one of those napkin-folding classes."

Akira tried to stifle a giggle. "No, I really don't. It's actually a cooking class, but you really don't have to come. Even though I hate the idea of going alone."

He groaned again. Of course he'd go with her.

"You can just come and watch. You don't have to participate."

He couldn't contain his grin. She had him wrapped around her little finger, and he didn't mind. Not one tiny bit. "OK, I'll come with you. But only under one condition. You can't mention the class to my uncle. He'll think I'm some kind of...wuss." Devon shook his head. "I swear, Akira, you're going to owe me after this."

She put her hand over his. "Thank you, Devon. I'll do whatever you want...in my room." She bit her lower lip, and Devon's control began to ebb. His body was no longer his own.

Their breakfast arrived just in time to rein his thoughts back in. They ate slowly, watching the ocean from the adjacent window and each other with guarded looks. After finishing off the last of his coffee, Devon took Akira by the hand and led her back to her shared suite. She opened the door and called out for her father, and to Devon's relief, he was gone. For the time being, they had the room all to themselves.

He leaned close and lowered his voice. "Do you want to pay up now?"

"I'd be more than happy to. What would you like me to do?"

Her words gave him pause. Even though she considered herself a professional entertainer and had assured him as much, he couldn't help wondering how many men she'd performed for in Japan and if her sweet, innocent demeanor was purely an act.

"Devon?"

He shook off his thought and took her by the hand. After finding a cushioned chair on the balcony, he sat down and pulled her onto his lap. He wrapped his arms around her waist and nuzzled her neck with the intensity of a lovesick teen.

"Ah...that's nice," she purred, turning her face away.

His cock hardened, and he knew she could feel it beneath her dress.

Akira let go a little sound of contentment. She dropped her legs over the side of the chair and wrapped her fingers around the back of his neck. He could see her panties again and couldn't resist touching her thigh. She leaned in to kiss him, adding heat to his hunger. He caressed her throat with his fingertips, and her pulse jumped. She arched her back just as a moan escaped her lips.

"Devon..." she whispered.

"I know, baby. Let me take the edge off." He teased her through her silky panties and then tugged them aside so he could put his fingers directly on her. She squirmed and whimpered softly. Then she covered his hand with hers, guiding his fingers toward her need—directing him like a skilled mistress on how to please her.

Devon wanted to drop to his knees. He wanted to lick her and suck her right there. Make her scream out his name and beg him for more. But this wasn't the right time or place. Someone could walk in at any given moment and catch them in the act. And the last thing he wanted to see was Mr. Hamada's shocked face.

Akira deepened her kiss and held him tighter. She arched her back one final time and whimpered, finding her release. Devon wrapped his arms around her and rocked back and forth. His cock wanted to burst out of his pants and explode deep inside of her.

"Mariko. Doko desu ka?"

Devon could hear a man's voice inside the suite. It sounded like he was speaking Japanese, and he had to be Akira's father. But who the hell was he calling?

Akira jumped off Devon's lap and adjusted her dress and panties. Her face was flushed, and her expression was stern and unfamiliar.

"My father's back. Don't say anything. Let me handle this."

"Who's Mariko?" Devon whispered. The bulge in his pants was extremely noticeable, and the sound of Mr. Hamada's voice wasn't enough to lessen it. He wanted to be reckless in front of this man—to pull Akira back so that he would know the true nature of their relationship. But there was no telling what this man would do.

"I'm on the balcony," Akira called out to her father. Then she looked back at Devon. "I'll explain later. Stand behind me and put your arms around me."

"Are you sure?"

"Never more so."

Devon got up and pulled her against him. Her father walked out onto the balcony and stopped short at the sight of them.

"Ohayou gozaimasu," Akira said. "How are you feeling today, Father?"

Mr. Hamada locked eyes with Devon. He was obviously not happy at seeing him there but kept his tone light with his daughter. "Good morning, Akira. I'm feeling much better. The pills the doctor gave me for my indigestion seem to have helped."

"That's good news, Father," she said.

"I even managed to take a long walk this morning."

Devon swallowed hard and pulled Akira a little closer.

"I ordered you coffee and pastries for breakfast," she said. "I wasn't sure what time you would be returning or how you'd be feeling."

"How very thoughtful of you."

Devon felt like prey that Akira's father was stalking. His eyes were drilling into Devon's skull and showed no signs of letting up.

Akira glanced at Devon and seemed to recognize the anxiety he was feeling. "The captain is giving us a tour of the bridge at eleven o'clock, but we're going to a cooking class before that."

"Of course you are," her father said, his anger apparent. "Let me guess. You're spending the whole day together."

Devon's arousal was no longer an issue. He looked at Akira, not sure what to say.

"Yes, we are," she answered, smiling. "I need to finish getting ready. We don't want to be late for class. Although I'm sure Devon won't mind."

He forced his lips to smile.

"It's good to learn new things." She took Devon's hand in hers and faced her father. "This is a wonderful opportunity to spend time with some of the passengers I've met on board. You did ask me to be more social, didn't you?"

He looked away and mumbled indecipherable words under his breath.

Akira looked back at Devon. "OK, then. I'll be ready in a few minutes." She leaned up and kissed him on the lips. Devon could feel her father staring and the heat in the room growing. "Please wait here." Akira left them together and disappeared into her room. Both men continued to stare at each other, neither saying a word.

After a few seconds, Devon could no longer stand it. "I'm sure you have a lot to say to me, Mr. Hamada. But I want you to know that we didn't plan for any of this to happen. We met and developed these feelings for each other. There was no motivation behind it." He paused. "I don't know what else to say to you, sir."

Despite Akira's request, Devon headed for the door and glanced back. He wanted Akira's father to say something—to confront him like any protective father would. Yet he didn't say a word. His disapproval was far worse than Devon ever imagined it would be.

"She's my daughter," he finally said. "You're not right for her. No one on this ship is."

"I know, Mr. Hamada," Devon said. "I understand your position, but I can't help how I feel about her."

"She really likes you." He said it as though it were another accusation.

"Yes...and I really like her. You have to trust me."

"Trust you?" He humphed and shook his head. "You have no idea what you're dealing with here."

Devon wasn't sure if he was hearing him correctly. "Then please tell me, sir. What am I missing?"

Akira exited her room, and Devon turned his attention to her.

"Is everything OK?" she asked.

Devon watched her father's stern expression. He waited for him to answer, expecting the worst.

"Yes, dear. Everything's fine. If you're happy, then I'm happy."

Akira touched her father reassuringly on the shoulder. "Believe me, I'm happier than I've ever been." She took Devon's hand and waited for him to open the door. "I'll see you in a little while, Father. You needn't worry. As I'm sure you're well aware, I've always honored my promises."

They left the suite, and Akira closed the door behind them. She reached for Devon's hand, halting him in place. "I'm sorry. Did my father give you a hard time about us?" She looked genuinely concerned.

"I think he's in shock, and I don't blame him. I'm a treasure hunter with no stability in my life, and my reputation isn't...well, let's just say he wouldn't be impressed. He probably sees me as an ill-bred, self-centered American. And I can't say I blame him. I'm only here because of my uncle, which makes me subpar dating material."

Akira caressed his cheek. "It doesn't matter what he believes. He's going to have to accept the fact that I want to be with you."

Devon looked down. "He thinks I'm planning to take advantage of you."

"Well, I hope he's right." Akira reached for his hand and squeezed it—a sign that she shared his feelings. They continued their walk and finally arrived at the room where the cooking class was gathering.

"Akira!" Dr. Bradshaw's voice was the last thing Devon was expecting to hear. He looked across the room to see him and Sara waving to them.

Devon groaned. *My God, are they connected at the hip?*

Akira smiled. "Seems they enjoy cooking as well."

"As well as what?"

"I'm sorry to tell you this, Devon, but I already knew they'd be here."

She held Devon's hand as they made their way to seats next to the dispiriting couple. Devon found the grin on Bradshaw's face as unnerving as seeing them there together.

Where the hell was his uncle anyway?

Bradshaw scratched his beard and eyed him suspiciously. "Fancy meeting you here, Devon. Akira told me she likes to cook, but I never thought I'd see you at one of these classes."

Devon gritted his teeth. "Does my uncle know you're here?"

Sara pursed her lips. "Besides being my doctor, Peter and I have been friends for years. It really doesn't matter what my husband thinks."

Bradshaw rested a hand on Sara's shoulder. "Well, I'm glad we got that straightened out. It's all about having fun, right?"

"Yes, of course," she said.

"Yeah, real fun," Devon grumbled.

Bradshaw kept his eyes on Devon. "They're teaching how to prepare appetizers in this class. I don't know if I mentioned it, but I love to play around in the kitchen and have received dozens of compliments for my gourmet cooking."

"Really?" Devon squinted at him.

"He's a natural according to the head chef on this ship," Sara boasted. "He was a quick study in our last class and became the center of attention."

Bradshaw looked extremely pleased with himself.

"You don't say?" Devon's competitive side kicked in.

"I think Devon is just going to watch," Akira explained to Sara.

"I changed my mind. Since I'm already here, I might as well take part."

Akira was all smiles. "Oh, I'm glad to hear that. I think it will be fun for all of us."

The instructor arrived in class and introduced Bradshaw as her star student from her previous session. Everyone clapped and made a big fuss over him. Devon was now determined to outdo him, no matter what it took.

After providing all their supplies and ingredients, the instructor divided them into four groups and explained what they would be doing. She sautéed onions, added spices, garlic, and ground meat, then stirred the mixture as it simmered on the cooktop. Next she filled square wonton wrappers and pinched them before dropping them into boiling water. When each serving was done, she set a sample before them with dipping sauce and waited for the happy appraisals to subside.

"So let's get started," she said. "Just follow my lead."

Bradshaw was able to keep up with her, and Devon did the same. They both finished with a large plate of wontons at the same time. The doctor seemed to be visibly surprised by Devon's quick learning curve and commented that his finished product looked even better than the instructor's.

"What did you do, Devon?" he asked. "Yours looks different."

"I changed two of the folds to give the wonton a more pronounced look."

Sara nodded her approval and continued to work. But Akira had overfilled her dumplings and added the meat juice and was struggling to keep them from tearing. She turned to Devon and giggled. "I'm not much of a cook. I guess it shows."

The instructor stopped in front of Bradshaw and Devon. "What have we here?" she said. She held a plate of Devon's finished dumplings in her hand so the whole class could see. "These look better than mine. What exactly did you do, Mr. Lyons?"

When Devon didn't immediately respond, Sara answered for him. "He changed a couple of the folds to give each piece a sharper appearance."

Devon's face warmed. So much for being anonymous.

"Very impressive," the instructor said. "Class, let's give this young man a round of applause." The whole class applauded, and Devon felt a little too exposed.

"Now let's taste them and see if they're as good as they look."
The instructor popped a dumpling into her mouth. She hummed
her approval and motioned for the class to take heed. "This is
what I'm hoping you'll all learn today. How to be talented chefs
and share your love for cooking with others."

Akira kissed Devon on the cheek. "You're very talented. And
I need your help."

He smiled and moved closer to assist her. He finished a half-
dozen pieces, and when he glanced up, he noticed that Bradshaw
and Sara were exchanging glances.

The instructor returned to the front of the room and
reminded everyone to turn off their stove tops. "Shall we continue?" She demonstrated how to prepare chicken satay, and
Devon was convinced that he could master this dish with no
problem at all.

Bradshaw smiled. "Let's see how good you really are. Do you
think you can make kabobs faster than me and get kudos for
how they look?"

Devon hadn't been interested in anything Peter Bradshaw
had said since the day he first met him. He was overdressed and
cocksure and boasted a little too loud. "How would you like to
make a wager, Dr. Bradshaw? If I can beat your time, you'll owe
me a favor. If I lose, I'll owe you one."

The self-assured look on Bradshaw's face told Devon that he
didn't think he could lose. "It's a deal." They shook on it, and he
checked the clock. "Let's see what you can do in ten minutes."

Devon chuckled and picked up his knife. "Anytime you're
ready."

"Go!" They both to set to work: chopping, creating marinade, dipping and sliding chunks of chicken onto short bamboo
sticks. When Devon's plate was full, he turned on his grill and
cooked the prepared meat to perfection. Meanwhile, Bradshaw

fumbled with his oversize pieces and added the wrong amount of soy sauce to his marinade. By the time his plate was filled, Devon was turning his kabobs over for a final browning.

"Time's up," Akira announced. She picked up a filled skewer from Devon's grill and blew on it before taking a bite. "Absolutely delicious! Looks like you owe him a favor, Dr. Bradshaw."

The doctor appeared to be genuinely surprised. "Yes, I guess I do. So what kind of favor are you after?"

"Oh, that waits to be seen. I haven't quite decided yet."

Akira whispered in his ear. "Let me pick."

Bradshaw arched a brow. "What are you two up to? You're enjoying this way too much."

Devon smiled. "Let's just say I love it when somebody owes me something."

Akira smoothed his hair above his left ear and whispered in it again. "Like when I owed you this morning? I think that ended up better for me than it did for you." A coy smile formed on her lips.

"That's where you're wrong, honey. I enjoyed it just as much, if not more than you did."

Bradshaw stood brooding. "Enjoyed what? Trying to better me? I can pose a new contest if you're up for it. Like a battle of wits…"

"Maybe another time. We have an appointment upstairs."

The class ended, and Devon and Akira bade their farewell to the instructor. Akira shook Bradshaw's hand while Devon and Sara stood apart, waiting. "I'm sure you're a great cook too… when there isn't pressure from everyone watching."

Bradshaw glanced down at his hand and nodded. His frown was hard to miss.

Sara tapped him on the arm. "Ready for bingo? They're giving a free trip away today."

They proceeded toward the atrium and turned right, disappearing from view, while Devon and Akira waited for the elevator doors to open. She laid her hand on his arm. "I had no idea you were a gourmet chef. That's a true gift indeed."

He flashed a quick smile. "I'm really not that great."

"I beg to differ with you."

The doors opened, and they stepped inside. Two couples were waiting, chatting about an unfamiliar passenger who had boarded the ship at their last stop. They found it extremely odd with only four days to go. When they reached their floor, the women turned to Devon and said in unison, "Have a great day!"

"Thank you. We'll try."

As they approached the bridge, the conversation between Akira and Devon turned to Captain Brice. "He definitely likes the ladies," she said. "Although I couldn't help noticing the ring on his finger."

"Well, that doesn't stop men like him."

Devon was surprised to see his uncle and Akira's father tucked into the tour. Mr. Hamada was attempting to look interested in an elderly woman's conversation while two others looked on.

Akira acknowledged her father's presence with a nod, then moved closer to Devon. She reached for his hand and held it tight in an act of deliberate defiance. "This should be fun."

One of the ship's officers opened the door and ushered them onto the bridge. While he greeted the group, Devon turned back to his uncle and kept his voice low. "Seems Mr. Hamada figured out our relationship."

"The two of you? No surprise there, son," Paul half whispered. "It appears that you didn't heed my warning after all."

Devon smiled. "The heart wants what the heart wants. Nobody can change that."

"You sure it's your heart?" Paul glanced at Devon's crotch, clarifying his meaning.

Akira linked her arm through Devon's and shushed him. "The tour's about to begin."

Devon leaned down and breathed in her ear, "I'm sorry if I've caused problems for you."

"You haven't. Don't even think about it." She gave him a pointed look. "Just make sure you stay close. I don't want the captain to drag me away."

Devon couldn't help grinning at her demand. "As you wish." He meshed her against him, and she giggled.

"Much better."

The captain asked to have everyone's attention, insisting that the women make their way up front near him. The elderly woman who had Mr. Hamada's ear was the only one who rushed forward. He got the initial flirting and innuendos out of the way, and then he launched into an informative and entertaining tour of the bridge. He didn't repeat any of the stories he had shared at dinner, leaving Devon begrudgingly impressed.

As riveting as the captain was, most of the passengers seemed to be more impressed with the 360 degree views from the windows and the fact that the bridge looked like the command center at Cape Canaveral. There were countless panels and gadgets for controlling every aspect of the ship, but Devon was more in awe of the sheer size of the steering wheel. He soon learned that it was mostly for effect, as the ship was fully automated, and wheels were a thing of the past.

When the tour was over and they gathered together out on the deck, Paul seemed to be in a jovial mood. "Why don't we all go to lunch together, Mr. Hamada? I'm going to be getting a treatment for my sunburn all afternoon so I can use a little company right now."

"It's Takashi."

"Excuse me?"

"My name. We seem to be close in age. No need for formalities on this ship."

"Oh, ah…yes…yes, of course," Paul stammered.

Akira turned to Devon. "Do you mind the company?"

He leaned toward her. "Of course not. I can't avoid your father, honey…not if I want to be with you."

"Thank you for understanding. He's stubborn and opinionated, but he's not unfair. Just give him some time to get to know you."

"I'll do whatever it takes." Devon pulled her closer. He'd do anything she wanted just to make her happy.

Paul suggested that they have lunch in one of the specialty restaurants, where it would be easier to get seats together at that hour. They decided on the pizzeria and found a corner table that could accommodate the four of them. Mr. Hamada didn't attempt to separate Akira and Devon, but he made it a point to sit directly across from them. Devon was being drawn under the microscope for the second time in a row. Last night he had been pretty sure that the intimidating man was watching his every move. And today, he had absolutely no doubt that was the case.

Akira seemed determined to ignore her father. She was extremely affectionate to Devon, touching him constantly, as she had a tendency to do. At first, Devon stiffened and kept his hands to himself. However, eventually he loosened up and wrapped his arm around her shoulder.

Devon swore he heard a growl coming from across the table. Then a low voice rumbled out. "So what are your plans this afternoon, Akira? Why don't you see what's available at the spa? I understand it's a very nice place."

If Hamada's intention was to keep them apart, he wasn't very subtle.

"Devon and I already have plans in town." She put her hand over Devon's and smiled. "When we get back, I have a surprise for him, but I can't share it right now. Not without ruining everything."

Her father's eyes were fixed on Devon's face, causing sweat to collect on his scalp. "Have fun, but don't forget about your responsibilities."

"I haven't forgotten, Father." Akira put her hand on Devon's thigh, and he instantly responded, in spite of her father's presence.

"Responsibilities?" he asked.

"I have a little chore that I need to take care of before the cruise ends." Akira locked eyes with her father, and a silent exchange took place.

Paul asked Mr. Hamada about Japan and his undisclosed occupation. Mr. Hamada responded by talking proudly about Japan's beauty and technology but conveniently omitted anything too personal. All the while, Devon noticed Mr. Hamada watching him out of the corner of his eyes.

Akira pushed Devon's hair back and whispered seductively into his ear, "Want to know what your surprise is?"

"I think we should wait until your father's not around." He put his hand on hers to keep her from moving it farther up his thigh. "I can't trust my reaction to anything you do—or say."

She giggled in his ear, and his body responded further.

"Good idea." She lifted her hand from his thigh and placed it on top of the table.

Captain Brice walked into the restaurant and filled a cup with coffee from the row of thermoses along the wall. Then he turned around and zeroed in on their table like a moth to the flame. "Well, hello there," he said, hovering above them. For the time being, his attention seemed to be focused on Mr. Hamada. "You must be Akira's father. With all the activity on this ship, we haven't had a chance to officially meet. You have a beautiful daughter there, by the way."

Mr. Hamada bowed his head slowly. Then he watched the captain from the top of his eyes, as if suspicious of his intent.

"I understand you sell antique swords and brought one along with you," Brice added. "I've always wanted one myself but never had the opportunity to look into it. To be honest, I wouldn't even know how to go about it." He smiled. "You know, this might sound a bit strange, but would it be possible to get your business card? My fifteen-year-old son has a birthday coming, and a collectible sword would make a wonderful gift."

Mr. Hamada kept his line of vision and voice low. "I'm sorry, but I didn't bring any cards with me."

"Oh, of course...of course. Well, if you get the chance, I would sure like to talk to you more. Maybe get some contact information before we part ways?"

Akira's father bowed his head again. It seemed he was anxious for the captain to move on. Fortunately, a group of young women walked into the room, stealing the captain's attention. "You all have a good day now," he said as he ventured off in their direction.

"Strange man," Mr. Hamada said.

"You're right about that," Paul added. "He definitely has a thing for the ladies."

Mr. Hamada actually smiled. Then he asked Paul about his profession and sat back silently listening as Paul expounded on details about his gallery and buying trips around the world. Mr. Hamada asked him about Mexico, indicating he would love to travel there one day, but Paul preferred to elaborate on the bargains he had found in Italy.

The meal finally ended, and everyone parted ways to pursue their own interests. Devon's uncle was getting along with Akira's dad, and everything was going smoothly—more smoothly than he ever dreamed possible. He looked at Akira and realized he had never felt so content, so excited about the future. How had he gotten so lucky?

She took his hand and squeezed it. "Let's skip the tour in Jamaica and head back to my suite. My father will be gone all day, along with most of the passengers on this ship. We'll have the whole place to ourselves, and it will be nice to have some time alone with you."

"But you sounded so excited earlier. Are you sure you want to stay on the ship?"

A shy smile touched her lips as she said softly, "Absolutely."

"So what do you have in mind?" Reminded of where they'd left off earlier that morning, he couldn't help but grin. Although his body would disagree, it really didn't matter where this relationship was headed, just as long as they were together.

Akira tilted her chin. "Putting on our bathing suits and relaxing on my balcony. You could sunbathe while we talk. I'll need you to help me apply sunscreen all over my body. And I'll help you. What do you think?"

He remained speechless for a moment, then chuckled. "You don't really expect me to answer that question, do you?"

"No." She smiled. "I just wanted to see how you'd respond."

14

REVELATION

Devon looked at himself in the bathroom mirror and considered his situation. When he came on this cruise, he'd never expected to fall in love. And yet here he was, displaying his physique in a flashy bathing suit for a woman he couldn't stop thinking about. After losing Serena, he had lost interest in workouts at the gym, but diving for deep-sea treasure, clearing decks, and carrying loads on board the *Stargazer* had beefed up his body and kept his six-pack in place—something Akira seemed to appreciate. He could allow himself to have doubts over her motive for testing his endurance, or he could focus on the fact that her hands would soon be rubbing lotion all over him. It was solely his choice, and with his suppressed libido reengaging, he chose to think of the latter, assuring himself that any warm-blooded male would feel the same.

He made his way to Akira's room and knocked on the door. "It's me," he called out.

"Come in, angel," she answered.

He entered and found her standing in the center of the room dressed in a skimpy blue bikini. It was completely unexpected with the conservative manner she had presented on a daily basis. He buried his surprise, but no matter how hard he tried, he couldn't take his eyes off her gorgeous body.

Akira smiled. "Can you help me?" She was trying to tie up her long black hair with a silky blue ribbon, but loose strands kept escaping. "I need you to hold my hair for me while I finish fixing it. OK?"

Devon moved behind her and did as she asked. His body had involuntarily responded to her skimpy clothing, and now his close proximity to her was increasing his response.

She finished tying her hair and then turned to hug him. The sensation of her bare skin against his made the situation worse. He knew that she could feel his excitement and see it the moment they separated. The swim trucks she had insisted he buy weren't going to provide any cover.

Akira ran her fingers through his hair, and he instantly realized that he was responding too quickly. He had no desire to scare her off and lose her for good. "You're incredibly beautiful," he said. He looked deeply into her eyes, an irresistible attraction developing between them. But was it only his imagination?

"And so are you." She pulled his head toward her so that she could kiss him.

God, she made him feel so good about himself. Happy and relaxed—and sexually desired. However, there was something holding him back. He knew where they were ultimately heading, but he wasn't prepared to go there. At least not quite yet. "So are we sunbathing?"

Her eyes twinkled with a smile. "Can't wait to get your hands all over me?"

Damn. How did she always manage to do it? Make him lose all control of himself? "If you really must know, it's all I've been able to think about." He pulled her close and loved the feel of her in his arms.

"OK, let's go out on the balcony. I moved a couple of lounge chairs into the shade. I burn even without direct sun. Do you mind putting lotion on me first?"

"It will be my pleasure." He sat next to her on the lounge chair. "You really are beautiful, Akira—and I mean in every way, not just physically." He gently applied the sunscreen to her face and then leaned in to kiss her lips. She put her hands on the back of his head to pull him closer and to deepen the kiss. Devon ran his hands down her arms. His need to touch her was overwhelming.

They broke their kiss, and Devon found the strength to speak first. "Akira." He kissed her nose. "I don't want you to burn. Let's get some sunscreen on you. Lie down on your stomach, and I'll start with your back."

Akira switched her position, and Devon began to apply the lotion to her shoulders and back. He touched her tenderly, matching the way he felt about her. She let out soft moans of contentment as he trailed soft kisses against her skin.

"I like how you apply sunscreen, Devon. So many added benefits," she cooed.

"Baby, we're just beginning." He continued to apply the lotion to her lower back and stopped when he reached her butt. It was so firm and round. He poured more sunscreen into his hand and worked on her thighs. She squirmed and made little sounds that made his cock harden more.

"Your hands feel so good, Devon."

He wanted to cup her butt in his hands but continued to work on her legs instead.

"How are you doing?"

"Time to turn over," he said. He knew it would be impossible to hide the effect she had on him when her eyes found their target.

"Kiss me, Devon."

He bent forward and kissed her quickly. Then he returned to his job, applying sunscreen to her arms and shoulders. He moved down her chest and stopped short of her breasts.

"Is there a problem? I don't want to burn." Her come-hither look left his cock throbbing. He applied a small amount of lotion to the parts of her breasts that were exposed. "You can untie my top if you'd like."

His hands were trembling as he tugged at the bow holding her top together. He pushed the material aside to reveal her perfect breasts. He couldn't stifle the moan that escaped his lips. "You're so beautiful, Akira."

"You really think so? I'm sure you've been with many women. I'm really not so different."

His voice was breathy in his ears. "That's not true. You're the most incredible temptress I've ever met."

He swiped his thumbs over her nipples. Akira gasped and arched her hips. Devon's cock was straining against the fabric in his trunks. He continued to caress her nipples as Akira whimpered.

"Devon?"

"Yes, Akira?"

"I like how you touch me."

"I'm glad, baby. I want you to feel good."

He brought his mouth down and flicked his tongue over each nipple, causing her to cry out. When he could no longer resist, he sucked on them slowly. She squirmed and moaned, and the ache in his cock grew. He slid his hands down her stomach to the edge of her bikini bottom and smiled when she arched her back again. "Just following directions, baby. I need to make sure your whole body is covered."

Akira smiled as he moved down to her feet and started to apply sunscreen to her ankles and calves. He separated her legs slightly to have better access to her thighs and planted kisses starting at her knees and stopping just short of her bikini bottom.

"Devon…" She choked out his name.

"Almost done." He applied more lotion to the sides of her thighs in slow circular movements and stopped when he reached her wet center. "Open a little wider for me, Akira. I don't want to miss anything."

She let out a desperate little moan and opened her legs for him. He buried his face between her legs and kissed the top of her bikini bottom. She cried out and grasped his hair in her hands.

He looked up at her and smiled mischievously. "Do you like that?"

"Yes, Devon. More, please…more."

He slipped his fingers under the top of her bikini bottom and then looked at her again.

"Don't stop, Devon. Don't stop."

He pulled the bottom off her and then positioned himself between her legs. She automatically spread them and squeezed her eyes shut, waiting for his next move. Devon was so aroused, he thought he would lose all control. He used his fingers and thumbs to separate her folds before dipping a finger inside her. "You want me bad, don't you?" He moved it in and out in a steady motion, increasing his depth and her wetness. She whimpered and squirmed again.

"Look at me, Akira. I want to see what you feel."

She did as he said, revealing a dark animalistic craving in her golden-bronze eyes.

"OK, baby. Time to make you happy." He put his mouth on her mound and gently kissed it. She grasped his head tighter and arched like a cat, intensifying his contact. He pressed the folds of her labia apart and swiped his tongue through them until he came to her swollen clitoris. Her scent enveloped him as he flicked his tongue wildly.

"Oh, Devon," she sobbed.

He spread her inner lips with his tongue and forced his way inside. As he continued his ardent assault, he relished the slightly bitter taste of her. He reached up and seized her ass with both hands, drawing her onto his tongue as he swirled it around her clitoris.

"Devon...oh yes...yes..." she moaned. She pushed his head down farther, urging him on. He knew exactly what women liked, and she was no different in this regard except for her incredible endurance. He teased her with his tongue and mouth mercilessly, licking and sucking...expertly increasing the pressure and intensity until she approached a frenzied state. Her whole body began bucking under him as he drove her over the edge. She arched her back one last, lingering time and cried out his name before collapsing back in the chair.

After a few seconds, she moved over and pulled him up next to her. He put his hand over her mound to help her ease down.

"Oh, angel," she half whispered.

"That good, huh?" He pushed a strand of hair out of her face and smiled down at her.

"Yes, that good." She had tears in her eyes, threatening to fall. "Thank you."

An intense feeling of tenderness washed over him, and he realized at that moment he would do absolutely anything she asked.

"Devon. Let me touch you." She had moved her hand between them and was stroking him through his swim trunks. His erection was immediate and intense. He thought he would come just knowing her hand was on him.

"Akira." His voice was hoarse in his own ears.

"Lie back," she instructed. "I want to take care of you the way you deserve." Akira sat up and made room for Devon on the lounge chair. She positioned herself between his legs and smiled. "Time to get comfortable." He helped her remove his trunks before allowing her to take control. She wrapped her hand around his cock and began stroking it from bottom to top. He was harder than he could ever remember in his life. He released a moan from the pure torture of the sensation. Then he felt the warm wetness of her mouth as she took him inside. Every nerve in his body seemed to concentrate on one single spot.

He moaned louder and instinctively thrust into her. "Baby…"

Akira swirled her tongue around the top of his shaft and then sucked on it.

Devon cried out and thrust again. "Akira, please…don't stop." He was already on the verge of coming, but she was relentless in her pursuit of his happiness.

She took his cock farther into her mouth and began to move up and down on him in a steady rhythm. Devon clutched the arms of the chair and clenched his teeth. "That's so good, baby." He held his breath when she used her tongue to stroke his shaft with every upward movement. "So good, baby. So good." Her hands held his hips in place as she increased her tempo, leaving him panting. Devon wanted to pull out but couldn't stop himself from coming. He clenched the chair arms even tighter and cried out as his body jerked and his seed poured out of him. Akira remained still until he was calm. Then she withdrew her mouth and laid her head on his thigh.

Devon wanted to hold her close. "Come lie next to me."

She moved up beside him and remained silent.

"Are you all right?" he asked. He kissed her repeatedly and was overcome with feelings of tenderness for her. "You've got to know that I'm crazy about you."

Akira nestled against his neck. "That's how I feel about you too."

His heart beat faster. They lay in each other's arms for a while—until Akira laughed.

"What's so funny?" Devon could feel the smile tugging at the corner of his lips.

"We never finished putting on sunscreen. I hope I don't burn in the wrong places."

Devon chuckled. "Your butt is the only spot that I didn't cover completely. I'd better check it for you."

Akira giggled as she got up from the chair. "Does it look OK?"

"Looks perfect to me, but let me take care of it just to be safe." He chuckled again, enjoying their lack of inhibition with each other. After pouring lotion on his palm, he applied a generous amount in a slow, sensuous manner and then pulled her onto his lap. He kissed her neck softly and inhaled her heady fragrance, reminding him how much he adored this woman.

"Devon, I'm going to put sunscreen on you too. Believe it or not, you need it." Akira extricated herself from him and took ownership of the squeeze bottle.

Devon lay back to take in the view of Akira's amazing body. "I believe you're right." He found himself enjoying her massage and display so much that his arousal became impossible to hide. He flashed a sheepish smile when her eyes met his. "Sorry. My body craves you."

"Mine feels the same way." Akira grinned at him. "But I think it's time for us to put our swimsuits back on. I don't want the neighbors getting curious or my father to walk in and see us this way."

Devon sobered at the thought. "You're absolutely right. He appears to have enough issues with me. I'm not interested in losing valuable body parts."

Akira glanced at the open glass door. Her father's covered sword was resting against the wall, just as it had been all day. "You have no reason to worry about him, Devon," she said. "All of his issues are with me. He's traditional in many ways and thinks I'm an incompetent child."

Memory struck a chord in Devon's brain. "Is that why he called you Mariko? Is that some kind of childhood name?"

Akira drew an audible breath. "What are you talking about? Where did you hear that?"

Devon picked up his swim trunks. "The day he walked in while I was here, I heard him call out a name...like he was expecting you to answer."

She looked down at the two-piece bathing suit in her hand, then back at Devon. "It's a name I was given years ago. When I was a geisha. I don't know why he would mention it now. He's obviously getting old and forgetful. My name is Akira Hamada. That's all you need to remember...to stay friends."

Stay friends? Her words were troubling. Could she dismiss him so easily? He wasn't in a position to ask, and losing her terrified him. "It's forgotten, Akira. You don't need to worry about me."

"I had a feeling you'd say that. You're the best thing that's ever happened to me. I want to enjoy every minute we have together."

Devon breathed a sigh of relief. "I know exactly what you mean." He smiled back at her, feeling a little less sure of himself but unwilling to admit it.

She pulled his head down to kiss him. It was long and deep… and powerful. Then she smiled. "I need to get dressed. There's some tea and cookies on the counter. I'll throw on something comfortable and meet you back here. OK?"

"Absolutely." He followed her into the living room and watched her cute little buttocks disappear behind her bedroom door. Then he picked up the plate of cookies and pitcher of iced tea and made his way toward the table on the other side of the sliding glass door. After setting them down, Devon remembered that he needed glasses and returned to the living room space to collect them. However, something halted him in his tracks. The sword Akira's father alluded to in the restaurant was only a few yards away. It would only take a minute to view it and might be the only opportunity he had.

Devon stepped up to it and loosened the gold-tasseled cord on the green silk covering. He pulled it free and discovered a black lacquered sheath inside, as smooth to the touch as Akira's skin. The handle was wrapped in a tightly woven black cord, and the guard below it featured an exquisite bamboo carving. Devon extracted the katana sword and was wowed by its polished carbon steel blade. There was no doubt in his mind that the exquisite hand-honed weapon could cut through a thick bamboo tree with a single strike and was sharp enough to slice paper. He'd never actually seen a katana sword up close—only in movies and magazines—and the feel of it in his hands was powerful. The ancient relic was as deadly as a revolver and represented the demise of warriors who were foolish enough to challenge the handler's blade. The image of an invisible foe formed in his brain, and soon he was wielding the blade before him in wild slashing fashion.

He balanced it in his hand and smiled. "Incredible." The weight was perfect. Whoever crafted it knew exactly what they were doing.

Devon suddenly realized that at any given moment, Akira or her father could walk into the room and witness him touching their prized possession. It was important that he return it unharmed to its original place as quickly as possible and respect their privacy. With that thought foremost in his mind, he turned the sword over and was in the process of sliding it into the sheath when his eyes latched onto a beautifully engraved marking on the blade.

M...as in the name Mariko. It couldn't possibly belong to her. The woman he'd come to know was sweet and innocent, not a female samurai warrior. The letter must have been etched into the blade by the sword maker or the original owner.

He slid the sword back into its silk covering, drew the gold cord tight, and leaned it against the wall where he found it.

"Mariko?" Mr. Hamada's voice reached him from the entryway. Her father's persistence in using the discarded name was confusing, especially after Akira's explanation.

She stepped out of her room wearing a long floral caftan and a tense, uneasy smile. "You're back so early. We were sunbathing and are about to have snacks on the balcony."

"Sunbathing? Here?"

"Why, yes. We decided to take a break from all the tours. Did you enjoy seeing the city?"

Akira's father eyed Devon before answering. "It was hot and dusty. There were people everywhere: in crowded shops and restaurants. Street urchins had their hands out, begging for money, and the poverty was impossible to ignore. Why anyone would want to go to Jamaica is beyond me."

Devon turned away from her father, hiding his pained expression.

"Now that you're back," Akira said, "you'll have more time to relax. Maybe even take a nap."

"Yeah, right."

"There's a special dinner tonight. It's semiformal, which means a jacket but no tie, unless you want to wear one."

Mr. Hamada grumbled. "I'm going to have a drink and watch TV." He stood next to the couch with his eyes fixed on Devon.

"Would you like us to join you?" Akira asked. "I can find a movie…"

Devon had misgivings about Akira's attempt to bring them together. But he was willing to do whatever she thought was best, even though he believed it was useless.

"If you don't mind, I'd like to speak to this gentleman alone," Mr. Hamada said.

Akira's eyes narrowed. "Is that really necessary?"

He pursed his lips and nodded.

Devon smoothed his hand over his taut stomach, wishing he'd had the foresight to bring a shirt.

Mr. Hamada walked toward the large balcony and dropped into an outside chair. Devon followed and glanced at Akira before closing the sliding glass door behind him.

"It appears that you spent the afternoon in my daughter's room," he said. "Am I correct?"

Devon tensed. "On your daughter's balcony." Guilt gripped him. He knew full well that the man's insinuation was true.

"What were you doing there that you couldn't do here on the living room balcony, Mr. Lyons?"

This was much worse than he was expecting. He didn't think Akira's father would pry so deeply into his daughter's business, especially with her being a grown woman with a mind of her own. "I care about her, sir," Devon said. "You have to trust me—and her. I won't do anything to hurt your daughter." He didn't know how else to answer.

"Really? And just how much do you care about her, Mr. Lyons?"

Devon managed to hold his stare. "I know you don't want to hear this, but Akira and I have a special connection. It's something I've never experienced before."

Mr. Hamada angled his head. "You're not seriously telling me that you've never been in love before?"

Devon glanced down before answering. "There were others. But the feelings I had for them could never touch what I share with your daughter."

The old man seemed to be taken aback by his honesty, or perhaps it was something else. He crossed his arms and studied Devon with a scrutinizing look. "You understand this is merely a shipboard romance, Mr. Lyons. When we arrive at our last port, it all comes to an end."

Devon remained steadfast. "It won't end for me, sir. Especially if your daughter feels the same way."

The sliding door opened, and Akira appeared. She stood before them, searching their solemn faces for clues. "What's going on out here, gentlemen?" she asked.

Mr. Hamada said nothing, but there was a sudden twitch in his neck, jerking his head to one side.

"I need to change my clothes," Devon told her. "It's getting chilly out here."

By the troubled look in her eyes, the reference wasn't missed.

"I'll be in my room getting ready if you need me." Devon kissed her on the forehead and strode toward the door, feeling his confidence drain with every step. He was in the hallway when the door opened again.

"Devon, wait!" Akira was suddenly at his side. "Don't let anything he said affect you. He's just a protective parent—the only one I have."

"I suppose that's why he's determined to keep us apart."

"How so?"

"Because he doesn't think I'm good enough for you. And right now, I happen to—"

Akira's finger was on his lips shushing him. "Nothing will change the way I feel about you. Nothing. Don't ever forget that."

Her words hung in the air, sounding so final. So absolute. Not until that day had Devon considered the possibility of losing her. Not after growing so close so quickly. He would never be ready to say goodbye—the mere thought made him hungry for air.

She pressed her hand against his chest. "I love you, Devon Lyons. I've never said that to anyone, but I'm saying it to you now."

His eyes met hers and held tight. "Are you sure? I mean… really sure?" She kissed him then, and at the touch of her mouth, any shred of doubt fell into bits. Along with that went his uncle's well-intended caution. Her arms went up around his neck, and her tongue brushed his lips. He deepened their kiss, and she opened her mouth, encouraging his tongue to meet hers. The ache in his loins rose up again, quicker this time and hotter than ever. When he pulled his tongue back, she followed. It was a move of instinct, not conscious thought. It amazed him that within her was this bold, lascivious creature: taunting and teasing, driving him to the brink. She tasted warm and tangy—like the strawberry drink she'd enjoyed on the bus, leaving him smiling from ear to ear.

She pressed her hands on the sides of his face, as if to hold him there, and he complied, remaining silent. She took his lower lips between both of hers and pulled, sucking gently. He released a soft moan against her mouth, and a shudder rocked his body. His heart was racing, threatening to burst through his chest.

He drew her closer and slipped his hands behind her and onto her bottom. She rocked in her heeled sandals, smiling. He

KAYLIN MCFARREN

captured her mouth fully with his and pushed her backward two steps until her back was pressed flat against the door. Then he opened his eyes, and they stood there, gazes locked, rapid breaths mingling. "You're killing me, girl," he said. "Do you have any idea how much I want you?"

A bang in the hallway turned his head to the right. One of the maids whom he'd seen attending to Akira's room earlier that day had dropped a metal waste bin, sending it bouncing against the wall. She picked it up quickly and disappeared through the adjoining corridor, apparently embarrassed by her intrusion. Devon looked down at Akira and smiled. "I'm crazy about you... with an emphasis on crazy. Now go get ready before I take you right here."

He took a step back, and she turned away from him, searching her pocket for the room key. After finding it, she opened the door, and he swatted her butt playfully. "Get ready. We have dinner in thirty minutes."

She turned around, feigning an annoyed look. "Then stop distracting me."

The door closed, and he stood there smiling like a silly schoolboy with a huge crush and matching hard-on.

15

AFFIRMATION

Takashi had assumed his usual position, sitting on the sofa with his arms crossed. "I don't know what you think you're doing. That stupid fool is completely in love with you. I almost feel sorry for him, knowing that you're going to destroy him when this is over."

Akira dropped her bag on the table and moved toward the sliding glass door. The only indication that they were moving to a new destination was the wake caused by the plowing ship and shifting white clouds in the distance. "He won't be alone," she murmured.

"You've got to be kidding," Takashi groaned. "Have you forgotten why we're here? Romance was never part of the deal, Mariko."

She spun around on her heel. "Why do you keep calling me that? Are you intentionally trying to blow my cover?"

Takashi snarled. "If your boyfriend weren't always hanging around, it wouldn't be a problem, right?"

She chose not to answer, and he jumped up from his seat and began pacing about like a wild animal, growling under his breath. He was incapable of understanding someone as kind as Devon—a man who made her feel more alive than she had a right to be.

"Don't expect me to be at that dinner tonight," Takashi said. "I have no interest in knowing any of these people."

"Skip it then. But you need to show up tomorrow. If you continue to stay away, your absence will leave everyone asking questions."

Takashi stopped in his tracks. "What kind of game are you playing anyway? This isn't the way it's supposed to work. Eliminate Sara Lyons and Bradshaw and be done with it. Paul Lyons is merely a fool and had nothing to do with Keiko's murder. Isn't that what you said?"

"And do what? Dive off this ship and break our necks? Or, better yet, try to escape when we reach the next port and have the FBI and every police agency in the country searching for us?"

Takashi sat down.

"I told Yuki it was messed up when she gave me this assignment. I honestly think she put me here to get caught. She's convinced I'm responsible for her brother's death. That's the only thing I'm sure of."

"That doesn't make sense."

"No, it doesn't. But we're here now, and I'm going to do whatever it takes to bring Keiko's murderer down. Devon is my ticket off this ship and nothing more. Do you understand?"

Takashi nodded. "So what do you have planned for tomorrow?"

Akira smirked. "If you really must know, he arranged for a submarine tour. Then we're visiting a turtle farm and making a brief stop at the beach. He'll be wearing the new bathing suit I convinced him to buy. The same pair that has a hidden inside pocket. Yesterday I remembered the waterproof bug I packed and thought it might prove useful. I'm going to leave him and his uncle alone during our outing so I can listen in on their conversation."

"For what purpose?"

"To find out if Sara Lyons is capable of murder."

His brows gloomed at the mere mention of her name. "How are you going to get them to talk about that?"

"I'm planting a seed in Devon's mind. It will leave him questioning his aunt's behavior. Then his uncle will tell me everything I need to know without being aware of it."

Takashi looked down and seemed to be mulling over her logic.

"I just need to hear that she did it. I need to know for sure that we're killing the right people."

Takashi nodded.

"Then we're in agreement," said Akira. "So what do you have scheduled for tomorrow?"

"The concierge told me that Peter Bradshaw is going on a yachting and snorkeling tour with Sara in the afternoon. I'm tagging along to check out her swimming ability. If she's as unskilled as I suspect, drowning her might be an option."

Akira shook her head. "Fine. Do whatever you need to do."

"So I guess you'll be out late again tonight," Takashi said. The drawn look on his face brought to mind a concerned father, but she knew better than that. He was only worried about his own safety should he fail to please Mitsui-san.

"I have to change," she said. "Devon is meeting me downstairs in ten minutes. And by the way, is it really necessary to be so mean to him?"

Takashi snorted. "Think about it, Akira. If I ignored a man's advances toward my beautiful daughter, I wouldn't be much of a father, now would I?"

Akira shrugged at the offhand compliment. "From what I know of him, Yukio Abe wasn't much of a father either. At least that's what my mother told me before she ran off. But that didn't stop me from seeking revenge for his murder—and Kenji's death."

The corners of Takashi's lips turned down. "Is that so? Well, perhaps it would be best to keep that to yourself, Akira."

She smiled sarcastically. "The only thing sweeter than a secret is revenge, Hamada-san. At least that's what I used to believe. But I've only found misery for my efforts—a dull ache that I carry with me every day. In all truth, I have no one to blame but myself for my failures."

Takashi looked down for a long moment. Then his eyes lifted, and his voice dropped. "I have something important I need to tell you, Akira. Something that may change everything you believe." He paused, as if second-guessing himself. "But maybe now is not the time."

"Then keep it to yourself, Hamada-san. Nothing you can say or do matters. Not when it comes to me."

"What about Devon?"

"While we're on this ship, I intend to fulfill my obligation by whatever means necessary. And if by chance, I discover a small sliver of happiness, would it really be so terrible?" She choked on the words. "So unforgivable? Even if it's only for a matter of days?"

His eyes searched hers and surprisingly softened. "No, I guess it wouldn't be."

16

IGNORANCE

Akira almost bumped into Devon as she exited her room. When she tilted her head back to look up at him, a broad smile spread across his bronzed face, washing all her frustrations away. "You look as enchanting as ever," he half whispered. He pressed his lips gently to her forehead and gazed down at her, and the fluttering in her stomach grew.

She surveyed her blue silk halter dress and touched her long pearl necklace. "I hope this is all right for tonight."

"Every guy in the place will be jealous, I assure you."

She loved the way his breath caught, his hand finding its way to her lower back, pulling her tight against him. She kept one hand over his heart but allowed the fingers of her other to lightly trace up his collarbone before tangling in the hair at the nape of his neck. As she pulled him down to her level, she noticed for the first time that his eyes only closed at the last possible moment, drinking her in until she was too close to see.

And then his lips were on hers. What started out as gentle quickly heated as his tongue traced her bottom lip and finally slid inside. As she tugged a little tighter on his hair, he let out a deep groan. His hips pressed forward when she ended the kiss with her teeth teasing his bottom lip. She buried her face just under his chin and felt warmth emanating from his body. Then his stomach rumbled.

"You must be starving," she whispered against him, her lips tickling his neck. He shrugged, and she tilted her head back to look at him.

"Honey, I'm more than happy to delay our dinner. But if this show of affection continues, my hunger will only increase." His eyes were playful, hinting at more.

"I'm hungry too." She rose to her toes again to press a demanding kiss to his lips.

He pulled away and smiled. "If you insist on continuing this, I may have to take you back to my room and feed your appetite in other ways."

She found his hand and locked her fingers with his. Then she gave a small tug, and he followed without hesitation. "Dinner first," she said, smiling.

"Only if you insist." They reached the elevator, and she looked up at him. Heat rose to her cheeks, and her stomach somersaulted. No matter what lay in store for them, she hoped this incredible feeling would never go away. It was simply too precious to lose.

When they arrived in the dining room, Dr. Bradshaw, Sara Lyons, and Paul Lyons were already seated at the table.

Devon pulled out a chair next to them and smiled at Akira. "After you."

Dr. Hoffman and Vivian Ward arrived in dark blue attire and assumed their places across from Sara and Paul. For ten minutes, they chatted away. However, the last chair at their table remained empty, drawing attention to Hamada-san's absence.

Sara looked up from her half-empty wineglass and asked Akira, "Will your father be joining us tonight? Paul enjoyed their conversation this afternoon immensely and was hoping to discuss our trip to Japan in the spring." She patted his hand. "Right, dear?"

Paul looked down. "Yes, of course."

Akira flashed an uneasy smile. "He's been a bit under the weather but assured me he's fine. He might surprise us all by showing up."

Devon reached for her hand and held it under the table, away from prying eyes. "I'm sorry that he's not feeling well," he said. Although in all likelihood, he wasn't. Why would he be with the way Takashi was behaving?

Peter Bradshaw raised his forefinger, signaling for a drink from their waiter. "Hey, Marion...over here. You've got customers waiting."

The waiter's complexion darkened. Whether from frustration, humiliation, or downright disgust, it was impossible to tell. He approached the tuxedo-clad maître d' and engaged him in a short conversation before frowning and walking away. The maître d' assumed control of their table, appearing unfazed by the waiter's sudden departure. "Marion is handling another table. I'll take care of that bourbon for you, Dr. Bradshaw."

"Fine, fine. We're paying good money to get proper service. It's important for employees on this ship to remember that."

"Yes, sir. Was there anything else you needed?"

For a few seconds, Akira wondered if their waiter would be the next victim on this ship.

"Just our drinks. Pronto," Bradshaw said.

Akira looked at Devon and mouthed the words, *"Are you kidding?"*

Before anyone in their group could respond, Bradshaw sent the conversation in a different direction. "Did any of you know that Devon has a hidden talent for cooking? Even the instructor was impressed."

Everyone stopped whispering to listen to the doctor, but Devon's glare told Akira that he didn't like where this was headed.

"Akira and Devon took a cooking class with Sara and me this morning," Bradshaw informed them. "If our chef doesn't deliver a great meal as promised, we can always send him to the kitchen to teach everyone a thing or two. Right, Devon?"

Bradshaw's hardy laugh left Devon frowning.

Akira laid her hand on his arm. "I was equally impressed. It takes skill to prepare food so quickly and with such delicious flavor."

Sara winked at Peter. "So I'm assuming you let him win—just like you did with Paul."

Akira squeezed Devon's arm in an attempt to keep him silent. "He competed with your husband?" she asked. "On this ship?"

"No, dear," Sara answered. "In Mexico. They attended a cooking class for resort members at the Villa del Arco. It turned into an enchilada-making contest. Silly, I know, but I thoroughly enjoyed watching it all the same."

Akira turned to Bradshaw. "It must be nice to take so many trips together. Somehow I assumed this was your first vacation with Mr. and Mrs. Lyons."

"Oh no," he corrected. "We've traveled together a great deal over the last six months."

Paul lowered his voice. "Actually, more than I'd care to recall."

Bradshaw leaned close to Akira so that only she could hear. "Don't believe anything that man says. He knows that my priority is to look after his wife—wherever that takes us. Mexico, Brazil,

Costa Rica, Italy. When she's happy, we're all happy." He looked at his charge and winked. "Right, Sara?"

"Oh yes, yes. Of course." She held her wineglass out to the waiter for a refill. Akira got the distinct feeling she would agree with anything Bradshaw said: good, bad, or indifferent. The fact that he was overly attentive to her and a constant traveling companion perked Akira's interest and added a new layer to the mystery of Keiko Mitsui's death.

It was time to be bold. "I understand a Japanese woman died mysteriously in Cabo San Lucas a few months ago," Akira began. "Were you there when it happened?"

A strange look flashed in Bradshaw's eyes. Then his reassuring smile appeared. "I honestly don't recall. But a better question is, why the interest, Akira? Did you know her?"

Devon's hand was now moving on her back. "Honey, why are you talking about this?"

"The wife of a wealthy businessman was murdered in Mexico. The story appeared in Japanese magazines and newspapers for weeks. I was just wondering if the doctor might know more details. He did mention being called in for consultation while vacationing there. Isn't that right, Dr. Bradshaw?"

The doctor cleared his throat. "If memory serves me correctly, the woman showed symptoms of bipolar disorder. She jumped from her balcony on the fourth floor into the swimming pool and struck her head on the bottom. I'm sure it was disturbing for everyone involved. But there was no mention of murder. At least not that I'm aware of."

"Oh yes. I remember that," Sara interjected. "We saw her on the beach the day before. She was traveling with friends and shopping for silver jewelry. In fact, she bargained a beautiful turquoise bracelet out from under me and was downright proud of it."

Bradshaw watched her from the edge of his glass.

"She was also the same woman who stole our lounge chairs by the pool," Sara continued. "We ended up in a terrible donnybrook. It was so embarrassing. That woman contacted security and tried to have us removed from the premises. Surely you recall that, Peter?"

The doctor rested his hand on her arm. "I must admit that my memory's not what it used to be. It's probably old age creeping up, turning me into a senile old man." His teasing smile didn't quite reach his eyes.

Sara shook her head. "Don't be saying that, Peter. You're brilliant, and everyone here knows it."

"No, I'm afraid that's not entirely true. I've survived to middle age with half my wits, while thousands have died with all of theirs intact." Bradshaw paused before chuckling. "That's a quote from *I, Claudius*: a 1976 BBC television show," he told all of them. "Seems there are a few things I still recall." Three waiters were rapidly approaching their table. "Ah, would you look at that," he said, diverting their attention. "It seems our salads are here. Should we order some more wine?"

Paul reached for the water pitcher and refilled Sara's goblet. Then he held the breadbasket before her, and she waved it away. The conversation started up again, touching on shipboard activities, but Akira was no longer listening. The relationship between Sara and her doctor had taken center stage. She couldn't help noticing that Sara seemed oblivious to her husband's kind gestures and charming remarks but practically gushed at everything Bradshaw said. As she glanced around the table, Akira found herself wondering if anyone else had realized this was more than a doctor-client relationship.

"Red or white?" Bradshaw asked no one in particular.

While he perused the wine list and discussed his selections with Sara, Akira rested her hand on Devon's thigh and whispered in his ear. "Is Sara the doctor's only client?"

"Come to think of it, I believe so. From what I've witnessed, they're totally inseparable."

Sara laughed and patted Bradshaw's arm. Their odd relationship was getting more interesting by the second.

"Is it unusual for a private English doctor to travel with his client?" Akira asked Devon.

"I thought it was weird too. But then my uncle reminded me that Sara can afford to buy whatever or whomever she wants, including judges, lawyers, and real estate agents. I guess it comes with being ridiculously wealthy. There are no limits, no exclusions, and no buffers apparently. But then I'm guessing you've come across people like that in Japan too."

Akira rolled her lips. "A few, but not to such an extreme." She could feel Bradshaw's eyes on her, raising the temperature in the room. It was important for her to pay close attention to what was happening but also appear disinterested. She leaned over to kiss Devon on the cheek while grasping his thigh more firmly. "Do you want to go for a stroll on the deck again tonight?"

The corners of his lips lifted. "Two inches to the left, and you'll know my answer."

Akira returned a sweet smile. While her eyes appraised his flawless features, her ears were tuned in to the conversation between Sara and her mind-bending doctor. She couldn't help wondering if this man was involved not only with Keiko's death, but also the waiter's suicide and the cocktail waitress's accidental drowning. There was no doubt that Sara had been watching from the railing when Adriane's body was recovered, but where was Bradshaw at the time?

Like Devon had said, they were always together: eating meals, taking classes, sightseeing. Except for that one time—the night when Bradshaw disappeared in Florida just hours before their departure. The Russian hospital director died mysteriously after a vicious attack by a mugger that same night. It still didn't make sense why Bradshaw had followed after her. What if she had done something to offend Sara, and the doctor was just crazy enough to kill her? What if that was his common practice on all those trips they took together and during all the years he'd spent treating her in England? The number of deaths in their wake could be in the hundreds.

Akira looked across the table and met his eyes. She smiled at him, but his intense stare forced her to look away. It was almost as if he knew what she was thinking. And Sara: poor, dim-witted Sara. She had to be his unknowing accomplice. The curly-haired, age-defying woman was high-strung and overindulgent, but too emotional to be a murderous ringleader.

Akira ventured a look in her direction. The merry matriarch was laughing again, brushing elbows with Vivian and winking at Hoffman across the table from them, unaware that the real joke was on her. At the opposite end of the table, Paul smiled on cue, playing the part of a doltish husband. With so many people dying around them, how in the hell did he not know? How could he remain calm and unaffected—and so blind to the truth?

17

INTRUSION

"Hello," Paul called out.

Devon was startled when he heard his voice. He'd been expecting to meet up with Akira on the balcony this morning. They had planned to get their first glimpse of the Grand Cayman Islands together, and he was anxious to see her.

Devon's stomach clenched. He almost forgot that his uncle was joining them. "My...you're up early."

"I didn't want to miss our tour. From the description, it sounds rather intriguing. And better yet, it means one less day in the sun."

Devon surveyed him. "So this isn't about Akira and me?"

"Son, give me some credit. I might give unwelcome advice from time to time, but interfering in your life has never been my objective. I just can't stand spending another day with Sara and Peter."

Devon almost felt bad for him. He would hate the idea of sharing Akira with anyone, especially with a man she secretly confided in on a daily basis. As it was, he remained uncomfortable touching her in front of his uncle. Yet for some reason, she didn't seem to have the same problem.

"Good morning, gentlemen." Akira walked through the open door and out on the balcony to greet them. She was wearing a short pink sundress that begged Devon to look at her legs. He swallowed hard and had to tear his eyes away before anyone noticed.

Akira smiled at Paul. "Did you sleep well?"

"Sara is always asking me that. 'How did you sleep, darling?' 'Did you get a chance to sleep?' 'Did you get any rest, Paul?' When you're my age, Akira, you're lucky to get four hours in, and even then, it's spent tossing and turning."

Devon glanced at Akira. "Yep…as optimistic as usual."

Paul moved to the cabin's large picture window and stood looking out toward the front of the ship. "This is a strange place," he said. "The people on this ship have been up since sunrise, but they just sit there."

Devon shrugged a shoulder. "No place to go."

"Right. Nothing to do."

"So what's wrong with that?"

"Don't ask me. It's just something I don't understand."

Devon joined him at the window. "Well, this is a day of firsts."

"How can you sit around and do nothing all day?"

"You've never tried it?"

"Why would I want to?"

"Maybe to relax?"

Paul heaved a heavy sigh. Outside, a hungover partyer walked across the deck and sat down where a female housekeeper was sweeping. He crushed his cigarette under his heel, resulting in the woman glaring at him for endless seconds. When he turned away, she used her broom on his backside, prodding him to move on. Bystanders stood around laughing, and the angry, middle-aged woman glanced up at Paul before continuing her tedious chore.

He continued to stare at her. Then he asked Devon, "Does that woman look familiar to you? The maid with the broom?"

Devon took a quick look. "Not that I know of. Why?"

"No reason. Anyway, it's all pointless. Floating around on this ship."

"You've never seen people with nothing to do?"

"I've never thought about it." Paul glanced up at the clear blue sky.

"Are you telling me you've never been on a cruise before? I just assumed that—"

"No, I haven't. Can't you tell?"

"Well, it's a vacation. Try to relax."

"Like them?"

"People who work hard like to play, especially in the sun."

"They sit outside all day wasting time better spent on work."

Akira joined them and smiled. "Are you always this agreeable in the morning?" She reached for Paul's hand and looked up into his eyes. "You never smile when you should, Mr. Lyons. There are good things in this world. Nice people and great reasons to be happy."

He withdrew his hand. "Not for me."

Akira turned to Devon and half whispered, "Did something happen last night?"

"I don't know." His attention returned to his uncle. "What's really wrong? Why are you acting so strange?"

Paul glanced at Akira. "I'm sorry. It's a long story. One I'd prefer not to share, if you don't mind."

Devon noticed Paul's pained expression, which vanished as quickly as it had appeared. "Perhaps a hot meal will make us all feel better," he said. "Should we go to the buffet for breakfast?"

They looked at one another and agreed. After arriving at the lido deck, Akira and Devon wove their way through the food line and found a table near a window so that they'd depart on time. Paul seemed to be overwhelmed by the variety of choices, which resulted in his taking much longer than necessary.

Devon pushed his food around with his fork. "I hope you don't mind my uncle coming along."

"Not at all. I'm happy to spend some time with him," she said. "Although I was looking forward to having you all to myself."

"Geez. Maybe we should just skip the tour and find a quiet place on the ship."

Akira smiled. "It will give you something to look forward to later."

Devon moaned. Wasn't that the same thing she'd said after kissing him goodnight in the hallway? Just before her scowling father opened the door.

Paul chose that moment to arrive at the table with two huge plates of food. "Am I interrupting something?"

Akira and Devon exchanged glances. "No, we were just discussing what we might do later," he said.

Breakfast went better than Devon had expected. He didn't know if it was because Paul was so engrossed in his food or because he was showing signs of accepting his relationship with Akira. Either way, just being in Akira's company was a blessing.

When the meal was over, they went back to Devon's suite to get ready. His uncle disappeared upstairs while Akira lingered in the living room.

"I need to see you in private for a minute," she said. She led him to his room, leaving Devon feeling a bit nervous with Paul a short distance away. "I didn't get a chance to greet you properly this morning." Her arms slid around his neck, and she lifted up on her toes. Her tongue tangled with his, and he moaned at the desire that raced through him. His hands itched to roam her body, but he couldn't. He had to be satisfied with this.

He plundered her mouth, and she whimpered with pleasure, sending him soaring to the heavens. He drew his hands up her bare arms and settled them on her shoulders before sliding them back down again. Her skin was like satin to his touch. His fingers traced along the delicate bones at her neck, and then he cupped her face between his palms. He shuddered as she arched even closer into him. He was weighing the consequences of whether he dare go any further when Akira pulled back.

She slid her hands from his neck and flattened them against his chest in a telltale sign. Reluctantly, he lifted his head. His breathing was fast and shallow, and he noted that she was struggling with hers too. He forced himself to drop his hands and step back from her. As usual, the bulge in his pants became noticeable. More than anything he wanted to ditch the tour and throw her down on his bed right then and there.

Akira smiled. "I'd better go get ready. We don't want to miss the tour." She turned to leave, and Devon reached for her hand.

"Thanks for being so understanding. My uncle can be a real handful, and having him along won't be easy. As far back as I can remember, he's always distrusted people. Maybe because he wasn't trustworthy himself. Anyway, he'll come around after spending more time with us. You'll see."

Akira looked away. "So it's true. He doesn't like me."

"Oh God, no. You're perfect. It's not about you. He's been doubting my judgment for years. That's one of the main reasons why I didn't want to come on this trip."

She lowered her chin. "Then why did you? I mean if you don't get along…"

"I don't know. He said he wanted to make up for the past, and I just took him at his word."

Her eyes dusted the carpet. "I understand."

"I hope so, because the way I see it, if I hadn't come on this trip, I would never have met you." He took her hand and kissed her fingers. "Despite everything, you're the best thing that's ever happened to me."

Akira remained silent for several seconds. Then she tipped her head to one side. "I feel the same way about you." She stepped away and picked up his new swim trunks from the top of the dresser. Then turned back around, holding them out to him. "Make sure to put these on. Then we won't have to worry about changing later. OK?"

"Sure, honey," Devon said, smiling. "Whatever makes you happy."

18

TO HELL AND BACK

Paul finished getting ready before heading out to meet Devon and Akira. They made their way to the gangway to board the tender that was ferrying them to the harbor. The water was a little rough, so he held Akira's bag while Devon and a crewman helped her board. When they arrived at the dock, they were ushered to the ferry that would take them to the submarine.

Paul smiled at them. "How'd you two choose this tour? I don't think I noticed it originally. Haven't got a clue why I overlooked it."

Devon said, "We thought it sounded intriguing."

The ride to the docking area was fairly short. Devon climbed down into the submarine first and then helped Akira and Paul down. The tight quarters required them to switch places so that Devon was sandwiched between them.

Akira whispered in Devon's ear, "I suddenly feel nervous."

He took her hand in his and whispered back, "So do I."

She leaned forward. "Your uncle looks nervous too."

Devon turned to Paul. "Akira wants to know if you need me to hold your hand. She thinks you look nervous."

Paul laughed. "I think I'm getting the raw end of the deal here, son. You get to hold Akira's hand, and apparently I get to hold yours."

"Akira thinks it's a good idea." Devon squeezed her hand, and she grinned.

Paul laughed again, and something shifted inside Devon. It was the first time his uncle had joked about their relationship. It was a good sign and a chance to fully relax.

The submarine pilot addressed them over the loudspeaker. He reminded them about the safety features of the vessel and explained that it was naturally buoyant. If there was any kind of a problem, the sub would simply rise to the surface. The vessel began its descent, and within a couple of minutes, everyone's nerves had calmed. They were in a new, fascinating world filled with amazing landscapes and colorful, exotic marine life. Paul seemed to be having the time of his life, laughing and making comments about the coral-covered rock formations. He had the enthusiasm of a child—a behavior Devon never thought possible. As their tour continued, Devon felt as if he were seeing things in a whole new light with both of them by his side. He placed a hand on Akira's thigh and smiled.

When the ride was over, they boarded the ferry again. Akira leaned against Devon and wrapped both of her arms around his waist. He put his arm around her shoulder, keenly aware that Paul was standing across from them. She slid her hand under his shirt and caressed his back. Her touch instantly aroused him, and for some unexplained reason, she seemed to enjoy teasing him and picking the most awkward moments to do so. Even with his hand on her shoulder, she managed to slip her fingers under the back waistband of his trousers and keep it there.

"Akira." He tried to whisper a warning to her, and she smiled. "Just checking to see if you're wearing my new swim trunks."

Although Devon didn't look up, he could feel Paul's eyes on him. If she was hoping to gain his approval, she was definitely going about it the wrong way.

Akira removed her hand and moved it up to comb through his hair. She knew the effect that had on him but didn't seem to care. "Your hair got all mussed up from the wind. I'm just straightening it for you." He caught her eye, and she bit her bottom lip. He could feel his arousal increasing and gave her a warning look. She simply smiled.

When they arrived at the dock, they were ushered onto a bus for the next leg of their tour. Devon and Akira sat together, and Paul sat across the aisle from them. Playing the gentleman, Devon made sure she had a window seat so she could enjoy the view.

"I couldn't help noticing that you have your bag with you again," Devon said.

"Ah yes." She smiled and reached in to pull out sunscreen. "Would you put some on my face for me?" She handed him the tube.

"Of course." He began to tenderly apply it to her face and gently rub it into her skin. He could feel Paul watching him the whole time and couldn't help wondering what his uncle was thinking. But that didn't detour him. When he finished her face, Devon continued to cover the exposed skin on her shoulders, her back, and then her arms. When he was done, Akira took the tube and began applying lotion to his face, stopping to kiss him along the way. The whole process was very sensual but extremely uncomfortable for Devon with Paul looking on. There was something extremely intimate in the way they touched each other, even though they tried to make it seem as casual as possible.

Akira didn't seem the least bit inhibited by his uncle's presence, and Devon admired that about her.

"Do you want some sunscreen, Mr. Lyons?" Akira called from across the aisle.

Paul looked over and met Devon's eyes. "Yes. Thank you, Akira."

Devon handed the tube to him and held Paul's gaze.

The tour guide began to speak. Paul broke eye contact with Devon to look up at her. She explained to them that they'd be making three stops along the way and relayed an entertaining account of the sights they were seeing and some fascinating stories behind them. Everyone relaxed, and several passengers fell asleep.

They arrived at the turtle farm first, and the sun was beating down hard.

"Did you bring a hat, Mr. Lyons?" Akira asked.

Paul looked sheepish. "I forgot. When I changed my tour, I didn't realize I'd still be in the sun."

"Not a problem," she said. "You can borrow the extra one I brought. But that means your nephew won't have one to wear." She handed the hat to Paul. "Sorry, Devon."

He had a huge smile. "No need to apologize, honey. I'm sure I'll be fine. My uncle needs that hat more than I do."

"You don't honestly expect me to wear this, do you? It's a woman's hat." Paul looked incredulous, making it impossible for Devon to wipe the grin off his face.

"Devon wore it," she explained.

Paul looked at his nephew. "You wore this? I bet that was quite the sight. I hope you took photographs, Akira."

Devon grimaced. "No, she didn't. But you might not get off so easy."

"Akira..." Paul's voice was pleading.

"Sorry, Mr. Lyons, but you need to wear it. Your wife would never forgive us if your sunburn became worse."

It seemed she wasn't about to give in. He put the hat on, in essence admitting defeat. Devon couldn't suppress his laughter. His uncle glared at him, then busted out laughing as well. "It appears your young lady has more muscle than the two of us."

Devon looked fondly at Akira. "Indeed, she does." He leaned close to Paul. "Determination is one of the things that attracted me to her."

"I know exactly what you mean. When she gets her mind set, there's no turning her. Just like my temperamental wife."

"Are you talking about me?" Obviously Akira hadn't heard a word, or she would have had a strong reaction. Devon grinned at her, and she smiled back. "OK, OK...I won't ask," she whispered in his ear. "But I insist you tell me later."

He put his arm around her waist and whispered back, "We'll see."

The tour guide directed everyone to one of the park staffers, who was scheduled to give them an educational overview of the farm. They followed her the short distance to the breeding area, and Akira insisted that Devon join her under her umbrella. He had no objection, since it meant they had to stay very close together.

As it turned out, the tour was fascinating. Turtles ranged from newborns to creatures weighing up to six hundred pounds, and they got a chance to hold the babies. Akira took photos, and Paul seemed to have forgotten that he was wearing her hat, leaving Devon slightly amused.

At the end of the tour, they had free time to grab a bite at a restaurant located within the park. They sat outside on a covered deck and had tropical fruit punch, jerk chicken, conch fritters, and a mixed variety of seafood appetizers. The sound of a splash turned their heads, and they spotted several turtles in the nearby lagoon paddling about, leaving them all laughing.

They returned to the bus and began the drive to their next stop. According to the tour director, they were visiting a place called Hell, which was just a few miles away. The name proved to be hilarious to everyone on the bus. They'd have time to take photos, visit the Hell post office, and purchase souvenirs if they so desired.

Hell ended up being an outcropping of unusual black limestone formations jutting out of the landscape. The origin of the name was up for debate, but it made for an interesting tourist attraction. Paul had a grand old time meeting the red-suited town "devil" and exchanging corny sayings. "Where in Hell are you from? Is it hot as Hell? What in Hell do you do for a living?" The conversation continued as Devon and Akira snuck away to investigate the region's geology and read signs explaining myths surrounding the site.

She rested her hand on his forearm. "Your uncle seems to be enjoying himself."

"I know; it's crazy. He's always been quick to judge people and point out the negative side of every situation. I don't think I've ever seen him so relaxed." Devon took her hand and kissed it. "He's always been concerned when it comes to my welfare. And with my past, I can't say that I blame him. I just hope he realizes how much I care about you." He grinned at her, and she grinned back.

Paul joined them. "What the hell are you two up to?" He smiled and showed them the miniature devil he had purchased in the gift shop. "Akira, take a couple of photos of Devon and me. I want some in front of the signs with Hell on them."

"I'd be happy to," she said, smiling.

"Dang it," Devon quipped. "You know how much I hate photos."

Paul pulled Devon away from Akira's side. He put his arm around his nephew's shoulder and directed him to various spots for photo ops. She followed them around, snapping away. Then Paul offered to take photos of Akira and Devon near the rock formations and in front of his favorite signs. He even managed to get one with the town's designated devil.

The tour guide put the fun to an end when she called them back to the bus. They were headed to their last stop, which would allow them a couple of hours on a beautiful beach to sunbathe, swim, or just relax in the shade.

Devon found a quiet spot on the beach for the three of them. They rented a large umbrella and a couple of lounge chairs. Akira spread out a blanket while Paul purchased cold drinks from the local snack shack. They'd worn their swimsuits under their clothing, so it didn't take them long to get ready. With Paul and Devon ensconced under the umbrella, spread out and sipping away, Akira took the opportunity to scour the beach for seashells and polished stones. She assured Devon she'd be fine on her own and would return shortly, giving them plenty of time to swim.

When she was out of earshot, Paul turned to Devon. "I'm surprised by how much you two have in common. You're different in so many ways. But what amazes me even more is how openly affectionate she is. I mean…from what I understand, Japanese women tend to be shy and conservative. They don't publicly display their emotions. And yet Akira makes a point of—"

Devon was quick to cut him off. "Since when do you know so much about women?" He suddenly realized his uncle's show of approval was purely an act. "Akira is not like anyone else. She's very special and means the world to me. I think it's time you accepted that."

Paul frowned. "It was not my intention to cause problems. I was merely making an observation. I'm sure Akira is a wonderful woman. Even though she came into your life quickly and we know very little about her. I just want to remind both of you that this trip will be ending soon. Unless you're relocating to Japan or she's moving to California, you're going to have a hard time building a future together." His uncle sighed. "I live with Sara in the same house, and even that poses a challenge."

Devon considered his uncle's harsh words. He and Akira had talked about every subject under the moon, although the focus seemed to rest solely on him. Despite his need to know more about her, Akira's secrets were her own. "OK, you're right. It's only been five days," he confessed. "But that doesn't change how I feel. We're both adults, and our relationship is between us. No one else needs to get involved. Not you...not even her father."

"I'm afraid you don't understand the Japanese culture, son. Her father's approval and opinions are essential to Akira. If they weren't, he wouldn't be on the ship." Paul looked down, shaking his head. "For some unknown reason, he's been sitting back, allowing Akira to behave in any manner she pleases. But that doesn't confirm his acceptance of her lifestyle or the people she chooses to spend time with, including everyone in our suite."

"And what about Sara?"

"What about her?"

"Aren't you concerned about the way she behaves with Bradshaw? He's so disrespectful when you're around. I know it's none of my business, but something isn't right about him. Don't you feel it?"

Paul shut down and stared out at the ocean.

Before long, Akira crossed the beach and headed toward them. Despite his resentment over Paul's involvement and his uncle's reaction to his harsh words, Devon was left with plenty to think about.

While Paul silently watched, Akira set her bag down next to Devon and began twisting her hair—trying to tie it up the same way she had the day before. "Can you help me?" she asked him. Devon stood and helped her fasten it, and she gave him a quick kiss on the lips. He could feel Paul's eyes on them the whole time.

Devon returned to his chair. Akira sat between his legs and passed back the tube of sunscreen. Without being asked, he slowly and tenderly applied lotion to her shoulders and back. It took everything in his power to control his response to touching her. Akira took the tube from him and covered the rest of her body. And all the while, Paul continued to watch them.

Akira stood and made Devon slide forward. Then she climbed onto the chair behind him. "I think you need some lotion too." She started to rub the sunscreen on his back but didn't stop there. Her hands moved to his shoulders and over his biceps. Much to his chagrin, she put her arms around him and began to rub lotion on his chest and stomach from behind. His body involuntarily reacted, adding heat to the moment. She leaned forward and nibbled on his ear.

Devon was losing all control. He searched desperately for something to distract him. Thankfully, Paul's feet were in his line of vision. The man had the most unattractive toes he'd ever seen, and Devon was grateful for the discovery.

When Akira got a little too low on his stomach, Devon grabbed her hands. "I'll take it from here, honey." He brought her hands up to his lips and kissed them. Taking the tube in hand, he finished applying the sunscreen himself. Even from where he sat, he could feel Paul's eyes studying them.

Akira took his hand and pulled him up off the chair. "Devon and I are going for a swim. We'll be back in a little while."

"Yes, of course." Paul smiled at Akira and briefly caught Devon's eye. The warning he found there was clear. *Don't do anything to embarrass yourself.*

Akira led him to the water. It was crystal clear and had varying shades of blue and green. She smiled and told Devon that the water was almost as beautiful as his eyes. Then they walked out into the ocean hand in hand until their bodies were completely covered. She wrapped her arms around his neck and kissed him. "Alone at last," she murmured.

He kissed her back, keenly aware that Paul was watching from a distance. "You're not uncomfortable being affectionate with me in front of my uncle. I admire that about you—not caring what anyone thinks."

Akira kissed him again. "I'm not going to hide how I feel about you. And besides, your uncle is the one who has a problem with it." She lowered her voice. "Or perhaps with me. But I like being affectionate with you."

"And I like it when you are, baby. I wouldn't want it any other way. I just feel as though he doesn't approve when he sees us touching each other. And what about your father? How does he feel about me?"

"It really doesn't matter, does it?" Akira ran her hands over his chest. "I actually think it's sweet that you worry so much. It tells me how much you care about me." She blushed. "I like you exactly the way you are, Devon. You make me feel special—and sexy. I've never sensed that about myself before."

He must have looked incredulous, because it was the way he felt. "I don't think I have anything to do with that, honey. You're an extremely beautiful, sexy woman." He ran his hands down her arms and then pulled her against him to feel his arousal. "Every time I see you, my body responds whether I want it to or not."

She smiled shyly. "I know. So does mine. I want to share that feeling with you every time we're together. I don't know why it happens, but I'm completely uninhibited with you. I've never felt this free and comfortable with anyone. You have to believe me."

His heart began racing. He pulled her closer and leaned in to kiss her. Akira wrapped her legs around his waist so that his cock was pressed firmly against her. Devon moaned in her ear. "Ah, baby."

She rocked her hips. "I want you—in every way," she whispered.

He moved his hand between their bodies and pushed the center of her bikini bottom aside so that he could touch her. Everything that Paul had said was wiped from his brain. He didn't care what anyone thought, only about pleasing this woman.

Akira clung to him more tightly and whimpered. "We should wait until later."

Devon continued to caress her. "I want you to feel good." He continued to stroke her clitoris as she clung to him with her face pressed against his shoulder. She moved against his fingers in unison until she was pushed over the edge. Then she moaned her satisfaction. Her body relaxed as the tension drained from it.

"How was that, honey?" He kissed the top of her head.

"Incredible." She wrapped her legs around him and continued to cling to him. "I thought you were uncomfortable with touching me in front of your uncle."

Devon pushed into her and moaned. "I can't wait until we're alone." His erection was straining against his swimsuit. "Thanks to your hot little body, I won't be getting out of this water any-time soon."

"Anything I can do to help?"

"Wrong question, baby." He loved to feel her against him but needed to cool down before hitting the beach. "Let's race each other."

"Oh, I'd love that. I'm a pretty good swimmer."

"I'm not too bad myself." Devon grinned. "Let's see if you can come within five feet of the woman in the pink hat. The one floating over there on the blue raft."

"Got it." Akira dove into the water and began swimming. Devon followed her lead and stayed neck and neck with her. They arrived together, laughing.

"Looks like a tie," she said.

They continued to race each other, always coming within a few feet of each other, and kissed each time they stopped. Devon scanned the shoreline looking for Paul and found him sitting under the umbrella where they'd left him. "I think it's time we got out of the water. Need time to dry off before we head back."

"Agree. By the way, what does Sara think of me? Somehow I get the sense that she doesn't approve. And with anyone who displeases her dying, I'd hate to think I'm next on her list."

Devon stopped in his tracks. "What are you saying? That my stepaunt is a murderer?"

Akira paused before answering. "Have you even considered it? I mean…it does seem strange that people are dying on our ship, and she manages to remain unfazed, at least until Bradshaw disappears. Which brings up another question: Why would the director of a hospital pay the cost for a cruise and then forfeit the price on the very night the ship departs? What if I told you something happened to her too?"

"Like what?"

"She was murdered by a mugger."

"Really? And you know this how?"

"My father told me. He read it on the Internet. But I really think it was Bradshaw who did it."

Devon chuckled. "My goodness, Akira. Your imagination is almost as vivid as my uncle's. If I didn't know better, I'd peg you for an undercover cop or a tabloid reporter."

Akira was suddenly serious. "I know it sounds silly. But just think about it, OK? This guy could be dangerous."

He took her hand and kissed it. "The last thing you need to worry about is someone trying to lay a hand on you. Aside from me, of course."

He walked her across the beach and halted in front of Paul's chair.

"Nice job, Devon," he said. "I didn't think you had the stamina to keep up with her." He winked at Akira. "Holding back, huh?"

"How'd you know?" Her lips slightly curled.

Devon snorted. "Hey, give me a break. I've been swimming for years." Then he glanced at Akira. "You OK?"

"Of course." She wrapped her arms around his waist from behind and pulled him onto the lounge chair, leaving him pressed up against her. She smoothed his hair back with her hand and smiled. "That was fun."

"It sure was," he said. "I just hope you didn't get too much sun."

They ordered drinks, and Akira escaped to the bathroom to change into dry clothes. While she was gone, Devon considered her remarks about Bradshaw and accusations regarding Sara. It wouldn't have taken much to get his uncle riled up over their outrageous behavior or to feed his growing paranoia with the questions Akira had asked. As it was, any day involving relaxation was rare and far between for Paul, and ruining his day was pointless. At least that's what Devon believed.

Paul leaned back in his seat with his large fruit punch and smiled. "I don't ever want to leave. This place is incredible."

Devon watched the waves crash on the beach and the sand castles children had built being washed away. "I'll never regret coming here. That's for sure."

The tide withdrew, and people began collecting their things. The man at the snack bar was calling out, "Final orders!"

Paul looked at Devon. "She is an incredible woman. Akira, I mean. I really hope it works out for you two."

Devon took a long sip from his cup. "I appreciate your kind words, Uncle Paul. But I have no idea where this is leading. It's so complicated right now. If she agrees to come back with me to California, we might have a real shot. But I know her father will never agree."

"I understand a woman's loyalty to her father, but she isn't a child," Paul reminded him. "She needs to stand up for herself, and that might cause some upset. But if she loves you, I'm sure it will work out."

They sat quietly for the next ten minutes, watching the waves rise and fall and relishing the warmth from the late afternoon sun. When Akira returned, they gathered their belongings, piled back into the bus, and returned to the ship. Devon walked her back to the door of her suite, and they agreed to meet at their usual time for dinner. She gazed up at him and smiled.

"It's formal tonight. Good thing I brought extra dresses."

Devon took her hand. "I'd love to skip dinner altogether. There's nothing I'd rather do than lie in bed with you, making love for the rest of the night." He leaned his forehead against hers. "You know I'm nuts about you, angel." He laid his hand on her cheek and traced her nose and lips with his thumb. "If you give me the chance, I'd love to prove it."

God, she's so beautiful, he thought to himself. *How did I get so lucky?*

Akira had a remarkable way of bringing out a combination of lust and tenderness in him that he didn't know quite how to express. His attraction to her was more than physical. There was a deep, soulful connection that couldn't be denied. Even though it had been less than a week since they'd met, to Devon it was as if they'd known each other for years.

Akira ran her fingers through his hair. "Everyone will be expecting us, silly. You'll just have to wait."

"In that case, why don't you have your father join us? I'm beginning to feel guilty for keeping you all to myself."

She looked down, gnawing her bottom lip. Something was obviously troubling her.

"Is…is everything OK?"

"Yes, of course. Why wouldn't it be?"

"I don't know. I just got a sense that—"

Akira placed a finger on his lips. "I'm fine. Now go get ready, and I'll do the same."

"OK, OK. I'll be back for you in one hour with or without your father. Just as long as you're with me."

She smiled sweetly. "Where else would I be?"

19

MASTER PLAN

Takashi's anger was apparent by the look in his eyes. He followed Akira into the living room and perched himself on the edge of the sofa. She knew a lecture was soon to follow, and aside from her bedroom, there was no place in the suite to hide. "I could hear you and Devon in the hallway. Haven't you listened to anything I've said? Since we got on this ship, I've been urging you to keep your relationship real—not some stupid fantasy cooked up in your brain."

"You forget. I'm just playing a part, Hamada-san. Exactly the way I've been trained to do."

"Well, then you're a better actress than I thought—and a lousy detective. If you don't get a confession out of Paul Lyons tonight, then I'm making the final call. They're all going to die tomorrow—one after the other. Sara Lyons, her husband, and Bradshaw. As far as I'm concerned, they were all involved anyway."

"That's crazy!"

"You killed three men before you got here, didn't you? How crazy was that?"

"I had no choice. It was my life or theirs."

"And how has that changed?"

Akira's first instinct was to grab the sword and use it. She wasn't the type of person to let anyone threaten her. Not after the life-altering experiences she'd been forced to go through.

Her eyes met Takashi's, and a shiver ran through her. She was scared, exhilarated, and weary all at once. Every encounter with him tested her endurance—her ability to stay silent, meek, and compliant. Then she noticed the handwritten note he held. Mitsui's signature practically jumped off the page.

"You *do* know the reason why I came on this trip, don't you?" Takashi asked.

Akira's breathing quickened. "I only suspected it. But it seems you've confirmed it."

"Confirmed what?'

"That you intend to kill me."

Takashi barked a loud laugh. His dark brows, one of which was split by a thin scar, furrowed, making him look almost devious. "What gave you that idea?"

"Why else would a cleaner come with me? Mitsui-san expects me to take care of his business and handle the resulting messes. That was part of the punishment I received after Kenji's death."

"Yeah, I heard the story about how you tried to kill him— right after your landlord beheaded Kenji. I don't know why you believed Mitsui-san was involved." He shrugged. "Anyway, it was a real shame about your danna. I actually liked him, and I can't say that about most people."

Akira looked down. "I guess I wasn't thinking clearly at the time."

"Obviously."

"Then you probably also know that Mitsui-san refused to forgive me."

Takashi chuckled. "I can't say that I blame him. You tried to poison the man, Akira. You're lucky to be alive."

She looked at him sideways. "Then why are you here, Hamada-san? Obviously, you've been given orders. They're right there in your hand—plain as day."

He glanced down at the paper, then back at her. "Because my responsibility is to finish this job. Mitsui-san asked me to bring your sword to test your loyalty. Nothing more, Akira or Mariko or whatever you want to call yourself. He never expected you to kill anyone on this ship, only to identify the mark. That's where I take over. When we reach the last port, the bag that's hidden in the safe next door and the passport inside it belongs to you." He slipped off his necklace and dangled it before her. "It's the key to your future, Akira. Do the math. It's all about Zakura-kai symbols and numbers."

"I don't understand. What does that mean?"

Takashi smiled. "Although you might find this hard to believe, you were always Mitsui-san's favorite. More important and significant than he originally believed. Just trust that he knows what's best for you."

Akira was lost in the meaning of his words. But they really didn't matter anyway, not to her. All she cared about was her freedom—the opportunity to move on with her new life. "So this is my last job? With no strings attached?"

"That's what I said, isn't it? When all this is over, he wants you to be happy—to make the right choices for everyone. Now stop being stupid and get ready for dinner. And do what you were sent here to do."

Akira couldn't help herself. She threw her arms around Takashi's neck and hugged him with all her might.

"Enough, enough," he grumbled, shrugging her off. "We're not done yet. Open your hand." He pressed the key into her palm. "Keep that in a safe place. Somewhere no one will find it. When the time is right, find the bag I brought with us and use it the best way you know how."

"Yes, yes, of course. Whatever you say," Akira said, smiling. "I'll be ready in a few minutes. Are you coming as well?"

"In due time. Now get ready, and for God's sake, try to remember why you're here."

Akira rushed into her room and pulled out the prettiest dress she owned. After taking a hot shower and blow-drying her hair, she set to work on making herself as attractive as possible. Twenty minutes later, she walked out of her bedroom holding a pair of high heels in her hand.

Takashi was standing in front of the wall mirror, adjusting his black bow tie. His eyes widened, and his jaw slacked as she approached.

"Is it too much?" Akira glanced down at her plunging neckline and then back at him.

"You look amazing. Every woman on this ship is going to hate you."

Akira smiled shyly. "I certainly hope not. Anyway, I don't want you to worry about this job. Just give me forty-eight hours to find out who was behind Keiko's death. We can end all of this during the white night party, while everyone is distracted on the pool deck. I won't disappoint you, Hamada-san. I promise."

Takashi blew out a long sigh. "I'll be counting on that. Don't make me regret trusting you."

Akira bowed. "I'll see you downstairs." She walked into the hallway with a soft smile, unaware of the deadly threat lurking close by.

20

TRUTH BE KNOWN

Devon stood speechless in the open doorway as Akira walked past him looking sexier and more beautiful than he'd ever imagined possible. His vision traveled from her gorgeous smile to the split in the front of her formfitting emerald gown. He stepped toward her, and for the first time since they met, he was at a loss for words.

Her breasts were partially exposed, begging to be touched, and his body was responding accordingly. A strand of her hair had fallen across her cheek, and he brought his hand toward her face to brush it away. He held her gaze in a prolonged moment, unaware of anyone else in the room. There was only Akira and the sense of wholeness—of unadulterated joy. Nothing in the world could ruin that moment, not even his uncle's presence. This woman was his for the taking, and he wanted the world to know it.

As if reading his mind, Paul announced that he'd meet them downstairs, leaving the two of them alone.

"Akira, before we go to dinner, I have a gift for you." Devon handed her a small blue box wrapped with a white ribbon. She untied it and removed the top as he watched her every move. Inside the box was a radiant two-carat pink sapphire, mounted on a polished silver band. "I wanted to give you something special, but I couldn't decide on what. Then I thought about your incredible lips and how much I love kissing them. That's why I chose a pink stone. Do you like it? If you don't, we can always exchange it."

"Devon," she whispered, "I love it—and you. Thank you for this, for everything you've made me feel."

He slipped the ring onto her finger and said, "Always." He leaned in to kiss her, and even though they had done it so many times before, it took his breath away. He could feel his heart pounding in his chest. It was the way he felt when she touched his hand and kissed his cheek the first time. The way he felt when she curled up on his lap and wrapped her arms around his neck, kissing him over and over again. It was the constant stirring inside of him that only Akira could create—that made him happy to be alive.

He reached for her hand and kissed the top of it. "I know you're not a big drinker, but do you think tonight warrants a toast? I ordered a special bottle of champagne for dinner that will be waiting on ice."

"You think of everything," she said, smiling.

They took the elevator downstairs, and Paul greeted Devon enthusiastically in the dining room, putting his arm around his shoulders. "That was quite a day," he said. "Thanks for letting me tag along."

"Didn't have much choice," Devon said, smiling. "Although Akira didn't seem to mind." She took his hand and squeezed it, and he squeezed her hand in return.

They were the first to arrive at their table, and Devon helped Akira to the best seat and sat next to her. Paul sat on the other side of her. Sara and the rest of their party arrived minutes later, and everyone began to animatedly share stories about their day on Grand Cayman.

Bradshaw's booming voice and hearty laugh soon became the main focus. "I heard that Paul and Devon went to Hell today. Run into anyone I know?"

Despite Devon's misgivings, Paul gave them the lowdown on their tour. "Akira, show them the photos." She pulled out her phone and did as he requested, while Devon grimaced.

Vivian laughed. "Nice hat, Paul. We need to go shopping together."

"It's Akira's. She insisted I wear it to keep from getting too much sun. If I wasn't there, she would have made Devon wear it again. But to tell you the truth, I look better in it." Paul almost choked on his own laughter.

Hoffman chuckled. "I'd pay to see that." He turned to Akira. "You must have some great photos."

Devon didn't give her a chance to answer. "You won't find any photos of me."

"Yeah, I bet." Hoffman laughed even harder.

Sara ignored Devon and looked at Akira. "I bet he looked adorable."

She giggled and put her hand on Devon's arm. "He did. But he always does."

Paul smiled. "We actually had a lot of fun. Who knew that my nephew could be such good company?"

Everyone laughed at Devon's expense, but he didn't mind. He'd obviously made headway in his relationship with Paul and could suffer a few lighthearted indignities. Besides, Akira was enjoying herself, and that's all that mattered to him.

Dinner went by quickly and without negative occurrence. Paul was in high spirits for a change, and it was obvious how much it meant to Sara. Devon hoped it would continue in that vein, making the trip all the more pleasant. However, the long, somewhat stressful day was catching up with him.

As if she knew what he was thinking, Akira leaned toward him and commented on her own state of exhaustion. "I'm feeling a bit tired. Would you mind if we went back to your suite and sat out on the balcony? I don't think I can manage anything else today."

"You read my mind." He helped her stand and bade everyone good night. Then he put his arm around her waist and walked her to the elevator. "I have to attend to a small matter. Here's an extra key to my room. Why don't you head back to your suite and change into something comfortable? I'll meet you at my room shortly."

"Thanks, angel. I'll see you in a little while." She kissed him on the cheek and stepped into the elevator. The doors closed, hiding her coy smile.

Devon made his way to the sundry store. He'd known from day one that he hadn't planned well for this cruise. He didn't bring enough casual clothing, forgot about sunscreen, and hadn't thought to bring a hat. Those oversights were due to his lack of interest in this trip, and meeting someone as beautiful as Akira was something he had never foreseen. However, their relationship was moving rapidly, and he wanted to be prepared if things continued in the direction they were going.

He scanned the store shelves to no avail and decided it was best to ask the male clerk behind the counter. "Do you sell condoms here?"

The clerk looked surprised but quickly recovered. "Yes, sir. Do you have any special requirements?"

Devon was thrown. "No, just give me your most popular brand."

"Regular, large, or extra large?"

"Large." Devon was anxious to get this purchase completed.

"We only have one type in that size, sir."

"That's fine. Just give me what you have."

"That will be nineteen dollars and thirty-five cents, sir."

Devon handed him a twenty-dollar bill.

"I'm afraid we don't accept cash. But you can charge it to your Sea Pass card."

Devon was taken back. "I don't want to charge it to my room. I'd like to pay for this separately."

"I'm sorry, sir," the clerk said. "You have to use your Sea Pass for all purchases on the ship. We don't have the option for any other forms of payment."

This would never do. He couldn't charge condoms to the suite. His uncle would be the one reviewing all the room expenses before paying them.

"Hello, Devon. Imagine meeting you here." Bradshaw's voice was the last thing he needed to hear. "Can I help you with something?"

Devon turned to block his purchase and groaned to himself. Then Mr. Hamada entered the store and picked up a magazine. "I'm calling in my favor, Dr. Bradshaw," he said between gritted teeth. "I need you to charge my purchase to your room—no questions asked." He could see the questions immediately form in the man's eyes.

"Just charge it," Bradshaw told the clerk. Then he turned to Devon. "What are you two up to?"

By now, Akira's father had noticed them and was heading over. Bradshaw glanced at the counter and saw the condoms. He chuckled and gave Devon a slap on the back. "It's good to see young people being responsible." Then he saw Akira's father and gave Devon a warning look.

"What are you doing here? I thought Akira was with you." Her father looked extremely concerned.

"I'm meeting her at my suite. We're going to relax on the balcony before calling it a night."

Mr. Hamada's brow furrowed. "Your suite? What's wrong with ours?"

"Nothing, sir. It's just more convenient."

"For what?"

Devon had no answer. He noticed that Bradshaw was now holding a bottle of iced tea and the condoms in his hands and was anxious to get out of there.

"Just try not to keep her out too late."

Devon nodded. "Yes, sir." He bought a pack of gum to make it look as though he had a purpose for being there. To his relief, Mr. Hamada remained in the store, looking at items on the shelves.

When Devon arrived in the passageway, Bradshaw pulled the package out of his bag. "Let's take a look at what I purchased." He began perusing the label in open sight of anyone who might have been watching.

Devon was getting impatient. He held out his hand. "Please give those to me."

"Glittery-gold and silky smooth." Bradshaw couldn't suppress his laughter. "You really are filled with surprises, young man. Let me see." He turned the package over. "They glow in the dark?"

"Give them to me!" Devon grabbed the condoms from Bradshaw's hands. He stared at the package and groaned. Bradshaw hadn't been joking. "The clerk said this was all they had. I hope it isn't real glitter."

The doctor exploded with laughter. He took the package back and checked it again. "Appears to be just a design."

Devon sighed. "Not a word of this to anyone, Dr. Bradshaw. That's part of our deal." He tried to glare at him but ended up laughing himself. The whole situation was ludicrous, to say the least.

"OK. Not a word from me." Bradshaw made a motion of zipping his mouth.

Devon stared at him for a second and then extended his hand. "Thank you. They don't accept cash, and I don't think my uncle is interested in contributing to my sex life."

Bradshaw seemed genuinely surprised that Devon had confided in him. He even admitted that he was flattered by his trust. "Anytime, son. If it makes you feel any better, I think your uncle is coming around. He seems a lot more comfortable with Akira and the idea of the two of you together."

"We've definitely made some progress, but her father is another story altogether. I don't think he'll ever accept me." He offered a weak smile. "Well, good night, sir. I don't want to leave Akira waiting any longer, and I'm sure you have other plans."

"Actually, I'm meeting everyone in the casino, so that should allow you some extra time on your own. Personally, I haven't had much luck with the ladies. The only one I thought I had a chance with left me waiting at a hotel." He smiled and walked away, leaving Devon slightly surprised.

I guess you really don't know anyone. Devon put the package of condoms in his jacket pocket and walked quickly toward the elevator. Kindness was the last thing he'd ever attribute to Bradshaw.

21

OBSERVATION

The watcher stood at the end of the fifth-level passageway, waiting for Akira Hamada to reappear. She had been inside room 501 for more than fifteen minutes waiting for Devon Lyons, an innocent victim in the scheme of things.

Aside from her beauty and poise, there was nothing unusual about this vexing creature, which made the mystery of her all the more intriguing. Through observation, the watcher had become aware of the fact that she possessed a magnetic personality, attracting the attention of everyone around her. However, she offered very little about herself by way of conversation and idle chitchat. Instead, what she did best was make everyone feel empowered or validated by their beliefs—a marvelous tactic when one came to think about it.

Remarkably, this mysterious woman had developed two personas: a sweet, jovial exterior concealing a dark, evil soul. The adjoining door between an empty room and the suite she occupied with her father had been left slightly ajar by the housekeeper, making it possible to overhear her surprising reveal. As it turned out, she was a well-trained paid assassin who had been sent there on assignment. But she was currently in a holding pattern, determining her correct target. The deception she was engaged in would have been applauded, even encouraged, if not for the fact that Devon Lyons would be written off as collateral damage. In the watcher's mind, corrupt, shameful beings deserved what they got, but innocent bystanders were a rare commodity, needing to be protected at all costs.

A noise traveled from the opposite end of the hall, indicating someone was rapidly approaching. For the watcher, it would be easy to vanish and remain undetected, but there was something vaguely familiar about this man. His white slacks, gray shoes, and navy-blue jacket said very little about him, but the distinct scent of Old Spice traveled with him, lifting fine hairs on the watcher's neck. His dark hair was long in the back and combed over the top in the same unflattering fashion.

He glanced over his shoulder and cocked an eyebrow. "That's one angry woman," he said. The corners of his mouth twitched in a suppressed grin.

"Who are you referring to?" The watcher had thought that after the years of dealing with self-serving imbeciles, all the squeamishness from looking into their faces had passed. But tonight, that wasn't the case.

"The woman in line before me. She's been making ridiculous claims, insulting passengers, and basically pissing everyone off."

"I don't handle customer service," the watcher said, "but if you give me a description of this woman, I might be of some assistance."

"Auburn hair, thin red lips, round face, brain-dead eyes. I estimate her to be in her late sixties."

"Hmm...not sure about that one." Privately, the watcher suspected it was Sara Lyons, causing problems as usual. But there was no point in confirming the suspicion. "Of course, one must feel sorry for the dissatisfaction she's experienced, even though she—"

"I don't," the man interrupted. "She nearly ruined my supper last night insisting that I give up my seat, since she was certain she was of a higher caste than I."

The watcher was slightly amused. "So did you?"

"Do what?"

"Forfeit your seat?"

"I did *not*," the man said indignantly. "I'm not living in Europe, nor are we anywhere near that woman's country. So why should I bow to English customs? And then this morning, she cut in front of me as we waited outside. Her husband had to make excuses to everyone before dragging her off to their room." The man blew out a sigh and smiled. "I confess that I'm relieved that there are only three more days to deal with her as a fellow passenger."

"Ah," the watcher said, using a noncommittal voice. The grin, the angle of the man's jaw—it suddenly became clear why he looked so familiar. He was a doctor at the Hartwood Hospital— an antiquated asylum built in a location specifically chosen for its isolation. It was opened in 1895 and quickly gained a reputation as a cutting-edge treatment facility for mental illness, where patients underwent therapies like electric shock treatment and lobotomies. As with many other hospitals in the area, it closed in the 1990s, after a new health-care law was enacted. However, the last two wards, where the watcher had resided for over ten years, remained open until 2010, when the building was declared uninhabitable.

"You're Dr. Emil Sacco from Malta," the watcher said.

The man acknowledged this. "How did you know? Have we met?"

"Yes. A number of years ago. We exchanged points of view at a treatment facility in Scotland."

Sacco's brow furrowed. "Scotland, you say. The old sanitarium?"

The watcher nodded, amazed at how easy it was to forget the neglect he had allowed and the physical abuse he had inflicted on half the patients living there. After receiving a substantial bribe, he took it upon himself to label the watcher an unsalvageable mental case—incapable of functioning in the outside world.

"I'm sorry; I don't recall meeting you," Sacco said.

How very convenient, the watcher thought. "So might I ask the reason for taking this trip?"

"My grandmother passed," he said, eyes that had previously been amused now sober. "I never knew her, and no one can tell me much about her. I was invited to join this medical cruise conference and was hoping to learn more about her from Dr. Bradshaw."

Dr. Bradshaw. The name made the watcher's skin crawl. This man was the greatest villain of all. "Was she one of his patients?" the watcher asked.

"Yes, in fact, she was. But I'm finding it difficult to speak to him. I left several messages to no avail. I suppose he prefers not discussing private matters while on vacation. And I can't say that I blame him. But it would be nice to hear what he has to say."

"Well, I wish you good luck in your pursuit, Dr. Sacco." The watcher made a small bow, feigning politeness.

Sacco smiled in return and bowed respectfully. "I thank you," he said. "Perhaps we can sit down before the end of our journey and revisit our discussion."

The watcher's lips played with a smile. "I'm sure you'd find it rather amusing. If you'd like to share your room number, I can leave you a message regarding the best time to meet."

Sacco nodded. "I'm staying in room 307. I'll be tied up in the morning, but I'm sure I can find an opening before lunch."

"The ship will be at sea all day tomorrow," the watcher said. "There are lots of activities aboard: rock climbing, cooking classes, bingo. And of course, there's the white night party on Friday. Do you have anything special planned, sir?"

"No, I'll be staying in my room, ordering in. I've had my fill of this ship and the people on it."

"Hmm...sorry to hear that. I suppose cruising isn't for everyone."

"Yeah, well, I only came because I was invited. Normally I avoid confined spaces and overpriced tours." Sacco wiped his nose with the back of his hand and sniffed, reminding the watcher about his coke habit. Several of the patients at Hartwood had witnessed him injecting the drug into his arm and occasionally sniffing it. "By the way, did you hear about the accidents on this ship? Personally, I have an abiding wish to die old in my bed. Preferably after a long and boring life selling pharmaceuticals."

You don't say? "Is that what you do for a living? I was under the impression that you were a practicing physician."

"I was at one time. But I find it less stressful to visit them rather than be one."

The watcher allowed a small smile to form and said in the kindest voice possible, "I'm sure you're very good at your job, Dr. Sacco. I'll be looking forward to hearing more about it during our talk tomorrow."

The watcher moved aside, allowing the arrogant man to pass.

"If Dr. Bradshaw shows up," he said, "let him know that I'm looking for him."

"Why, yes, of course."

Sacco brushed the watcher's coat as he passed, awakening a buried emotion.

"I'm sure he'll be dying to see you," the watcher murmured to the man's back. But there was no sign that Sacco had heard. And even if he had, the meaning of the words would be lost on him.

It was time to move on to more interesting scenery and to leave a farewell gift for this abominable blowhard.

22

AT LAST

When Devon arrived at his suite, Akira was there, patiently waiting to greet him. She had traded her low-cut dress for a short black skirt and semisheer blue top with matching lace trim. Her feet were bare, and her long black hair fell over one shoulder, reaching clear to her waist. She held a frozen chocolate mint popsicle in one hand and moved it in and out of her mouth in a provocative fashion.

Such a tease.

"Mm…tastes good," she said. "Want some?" He smiled and shook his head, watching her devour the icy treat. A tiny drip traveled down her chin, and he used his thumb to catch it before licking it away.

She smiled. "Did you finish your errand?"

"Yep." There was no point in elaborating. After loosening his tie, he removed it and draped it over a chair.

She held out her sticky hands. "Do you mind if I freshen up?"

"Go for it." She walked into the bathroom and rinsed her hands in the sink. While he waited for her, Devon slipped off his shoes and socks and set them inside his bedroom, mindful of Sara's obsession with neatness.

Akira returned and smiled at him. "Let's go out on the balcony. It's so beautiful tonight. We can relax better out there." She took his hand in hers and led him outside. "Why don't I help you get more comfortable?" She pushed his jacket from his shoulders. He finished removing it and tossed it over one of the lounge chairs. Then he turned back to her. She grinned in delight at the hiss she elicited from him as her fingers slipped under his shirt and played with the waistband on his pants. While he remained still, watching her, Akira frantically unbuttoned his shirt and pushed the fabric as far down his shoulders as their positions would allow. She smoothed her hands across his broad chest, and a fresh curl appeared on her lips. Her fleet fingers quickly unfastened his pants and began tugging the front apart so that she could slide her hands inside his boxers and against his skin. His flesh was fever-hot, and when his body jumped in reaction to her caress, her fingers grazed the top of his hard length. She closed her hand around it and ran her thumb back and forth across the sensitive tip.

Devon moaned against her breast, his hands clutching her waist and backside. He stood up straight, taking his hands off her just long enough to shrug out of his shirt and pull his undershirt over his head. Before the fabric hit the floor, he pulled her back into his arms and yanked the hem of her blouse out of the top of her skirt. As she ran her hands over his biceps, he reached behind her to unhook her bra and then unfastened the clasp holding her skirt around her waist. She melted against him and followed his earlier example, trailing teasing kisses across his shoulders, up his neck and ears and down his jawline.

When his mouth found hers, she kissed him greedily. Her hands slid down his back to push his pants down his muscular legs. She dug her fingernails into his backside, smiling against his mouth as she elicited another hiss of pleasure from him.

Devon grabbed the skirt he'd already loosened at her waist and tugged hard, letting it fall toward the floor on the balcony. While running one hand up her back into the mass of silky soft hair, his other hand discovered there was nothing to block his exploring hands. A smile curled his lips. *No underwear?* He cupped her hip and pulled her tight against him. "Seems you forgot something." His hard cock pressed against her thigh, demanding her attention.

She nipped at the skin on his shoulder. "I want you out of those pants," she whispered in his ear.

He stepped back from her long enough to remove his slacks and secure from his pocket the condom that Bradshaw had purchased. His cock was throbbing, and his heart was racing with the anticipation of being inside of her.

She looked down at the source of his pride, and her eyes widened. "Is all that for me?"

"Every inch." The right corner of his mouth lifted. It felt great to be admired—even if it was only for the size of his dick.

She noticed the sparkling packet in his hand and grinned. "Is that gift wrap? I had no idea we were celebrating the Fourth of July."

He had no interest in explaining how he'd acquired the glittery condoms, only in making good use of them. "I hope you don't mind. I didn't come prepared, and it was all they had in the store."

Her smile was becoming a permanent feature. "Gold has always been my favorite color."

Devon almost laughed. Talk about surprises. Apparently this girl had a kinky side to her.

Akira took the package from his hand. "You know, maybe we'll try them one day."

Devon's mouth slacked. "One day? Do you mean that we're not going to—" He hated saying the word *fuck,* but inside his brain he was screaming it.

"I'm on the pill," she said. "For medical reasons. I didn't want you to think I was expecting to need it."

Devon pulled her close. "Honey, it's all right. You don't have to explain anything to me."

"I know. But I should have told you sooner. There just didn't seem to be the right time or place."

"Well, it's not exactly dinner conversation, is it? Especially with my uncle and aunt always around."

She flashed a quick smile. "Now where were we?" She positioned him in front of the lounge chair and gave him a gentle push. He fell back into the chair, and she climbed onto it, slowly straddling his lap. She placed her hands on his shoulders, leaving her face an inch from his. "So I assume your weapon comes fully loaded?" Her warm breath—an aroma of mint, chocolate, and that uniqueness that was Akira—washed over his nose, causing him to twitch. Akira looked down between her legs and smiled.

"Let's just say it's been building up for a while."

"Hmm...how 'bout we do something about that?" Akira reached down and played with his balls with her left hand while stimulating herself with her right. Devon let out a soft moan. She grabbed the base of his shaft firmly and wrapped the fingers of her other hand around the top. Then she began pumping his shaft slowly. He closed his eyes and bit his lips, trying to hold back. She kept her bottom hand on the base, just a little firmer each time she pumped, adding speed and tension until he was about to explode.

He reached for her hand to stop her. "You're killing me, baby. I won't last if you do that."

"Don't you want me to make you happy?"

"Not that way." He held her hips, guiding her onto him. "I want this." By the feel of her wetness, she was more than ready. After a few seconds of adjusting to each other, Akira began to raise and lower herself on him. The fullness inside of her coupled with the friction caused by her movements left her whimpering and his heart pounding. To his amazement, the sweet, charming girl he had come to know had hidden talents, the likes of which no one else would ever know. Not if he could help it.

She tipped her head back and closed her eyes, riding him like a rodeo pro. "Ah, nice...so nice..." she cooed. He met her movements, proud of how much he could please her. She pressed her breasts against his chest and clutched his shoulders with both hands while rocking her hips back and forth in a steady rhythm.

His voice sounded husky in his own ears. "My God, you're amazing. Why didn't we do this sooner?" His fingers dug into her hips, and she bit her bottom lip, suppressing a moan.

"Oh yeah...that's it. That's it." She quickened her pace and began to raise herself higher and push down harder. The increased pressure against her clitoris made her whimper each time she pressed into him. Devon groaned as her body gripped his cock with each thrust. He kept one hand around her waist to steady her, raising the other to cup what he was sure was the most beautiful face he'd ever seen. She turned her cheek into his caress as she closed her eyes again. A soft smile touched her mouth as she pushed her hips forward, leaving his body quivering with the sensations she invoked.

A low raspy groan escaped his lips. He wanted to hold on, make this last forever. "Look at me," he whispered. She lowered her chin and raised her lashes, gazing at him with dark, dewy eyes. She pushed a wayward shock of hair back from his face before leaning forward to kiss him on the forehead.

"You're incredible," she murmured. "As good as you look."

He grazed his fingertips over her cheekbone before sliding them across her lips and down the curve of her neck. They traveled across the expanse of her breasts as she quickened her pace, testing his endurance.

"I don't want you to forget this," she said. Then more softly, "Or me."

Devon groaned again as her body gripped his cock even tighter and pumped it with every movement. He had both hands on her waist now, thrusting into her with determined purpose.

"Yesss…" she hissed. Her soft moaning told him that she was approaching the edge, and he was nearly there himself. He had to bite his tongue to hold on longer.

"So close…so close…"

He thrust faster and harder, and her soft moans matched the rhythm of his strides. She threw her head back and cried out as her spasms took hold, sucking the semen from his cock and jolting his body with spontaneous impulses over and over again. The intensity was unlike anything he had experienced before.

Akira collapsed against him. He was still inside of her and wanted to stay there forever.

"Baby." He ran his fingers through her hair, still breathing heavily. "We have something special between us. Physical and otherwise."

"I know. I've known it all along." She kissed the top of his chest and looked up to meet his eyes. "I've never been this happy—not ever."

"Me either." He stroked her back, cherishing everything about her—every moment they'd shared together. He was about to bend down and kiss her when he heard a sound coming from inside the suite. The front door had been opened, and to their mutual horror, footsteps soon followed.

"I'm going to sleep like a log," Sara said. "Darling, close the curtains before you come to bed."

Devon watched Akira's eyes widen as Paul stepped up to the patio window and stayed there a few seconds before drawing the blinds shut.

"It's taken care of," his voice answered. "I'm going to grab a bottle of water and be right up."

Akira's body tensed, automatically flinching away from Devon. Acting on instinct, he grasped her hips firmly to keep her in place. She looked at him in shock. He raised a hand to pull her head down so that he could whisper softly in her ear. "They don't know where we are, but if you make any noise, we'll be caught for sure. We just have to stay here for a while."

She released a small sigh of frustration. But after a brief moment, she nodded her agreement. She pulled back just enough to meet his gaze, her lips pinched together in concern. His questioning expression brought her close to his ear. "I think he locked the door. How are we going to get back inside?"

Devon smiled. "I guess we'll be sleeping out here tonight." He nibbled her earlobe, and she dug her fingernails into his shoulder, trying to push him away.

"What if my father comes looking for me? Did you even think of that?"

He shrugged a shoulder, enjoying the frustrated look on her face. "You're my girlfriend, and we're over twenty-one. That makes us both legal in my book." Devon smiled. "As far as I know, we're not doing anything half the people on this ship haven't done before—and are probably doing right now." He stared at her luscious lips and felt himself getting hard again. How was that even possible?

"You're making me crazy," Akira murmured. "I don't know why you think that...oh!" His thumb was strumming her nipple, and his mouth was back on her neck, tasting her skin. She dug her fingertips into his shoulders. "What are you doing, Devon? You have to stop this..."

He looked into her face, smiling with satisfaction at her passion-drugged expression. "Can you feel it? Inside of you?" Devon half whispered. "I can't help it, you know. You have this effect on me." He tugged a lock of her hair, bringing her face close to him once again. "I can be quiet if you can," he challenged her. When her eyes widened in surprise, he quirked an eyebrow at her in the way that seemed to amuse her. She bit her lip and tilted her head to one side, studying his face. He grinned at her, silently daring her.

"All right. Two can play this game," she said. Akira shifted her weight in his lap and began rocking back and forth again. She pressed against the full length of him inside of her and used her pelvic muscles to clamp down and squeeze tight. He closed his eyes and gasped for breath. She pressed her finger against his open lips and continued her tantalizing assault. When he opened his eyes to look at her, she placed her forefinger against her own mouth and shook her head slowly. In answer, he gripped both of her hips firmly, holding her in place. He shifted his hips and drove himself deep inside her, causing her to let out a silent gasp. Then while keeping one hand on her lower back, he flipped her over on the cushion in one quick motion. He ground his hips into her, causing her to whimper. Then he adjusted his thrusts, varying from slow to erratically rapid.

By the dazed look in her eyes, Akira was lost in pure ecstasy. She lifted her hips to meet him, urging him to keep going. "Deeper, Devon," she murmured. "Go deeper."

"OK, baby. If that's what you want." He put one of her legs over his shoulder and got on his knees. Putting one hand under her butt, he pulled her closer and drove himself into her core, reaching the upper wall inside of her. A loud moan escaped her lips. He continued thrusting, hitting the G-spot every time. She was gasping for air and clinging to him for dear life.

"Oh yes...yes. That's it...that's it..." Her voice trailed off, but she was still fully engaged. He drank in the sight of her body wrapped securely around him. He would make this a night to remember—for both of them. Instead of going faster, he slowed down a bit and thrust a bit harder, staying deep for an extra second or so. Then he pulled all the way back until the tip of his member was barely in. He would let her desire for speed create a crescendo effect, so when he thrust faster, she was absolutely focused on it. And just as he predicted, she began begging for more. He returned to a constant rhythm, amazing himself by his sheer willpower. As three minutes became five, it became increasingly difficult to stay quiet. Yet the rapturous look on her face and the feeling of her warm, slick body below him was more than enough reason to keep him from crying out.

Her fingers dug desperate grooves into his shoulders and back as she moved her hips to match his pace. Her body ground into him, and his passion spiraled upward until everything else disappeared. As if reading his thoughts, her eyes glossed over, and her lips slightly parted. Her body shivered before setting loose a series of cock-grabbing spasms.

Akira's climax was his undoing. He held her tight as he spilled himself into her. After a few seconds, she opened her eyes to gaze up at him, and Devon looked at her lovingly. "You win."

She pushed a stray lock of hair behind his ear and leaned forward to kiss his temple. "I know," she whispered before placing a soft kiss on his lips. "I always will."

His arms tightened around her. "I love you, baby." He leaned down and shared a long, lingering kiss. Then they rolled onto their sides. She nestled her head against his shoulder, and they stared up at the dark, cloud-covered sky. If there was a heaven in this world, by God, Devon had found it. He looked at her perfect profile, feeling a rekindled warmth in his heart he never imagined possible. Not since losing Selena.

After a long moment, he began to hear noises from inside the suite again. They'd been so caught up in their liaison that they had forgotten about the fact that they weren't really truly alone.

"Devon has a key," Sara called out. "Stop worrying about him. I'm going back to bed, and if you expect to join me, you'll be upstairs in the next three minutes. Is that clear?"

A few more seconds passed before the blinds were pulled back. The door opened slightly, and Devon grabbed his jacket from the neighboring chair. He threw it over both of them, barely covering his ass.

"It's going to get cold out there," Paul said. "It might be a good idea to call it a night."

Devon looked down at Akira, gnawing her lip. "Sounds good," he called back, thankful that Paul had the common sense to stay inside.

"I'll see you in the morning," Paul added. "And by the way, if you run into that beautiful young lady you've been keeping company with, can you please thank her for putting up with me today?"

Devon smiled. "I sure will."

"OK. Well, I'm off to bed then. Sleep well."

Akira met Devon's amused gaze and shook her head at their foolishness. His grin broadened before kissing her forehead. They listened as Paul's retreating footsteps plodded upstairs.

When his bedroom door was shut firmly, the only remaining sound on the balcony was soft music coming from a lower deck. Devon separated himself from Akira and dared to peek into the room to make sure they were truly alone. She sagged against him and gazed up at him in relief.

"Guess we have to be more careful next time," he said, referring to his uncle.

She covered her mouth, stifling a giggle. "I can't believe we got away with that."

"You think so, huh?"

"Yes. Don't you?"

"Not entirely. I left my tie on the living room chair. I'm sure my uncle noticed it." Devon gathered their clothes and handed off her belongings. "Do you regret this?"

She composed her features into a "deep thinking" expression before permitting a smile to brighten her face. "Not at all. And you?"

"Do you even have to ask?" He put on his boxers and watched her as she stepped into her skirt and pulled it up, hiding three small tattooed stars on her right hip—alluding to her playful spirit. She slipped her arms through the straps of her bra and secured it before putting on her blouse.

Akira tilted her head to one side, a smile playing across her features. "Why are you staring at me?"

"I just can't seem to get enough. Do you mind?"

"Not at all. But now it's back to normal for both of us. There's no reason for anyone to know what happened here tonight. Don't you agree?"

Devon puzzled over her words. He had no intention of sharing intimate details with anyone, although keeping a muzzle on Bradshaw could prove a challenge.

Akira reached for his hand. "Please understand, Devon. I'd like nothing more than to sleep with you tonight and wake up in your arms. But it's just not—"

His finger was on her lips. "Then stay with me, baby."

She held his hand. "I can't. Not if we want to be together again."

Devon studied her solemn face. *Was this about her father again? The angry asshole who hated his guts?*

"If you can behave yourself," she said, "I'll find a way to be with you."

Devon slid the door open. He looked into the living room, verifying the coast was clear before turning to her. "I guess I can keep my hands to myself. But it won't be easy."

Akira wrapped her arms around his neck and kissed his cheek. "It won't be easy for me either."

23

REASSURANCE

As he prepared himself for the day, Devon never stopped thinking about Akira. With only three days left before arriving in Florida and their homes thousands of miles apart, their romance was destined to fail unless one of them was willing to sacrifice everything. The thought weighed heavy on his mind, dampening the joy he felt at finding the love of his life.

"What's wrong?" Paul asked. He was seated in the living room, drinking a steaming cup of coffee, looking more serious than usual.

Devon rubbed his jaw. "What are you talking about?"

"You seem to be deep in thought, so something must be bothering you."

"No, it's nothing. Just thinking about my job and the work I have waiting."

Paul nodded. "If you say so. I didn't get a chance to tell Akira good night, but then I guess the two of you were anxious to be alone." The tone in his uncle's voice had an edge to it that Devon hoped he was imagining. "Did you enjoy your evening?"

"Yes, we had a great time." Devon kept his eyes on Paul, hoping to reveal nothing.

"You both must have been extremely tired."

Devon had no idea where Paul's questions were leading. "Yes, yes, we were." He felt like a mouse being toyed with by a clever cat.

"I thought as much. I found your tie on the chair in the living room this morning." Paul handed it to him.

Devon sighed. "Uh...I couldn't wait to get it off last night. You know how much I hate dressing up."

"Yes, I know. You must have felt the same way about your sock. I noticed it on the balcony when I stepped outside." He pointed to it on the lounge chair.

Devon swallowed a little. "I suppose I'm getting used to going barefoot."

Paul nodded thoughtfully. "Do you also prefer going without pants. Your belt was under the chair. Seems like a strange place to leave it."

Devon searched for an answer. "Accessories can be very constricting...a belt being one of them."

"I see." Paul took a sip from his cup and continued to stare at him. An endless minute passed without either one of them saying a word. Then Paul broke the silence. "Oh...and I think you dropped these." He held out a package of condoms.

Devon could feel his face warm. "Yes. Yes, I did." He took the package and slid it into the back pocket of his shorts. *Christ almighty...what is he hoping to accomplish?*

Akira chose that moment to use the extra key Devon had given her, perhaps hoping to surprise him. She joined them and was positively glowing. The sight of her made his uncle smile, despite the fact that Devon was watching. She gave Paul a quick hug and kissed Devon on the lips, adding a few degrees of heat to the room.

"I'm absolutely starving this morning," she said. "Let's go to breakfast. Do you want to join us, Mr. Lyons?"

"Sara went for a walk and should be back in a few minutes. She prefers dining in, and I'm sure the two of you would like some time alone."

"If you really don't mind…" Akira said.

"No, of course not. Run along and enjoy yourselves."

Devon nodded. "I'll catch up with you later, Uncle Paul."

On the way to the dining room, Akira carried the conversation. It was obvious that she was happy, and Devon's heart was light knowing he was responsible. At least he hoped so.

They got through the buffet line and found a table outside in a shady spot. Then Akira put her hand over his. "Is something wrong, Devon? You're not regretting last night, are you?"

Devon's heart almost stopped. "I want to spend every night with you. To feel your body next to me and wake up with you in my arms. How could I ever regret being with you, Akira? You're the best thing that's ever happened to me."

Akira smiled, and his heart skipped a beat. Then he became suddenly serious. "I don't want to embarrass you, but my uncle found my belt and the package of condoms on the balcony this morning."

For a moment, she looked concerned. "What did he say?"

"Not a whole lot, actually."

"Well, I'm sure he doesn't think we're sitting around holding hands all the time. Does he?"

Devon shook his head. "I think he'd like to believe that's all we're doing."

"He's seen us kissing and touching…being openly affectionate with each other." She squeezed his hand. "Last night was about expressing our feelings. Unless you believe it was a mistake."

"Are you kidding?" Devon wanted to pull her onto his lap and remind her how he felt. "I think his love life has gone to pot and he's jealous. He knows we're happy and he's not. Anyway, it doesn't matter. I just didn't want you to be caught off guard if he should say something."

Akira leaned forward to kiss him, and then she giggled. Devon started to grin. "May I ask what's amusing you now?"

She giggled more. "I'm sorry, but the thought of him finding those glittery-gold condoms is just too funny. He must really be wondering about you."

Devon had to laugh. His uncle viewed him as a conservative and very controlled person. He couldn't imagine what Paul thought of him now. "Well, when you put it that way, it is pretty funny." He leaned forward and kissed her.

Paul cleared his throat as he approached the table. "Seems Sara has another appointment with Bradshaw, and I'm on my own again. You don't mind if I interrupt your private time, do you?"

Akira smiled. "You're not interrupting, Mr. Lyons."

Paul seated himself and looked into her eyes. He asked her the same question he had asked Devon. "So you two had a nice night together?"

"Yes, it was the perfect night." She looked at Devon and placed her hand over his.

"What did the two of you end up doing all evening?" Paul's question surprised Devon. Paul usually reserved these pointed questions for him.

"We spent the evening enjoying each other's company. The way any grown couple would do." Her eyes were still locked with Devon's. "How did you end your evening, Mr. Lyons?"

"I spent some time in the casino again with Sara and her friends. But Sara was tired, and we came back to the room early.

I was surprised that Devon was alone on the deck and you had already gone to your room."

"We were tired too," Akira said. "That's why we didn't go out last night." Devon was awed by how composed she was while dealing with his uncle.

"So what do you two have planned for today?"

Akira squeezed Devon's hand. "We haven't discussed it yet, but I was thinking that it would be fun to go to the art auction this morning. What do you think, Devon? Are you game?"

"You know I'm willing to do whatever you want, honey. Are you planning to buy a piece of art?" Devon was thankful that she hadn't mentioned napkin folding or the flower-arranging class on the lido deck.

"No. I probably couldn't afford it. I'd just like to see how an auction works."

"Well, then I'm more than happy to go with you. Who knows? I might even find a gift for my sister."

Akira turned to Paul. "What about you, Mr. Lyons? Were you planning to go?"

"Nope. I'm laying low today. Ben and Vivian are joining me by the pool to read and relax. Then we're going upstairs to play in the bingo tournament. Sara and Bradshaw will probably be there too. As I'm sure you're aware, they both love winning money."

Akira smiled. "Do you want to join them, Devon?"

He bit off a frustrated huff. "No, baby, I don't."

She looked disappointed. "Why not? I think it would be fun."

Devon couldn't say no to her no matter how much he wanted to. "You're determined to torture me, aren't you?"

She angled her head. "You know, I'm very good at getting my own way."

"Yeah, so it seems." Devon shrugged a shoulder. "All right. I'll think about it."

Akira smiled. "Then I'll consider that a yes."

"Whoa, wait a minute. I'm not *that* easy." Devon gave Akira a stern look that sent her into peals of laughter.

Paul chuckled. "It appears that she has you whipped, son."

Devon's lips twisted into a wry smile. "I was hoping to keep that a secret."

The tension in the air vanished, and the rest of their meal was filled with lighthearted conversation. When they returned to the suite, Paul asked Devon to speak with him out on the balcony. He hesitated, expecting the worst, but then Akira gave him a reassuring look before heading off to her room.

Paul gestured at the lounge chair, but Devon elected to stand. "So what is it, Uncle Paul? I hope this isn't another lecture about the mistake I'm making."

He looked at Devon thoughtfully for a few seconds before answering. "Listen, son," he began, "I don't want to know what's going on between you and Akira. I realize that it's strictly between the two of you. But…" He hesitated. "There's really no easy way to say this."

"Say what?"

"That I noticed you didn't open the package of condoms yet. Before you do, I just want you to think about what's going to happen after this cruise ends. Akira is a very special young lady, and she obviously cares a great deal about you. But from what you've said, there's very little you know about her. I'd hate to think what would happen if things progressed and someone ended up getting hurt."

It dawned on Devon that Mr. Hamada was probably thinking the same thing. And yet Devon couldn't alter his course, not when it came to Akira. After losing Selena, he had valued the privacy of his soul far more than the intimacy of a sincere connection. He had put up a big front, playing the part of a disingenuous lover, distancing his feelings at all costs. In his mind, he had convinced himself that true intimacy would lead to his undoing. Yet here he was, defending the very thing that could destroy him.

"I already told you that I'm serious, Uncle Paul. This is not a fling. I can assure you that Akira and I will find a way to work things out."

Paul nodded. "I truly hope so. I can tell you from my own experience that it's easy to get carried away. You can want something so bad that all common sense vanishes."

Devon glanced out at the sea. He knew he still had a lot of problems, not the least of which was trusting another woman. And yet, the thought of losing Akira forever scared him more than he was willing to admit. During their talks, she had expressed interest in California and alluded to her strong desire to move there. But making that decision and sharing it with her father or anyone else remained in her hands, not Devon's. Unlike any romance he'd ever experienced, she held the reins and could cut him loose at any given moment.

"OK, then," Paul said. "It's going to be hard for me, but I'm going to back off for your sake."

"Thank you." Devon extended his hand. "I'll do whatever it takes to make her happy."

They shook hands, and Paul smiled. "I hope that includes you too."

Devon was anxious to end their conversation. He preferred his privacy when it came to personal matters and had been forced to reveal more than he cared to about himself with a number of people on this trip.

"So are we done here?" Devon asked.

Paul cleared his throat. "Just one more thing."

"Yes?" Devon braced himself.

"Glittery-gold? I really don't know you at all, do I?" Paul sounded incredulous.

Devon groaned. "No comment, Uncle Paul. Let's leave it at that."

"You got it."

Devon returned to his room feeling slightly less sure of himself. He pulled off his torn jeans and tank top and selected clothes he thought Akira would like better. After rolling up the sleeves on his blue striped shirt and tucking it into the top of his gray slacks, he looked at himself in the mirror. Tonight, when all was said and done, he needed to be sure of her feelings—to know, without a doubt, there was a future for them together. Not just words said in the heat of the moment or to anyone who happened to ask, but real, concrete plans they could implement and openly share. But dare he ask? If he came across too strong, he could send her running, and then where would he be?

Devon stepped into the living room and was surprised to see Akira back. It was remarkable how quickly she could change and look prettier with every reappearance. She was sitting on the sofa next to Paul dressed in a cute yellow dress with tiny black dots, and her hair was tied up in a ponytail, making her look half her age. When she saw Devon, her face lit up with a huge smile, and she stood up in her black strappy sandals.

"You look so nice," she said, "except for one tiny thing." She approached him and leaned up to brush some loose bangs away from his eyes. "Ah, now that's much better." Then she looked back at Paul. "Maybe we'll see you at the bingo tournament later today."

"I'd like that." He smiled at her and nodded to Devon. "Have fun at the art auction."

"We will," she said, linking her arm through Devon's. She led him out of the suite and partially down the corridor. Then she pushed him against the wall and kissed him.

When they parted lips, Devon grinned at her. "What was that for?"

"For whatever you said to your uncle. He seems to feel much better about our relationship. In fact, he even called us a couple."

"I think the condoms he found may have been a clue," Devon teased.

She smiled. "All kidding aside, angel, I think it's true. Maybe seeing them made him realize we're more than just friends."

"Especially with glittery-gold condoms."

"He didn't actually say anything about those, did he?"

"I'm afraid so."

"Oh my goodness. What did he say?"

"He commented on them and said he obviously doesn't know me at all."

"Or me. I thought they were very exciting."

Devon forced a smile. "Anyway, it's not important. He has his own issues to worry about."

Akira kissed him again. "I hope it's nothing too serious. Does it involve Sara and Dr. Bradshaw? They seem to spend a lot of time together…"

"To tell you the truth, honey, I'd rather not think about it."

They took the elevator to the observation level, and Devon glanced at his watch. "We're a little early for the auction. We could go inside and look around or take a stroll on one of the decks."

"It's such a lovely day," she said. "Let's go outside."

"Sure, whatever you'd like. I enjoy being with you, Akira. It doesn't matter what we're doing or where." He pulled her closer.

"Do you mean that? I mean...*really* mean that?" She looked expectantly at him.

"Yes, of course, I do." He gave her a mischievous grin. "Though some things are more fun than others."

"I have to agree with you there." She smiled seductively, and his body immediately responded. He was putty in her hands, and she seemed to know it.

They continued walking and talking. When they got to a quiet spot on the deck, they stood together at the railing, looking out over the water. Devon's mind was filled with dozens of questions prompted by his uncle's remarks. "What did your family think about you being a geisha?" He was curious about her past and wanted to know as much about her as possible.

She held onto the railing with both hands and stared into the distance. "My mother was very proud. I had a gift for languages and taught English to young women inside the house where I lived. When the seasons changed, I wore different kimonos: some of them had pink flowers, others had white cranes and copper leaves. They were so soft and beautiful." She closed her eyes, as if being transported to another place. "There were parties and formal affairs that I would be invited to by celebrities and businessmen. I was often asked to dance and play instruments—charm and entertain everyone there." Her eyes slowly opened, and her voice lowered. "But I no longer live in that world. I look after my father in this one."

"He wasn't concerned about your love life back then?"

She paused, as if collecting her thoughts. "No. He wasn't involved in my upbringing or with any of the people in my life. We've only recently become reacquainted, which is why we're on this trip together." She turned toward Devon. "Now it's my turn to ask. Why do you think your uncle is so interested in me?"

"Is he? What exactly did he say?"

Her gaze lowered. "He likes to ask questions. Lots of them. And some that are impossible to answer. Is that why we're having this conversation, Devon? To make you feel better about me?"

Devon lifted her chin with his fingertips, bringing her eyes to his. He spoke in a hushed tone to match her soft voice. "The only thing that matters right now is how much I care about you."

"What about before we met? Did you find any level of happiness in being alone?"

Devon thought about that for a while. "I had more or less reconciled myself to being alone. I never expected to meet anyone special, so I made a life for myself. I filled my days and nights with research books and long ocean trips. I worked hard and played hard and never looked back. At least I tried. But after meeting you, I don't want to be alone anymore. I want to be with you, Akira."

"And I want to be with you." Her eyes locked with his, and once again, Devon felt as though they had reached a new point in their relationship. The way she was looking at him assured him that she felt the same way. And although they had not been able to formulate the words to express how they were feeling, these few simple words seemed to say so much.

"Really? Do you mean it?"

She lowered her eyes and said nothing, as if debating what to say. "So what is going to happen to us?" she finally asked.

Devon moved closer and wrapped his arms around her waist. Akira's eyes lifted. She kept her gaze firmly locked on his, waiting for an answer.

He brought his lips close to her mouth. "That's simple, honey. I want to be with you, and you want to be with me. I think that means you and I are going to find a way to be together. Agreed?"

She took the initiative, kissing him long and hard.

When they separated, he stepped back and asked, "Is that a yes?"

She smiled but gave him no answer.

"So what do you say? Are we going to find a way to make this work?" He stared into her eyes, hoping for the right word.

It seemed like an eternity before she answered. "Yes."

Devon's heart beat faster. Deep down he knew they were meant to be together. He just didn't realize how much he needed to hear it said aloud—until now.

24

PICTURE PERFECT

Devon and Akira walked slowly hand in hand to the art auction and kept looking at each other, smiling. He was ecstatic over her promise to make their relationship work and couldn't think about anything else. They traveled down a long corridor, and Devon squeezed her hand.

"We need to discuss plans for moving you to California." They had done little more than brush over the subject, but he was already thinking about how much he was going to miss her until she got there.

"I'm still trying to figure out how to coordinate everything. I mean…it's a huge step for both of us. What if you decide it's not right? We haven't known each other very long, and I'd hate to think that—"

Devon stopped walking and took both of her hands in his. "It will work if we want it to. When I said we were going to be together, I meant it, Akira. I'm looking forward to spending every possible moment with you."

She smiled and raised her face to kiss him. "I just know you have a busy life. Being with me might be very difficult."

"Baby, I spend a lot of time on the *Stargazer* because I don't have anything to come home to. You might have to remind me that I need to get some work done once in a while." He looked into her eyes and wanted to say more but wasn't sure how. "Is your dad planning to come with you?"

Akira hesitated. "We haven't had time to discuss it."

"Well, you might let him know that I have a two-bedroom apartment located above a library. It's completely furnished and unoccupied, so you could both stay there as long as you like."

"Over a library?" She smiled. "That would be very convenient, since I love to read." She paused. "Maybe I could rent it from you until we find a place to live."

"It's yours if you want it, Akira. I think you'll like it, but you can decide after you've spent some time there with your father." He wanted to be with only her. But if her father was part of the package, he'd have to find a way to make it work.

She put her arms around his neck and kissed him again. "I'm going to have you over for a special dinner real soon." She blushed slightly. "And other things, of course."

Devon smiled. "I don't know how your father would feel about that."

Several passengers stepped around them in a hurry to see the auction.

Akira took Devon's hand. "It's fun to dream about these things, but we really need to get going." She led him into the observation level, where stacks of art waited. They walked inside the room, where chairs sat in a collective group and easels were covered with surrealistic paintings depicting Grimm fairy tales. A waiter offered them glasses of champagne, and Devon took a glass for each of them.

"Do you think you can drink this now and still have a glass of wine later?" He gave her a mischievous grin as he said it. "You may have to spend the night with me if you get too dizzy to find your room."

Akira smiled. "I may have to spend the night with you whether or not I have anything to drink."

The way she looked at him and how she said it made his body respond more than he deemed appropriate. He whispered in her ear, "Did I tell you already that you have the ability to move me in the right place at the wrong time?"

"Mr. Lyons!"

Devon groaned. This couldn't be happening. What was Bradshaw doing here?

"Sara, Vivian, and Dr. Hoffman are all here," Akira said. "This should be fun." She grabbed his hand and pulled him toward them. "Oh, it looks like your uncle decided to come too. How nice is that?"

Devon silently groaned. This was not what he had in mind.

"Thank you for inviting us," Vivian said. "We were planning to relax outside, but this sounded much better. Right, Ben?"

"Huh? Oh yeah."

They all positioned themselves on comfy swivel chairs, making it possible to view each piece while sharing their points of view.

Devon turned in his seat, facing his uncle. "What are you doing here? I thought you had other plans."

"Sara wants to buy a print of Alice in Wonderland's Tea Party that she saw on display, and she insisted I come along. She said the Mad Hatter looks like me." Paul twisted his lips.

Devon thought he might be ill. "Really? How sweet."

The auctioneer called everyone to attention. He explained how the bidding would work. Then the first piece was presented, and the bidding began.

Devon whispered to Akira. "Why do you think Bradshaw's here? Is there a rare piece of art he's planning to buy?"

Akira smiled. "Last night I heard him say that there's a series of animation cels from Cinderella he wants. They feature the three stepsisters from the movie."

"Are you kidding? Is that why we're here? To watch him buy Disney art?"

She released a quick laugh, and the auction proceeded. They all seemed to enjoy it even though they weren't bidding. Then the Cinderella cels finally came up, and Bradshaw sprang into action. There was another man interested in the same cels, but he dropped out rather quickly when Sara's scowl caught his eye. Bradshaw ended up getting the pieces he wanted and announced that he got a good deal.

The auction continued, and eventually several prints and paintings of Sleeping Beauty were featured. Devon noticed Akira tensing beside him and took her reaction as interest in the collection.

"That's such a beautiful scene." She sighed as the painting of Prince Charming leaning down to kiss his sleeping princess was placed on an easel.

When there were only two people left bidding for it, Devon put in a bid that was substantially higher than the others. Akira gasped. His bid was the winning offer, and the painting was sold.

She put her hand over his. "I hope you didn't buy that for me, Devon. It was too expensive."

He smiled. "I bought it for the apartment. It needs some art on the walls."

Sara turned to Paul. "I told you so."

"It's for a furnished apartment I own," Devon told her.

Sara puffed. "What man in his right mind would buy a Sleeping Beauty painting?"

Akira took Devon's hand. "A man who wants to be kissed." She leaned forward to kiss Devon on the cheek, leaving Sara scowling once more.

Four uniformed officers arrived in the room, surprising everyone. One of the men stepped forward to make an announcement. "Is Dr. Bradshaw here?"

Peter glanced at Sara before lifting his hand. "That's me."

The officer continued, "The gentleman who was planning to meet you this evening was found in his room...indisposed. Would you mind coming with us?"

Bradshaw abruptly stood. "Not without an explanation. Who is this about, and exactly why am I being singled out?"

The four officers exchanged looks and whispered among themselves. Then the same officer spoke. "I'm not sure this is the right place to discuss this matter. Perhaps it would be best if we spoke privately?"

"There's nothing you could say that would embarrass me," Bradshaw bellowed. "Now tell me what this is about before I involve the captain."

"All right. If you insist," the officer said. "One of the maids discovered a colleague of yours on the floor of his room with his face covered in a white powdery substance. The ceramic bear he purchased in the Cays was used to carry this aboard, and unfortunately it wasn't detected before Dr. Sacco overindulged himself."

Devon was at a loss. "Are you saying he overdosed on coke?"

The officer hesitated before nodding. "I'm sorry, Dr. Bradshaw, but your name was in his belongings, and we have a record of him trying to reach you. If you could come along and answer a few questions, we would greatly appreciate it."

Bradshaw huffed. "Perhaps it would be best if I called my lawyer."

Sara stood, appearing more indignant than usual. "What is going on here? This man has been with me all day. He doesn't deserve to be treated this way. Do you even have any idea who you're dealing with?"

The officer raised his hand in front of himself. "We simply need the doctor's assistance in identifying this man. He obviously took his own life, so there's no reason for you to get upset, ma'am."

A second officer stepped forward. "Please. After you, Doctor."

Bradshaw glanced at everyone in their group before assuming the lead. He disappeared from the room with the officers following. Within seconds, the room was buzzing with gossip and being fed with Sara's explosive remarks. All the while, Paul sat quietly watching—showing no concern over the strange turn of events.

The auctioneer approached Devon and asked him to sign for his purchase. They moved to his desk and made arrangements to have the painting shipped after arriving in Florida. When Devon returned to where Akira was seated, Sara was gone, along with Vivian and Dr. Hoffman. Only Paul remained at her side.

"So what do you make of all that?" Devon asked him.

Paul chose not to answer. Instead, he extended an invitation. "I think there's something I need to share with both of you. While Sara is out of the room, would you mind joining me downstairs?"

25

THE REVEAL

Akira leaned forward on the sofa, puzzling over the significance of each item spread across the table. She fingered through piles of hair clips, fountain pens, cuff links, buttons, pipes, watches, coins, and necklaces. There were at least fifty odds and ends of every shape, color, and size. There seemed to be no rhyme or reason for any of it. Then her eyes latched on to a large black enamel brooch engraved with a gold dragon—a one-of-a-kind piece that didn't belong here. She picked it up and studied it carefully. Then she flipped it over and blew out a closely held breath.

"Where did you get these?" she asked Paul.

"They belong to Sara. She calls them her tokens—whatever the hell that means."

"Tokens? She actually used the word *tokens*?"

"Yes, and she'd freak out if she knew we were touching them."

Akira eased back in her seat. "Who else knows about these?"

"Oh, I'm sure Peter does. I overheard them plotting last night. Sitting right there with their heads together, talking about their next vacation. They're planning to go to Japan, you know—the second week of March. Can you imagine all the havoc they'll cause there?"

Akira shook her head. "No, I...I can't."

"He's been hypnotizing her for years, supposedly to cure her migraines. But they never seem to go away. I've tried to separate them by threatening to leave her a dozen times, but she keeps bringing him back into our lives."

Devon chose that moment to return. He walked into the room with a bottle of champagne, two glasses in his hand, and a frown on his face. "I see you're back at it again, Uncle Paul. Blaming your wife for killing people. I thought we agreed that she was incapable of hurting anyone."

Akira stared at Devon in disbelief. "Again?"

Paul waved his hand above the table. "Then how do you explain all of this?"

Devon glanced at Akira and the items spread out before her. "So she collects weird stuff." He shrugged. "What's wrong with that?"

"It's not the fact that she has them or how strange they are," Paul said, dropping into a chair. "It's how she acquired them."

"Which is?"

Akira looked up at Devon. "By killing people."

Devon laughed. "You guys are being ridiculous. Sara isn't a murderer."

Akira picked up the dragon brooch. "Then how did she get this? It belonged to the Japanese woman who died in Mexico. The one I told you about." She flipped it over and held it before him. "Her name is engraved on the back—plain as day. And now it's here."

Devon was silent for a moment, then he lowered himself onto the sofa. He set the champagne bottle and glasses down on the floor, his eyes never leaving the table. Then he turned to Akira, searching her eyes for the truth. "Are you sure? Really sure? I mean, is there any possibility that it was given to her?"

Akira shook her head. "No, there's isn't. Keiko Mitsui would never give her brooch away. Especially to someone she'd been fighting with."

Devon's face paled. "Holy shit. She really killed all these people? But how is that even possible?" He turned to his uncle. "Do you think Bradshaw was involved? Could they be planning to kill someone else?"

"I wouldn't know," Paul answered." I heard them discussing their next trip, and that was bad enough."

"Next trip?" Devon shook his head. "Your wife and her crackpot doctor are murdering people, and you're upset about them planning a vacation without you? God! Tell me we're not related."

Akira's hand was on his arm. "Devon, calm down. There's nothing to be gained by attacking your uncle. He's the one who brought this to our attention."

Devon jerked his arm away and jumped to his feet. He started pacing back and forth in the room. "What are you going to do? You have to tell someone." He stopped abruptly in front of his uncle. "They need to be arrested right away. Before they do it again."

The door opened, and Sara walked in smiling, with a shopping bag in her hand. "Do what again, dear?" Her eyes landed on the eclectic collection spread out before them. Her jaw slacked in disbelief. "Oh my goodness!" She dropped what she was carrying, rushed to the table, and began wringing her hands. "What have you done?" she asked no one in particular.

Devon huffed. "*We've* done? What the fuck have you been doing?"

Sara gasped and looked hard at Paul. "How can you let him talk to me like that?"

Paul folded his arms across his chest and stared at Sara, not saying a word.

Akira turned to Devon. "What do you want to do?"

"If we call security, they'll haul her away. Won't they?"

Sara was crying so hard she couldn't speak. She was actually blubbering. The only words she got out were, "What gave you the right…to touch my things?"

While everyone watched, she picked up the jar and began putting everything back inside. Akira put her hand on Sara's shaking hand, stopping her movements. Then she looked into her brown eyes, searching for a sliver of rationality. "Where did all of these come from? Did you find them yourself, or did you have help getting them?"

Sara lowered herself to the floor and sat there, motionless except when a sob came up into her throat and shook her. The lines on her face bespoke repression and even a certain strength. But now there was a dull stare in her eyes—a glaze fixed on empty space. It was not a glance of reflection but rather indicated a suspension of intelligent thought. There was something coming to her, and she seemed to be waiting for it fearfully. What was it? It seemed too subtle and elusive to name. Her bosom rose and fell tumultuously as if she were beginning to recognize this thing that was approaching to possess her and she was striving to beat it back with her will—as powerless as her two white slender hands would have been.

Then two little whispered words escaped her slightly parted lips. She said them over and over under her breath: "My memories…my memories." The vacant stare and the look of terror that followed it vanished from her eyes. They stayed keen and slightly brighter, and every inch of her body seemed to relax. She looked at Akira and smiled softly, creeping Akira out. "They were given to me for safekeeping," Sara said. "They're pieces of the past. Fragments of my dreams. It's important to keep them locked away, or I'll lose them."

Akira looked at Devon, then back at the frail woman. "Lose what, Sara?"

"Memories of all the people I've met."

Akira kept her voice soft. "And what happened to these people? Are they still living?"

She shook her head. "Oh no. They're gone. Every one of them."

Akira nodded. "I see. And what about the black brooch? The one with the dragon on it? Where did it come from?"

Sara smiled again. "From Dr. Bradshaw, of course. He left it on my dresser as a gift. But I don't know exactly why. Maybe it came from one of his memory jars, and he forgot to tell me."

Akira looked at Paul. "I need to make a quick phone call to my father. I don't want him to be worrying about me. Can you help Sara put everything back? I won't be long, I promise."

Devon followed Akira outside and closed the balcony door behind him. He stood back, watching her type a text message into her phone. When she was finished, he asked, "Should I call security? Do you think they'll arrest Bradshaw?"

Akira was slow to answer. "For what? Keeping memory jars. Because that's all they've done as far as we know, isn't it?"

"But you heard what Sara said about the dead people."

"Yes, I know. But if the laws in your country are the same as mine, there's nothing anyone can do. If Bradshaw is confronted, he could claim he found everything on the ground, in the trash—wherever he wants. Which makes me wonder how many jars he has in his collection and how many people he might have killed."

"Crap. I never thought of that. He's probably been at it for years."

Devon looked back at his aunt, standing next to Paul. She was holding her jar with both hands, thanking him profusely for his help. "Do you think she's crazy, Akira?"

"With all the hypnotherapy Bradshaw's performed, it's impossible to know for sure."

Devon let out a sigh and exuded a more composed demeanor. "While we're on this ship, we need to act like nothing has happened. If for any reason Bradshaw believes we're on to him, he might disappear, and then none of us would be safe."

Akira watched Sara walk upstairs to her room. "So the next question is, how do we keep a murderer from killing again?"

"There's only one answer," Devon said. "We never let him out of our sight."

26

HIGH STAKES

Sara and Bradshaw were back at it, monopolizing the conversation throughout dinner with their wine critiques and personal interests. No mention was made about the corpse in room 307 or Sara's remarkable comeback after sharing her secret, making it difficult for Devon to appear calm and unaffected. His hands were clasped, but Akira could see his fingers working nervously around one another. At the same time, her stomach was churning over the text message she'd sent. With no word from Takashi, her foremost concern rested on his whereabouts and the actions he had promised to take.

She whispered to Devon, "Are you OK?"

After a long gaze, his hands fell apart, and he murmured, "I don't know," as if speaking only to himself.

Akira reached for his hand under the table. She squeezed it and smiled at him, masking her worry. "Let's visit the casino," she suggested. "It might be a good idea for everyone."

Devon nodded. "I usually break even. I'll play any game, just as long as you're with me."

"Excellent suggestion, Akira," Dr. Hoffman said. "I'm feeling particularly lucky tonight."

After finishing their desserts and coffee, they walked down the corridor and approached one of the placards advertising various activities on the ship. Dr. Hoffman pointed out the scavenger hunt taking place right after the last show in the theater. "I couldn't help noticing that it's for adults only."

"Now that should be fun," Vivian agreed. "Let's do it after a few pulls on my favorite machines."

"Guess it's been a while since you've played," Devon said. "The slots are computerized now."

Hoffman read notes about the scavenger game before turning to Sara. "Seems it involves things that might or might not be carried on your person, which means that giant purse of yours will probably have everything we're looking for. So our team should be a sure win."

Devon coughed. Then he looked at Akira. He must have read the warning in her eyes, because he quickly added, "Yep, a sure win, Doc."

They all walked into the casino, with Bradshaw and Sara in the lead and Paul trailing far behind. Stepping up to the blackjack table, Devon bought in with his ship charge card after promising to reimburse his uncle. Then he sat down to play. Akira joined him for a few hands after receiving a dozen chips and making a mental note of Bradshaw's location, which turned out to be a good thing in the long run. Every time Devon lost a hand, she won, and surprisingly Bradshaw never left his seat. So the time spent on the table was just as Devon had said: breakeven.

"Would you like your chips back?" she asked.

"All yours. Do with them what you will." He stayed at the blackjack table, but she took her winnings and moved to the slot machines, where Sara and Vivian were plugging away. Devon continued to play for ten minutes, then he stood and walked around, watching other passengers play various games ranging from craps and roulette to Texas Hold'em. He finally settled down in front of a slot machine a short distance away and began pushing buttons.

A siren went off on Akira's machine, drawing the attention of everyone in the room, including Devon.

He walked up behind her and leaned down. "Hey, gorgeous. Looking for a good time?"

Akira stared at the blinking lights and dancing joker, fascinated by what was happening. "Sorry, stranger," she said. "I'm having all the fun I can handle right here." To her amazement, she had won more than $1,000 without knowing what she was doing.

"How much did you put in?" Devon asked her.

"Twenty dollars."

"I think it's time to cash out."

"But why would I do that? I'm winning."

"After you hit the jackpot, it's easy to keep going and lose."

Akira laid her head back against him. "OK." She punched the cash-out button, and he took her ticket to the cashier to collect her reward.

"Congratulations, honey," he said, handing her a stack of bills. "You're one of the big winners in this place."

"Me too!" Bradshaw announced from behind them. "Eight hundred dollars richer here." He laid a hand on Devon's shoulder and smiled. "Should have stayed on that blackjack table, son."

Devon shrugged off his hand. "Yeah, right."

"Aw, come on," Bradshaw said. "Don't be a bad loser. Let me buy you both a drink." He waved over the cocktail waitress and ordered a bottle of champagne. "Make sure everyone in our group gets a taste." He watched the waitress walk away in her black shimmery minidress and grinned from ear to ear. "Now that one's worth keeping."

Devon turned away from him and met Akira's eyes. *Asshole,* he mouthed.

"You're right about that," she said, lifting Bradshaw's brows. The cocktail waitress returned and handed out filled glasses. Akira drained hers while Devon watched, and then he followed suit. Bradshaw guffawed and mimicked their actions.

The glasses were filled a second time, and somehow Akira got it into her head that the good doctor would be incapable of harming anyone if he were inebriated and had to be escorted to his room. She whispered the idea to Devon, who wholeheartedly agreed. Before long, the wine was flowing in a nearby bar, and the voices of everyone in their party were amplified, along with their laughs. Then Vivian delayed their well-laid plans by reminding everyone that the scavenger hunt was about to begin.

Devon and Akira followed their group into the theater and located seats near the back.

The cruise director stepped up on the stage and took the microphone. "Hello, everyone. We will be starting shortly, but first, here's the deal. We are going to divide into teams of ten to twelve players." He pointed toward stage left and continued. "This is the first group." Then he pointed at the next table. "We've got a second group right here. Let's get going now. We want to get started soon."

Before long, there were five teams, equally divided. Each team was given a large placard with a number from one to five. Devon and Akira were in team five along with the rest of their group.

"Now I will call out an item that I want brought to the stage," the director said. "The teams will hold it up with their number and rush to the stage. I will announce the numbers as teams arrive, and my assistant will write them down. The highest final score will result in winning six hundred dollars and discount coupons for future vacations for everyone in your group. So let me make sure you all understand. If I ask for someone to bring me a motorcycle, for instance, the first team to deliver it will win first place for that round and the second team with the closest time wins second place. My scorekeeper will keep track, and the team with the highest score at the end of the night wins our grand prize. Does everyone understand?"

Heads nodded in the room.

"Then let's get started."

Dr. Hoffman leaned forward. "Let's beat the pants off everyone. OK?"

Paul took a step back. "If you don't mind, I'm going to sit this one out and let the rest of you go at it."

"Suit yourself," Bradshaw said. "Come on, Sara. Let's show them how this game is played."

The cruise director glanced at his paper. "I need someone to bring me…a police whistle."

Akira turned to Devon. "What?"

"A whistle."

Surprisingly, Vivian had a real police whistle in her bag. "You're the runner," she told Akira. Following the directions, she bolted for the stage with their number in the air.

"Now that's how it's done," the director said.

Akira rejoined her group, smiling at Bradshaw.

"The next item is…a wooden pencil."

Hoffman handed one to Akira. She sprinted toward the stage and returned once again with a subtle smile on her face. "You're really good at this," she told them. "I packed clothes in my luggage and never considered needing…other things."

The third item turned out to be a small spiral notebook. Sara rummaged through her bag and shook her head. It seemed Devon couldn't resist asking, "You sure you don't have it?"

Surprisingly, Vivian reached into her bag and pulled out a notebook. "I do!"

"You're kidding," a man beside them grumbled. Other team members were now frowning, and a few were threatening to quit. Akira thought the game might be striking too close to home to involve Paul. She spotted him near the rear exit, talking to Felicia, the woman who was maintaining their rooms. She couldn't help wondering what they had in common, aside from their obsession with towels.

"It's not over yet," the director said. "I'm doubling the points and adding three bottles of wine to the winning pot. So don't give up yet." Smiles returned in the room, and the items in the hunt became more generic. "Bring me a photo ID that is not a driver's license."

Bradshaw handed over his hospital badge, and once again, Akira ran to the stage. But a player from another team was there first with a passport. And the next item proved to be more difficult.

"A stick of chewing gun that has real sugar." The room was filled with movement as every team member searched pockets, bags, and purses. A woman from an opposing team charged by, waving a stick of gum above her head. The game continued, with toenail clippers, a pocket comb, a can of hair spray, and a large rubber band. It seemed that whoever created this crazy game was determined to cause as much havoc as possible.

Then the director made an odd request, explaining the adults-only rule. "I would like a man to bring me a pair of women's panty hose." Laughs erupted, and it appeared that an attractive young lady from the fourth team was the only person willing to contribute to the cause. She was in the process of tugging them off when Bradshaw decided to be creative by picking her up and carrying her to the stage.

"Technically, it's correct," he told the director, who soon realized it was pointless to argue with him. Their team got the score; however, the second team jumped ahead when the cruise director asked for birth control pills.

Finally, the last item was announced. "I need someone to bring me a woman's bra...*not* being worn."

Sara covered her breast with both arms, and Vivian said, "Absolutely not."

Devon laughed and told them all, "During my college days, if you asked me, I could give you a dozen. But I don't have a single one right now." He looked at Akira and noticed that she had unfastened her bra and was in the process of sliding her straps through the arms in her dress.

She handed it to him along with their number and shouted, "Run!"

He beat out two teams, and their group received the highest score in addition to all the winnings. To everyone's amazement, Bradshaw said it would only be fair to divide the money among them and enjoy the wine together. So they agreed to return to the bar they had left before the game had started.

Devon held Akira's bra before her and asked, "Do you want to go to the ladies' room and put this back on?"

"No, I'm good," she said. "I don't really need it right now. You can hold on to it."

She walked ahead of him, and he tucked it into his coat pocket. "It's becoming a real challenge to keep up with Bradshaw," he confessed. "To be honest with you, I don't know how much more I can drink."

Akira looked over her shoulder. "You might consider ordering vodka and letting the waitress know it's a signal for water. She's been helping me out for the last hour. It's important to keep our heads straight and our eyes fixed on Bradshaw."

"For how long?"

"Until he wanders back to his room."

"Then what?"

The image of Takashi holding her upraised sword formed in Akira's mind. She stopped walking and turned around. "He'll be dealt with."

He reached for Akira's hand and kissed it.

As they walked into the bar, she realized their group had already been seated, but the doctor was still standing, ordering drinks from the bartender. He regarded Akira for a few seconds, and then a slow smile spread across his lips. "Come on, children. Don't keep everyone waiting."

Vivian patted the seat next to her. "Sit with me, Akira. I have to tell you my good news."

Akira dropped into the booth and looked around the table. Paul had his arms crossed over his chest, and Hoffman was grinning. Whether it was the result of the prize money they'd been awarded or the discounted fare, Akira had no idea and no interest. But he was obviously feeling no pain.

Vivian was positively giddy. "Peter said we wouldn't have won if not for my bag of goodies. He's giving me one of his memory jars to keep all my treasures in."

Akira glanced at Devon. "Memory jar?"

Bradshaw chuckled. "It's a way to display your keepsakes. You know, those things you want to keep close to you. Personally, I use mine for quotes and favorite sayings. You never know when you might need one for a speech. And as I'm sure you're all aware, my memory is somewhat lacking."

"I have one too," Sara volunteered. "Peter encouraged me to use it after losing my husbands and daughter. It's helped me cope with the tragedies in my life and is filled with all kinds of wonderful things. It's a great way to remember them—and other special friends I've lost."

Paul was frowning. "You don't say. If your tokens are reserved for your family and friends, then how did Gwen's earring end up inside?"

Devon was holding Akira's hand, squeezing it tight, waiting for an explosion to erupt.

"Oh, I found that in our bed, dear."

Akira watched the color drain from Paul's face.

"It has no meaning for me," she added, "but I know it does for you."

Paul's humiliation was apparent. He excused himself from the table, leaving Sara happily chatting away with Vivian, oblivious to the discomfort she had caused.

Akira glanced at Devon. He looked as stunned as she felt. It seemed they had jumped to conclusions and misjudged Bradshaw and Sara. However, there was still one token in Akira's possession that hadn't been explained away. If Bradshaw was innocent of any wrongdoing, how did he end up with Keiko's brooch, and why did he give it to Sara?

Akira turned to Bradshaw and hesitated before asking, "What about the black dragon brooch? Where did you get it?"

Bradshaw surprised her by smiling. "Oh, that. I found it on the ground in Mexico and left it on Sara's dresser. I just assumed it belonged to her. Do you know who the rightful owner is?"

Akira's throat was constricting. She picked up her glass of water and took a huge swallow, realizing too late it was vodka. She choked and squeezed out, "Yes…I do."

"Mystery solved," Bradshaw said, beaming. He excused himself to use the bathroom, and Devon followed after him. Akira pulled her phone from her purse and glanced down. She noticed the battery had died and realized she had no choice but to make a mad dash to find Takashi before he killed an innocent man.

27

FISH BAIT

Akira took the elevator across from the theater, dazed from the four glasses of wine and shot of vodka she had consumed. A few seconds passed, and the doors opened before her. She stepped out into the empty hallway and couldn't figure out which direction she was facing, let alone which way to proceed. She looked down and realized the carpeting under her feet had red and blue medallions—not the gold and blue diamonds she'd become familiar with seeing. After making numerous trips to various restaurants, she realized she had gotten off on the right floor but on the wrong end of the ship. The enormous staircase on her right led to the upper and lower levels, which should have made it easy to find her way back to her room. However, her explorations on the ship had proved that not every floor had immediate access to the passenger levels; many were blocked by restaurants, lounges, and shops.

Akira decided it was best to start over—to backtrack the way she had come. She pushed the elevator button and waited for what seemed like an eternity. Then a slight sway in the ship's motion caused her stomach to lurch. She needed fresh air to avoid further humiliation. A glass exit door stood waiting a short distance away. She slid it open and stepped outside. Oddly, all of the overhead lights above the walkway were out. It was impossible to see more than ten feet in any given direction. She gripped the safety railing and gazed up at the sky, drawing long, deep breaths. A sudden breeze whipped at her hair, tugging tendrils loose from her pinned-up hairdo. She wrapped her arms around herself, warding off the chill, and was about to return inside when she heard the sound of a voice.

"Is someone here?" a man called out. "Oh, there you are. It's so dark, I almost didn't recognize you." It was Peter Bradshaw, of all people. His gruff voice was unmistakable, but how did he end up here? Devon had followed him to the restroom just before she left the bar. Was Devon standing out here as well?

"Do you need help getting back to your room?" Bradshaw asked. "It's easy to get turned around on this ship. I've been doing it all week."

Akira realized he must have seen her. She was about to answer when his voice sounded again. "What the hell are you doing with that? Throw it away before someone gets hurt."

She froze in place, using the darkness as her shield. Who was he talking to? Devon?

"No!" Bradshaw yelled. "Don't do it! Listen to me...please!"

Pew. Akira recognized the firing of a gun with a silencer. There was a brief silence, and then the sound of a splash. Her mind begged to know what had happened, yet she didn't dare move. The murderer was only twenty feet away, and she had no interest in being his next victim. A sliding door hit its metal casing, alluding to his rapid escape. Her peripheral vision catch sight of a long, dark raincoat disappearing inside an open elevator. The door closed quickly, concealing his identity and transporting him to who knew where.

The sound of heavy, slow footsteps turned Akira around. It was a uniformed officer doing his nightly rounds. "Oh, good grief," he said. "It seems we have some nonworking lights out here. I'll need to get this addressed right away."

Akira shivered. "I...I seem to be lost. Would you mind helping me? My room number is 670. I believe I got turned around after leaving the theater."

"Happens all the time, miss. You need to go down one level, pass the pool, and then take the elevator to the sixth floor. Better yet, why don't you come with me, and I'll help you find it."

Akira walked with him until she arrived at her room. After watching him leave, she stepped inside and instantly became aware of Takashi's presence. He was sitting in the armchair with the table lamp on. His arms were crossed as usual, and a frown was darkening his face. "What took you so long?" he snapped.

Akira dropped onto the sofa. "Were you outside on the sixth floor of C level just before I got here?"

"No. Do you think I'm a magician or something?"

"Well, someone on this ship is. They disappeared in a black raincoat after shooting Bradshaw."

"What? Are you serious?"

"There's no doubt in my mind."

"So what did they look like?"

"I don't know. It was dark. I couldn't see their face."

"Then how can you be so sure he's dead?"

"I heard the sound of a silencer and a splash below the railing."

"Was anyone else there?"

"Not that I could tell. The duty officer showed up and made a comment about all the lights being out. He seemed to be as mystified as me."

Takashi scratched his head. "If Bradshaw is really dead, then our job here is done. Someone just saved us a lot of work."

Akira didn't know how to tell him that Keiko's murderer was still on the loose and her death had yet to be avenged. She looked down at the black pearl ring on her left hand. It was a token from her employer and a constant reminder of her obligations to the Zakura-kai organization—obligations that never seemed to end.

"It's not over," she said.

Takashi huffed. "What are you talking about?"

"It wasn't him. He didn't kill her."

"Of course, he did. You're acting stupid. Go to bed, Akira. You're making me crazy."

"I'm telling you it wasn't him. It was someone else."

"Who?" Takashi's eyes darkened.

"I don't know. But I have a feeling they've been playing us the whole time."

Takashi looked down, shaking his head. "What do you expect me to do? I can't go back to Japan and say we failed. Do you have any idea how Mitsui-san would react? Our lives would be worthless."

Akira swallowed hard, knowing Takashi was right. But she couldn't get rid of the thought of someone else stepping in to finish their job.

"Whether it's true or not, Bradshaw did it," he said. "He's the one who killed Keiko Mitsui, and we took care of it. Understand?"

Akira nodded.

"We're not going to talk about this anymore. Now go to bed. And don't bring it up again."

Akira retreated to her bedroom and closed the door quietly. When Takashi could be heard moving around upstairs, she lay down on her bed still wearing her dinner dress. Thoughts of the faceless assassin continued to plague her. Was it a man or a woman? Someone Bradshaw had pissed off, or a lunatic randomly killing people? There was no way to know for sure. Not on a ship this size and with the number of passengers it was carrying.

There were only three days left before the ship reached the coast of Florida. Even if she escaped in America, once Mitsui-san figured out they were lying or word reached him that the real murderer was still alive, she would be spending the rest of her life looking over her shoulder.

Akira slipped out of her dress and pulled Devon's blue T-shirt over her head—the one she had secretly taken. It was too late tonight to call him, especially with his aunt and uncle staying in the same suite. But first thing tomorrow, as soon as she could get him alone, she needed to confide in him and enlist his help—if she had any hope of staying alive.

28

TRUE CONFESSIONS

At breakfast, Akira could sense the tension between Sara and Paul. Something was going on. They had barely said more than a few sentences to each other, instead opting for half-spoken, pointed words and silence. It was awkward, especially with Dr. Hoffman and Vivian Ward present. Just yesterday, they had all been laughing and chatting away at dinner and throughout the scavenger hunt game. Although she couldn't keep up with their high-spirited conversations in the bar, Akira could definitely feel the shift in their relationship today. Whatever the cause, she tried her best to ignore it, but eventually it spilled over her like oil—spoiled and a bit disgusting. She watched as they both trudged on ahead of her and Devon toward the Omni Theater, stopping only long enough for Dr. Hoffman and Vivian to catch up with them. The whole time, all Akira could think about was Bradshaw. With Sara's blind commitment to him and their surprising reveal, it was easy to assume that late-night feuding had erupted in the Lyonses' suite. It was going to be a challenge to draw Devon aside and broach the subject of the doctor's whereabouts and the possibility of his involvement. But she was determined to enlist his help, even if it meant confessing everything.

When everyone was seated, the cruise director introduced the promotional movie for their new ship and Alaskan cruise. As one might imagine, he got the room excited over the possibility of winning two free tickets simply for being present. Akira had no idea why she and Devon had agreed to come here in the first place other than to demonstrate their unity and some type of normalcy while trapped on the ship.

The video rolled, and halfway through Akira remarked, "It's beautiful." She glanced over to see Devon smiling at her, his expression soft and gentle. She smiled back, trying to pretend she was happy and hoping she wouldn't be called on it.

"I can see why tourists want to go there," he said.

On the screen, eagles soared across blue skies and over lush wooded landscapes. Ice caps broke off and dropped into crystal blue waters. As pods of whales rose into the air and their babies followed, Akira's heart softened, and for a moment, it was as if she'd been transported to a plane of existence where colors exploded into her world. Devon sat next to her with the same look of wonder on his face, as if the magic of nature were something he was seeing for the first time.

He turned to her and offered a sheepish smile. "Despite everything," he said, "I'm glad we're together."

Paul grunted a few feet away. He dug into a plastic bag to fish out the bottles of water he'd brought with him. Then he handed each of them one and returned his attention to the screen.

Akira brushed her right hand up against Devon's, tangling her fingers in between his. He let go of a soft breath and glanced at her. His lips pulled back into his favorite secretive smile, and her heart turned over in her chest. It was the kind of look he'd reserved for their talks and the quiet moments that were just for them.

Paul called out to him in a hushed tone. "So I heard you were going to Albuquerque next month."

Akira was jolted out of her thoughts. She watched Devon nod. "Yeah. I'm hooking up with my sister and her husband, Chase. They're giving a presentation on new recovery techniques at the North American Oceanautic Conference. Then we're taking *Stargazer* and the crew down to Rocas Alijos on a recovery expedition." Devon turned to Akira and smiled. "I'd sure love to have you come along if you're up for it."

Akira turned away. It was one thing to ask her to be with him on a trip to California, even going so far as to offer the use of his apartment. But it was entirely different from asking her to be part of his life by going to New Mexico and sharing a serious commitment she wasn't prepared to address. Plus, there was still the matter of meeting his sister and brother-in-law—a couple who knew secrets about her past after meeting her in Japan on their treasure-hunting trip three years ago. Akira had never thought it important to acknowledge their relationship after hearing Devon mention their names, since she had no intention of seeing them again. However, reentering their lives during his trip would make it impossible to avoid discrediting herself by confessing the truth to Devon. In the meantime, she could continue to make vague promises to pacify him on the first count. At least until the ship reached its final port.

"Akira? What do think? Would you like to see New Mexico?"

She tried to hide her trepidation by staring at the snow-capped landscape on the theater's enormous screen. But Devon tugged on her arm, insisting on an answer.

"That's a very kind offer. But I'm sure your sister wouldn't appreciate you bringing me along."

Devon turned to face her. "Rachel's amazing. She wouldn't mind at all. In fact, I think you two would hit it off great."

Akira wanted to cry. This was everything she desired: a decent, caring man, a home in the sunshine, and a life away from the shadows of her current job. And she couldn't have any of it. Not ever. What could she possibly say? "Well, there's still my father to consider. I don't think he would approve of me going off—"

Devon dropped back in his seat and stared at the screen. "Oh, I didn't even think about him. I was just imagining how fun it would be doing all the touristy stuff together."

Akira let go of a little breath. He was in love with the innocent Akira—the woman who was willing to do anything to hold on to him. She wondered wildly if he'd still love her if he knew what she really was.

She forced a smile. "I'm sure it's wonderful there."

He lifted a brow but said nothing. Akira could feel him waiting for her to elaborate, to correct her reaction in some way, and yet he kept silent.

"Devon?"

He stared straight ahead. "Well, then I guess we'd better enjoy the next forty-eight hours. There's no telling when we'll see each other again."

Akira didn't know what to say. He was obviously disappointed, but she'd grown tired of making false claims and promises she couldn't keep. "I'm sure you'll have a great time with your family."

Devon remained stone-faced. "Yeah, right."

She tried to swallow, but her throat was dry. They had enjoyed each other's company for the last eight days, and she felt herself starting to need him all over again. Not just those moments of desire, but those private moments where they grew closer with little conversations and soft kisses stolen in between words. She wanted to wake up every morning and see his smiling face. She wanted to witness the world through his eyes and experience the adventures he had shared. To know what it meant to be normal and happy, surrounded by family and friends. Akira took a deep breath and released it slowly. She wanted a miraculous, unattainable dream. She wanted a life with him—forever.

Vivian turned around in her seat. "Would you mind if I take a picture of you two?"

"Sure," Devon said. He wrapped his arm around Akira's shoulder and drew her close, while she tried her best to ignore the wonderful way he smelled. A sad smile tugged at her lips, and her mind wandered as she thought about Devon's soft kisses and the evaporating hours.

"This has been the best vacation ever," Vivian said. "Don't you agree?"

They both nodded, but Akira's heart ached with the thought of it ending too soon.

"Now don't let me forget to get your addresses. I'll send you copies." Her brow lifted. "And maybe we could even stay in touch?"

Devon smiled. "Yes, of course."

Akira realized it was selfish and foolish and even delusional on her part, but she wanted to enjoy as much time as she could with Devon before saying goodbye. Yes, she had chosen Devon to sort out the mystery of Keiko Mitsui's death, and she was relieved after discovering Sara and Paul were not involved. But strangely, the time spent on this ship held more meaning for her and Devon than anyone else.

He hooked his fingers between hers and displayed a little smile as they left the theater and split off toward the observation deck. She kept her eyes level, trying not to focus too hard on how he made her feel. Whatever this was, it would always be with her: the sense of wholeness and longing she could only dream about until now. But time was running out quickly, and the truth was begging to be told. She needed to share what she had witnessed and ask for his help.

They sat down on club chairs in the corner of the room across from the massive windows at the front of the ship. Akira leaned forward and took his hands in hers. "About last night—"

Devon cut in before she could finish. "Can't we just enjoy each other's company? Do we need to talk about that now?"

She studied his solemn face and realized something was wrong. "What is it?"

Devon was quiet for a long moment, then he begrudgingly shared his thoughts. "Sara showed up on the bridge early this morning and told Captain Brice that Bradshaw was missing again and if he didn't send a search party right away, she was going to have him charged with dereliction of his duties."

Akira dropped back in her seat. "That's terrible."

"Oh, it gets worse. He claimed she was crying wolf again to get attention and that Bradshaw used their personal relationship to leave the ship in the Cays. He said Peter was probably hiding to avoid her, and who could blame him? Then she blew up and threatened to sue the company, and Brice stormed off in a fit. According to my uncle, it was a pretty ugly scene."

Akira noticed a cocktail waitress working her way toward them. "Did you follow Bradshaw to the bathroom last night?"

Devon rubbed his jaw with the back of his hand. "Yeah. I was kind of hoping you wouldn't bring that up. I spent an hour in the head—sick as a dog. I've never been good at mixing booze, especially when champagne is involved."

She realized how ridiculous it was to consider for even one moment that Devon was capable of murder. He was the last person who would own a gun and certainly wouldn't shoot someone if he did. But she still needed to ask. "So…you didn't take the elevator to the sixth floor?"

Devon waved off the waitress. Then he turned back to Akira. "No. I went back to my room and crashed. Why do you want to know?"

Akira glanced down at the carpet and debated how to answer. "Well, Bradshaw is definitely gone. I can attest to that." She was silently wondering how much to share.

"What do you mean?"

"He was murdered last night. Someone shot him, and he fell overboard. The lights were out, so I couldn't make out who did it."

Devon grabbed her arms and held tight. "You were there? Jeez, Akira. Did they see you?"

"No, I don't think so. Whoever it was had on a raincoat and wore a hat covering their face. Anyway, I need your help to find out who it was."

Devon's eyes grew wide. "Why? No one is expecting you to be Nancy Drew. You need to call security and report what happened."

Akira shook her head and lowered her voice. "I can't."

Devon edged closer. "Why not?"

Akira gnawed on her lip. She wanted to tell him everything, come clean for once in her life. But how could he possibly understand? She was sent there to murder Bradshaw, and now she was trying to solve his death. What the hell was she thinking?

"Baby…tell me." His eyes were pleading. "What's going on? What are you hiding?"

Takashi's words came rushing back to her. *Don't bring it up again.* If he found out she was working behind his back, he would be furious. And what about the investigation by shipboard security into Bradshaw's death? She could be dragged in as a witness. Damn it! Takashi was right. She should have kept her mouth shut.

Akira swallowed hard. "If I tell you, you'll never want to see me again. I know it."

He stiffened in his seat. "What are you talking about? I'm crazy about you. Nothing will change that."

Akira looked deep into his eyes, and her heart ached. She couldn't bear to hurt him, not ever. "I can't be involved," she finally said. "My father would never allow it. I just want to know who it was."

Devon took her hands in his. "I don't want you to feel guilty for not saying anything. You were frightened and didn't know what you should do. Obviously, someone wanted Bradshaw dead, but the fact is neither one of us is a detective. It's perfectly understandable if you don't want to be part of this, but I can report it. I can tell the officers that I was there when it happened—that I only saw the raincoat and hat."

"What about your aunt? She's going to be devastated."

"I guess I'll be telling her too."

"God, Devon…I'm so sorry. This shouldn't all fall on you."

"It's all right. I can handle it. I'll make a few calls and be right back. Don't go anywhere." They both stood up at the same time, and Devon hugged her. He motioned for her to sit, then he walked into the adjoining room and stood before a round pedestal table. He picked up the receiver for the phone and turned his back to her before making his calls.

A movement off to the right caught Akira's eye. It was Takashi. He was sitting on the opposite side of the room, watching her from the top of his coffee cup. Akira swallowed hard as he rose from his seat and crossed the room. He stood in front of her, and she came to her feet. "Akira-san," he said respectfully, taking a deep bow.

Akira regarded him with the same amount of respect and also bowed. "Hamada-san. How was your breakfast?" she asked, her nervousness noticeable. It only intensified as he rose from his deep bow to make eye contact with her. "Was there something you needed?"

"I couldn't help noticing you talking to Devon. You seemed rather upset this morning. I hope I didn't make a mistake in coming here with you."

Akira shook her head. "No...you didn't." She stared straight ahead, avoiding his eyes. She needed to stay calm and share nothing—only what was absolutely necessary.

He waited a few seconds before adding, "Just remember what I said. We both want to leave here without any problems."

Akira nodded and kept her eyes down. After a few more seconds, he walked away. Her heart was still racing as he boarded the elevator and disappeared from view.

Devon came back and blew out a breath. "OK, that's done." He dropped into the seat across from her.

"Is someone going to investigate?" she said.

"That's what I was told. The FBI will probably be here sometime today. I was told not to say anything until they arrive."

"What about your aunt?"

"My call was transferred to the captain. He thought it would be best if I waited."

Akira tendered a weak smile. "Yes, of course."

"Now let's forget about everything else for the moment and talk about you and me. I don't know what's going to happen when this trip ends," he said. "Obviously, I don't want to lose you, but going to Japan is out of the question for me. I don't know if you'd be willing to live on the *Stargazer* or in California—or how your father will react with me taking you there. But I've been thinking about this for days now, debating what to do. Trying to come up with a reasonable solution—a way to make everyone happy. And there's only one answer that comes to mind." He took her hands in his and leaned forward in his seat.

Her heart skipped a beat. She could hardly breathe.

"From the first moment I laid eyes on you, I thought you were the most beautiful woman I'd ever seen. And when you spoke, I fell in love with the sound of your voice. We've had some incredible moments over the last week, and we've enjoyed some unforgettable experiences together. But I want to share many more with you, honey."

Why was he doing this? Akira was sweating bullets. No matter how much she cared, they could never be married. She would have to disclose her true identity and explain away all her lies. And then there was her occupation to think about.

"I've never felt so strongly about anyone." There was a confident tone in his voice and a gleam in his eyes. "And I don't want our time together to end." He smiled and looked down at the pink sapphire on her finger. "So tell me, Akira Hamada, will you—"

Akira opened her mouth and blurted, "I can't marry you!"

Devon shook his head and dropped back into his seat. "Who said anything about marriage? I was going to ask you to move in with me."

She realized too late the mistake she had made and scrambled for an explanation. "I'm sorry, Devon. I just overreacted. You see, I was thinking about the man I was contracted to in Japan. It was for financial reasons and impossible to refuse. When you said those words, it just all came rushing back, and I…"

Devon slumped in his seat. "Contracted? Like a business arrangement? You became a mistress to another man? But you told me that only happens in movies. That it's…not real."

"I'm truly sorry, Devon. It happened two years ago, while I was living in Kyoto. Then Kenji died, and I was so confused—"

"Did he pay you to sleep with him? Like a prostitute? Is that what you're telling me?"

"I'm trying to explain, but you're making it so difficult."

His disbelief turned to anger. "Was this only a game for you? A way to amuse yourself on this ship?"

"No! It was nothing like that. I love you, Devon."

"Yeah, right. Just not enough to marry me."

"That wasn't your question!"

He huffed. "No, but it was your answer. And what the fuck does it matter anyway?" He stood up to leave and glared down at her. "My uncle said I was making a huge mistake. I just wouldn't listen to him."

"You don't mean that."

Devon laughed in spite of himself. "I do. How ironic is that?" He turned away from her and started toward the elevator.

She ran after him. "Please understand, Devon. You're the most important thing in my life. I don't want to lose you. But I'm not the person you think I am."

He shook his head in disgust. "You witnessed Bradshaw's death and said nothing all morning—not at breakfast or during the movie. And now I find out you were a paid mistress. What other secrets are you keeping, Akira? Next you'll be telling me that you're a convicted criminal or some kind of spy." He stepped inside the elevator and looked down, avoiding her eyes.

"No, Devon." Her voice was barely a whisper. "I'm far, far worse."

His eyes came up, and his hand followed, blocking the elevator door. "What did you say?"

She turned away and ran from him, shutting out the world and everyone in it.

"Akira!"

She squeezed through the crowd and ducked into the closest bathroom. Then she locked the door and crumpled to the floor. She was torn and broken by her own deception. Lost in the game she had played. She had allowed Devon to enter her spirit and stroke her soul, where everything was love, sensation, and surrender. He had cracked her shell wide open, exposing her vulnerability. It had never occurred to her that the emotion he stirred was really love—not meaningless sex forced upon her by a brutal lover. Not until it was too late.

The way she wanted him was blinding. As if she couldn't see what was really happening, only what she wanted to happen. She suspected that he would always seek to minimize the risk of being split open himself and his own secrets revealed. And yet somewhere deep down in her labyrinth, her intricacy, in the darkest part of her soul, she relished the mayhem—the damage she was capable of inflicting.

Oddly, she enjoyed a sense of privilege for having such passion in her life. Of witnessing firsthand what it meant to be stirred to the core—in the place she dared not enter. The place she had all but forgotten. But now the drama was over as quickly as it had begun. Devon's eyes were cold and dark. His angry words were vicious. He laughed at her cruel dilemma and called her a whore. And even yet, she looked for love hiding in his eyes, in his face, in his stance, and she found nothing but disdain. Upon seeing the truth, her heart stopped, and her perfect world crumbled.

Akira reached for the sink and pulled herself upright. She looked into the mirror and ate the tear that had escaped her eye. The kind, innocent soul Devon had taken her for was gone, replaced by a smarter and much wiser villain. Mitsui-san would be happy to know that his favorite assassin was back, ready to act on his orders.

29

FORGIVENESS

Day after day in his office at the stock brokerage firm, Devon had listened to stories about men and women messing around. They led secret lives and hid them from their marriages. They went through wretched divorces, inflicting pain on their children and their children's children. Sometimes they made desperate, tearful, sweaty efforts to hold on to the shreds of their lives. But their spouses never got over the betrayal. They could never forgive the deception or overcome the thoughts it invoked. His associates told him it was all about a quick thrill and the furtive moment of romance. Some of them would say they didn't remember making the decision that tore their lives apart. It just happened, they had claimed. And sometimes they didn't even know they were being unfaithful.

From the outside looking in, it was insane. How could anyone risk everything for ten minutes of personal gratification because their expectations weren't met? When he was eight years of age, that's when his mother had shown him how easy it was to run off with another man and leave her children behind. As a result, trust would always be an issue. There was simply no way around it.

Even when the woman he loved wasn't to blame.

Devon mulled over her words. *I was contracted for financial reasons.* Isn't that what she said? *It was impossible to refuse.* Surprisingly, the same scenario applied to his uncle, and Paul was still in his life.

Akira hadn't cheated on him. Just neglected to tell him the whole story—to tell him about the unimaginable life she had led. But that wasn't the problem. The real kicker came when she had refused to go with him to Albuquerque, because he knew California would come next. In all truth, Devon had pushed her away before she could dump him. It was just easier that way.

Or was it?

Years of resentment had gotten the better of him, turning him into a heartless bastard. There was no other explanation for how badly he had behaved. Devon had spent the last eight years of his life hoping to find his soul mate: the perfect person to make him feel whole. How many times did Akira say she never felt as deeply about anyone the way she did with him? How many times did he tell her that he felt the same way? They both had failed at love time and time again but had somehow found it in each other. Akira's adoration was the gift he'd been given and had thoughtlessly thrown away. And over what? His past?

At that moment, all he could think about was the pain he would suffer at not seeing Akira again. Not feeling her hands, her lips, her body against his. Not hearing her voice, her laughter, her soft whispers in his ears. *Damn it all!* He would go anywhere with her. Even climb the highest mountain in Nepal, if it meant they could be together. So why the hell was he here, acting like a fool, when he could be with her?

Devon picked up the phone and called Akira's room. It rang again and again and again. He called the customer service desk and sweet-talked the clerk into having Akira paged. After ten minutes, the woman's voice came back on the line to tell him, "I'm sorry, but she doesn't seem to be answering."

"Do you have any idea how I can find her?"

"I don't know, sir," she said. "I can't really say."

Devon wanted someone to reassure him that he hadn't made the biggest mistake of his life. That there was a way to erase everything he had said. He called her room again and let it ring a dozen times. Then an automated voice came on the line instructing him how to leave a message.

Not knowing what else to do, he went downstairs and visually scanned restaurants and rooms from one end of the ship to the other. He was about to enter the elevator for the third time when Vivian Ward and Ben Hoffman took shape before his eyes.

"Well, would you lookie here," Vivian said, stepping off the elevator. "Everyone is searching for this young man, and he magically appears before us."

"Everyone?" Devon hoped she was referring to Akira.

"Yes, your aunt and uncle. Well…mainly your uncle anyway. That aunt of yours can be a real shithead when she puts her mind to it."

Hoffman twisted a smile. "I'm afraid I'm inclined to agree. Sara has been on a tirade ever since Bradshaw disappeared. I honestly didn't have the heart to tell her."

Devon tipped his head to the side. "Tell her what?"

"The truth. Your uncle shared it with me during breakfast. He swore me to secrecy, although I'm not exactly sure why. The fact is, I've never been good at secrets. Most of the folks who know me are well aware of that."

Vivian elbowed Hoffman in the side. "Ben, get to the point."

"It seems a man's body was found by a fishing boat early this morning. The police called Captain Brice and said they were having a hard time identifying the guy—especially after the sharks made good use of him. Anyway, your uncle thinks it might have been Bradshaw, but the coroner hasn't confirmed it yet."

Devon blew out a breath. "How did my uncle find out?"

"The head of housekeeping told him. She knew the doctor and Sara were good friends."

"Well, my aunt's going to be devastated. That's for sure."

"I know," Hoffman said. "I suppose that's why your uncle wants to wait until we arrive. There's no reason for everyone on this ship to witness her meltdown."

Devon agreed. "Have you seen Akira?" He knew she would want to hear the news, even as bad as it was.

"We saw her about thirty minutes ago, heading toward the library. You might try venturing that way."

"What's wrong?" Vivian asked. "Did you two have a lovers' spat?"

Devon rolled his shoulders, like he was working out a kink. "Yeah, something like that."

She patted his arm. "I hope you figure it out. You make such a nice couple."

A cocktail waitress approached Devon. "Would you like your regular, sir? I'm sure I can find that special bourbon you like."

"No thanks, Judi." She walked back toward the bar, where two heavy hitters were waiting. It wasn't until that moment that Devon realized the positive influence Akira had on him. The fact he couldn't remember the last time he threw back a shot was remarkable in itself.

"Well, I can tell you one thing for sure," Hoffman said. "I'd hate to be Captain Brice right now. He's going to have a hell of a time explaining why he didn't involve the police with so many people dying on this ship."

Vivian sighed. "Maybe he didn't want to ruin anyone's vacation, dear."

Devon almost laughed. But Hoffman had a valid point. After four deaths, Devon would have expected FBI agents to be crawling all over the place. And yet there were none to be seen.

"So I guess I'd better get going," Devon said. "I'll probably see you tonight at the party."

Vivian beamed. "Oh, that's right. It's white night. I've been looking forward to it all week."

Devon was amazed at how easy it was to write off Sara's doctor. Even though he wasn't their best friend, they had socialized throughout the trip. Apparently the man was more irritating and self-serving than he had originally believed—especially when it came to his uncle. Which reminded Devon, he needed to give Paul a call. There was no reason to worry him needlessly. Not after hearing the news about Bradshaw.

Devon found a quiet place outside to park himself. He dropped down in a chair and was about to use his phone when he spotted Akira. His pulse quickened at the mere sight of her. She was standing outside by the railing, staring out at the sea.

He walked up behind her and was about to speak when she turned. "What do you want?" she asked.

"We weren't finished talking," he said back. "There's something I need to say."

"No, I think you've said more than enough." He reached for her hand, but she jerked it away. "I don't love you. I hate you right now!" Akira's eyes were filled with unshed tears.

"Honey, please, we can get through this. You'll see. It was just a mistake. I didn't mean what I said. We have a genuine relationship. It was just…insecurity talking."

"Insecurity? For what? Because I told you the truth?"

"No. Because I couldn't handle it." He was terrified of never seeing her again because of his actions, because she wouldn't listen to him and give him another chance. "I couldn't deal with the idea of you being with another man...with the thought of losing you because of your father."

"So you insult me and storm off. What were you hoping to accomplish by that? I can't pretend to be what you want me to be."

"You're perfect the way you are. I don't want you to change at all." He looked down, ashamed of what he had done. "I'm so sorry, baby. I hate apologizing. But I know when I'm wrong." He glanced at her and ventured a smile. "I sure hope you're not keeping track."

Akira remained silent for a long moment, giving Devon reason to worry. He was about to freak out when she laughed lightly and lifted a hand, resting it against his cheek. "I really should slap you, but I haven't got the strength," she said lightly.

"You have every right, you know." He turned to look down at her. "Akira—" He was cut off as she pressed her lips to his without warning. He widened his eyes. Much too quickly for his liking, she pulled away. Without saying another word, she placed her cheek on his shoulder, leaving him frozen in place. After a few moments of processing what had happened, he laid his head on top of hers. This was definitely not the way he imagined the day would end.

He slowly and awkwardly put his arms around her. "So am I forgiven?"

"Devon, let it go," she insisted, a fine crease forming on her forehead. She took a step back and looked away.

Resigned, Devon nodded. "So are you going to the party tonight? It's the last event before the ship docks."

Akira didn't speak for a few seconds, and he wondered if she had heard him. But then she turned to him and shared an unexpected smile. "I bought a white dress before coming here."

"Really? Will I get to see it?"

She didn't answer. Instead, she stepped inside the doorway and began walking toward a wall of elevators. He hurried to catch up as her heels softly clinked on the tightly woven carpet.

"You know, sometimes I don't think before I speak," he said.

Akira paused. "Yes, I've noticed."

"I never meant to hurt you," he said quietly. "That was never my intent."

She stopped walking and looked up at him. Her eyes glistened from unshed tears. "Stop apologizing, Devon. I forgive you."

"OK" was all he could say. He wasn't sure if she really meant it—if she still had deep feelings for him. It seemed not, by the way she was acting. But at that moment, it was all he could hope for.

30

DISASTER STRIKES

I t was the white night party—the last formal dinner at sea—and everyone had agreed to attend despite Bradshaw's absence. Sara was sitting at a table next to the pool on the ninth floor, working on her third drink. She had been complaining for more than ten minutes over him being written off by the crew and disrespected by everyone, including her husband. Oddly, no one seemed particularly interested in hearing about Bradshaw, not even when Sara mentioned his missing luggage and the personal effects taken from his room, eliminating all trace of him. It seemed he had done little to ingratiate himself with their traveling companions or any passengers on this ship, aside from Sara, of course. In fact, the waitstaff appeared to be relieved at not seeing him at their table, and the restaurant manager actually smiled after discovering his name wasn't on the reservation list.

Despite her training, Akira found herself obsessing over the murderer in their midst. She couldn't help wondering if the murderer were seated at a table nearby, watching all of them and considering who the next victim might be.

Devon reached for Akira's hand and looked into her eyes. "Should we send a search party?"

"For whom?" Akira was half expecting the FBI to show up at any moment, asking questions and stirring up tensions between her and Takashi. She knew an eruption would soon follow when Sara's worst nightmare was realized, and she couldn't figure out how Devon was staying so calm.

"Your father, of course." He leaned in and lowered his voice. "Did you notice that security has been beefed up tonight?"

Akira glanced around and spotted a few men in white uniforms near the exit doors. She considered telling him that they didn't look qualified or equipped to handle a murderer but thought better of it.

"I know your father isn't keen on parties or seeing me, which probably explains his delay," Devon said. "I just think it might be a good idea to keep track of everyone. At least until this matter is resolved."

The last phone message she received from Takashi said something about ordering more towels from housekeeping. He had also mentioned a gray-striped shirt he was planning to wear that he hoped was white enough for the party.

"Akira, should we be worried?"

She looked at the gold watch on her wrist. It had been twenty minutes since she left Takashi in their suite, much longer than necessary to change. What the hell was he doing anyway?

Concern must have registered on her face, as Devon was quick to volunteer. "Why don't you stay here with Sara while I check on him? He's probably in no rush to show up...with me being here."

Akira turned to Devon. "It's OK. Stay here with your family. I'll be right back." She rose to her feet, and he reached for her hand, holding her in place.

"You sure you don't want me to come with you?"

She couldn't help noticing that everyone's eyes were on her. "No. Please enjoy your dinner. I won't be long."

Devon's hand dropped away, but the worry lines remained on his forehead. "Call me if you run into any problems. OK?"

Akira walked toward the closest exit and nodded to one of the guards. Then she headed toward the closest bank of elevators. According to the lit numbers above two of them, one had stopped on the fifth floor and wasn't moving. The other was on the eighth floor, where the VIP rooms were located; it had stopped as well.

Damn it. Where was Takashi? What was taking him so long? She hurried toward the carpeted stairwell and began her descent to the sixth floor, taking two steps at a time. Akira's heart was racing. Just two more floors and she'd be there, demanding an explanation for his lateness.

Finally, she arrived at their room. She searched the entire suite, but her roommate was nowhere to be seen. The only clues to his disappearance were the empty hangers on his bed and a pile of wet towels on the bathroom floor. In the living room, her sword was still resting against the wall; however, it now sat at a slightly different angle. In all likelihood, a maid had moved it, making her feel foolish for leaving it in plain sight.

"Takashi, where are the hell are you?" Akira tossed in the air. She called the guest relations desk and asked if anyone had seen him. Just as she'd suspected, the inquiry proved pointless. The staff had thousands of passengers to worry about, and one misplaced father was not a priority. However, after paging him and receiving no answer, one of the clerks suggested using the service elevator to come downstairs and speaking with the security officer on duty. Akira was hesitant at first, but then realized she had no choice in the matter. After bumming a ride with the cleaning crew and their filled trash dumpster, she found her way to the lobby on the third floor. She stood behind an elderly couple for five minutes as they complained about room service taking so long and was about to give up her search when a young, dark-haired woman in a crisp white blouse tapped her on the shoulder.

"Miss Hamada? I'm sorry to bother you. Your mother has been trying to contact you all morning, but a block was placed on all calls to your room. I hope you don't mind that I took a message. I was planning to leave it under your door."

Akira was still stuck on the word *block* when the word *mother* registered. "My mother?" Akira hesitated before taking the white envelope extended in her direction. She nodded and waited for the woman to walk away before extracting its contents and reading quietly to herself.

Received word from Mitsui-san. Yuki Ota is traveling to America to join you. Tell Hamada-san to do whatever is necessary to come home safely. I miss you.—Oka-san.

What did it all mean? Why would Yuki come here? And why would Oka-san be giving directions? She didn't have a relationship with Yuki or any members of the Zakura-kai. The note made no sense at all.

Akira had to find Takashi—and fast. She racked her brain for clues to his whereabouts. It was now 9:00 p.m. on her watch. With the Internet café closed for the night, there was only one other place he could be: the Japanese restaurant at the far end of the seventh floor. He had been going there on a daily basis, devouring ramen, sushi, and pork dumplings. Akira must have missed him on her way down to their room.

She left the courtesy center and hurried toward the closest elevators. At least eight people were waiting for doors to open, and the ones that did were running full. The overhead light on the far left elevator was slowly moving down from the ninth floor, while the elevator next to it was still stopped. It had been on the fifth floor for at least ten minutes, giving the impression it was out of order. Not knowing what else to do, Akira hurried to the brass winding staircase in the open-air terrarium and began her rapid ascent. When she reached the fifth floor, she was blocked by a group of passengers at the top of the stairs, preventing her from reaching the landing and the restaurant on the seventh floor. According to what she was hearing, an incident had occurred inside the wall of the elevator that was stuck on the fifth floor.

She managed to squeeze between onlookers, excusing herself over and over again as she climbed the carpeted stairs. Eventually, she reached the front of the crowd and managed to steal a look. To her dismay, a gruesome scene was unfolding— something straight out of a Stephen King novel. A curtain of red streamed down from the top of one of the doors, and it sounded like a rainstorm inside the ship. Everyone was staring at the pooling blood on the floor, spreading at an alarming rate. Two crew members were trying to usher people back inside an adjacent restaurant, while another group stood nearby with cell phones raised high in the air, recording the shocking scene for posterity.

One man stepped around Akira and screamed at the top of his lungs, "God Almighty! What's happening here?"

As she stood watching, six crew members arrived and sealed off the foyer. A sign on a metal stand was placed in front of the blood-streaked elevator door reading, "Sorry! I'm not working."

Akira asked one of the crew members if he could tell her anything at all. He hesitated a moment before explaining that an Asian man had fallen into an open shaft on the sixth floor. He'd been trapped behind the wall when the elevator became operational on the fifth floor, beheading him and crushing his body.

Akira glanced around in a panic. There had to be dozens of Asian passengers on this entire ship; three of them were within viewing range. The probability that her partner was involved was extremely high, and yet it was essential that she stay calm and keep her wits about her. He could miraculously show up at any given moment, and seeing her physically shaken would only make her look weak, stupid, and incompetent.

One of the female passengers standing next to Akira wailed, "I want off this ship!" Another stood behind her telling a story to her friend about a woman's daughter going to the nightclub on this same ship less than a year ago. Apparently, the mother didn't realize she hadn't returned to their cabin until the next morning. Then she was called to the medical center and told that her daughter had passed away. Her naked body was found on the floor of a cabin that was occupied by four unknown men. After being forced to endure an additional two days on the ship before they could disembark and fly home to America, the young girl's parents learned that their daughter was date-raped and killed after visiting the bar.

Akira grabbed a crew member's arm and forced out the words. "Can you tell me about the man who died? I think he could be my father."

He stared at her wide-eyed, obviously shaken. "I'm...so sorry, miss."

She refused to release her grip. "Please. I need your help."

He glimpsed the faces in the crowd, then turned back to her. "There were two people: a man in a gray-striped shirt and a woman dressed in black. Some kind of scuffle ensued. She pushed him through the open door, and when I got here, it was too late."

Akira leaned closer. "Can you describe the woman? Anything about her at all?"

"She ducked away from the security camera, so I couldn't see her face clearly. But from what I could make out, she looked a lot like...you."

Akira fled from the scene, weaving around gawking passengers. She found another set of stairs outside and reached the sixth floor in a matter of seconds. Then she ran through the hallway leading to her suite. The mute housekeeper was standing outside her open door, restocking items from her rolling cart.

"Please come with me," Akira told her. "I need to talk to you...now." She walked into the room with the housekeeper trailing behind. "Are you here alone?"

The maid nodded.

Takashi was dead. Akira was sure of it. There were still two days left before the ship reached its final destination and nowhere on this ship to escape. If she didn't act quickly, she could be next. There was no doubt in her mind. She picked up the katana sword and turned around. The housekeeper shrank back like a wilted flower.

"I'm not going to hurt you," Akira explained. "I just need to ask you a question. Have you seen a Japanese woman on this floor? Someone who looks like me?"

Clare kept her eyes low and shook her head.

"I'm sorry if I frightened you, but it's very important that I know about this person." Akira laid her hand gently on the maid's forearm. "Please...I beg of you," she said, looking into her sad eyes. "If there's anything you can show me...anything at all..."

Clare gestured toward the connecting door between suites and pulled a master key from her pocket. She handed it off before stepping back and waiting. With thoughtful deliberation, Akira inserted the key and slowly opened the door. The room was dark and empty, and she breathed a sigh of relief. She closed the door behind her and maneuvered around the furniture, searching for the front door. After inserting the card key in the wall, the entry was instantly illuminated. She walked into the living room and nervously glanced around before exploring further.

The floor plan was an exact copy of her two-bedroom suite, with a second bedroom on the upper level. Nothing appeared to be out of the ordinary—nothing moved or touched or left as evidence for someone to find. As far as Akira could tell, there was no indication that anyone had been there at all. She turned on a lamp, keeping in mind that stealth was essential. No one passing by on the outer deck would notice a woman walking into a room and turning on a few lights. What they would notice, however, was someone holding a flashlight and wandering around in the dark.

As she continued to explore, she took everything in. It was a nice setup after all: comfortable, neat, and efficient. But now it was time to get serious. No one knew where he had hidden the mysterious bag he'd brought with him, just as Takashi had planned. But something told her it was here and she needed to find it fast. Most of Akira's colleagues in Japan hated the mystery behind discovery. They wanted searches to be over quickly so they could move on to other disturbing things. But she enjoyed digging through private offices, apartments, and houses. Looking for fibers of the personality she'd been sent there to erase. In a morbid, twisted way, it was a challenge both in seeing what they considered valuable and in hiding her tracks, which she had learned to do skillfully.

Purely out of instinct, she approached the coat closet on the main floor and opened it to peer inside. Two white terrycloth bathrobes had been neatly tied with their belts and hung on the metal bar for new registered guests to use. There was an ironing board, white plastic bags, and a large cloth sack for dry cleaning.

On the back wall was a small conspicuous safe standing wide open. But the item that drew Akira's interest the most could have been easily ignored if someone didn't know what they were looking for. Draped on a hanger behind the robes and dry cleaning bag was a black, ominous-looking raincoat—the same type Akira had seen the night Dr. Bradshaw disappeared.

Akira set it aside on the back of a chair and took her time going through each room, searching every place she could think of. She didn't expect to find what she was looking for in any of the downstairs rooms. In all likelihood, it would be somewhere in the upstairs bedroom, which seemed to be a favorite hiding place with most of the people she'd been forced to murder. She looked under the cushions of all the furniture before making her way upstairs. As she had done while working on other assignments, Akira searched the drawers in the bedroom first before opening the closet. Both were empty, aside from traces of dust, white plastic hangers, and a hideous, outdated rack for luggage. She kneeled onto the thick plush carpet and looked under the bed. And lo and behold, there it was: the safe Takashi had talked about. It was of medium size, gray and insignificant in appearance. Not a black, impressive vault like she had imagined.

Akira reached out gingerly and nudged the safe. It didn't budge. For whatever reason, it was locked into place. She examined it more closely and then moved under the bed to see behind it. Everything looked clear, and although it was unlikely, the possibility of it being rigged with a trap dawned on her, but only for a brief moment.

She remembered Takashi's words about Zakura-kai symbols and numbers playing an important role in her life. But what did it mean? There were three tiny stars tattooed on her hip, each with five distinct points, equaling the number fifteen. With nothing else to go on, she turned the combination on the safe to the right, landing on three. It clicked. She turned it to the left, passing the first number and stopping on five. It clicked again. The tricky part came with determining how to proceed. Fifteen could be seven plus eight or ten plus five. She closed her eyes and tried to remember any clues Takashi might have left behind. Then she realized she needed to keep it simple—just like the man she'd come to know. She turned the dial to one and then five. The lock clinked with its final number, and the catch lifted. She looked inside the safe and found the black bag containing the money he had left for her. But there was another item inside the safe—something she wasn't expecting to see. A small black box with another mysterious lock.

With all the secrecy behind the key Takashi had worn, she should have expected it to lead to a treasure trove. But there was nothing unusual about this box aside from the shape of the lock. She reached into the safe and pulled it out, finding it heavier than she'd expected. Then she closed the safe again and stood up. Whatever was inside had to be extremely valuable with all the safeguards Takashi had taken. It was even possible that he had died for it, yet only the murderer would know that for sure.

Akira retraced her steps through the suite, turning off the lights as she went. Tempted by curiosity, she stopped at the final one in the hallway and examined the box in its weak glow. She knew it was wrong to take the additional time, especially with Clare waiting. Yet for some unknown reason, she couldn't shut off the need to know.

What if the metal box were empty? What if he had died for nothing? What would she do then? Akira slipped her hand down the front of her dress and pulled out the necklace Takashi had given to her. With very little effort, the key fit into the lock perfectly. She turned it, flicking up the clasp. Then she opened the lid and looked down to see what was inside. Her eyes widened in disbelief. It was a bronze dragon holding a crystal sphere. But what did it mean?

The sound of approaching footsteps traveled through the walls. Akira lost her grip on the box, and it fell, landing on the floor with a heavy thud. The lid snapped shut, and the clasp fell over, sealing the strange object inside once again. In an effort to act quickly, she hid it on the top shelf of the guest closet behind the spare pillows, closed the door, grabbed the key, and hurried downstairs.

"Hello?" A woman's voice came from outside the next room. "Are you in here?"

Akira eased the door shut between the suites and pocketed Takashi's key in the raincoat she'd slung over her shoulder. Then she picked up her sword, keeping it close to her, and watched for the intruder to appear.

"Oh, there you are," Felicia said. "I've been searching everywhere for you." She rushed into the room and cornered Clare. "Is everything all right in here?"

Akira responded for her. "Yes, of course. We're both fine." Clare was cautiously watching her, and she wasn't sure what to say.

Felicia raised her brows, confirming her curiosity. If she was aware of the murder one floor below them, she wasn't letting on. "Well, then we best be off," she said. "Sometimes Clare loses track of time and works past her scheduled hours. It seems I'm always on the lookout for her."

Akira's hand tightened on the sword's grip. "Before you go, I need some help."

Felicia put on a soft smile. "What is it?"

"A Japanese woman recently boarded this ship. Her name is Yuki Ota, but she might be using another name. I need to locate her as soon as possible without alerting anyone."

"And why is that?"

"I believe she knows something about the accident downstairs."

"Accident?" The crease between Felicia's brows deepened. "What accident? Did someone get hurt?"

There was movement in the hallway just beyond the open doorway. Devon stepped into the light, making his presence known. "More like murder," he said. "The one involving Mr. Hamada." There was no telling how long he'd been listening, and Akira resented his presence.

Felicia's mouth sagged. "Your father was killed? That kind gentleman? Where? When?"

"On one of the elevators," Devon explained. "About twenty minutes ago." His eyes were on Akira, judging her reactions. "There are men downstairs checking cameras, trying to determine who was involved."

She chewed on the corner of her lip, debating what to do next.

"Oh my Lord! That's horrible!" Felicia bellowed. "That means the murderer is running around loose. He could be planning to kill again. It might not be safe on this ship for any of us."

Clare was cowering next to her, looking like a frightened child.

"Has the captain been notified?" Devon asked Akira.

"I'm sure he has."

"Then the FBI will handle this—as soon as they arrive." Akira almost laughed. Nothing was going to happen, and she knew it. The captain hadn't contacted anyone. If he had, the FBI would already be here, asking everyone questions, securing suites, and locking down floors. Brice was simply biding his time until the ship arrived in Florida and he could jump ship and safely escape.

"I think it would be best if you all went back to your rooms," Akira said. "There's no reason to get involved in any of this."

Devon glanced down at the sword in her hand and snorted in amusement. "So it was yours after all. I should've known." The seriousness in his voice was apparent. She looked past him, ignoring the scowl on his face. "There's a murderer on this ship threatening who knows how many lives," he railed, "and you're going to pretend to be Wonder Woman, single-handedly taking him down?"

Talking to him was a waste of breath, but Akira's inner voice urged her to go on. "This isn't something you need to worry about, Devon. Please go be with your family. I can take care of myself."

Although Devon didn't seem to notice, Clare's eyes were fixed on his face, studying him from every angle.

"You have no way of knowing that," he said. "If the murderer overpowered your father or whoever the hell he was, then they could take you down as well."

"I'm a skilled professional," Akira said, "fully equipped to handle this situation. Now please go back to the dining room and look after your uncle and aunt. And whatever you do, don't tell them what happened tonight. Just get them back to their room safely. I'll call you when I'm through. Can you do that for me?"

Felicia stood tall, but her charge was still huddling. "I don't understand," she said. "Why do you have a sword? Are you a Japanese detective or something?"

Akira's eyes met Devon's. "Yeah, something."

"Come on, Clare." The lead housekeeper beckoned. "Let's go back to our room and lock the door. We're staying there until this is over." She steered the mute woman toward the elevator, but Clare's gray eyes never left Devon, leaving Akira questioning her interest in him.

"Do you know her?"

"Know who?"

"That woman...Clare? Have you ever seen her before?"

"No, of course not. Why are you changing the subject? I hope you're not planning to do something stupid."

Akira dispelled her curiosity in light of his abrasive remark. "I can't tell you." She laid the coat over the back of a chair and leaned her sword against the wall.

"You're not going anywhere on this ship without me."

Shadows crawled over the world around her, and the thick tension in the air made it hard to breathe. Her mind transported her back to the bathroom floor on the observation deck, magnifying the pain of his cruel words. She turned away from Devon and stared at the floor, tightening her hands at her sides.

"Are you listening to me?" He grabbed her arm, spinning her around, bringing her right fist with her. She struck him hard in the jaw, knocking him out cold. Akira was stunned for a moment and stared down at his silent face, amazed at what she had done. It was a reflex action, not a deliberate attack. She would never do anything to hurt him, not ever. But on the other hand, she couldn't have Devon in the way. He would only complicate matters, and there was no telling what Yuki would do with him.

Akira grabbed his arms at the elbow and dragged him into the next room. It took every ounce of her strength to pull him onto her bed. She arranged his head on the pillow, then looked down at him, frowning. "Why did you make me do that? Damn it, Devon."

Akira shook her head at that. "Moron. It's a good thing I love you as much as I do." She leaned down and kissed his forehead.

"Now stay here. Do you hear me? I'll be back to look after you. I promise."

She untied her dress, letting it slide to the floor, and glanced back at Devon. "Too bad you're not awake now, huh?" She half laughed at her words. After searching in the drawers, she found her black jeans and a matching T-shirt. She put them on and found her black tennis shoes under the bed. Then she looped her hair into a knotted ponytail and surveyed her appearance in the mirror. The trained assassin was back, ready for action.

"I don't know where you are, Yuki, or why you found it necessary to kill Takashi," she said to herself. "But I'm going to find you and end this once and for all."

Akira returned to the living room and picked up the master key Clare had left behind. She opened the leather binder provided by the cruise director, ripped out the three pages diagramming the ship, and folded them neatly. If it took all night, she would search every room from floor to ceiling until she found the murderous bitch. But first, it was time to make plans. Akira needed to think clearly—to ready herself for her greatest challenge. She knew no one else had the expertise to do what Yuki had done or was more remorseless. Aside from the black, oversize raincoat she had taken, there were no clues in the neighboring suite to help guide her—no way to know where her clever adversary might be hiding or who her next victim might be. She needed answers and permission to proceed, and the only way to get them was by calling Zakura-kai headquarters in Japan.

Akira picked up her cell phone just as the phone in her room rang. It was the reception desk downstairs with an urgent message waiting. Something about an envelope with her name written on it. She hurried downstairs to accept it and tucked it into her back pocket without reading it. Then she waited before the elevator for what seemed like an eternity, anxious to get back to her room. She was eager to get on her cell phone and hear what Mitsui-san had to say after learning the horrible news about Takashi.

Devon rolled over and sat up, rubbing his jaw. He looked around the dark room and picked up Akira's dress from the end of the bed. Her perfume was emanating from it—the soft scent of lavender that followed her everywhere. He was stunned by the realization that she had actually hit him, taken him out with one powerful punch. *Wow.* It was surreal. Even though he had been on the receiving end of her pent-up anger, he was actually impressed by her sheer strength when it came to defending herself.

Devon walked out of her bedroom and noticed that the door to the connecting suite was slightly ajar. A beam of light passed by, and footsteps could be heard inside. Moving closer, he whispered, "Akira? Are you in there?"

While keeping a watchful eye, he opened the door wider and stepped inside. The blinds were closed, and the lights were out, making it nearly impossible to see. There were more footsteps coming from the next room, propelling his interest. He walked toward the sound, allowing his eyes to adjust slowly to the dark. Everything had become shadows, even the furniture, making it difficult to maneuver in each room. Edging against the wall, he flipped on a light switch and discovered it wasn't working.

Damn card keys.

"Akira," he called out again. What was she doing in here, and why wasn't she answering? Then it dawned on him—maybe it wasn't her. Devon stumbled a bit, trying to find the front door. He was preparing to leave when another sound stopped him in his tracks. Footsteps were now coming from behind him. He clenched his fists and waited until he sensed a presence close by. Then he spun around quickly, ready to battle whoever was in the room. He was instantly grabbed by the arm and slammed to the floor. Shocked by the sheer force of the attack, he stumbled to get back on his feet and quickly regained his composure.

Devon moved back out of range and looked around the room, his heart racing wildly. Before he could think twice, his attacker stepped forward, and his features became more clear. The man looked slightly older than Devon, Samoan, and definitely larger.

After realizing his arms were up and fixed, Devon got ready to beat the shit out of him. He had been in the ring with a great number of boxers and knew how to anticipate their moves. He swung his fist toward the man's broad nose, halting his attacker long enough to verify his injury. He took his hand away, revealing a smear of blood. Then he wiped it off on his pants, and his glare intensified.

Suddenly he pounced, sending both of them crashing to the floor. Before Devon knew it, the guy was on top of him, hovering over his face, pinning his arm to one side. Devon tried to push him off, but the maniac was as heavy as he looked. His fist smacked into Devon's lip, slitting it wide open and filling his mouth with blood. He swung again in rapid procession, connecting with Devon's neck, forehead, chest, and arms. Blood ran down Devon's face, but he wasn't about to give up. He threw a hook into the man's flabby side, causing him to yelp and roll over onto his chest.

Devon climbed onto his feet and dropped a knee into the guy's back. Then he slugged the man's head twice and banged it on the floor, hoping to knock him out. But the guy surprised him with a back kick to his nuts.

"Holy shit!" Devon yelled, falling to the floor in pain.

The guy was sweating profusely yet managed to get back on his feet. He lunged forward, and Devon delivered a series of blows to his rib cage. Then he shoved the assailant away. He retaliated by grabbing Devon by the neck and jammed his thumb into his throat, cutting off his air supply. He let go for some reason, and Devon rolled onto his side, coughing and choking—trying to get his breath. The guy stared down at him, and Devon thought it was finally over—that he was satisfied with the damage he had inflicted. But he was terribly wrong. The monstrous man leaned down and struck him full force across the face. Devon tried to get up but was kicked to the ground again. He grabbed a chair and tried to pull himself up, but his knees buckled underneath him. He looked up from his kneeling position and tried to focus on the face of the villain standing before him, but everything was disorientated, and a feeling of nausea overwhelmed him.

"Why?" Devon managed to whisper as the man stepped closer. "Why are you doing this?" He took another blast across the face, instantly knocking him out.

31

PREPARATION

After activating her Japanese SIM card, Akira pressed the listing for Mitsui-san's number and waited anxiously for him to answer his phone. It rang six times with no answer. She was desperate to act quickly but knew repercussions could result from taking matters into her own hands. She checked her e-mail messages and was surprised to find one waiting from a former friend and fellow geiko in Kyoto—a woman she had lost track of three years ago.

Please accept my condolences for the tragic loss of your Oka-san.
Everyone feels deep sorrow. You are in our thoughts and prayers.
Be safe, Mariko-chan. Love, Nori.

The message further explained that Mitsui-san was looking after everyone in the teahouse and would be spending a few days in Tokyo. He would make all the funeral arrangements after returning home tomorrow.

Akira stared at the message in disbelief. She checked the date on the forwarded e-mail and realized there had been some confusion on her address. No matter. She was heartsick over the loss of Oka-san and at the same time relieved to learn the reason for her inability to reach Mitsui-san. She pressed the number for her geisha sister in Kyoto, anxious to gain more information. But Tamayo didn't answer. Growing impatient, she tried the assistant housemother's number and was relieved when she picked up on the third ring.

"It was terrible," she said in Japanese. "I can't believe it. It's so unfair, so unfair."

Akira commiserated with her. "I agree. It's very sad. She was a kind, caring woman. This shouldn't have happened to her. I should have been there."

There was a pause, and then Akira heard a sound she couldn't identify, followed by an expletive from a man. It sounded as if Mitsui-san had suddenly snatched the phone away from the housemother. Without missing a beat, he asked her, "Where are you? Did you open the box I sent with Takashi?"

Akira was confused by his question. She told him that she was still at sea and would be returning to Florida soon. That Takashi had hidden it, but she managed to find it.

"Why would he do that? Where is he?" Mitsui-san was obviously upset. "He had specific orders. Why didn't he follow them?"

Akira explained how she had left the dining room and gone searching for him. When she couldn't find him, she was told by a crew member about his horrible death in the elevator.

"Why...that's wrong. So wrong!" Mitsui-san said. "Do you have any idea how it happened?"

She explained what she knew and her suspicion about Yuki, especially after receiving the note from Oka-san.

He was quiet for a long moment, and then he asked, "When did you get this note?"

Akira racked her brain. What was the time? She thought it was shortly before Takashi was killed. Only a few hours ago.

"Your Oka-san didn't write it," he told her. "It would have been impossible. "She...died right after you left Japan more than ten days ago." Mitsui-san's voice echoed in the room, or was it just in Akira's head? Her throat closed up; her eyes filled with angry tears. She scanned the room with a sweeping look and located her sword, resting against the wall in the far corner.

"Why didn't you tell me? I had a right to know."

"What? That I believe Yuki was involved? That's not important right now," he said. "Let's focus on one thing at a time. You were sent there to do a job. Is it done?"

Not important? How could he say that? How could he be so callous? The only reason she had come here was to keep Oka-san safe.

"Akira, listen! Is it done?"

"If you're asking about Bradshaw, the answer is yes."

"Good, good. Now I need you to be careful. Yuki is on that ship, and she wants you dead. It involves a matter I'd rather not get into right now. But I want you to take whatever steps are necessary. Do you get what I'm saying?"

"Yes."

"And about Takashi—I'll have some men waiting after you arrive. I want him brought back to Japan for the funeral. He deserves to be with his family and friends."

"What about Yuki?"

Mitsui-san was quiet. Then he said, "Leave her for the sharks." He abruptly hung up, leaving Akira more frustrated than ever. A flush of rage surged through her at the thought of coming face-to-face with Yuki. She had barely gotten over the shock of Takashi's death, and now there was Oka-san to think about. Why would Yuki kill a defenseless old woman? A person who never caused anyone harm? It made absolutely no sense at all.

Akira had to steel herself for the worst, knowing how exploitative and abusive Yuki could be. She was a blighter of a woman and didn't know what was off-limits and what was acceptable. Her loyalty was only to herself, never to any other person. As much as she must have hated Akira, Takashi and Oka-san didn't deserve to die.

It took a full minute for her to center herself and examine the note supposedly from Takashi.

Mariko: I know you hate that name, but it's the way I always think of you. I tried to call you six times today, but you didn't answer the phone. I can only hope that you get this note before it's too late. Yuki Ota is on this ship. I spotted her when everyone went sightseeing two days ago. I've been following her since then, trying to understand why she's here. The only thing I can figure out is that she knows about Mitsui-san's plans for you. I'm sure she's angry and extremely disappointed, but you're not to blame. Not in any shape or form. The best thing to do is to arrange a meeting with her and find a way to resolve this, even if it involves compromise. No matter what she believes, she needs to respect Mitsui-san's decision and honor his wishes in all things.—Hamada-san.

Takashi's message fanned the flames of Akira's anger. She recalled their verbal sparring matches, as well as their unspoken acrimonies—unspoken because he had no wish to upset her. Even so, Akira knew she needed to accede to his advice by meeting up with Yuki and reminding her about her coming break with the Zakura-kai. Takashi must have worried she wouldn't get his note in time. Did he know he was going to die? That Yuki was going to kill him? That Akira was in terrible danger as well? Her hand ached, and she looked down in surprise to find she had squeezed the note into a tiny ball. She smoothed out the paper like it would bring Takashi back, but the neatly written kanji just sat there, providing a painful memory of her partner.

It dawned on Akira that Devon was still sleeping in the next room, as quiet as a cat. She needed to check on him and make sure he was safe before leaving. There was no telling if she'd ever see him again, and it was important to tell him goodbye without him knowing what she was up against.

She walked into her bedroom and was surprised to discover he was gone. The bedspread was half off the mattress, and his white jacket had been tossed on the floor. No doubt he had woken up angry and stormed off in a fit. She would have to find a way to apologize—if he were willing to listen. But that would have to wait. Enough time had already been wasted. She needed to concentrate on what needed to be done.

After returning to the living room, she had the clarity of mind to call down to the reception desk and book a limousine to take her to the airport after arriving in Port Everglades. Then she drew the curtains, darkening the room. She closed her eyes and relaxed her thoughts through meditation, knowing she would need to be mentally prepared to face her greatest adversary. But then the strangest thing happened. She imaged herself standing on a cliff, engaged in heated argument with Yuki. The two of them charged at each other, and then Yuki spun around, backfisting Akira, sending her flying. She was falling from the cliff's edge, screaming in fear. She reached out and grabbed a tree root. She held on tight, willing herself to stay strong. Then she opened her eyes and looked around. A cold chill in the room left her rubbing her arms. Was it Takashi? Was it his ghost? Was he still looking out for her, even now?

32

TWISTED

Devon tried one eye slowly, opening it in the dim light. A black floor came into focus, and a deep darkness traveled far beyond him. *Christ Almighty!* How did he end up here? He rolled onto his right side, and dizziness assaulted his senses. His head hurt, but he had to get up. Had to—his uncle would be searching for him again, worrying that he had done something stupid.

Devon moved his legs and heard a clink. Something pulled at his left ankle. He dug the toe of his shoe into the uneven floor and tugged back. But whatever it was held firm. He twisted his body so he could see in the dimness. Was that a chain? Connected to his ankle? To a thick ring in the floor? This was ridiculous. The worst parody of a dungeon in the bottom of a cruise ship. If his head didn't hurt so badly, he would actually laugh.

The sound of distant steps caught his ear. Devon tried to turn, groaning when he lay on his left side, and his head touched the floor. He shut his eyes, clenching his teeth, fighting against the growing pain. The steps drew closer. One set? Two? Three? He waited, lying there, swimming in pain and cold, realizing something was wrong with his head. Was that Akira? Why had she done this? Sara would be pissed, yelling about the delay. The delay of what? Something important, he was sure of it.

Suddenly a hand was on his hair, grabbing a fistful, jerking him up and onto his knees. The chain tugged at his left ankle. His arms struggled to brace himself at the sudden movement, because something was holding them back. He moaned with his eyes closed, feeling dizzier by the second. His head was pulled back farther. He opened his eyes slowly, blinking at shapes and at the light overhead, which suddenly swung into view. His eyes teared up, and he struggled to stay on his knees. The hand held onto his hair and jerked his head again, pulling it back so that he was staring at the ceiling. He waited for what would come next, his heart pounding wildly in his chest. Something cold and sharp pressed against his throat. He shivered from the cold air moving around him. It was eating into his skin, causing little spasms. The jacket—the white jacket he was wearing would have been warm right now, especially with no shirt covering his chest.

A glistening knife danced before his eyes. "Devon. It's so kind of you to join us," a deep voice said. "I've been looking forward to entertainment all night." A face was near his—a man's, he was sure of it. He was holding Devon's hair in a painful grip, leering at him. He'd seen this face before, but where?

A woman's low laugh left Devon shivering more. "He's beautiful, Michael," she said. "Even with bruises, he's much prettier up close."

The man who had spoken to Devon laughed. "Better than me?"

The woman stepped into Devon's range of view and leaned over him. Her hand stroked his cheek and touched the left side of his head. "Oh yes. Definitely."

Devon groaned, turning away. She slapped his face hard, opening the wound on his lip. Warm blood filled his mouth and trickled down his chin. He swallowed, his breath coming in little shudders. His head ached from the vicious beating he had taken. *Shit.* Did he honestly deserve all this?

"Don't turn from me," the woman said. Her hand came back, stroking his jaw with one finger and trailing down his throat with one nail.

The guy she had called Michael moved the knife back before Devon's eyes. "You shouldn't get too close, Yuki," he said. "He's dangerous."

She laughed. "Dangerous? Don't be ridiculous. I'm the only threat here."

Michael waved the knife again, touching the tip of it to Devon's cheek. "By now, you're probably wondering why you're here, Mr. Lyons. It's very simple, you see. I just want to know where the money is. The bag Hamada brought with him on the ship." He leaned close to Devon, the knife moving down his throat, pricking at his collarbone. "It's not in the safe or anywhere in their room. Where did Akira hide it? She must have told you after he died."

Devon blinked, shaking his head. *Money? Hamada?* Snapshots flashed in his brain. Akira laughing. Her father frowning. Blood spreading across the floor.

Devon got another smack across his mouth, sending his head jerking back. The hand was still there, holding him by his hair.

"Tell me!" Michael shouted. "Don't be stupid. She's not worth it." Another smack, then another. Blood was trickling from both corners of his mouth, down his neck, and across his throat. His eyes rolled back in his skull, and his vision blurred. His deep groan sounded strange in his ears.

"He'll never tell you," Yuki said. Her hand was back, dabbing a tissue on the corner of Devon's mouth, simulating a sympathetic touch.

"Use the drugs," Michael said. "The ones you found in Bradshaw's room."

She shook her head, visible even in the dimness. "No. They'll only make him sleepy—and I need him to be wide awake for this." Her long, black, wavy hair swished down her back with every step. Her eyes were dark and striking like Akira's, but different. *Very* different. And there were three gold stars tattooed on the side of her neck, distinct and perhaps significant. He'd seen them before. But where?

On Akira?

"You're wasting time. If he doesn't know anything, then why are we bothering with him? Get rid of this fool and bring Akira here. She's the one with all the answers."

A low chuckle came from the woman, and somehow it was more terrifying than anything Michael had said. "He really *is* beautiful, Donley." There was a sound of soft clicking heels on the hard floor as she moved about. "So perfect." She touched Devon's hair and smiled. "Exactly what I need."

"You...need? What kind of game are you playing, Yuki? What about the money you promised to give me? If anyone finds out about this..."

"Don't worry, sweetheart. All I need is one day." Her hand was on Devon again, moving down his chest and causing an intake of breath. "Akira will come looking for him when she figures it out. Then I'll get what we both want."

Devon shuddered. His breath was ragged, and his body twitched from the cold. Yuki's hand moved over his stomach and down the front of his pants, as though she had every right to molest him. He turned away only to feel her fingers on his right nipple. She twisted it until he cried out in pain.

"Uhhh!" He squeezed his eyes shut and clenched his teeth. But no matter how much he wanted it, she wouldn't go away.

"I told you to never turn from me." Her hand was back at it again, touching and teasing. He blew out a breath and held still. "Much better," she said. Her hand was groping the front of his pants, measuring the length of his cock. "Ah yes. This is going to be fun."

"Fine," Michael said, sighing. "You've got ten hours. I have a first-class seat on a plane to Cuba on Sunday at eight fifteen a.m. If you don't deliver as promised, believe me: you'll wish you had."

Devon could hear him walking away. He needed to memorize his name. *Michael Donley*. Wait a minute. Was that the man who had greeted them when they arrived? Who had organized all the games and activities on the ship?

The cruise director on this fucking ship?

Yuki laughed. "Don't let anything he said affect you, angel. He won't live long enough to get off this ship. He's already served his purpose, but you have so much to give."

Three years ago, Devon had been physically tortured by a drug lord in San Palo. He could take the beatings if he had to and give as good as he got. But sex abuse was a different matter altogether—a game he had no interest in playing.

"Why are you doing this, Yuki?" he asked. "I don't know you, and I don't know anything about hidden money. I swear! Please just let me go, and we'll pretend this never happened."

She smiled. "Oh, aren't you sweet? I'd love to give you what you want, puppy. Truly I would. But I have needs of my own. And they don't involve Donley's money. What I'm interested in is much more important. I want to know about the box. The one

Hamada brought with him on this ship. I know that Akira tells you everything, Devon. She trusts you more than anyone in this world. Tell me where it is, and I'll let you walk out of here. I'll let you fly to New Mexico and go scuba diving for that treasure you're hoping to find."

What the hell? "You were listening to me? Where? When? How is that even possible?"

Yuki smiled. "Oh, you'd be amazed what I can do."

Devon had reached his limit. "I don't know anything about money or some goddamn box. And even if I did, why would I tell you?"

"Is that a nice way to talk, angel?" Yuki ran her fingers down the side of his neck about an inch below the base of his ear and rested them against his pulse. "Oh yes. I've heard you call her that. Sweet, wonderful, innocent Akira. Did you know she kills men for a living?"

Devon shook his head, refusing to listen. Yuki was lying—trying to deceive him to get what she wanted.

"I've been everywhere on this ship watching the two of you—talking about art, people, travel, and your aspirations. Jamming your tongue down her throat and your hands down her pants when you thought no one was around." She brought her face close to his. "You have no idea what a real master of sex can do. But you're going to find out very soon." She placed her palm on the side of his neck and bounced it a few times. And like a punch to his chin, blackness was instant.

A slow brightness was growing again, but this time there was something different—a soft pad under his cheek. Devon moved his arms slowly to test his restrictions and discovered nothing was holding him back. Was he free? Was it all just a crazy dream? He turned his head, opened his eyes slowly, and pulled himself onto his forearms. He was in a large elegant suite—a room unlike any he had seen before. Beneath him was light gold carpet, and across from him were red and gold curtains drawn shut. He moved forward and was instantly choked. Something was cinched around his throat, snatching him back. His fingers told him it was some sort of collar like a dog would wear. But there was no buckle, only a metal link at the front. It was connected to a chain, pinning him to the floor. It had enough length to allow him to crouch and kneel but not stand. He grabbed the ring in the floor and tugged it with both hands. There was no give. He braced his foot against it and blinked. Where the hell were his shoes? The chain dropped from his hands as he looked down at his pants.

"Holy shit," he muttered. "What the hell is going on?" His chest was still bare, but his legs were now covered. He was wearing black leather pants, snug and soft. A mesh metal jockstrap had been custom fitted and was tightly locked in place. He held up one of his wrists to the light, trying to determine if the black leather cuffs were soldered on.

Devon took a deep breath and let it out as a sigh. How long had he been like this...unconscious and sadistically bound? He touched his face and winced when his fingers reached his mouth. The fresh blood on his fingertips told him it hadn't been long. He remembered the slaps and a woman's dark brown eyes glaring at him—and being punched in the jaw by Akira. *Damn.* What was it with Asian women and their need for control?

There was a tall metal vase on the floor, polished and seamless. Devon moved closer and could make out a bruise on his cheek and chin. His bottom lip had a fresh cut and was slightly swollen, confirming the reality of his situation. He closed his eyes and sat cross-legged, holding his head. After his attacker finished with him, there were voices, hands grabbing him, rolling him over, and taking him somewhere.

To here?

He looked up again, rubbing his hands on his arms. He grabbed the chain holding his neck to the floor and tugged hard. There was no give. He braced his bare foot against the link and pulled again, arriving at the same ineffective result.

"Ah ah ah!" Yuki said cheerfully.

Devon looked up, still holding the chain. The woman was back again, eyeing him with a devious smile. She was wearing a red satin sleeveless gown, the neckline cut in a Mandarin style. Her black hair was pulled back into a tight bun and secured with a red-lacquered chopstick. Her nails were bloodred, and her lipstick matched, reminding him of a female vampire.

"Where am I?" Devon asked, his voice raspy in his own ears.

"You're in a private room," she answered. "It's called the Presidential Suite. A place Michael reserves for his *very* special guests." Yuki moved slowly around the living room space, motioning at a young, slender woman who was dressed in a black kimono. She rushed to her side and bowed her head. Yuki whispered something, and the frightened creature skittered away, returning with a tall, icy drink.

"Are you thirsty, Devon?" Yuki asked sweetly, crossing her legs in a black velvet chair.

Devon swallowed hard. "I don't understand. Why are you doing this?"

Akira rocked her foot nonchalantly. "I do love your accent. English? But just a hint. Perhaps you left England as a child? Or had parents in America who came from there?" She spoke as though they were at a tea party.

Devon hated crouching on the floor in front of her. He wanted to stand and was tired and sore. "Who are you?" he demanded to know. The smile left her face in an instant. She snapped her fingers, and the huge Samoan man was back. He grabbed Devon's chain in one hand and his left wrist in the other. He twisted the wrist up behind his back until his head hit the floor. Then he jerked at the collar. Something inside of it constricted, closing on Devon's throat and cutting off his air supply.

He bucked against the man, gasping for air, and fought against the pain in his head. He pushed against the floor with his right foot, trying to get some leverage against this oppressive beast, until black dots began forming.

Yuki nodded at the man who held him. The pressure eased, and Devon was left panting like a dog. But the beast kept him grounded by painfully twisting his arm back.

Yuki touched Devon's hair tenderly and smiled. "As to your question, it's not who I am, my dear Devon. It's who you are."

He frowned, gasping as his arm was jerked.

Yuki smoothed his hair again. "Poor baby. It hurts, doesn't it? I'm afraid it's going to hurt a lot more before we're through." Her hand continued to stroke his hair, while the man behind him held his arm until it was numb.

"Oh, I almost forgot," she said. "This is Cujo. I believe you met each other a few hours ago. He has a great right hook, but he needs to work on blocking. Don't you agree?"

Devon was pulled to his knees, his left arm still behind him.

Yuki stood, smiling pleasantly. She paced before him while she talked in a steady rhythm. "So you really want to know who I am, huh? Well, let's start with this. You may only call me ma'am or mistress. Whichever you prefer. I'm afraid those are the only options you have while you're in my care. As to who you are…why, Devon, you're my prisoner to use any way I desire." She halted her steps and looked down at him. "Until I grow tired of you."

33

For the watcher, there was great reason to celebrate Bradshaw's death. He was responsible for falsifying documents, kidnapping a child, fucking up his patients, and basically ruining a lot of lives. However, the true culprit was still breathing, along with her new bosom buddy. They had come close to preventing the doctor's richly deserved death by wandering about as drunken, mindless fools. Fortunately, the dark angel had arrived on the sixth floor just in the nick of time—accomplishing what the watcher could only dream about. However, these dim-witted beings would continue to be a constant irritation if not dealt with in a timely manner. The ship would be docking soon, and all its inhabitants would disembark, never to be seen again. The only chance to enact the watcher's final solution would have to occur during breakfast, since no one would suspect poison in their food.

It had been easy enough to travel through rooms, corridors, and passageways without drawing suspicion. But gaining access to the kitchen could prove more difficult, unless some naïve soul was an unwitting participant. It would have to be a simpleminded individual, incapable of believing that anyone would think about committing murder, especially when it involved two of the people around her.

Vivian Ward. She was the perfect dolt. There was no doubt about it. She lived in an imaginary wonderland: playing board games, tasting tidbits, and folding napkins into cranes, while the man she kept company with discussed his practice of destroying minds in his so-called mental health clinic.

Fortunately, during ocean-bound voyages around the world, there had been great opportunities for the watcher to visit exotic ports and learn about the magic of poisons. One of the most fascinating just happened to be blowfish, a delicious delicacy in Japan. With sushi being so popular in the dining room and one of Dr. Hoffman's favorite dishes, it would be so easy to add the neurotoxin the watcher had smuggled aboard. As the doctor gracefully gripped slivers of raw fish with his wooden chopsticks, dipped them into his small bowl of soy sauce and wasabi, and happily munched away, the poison would enter his bloodstream and begin its deadly process. How invigorating it would be to watch him drool and whimper while his respiratory muscles contracted.

Then there was that lovely salad ingredient—a delicious toxin discovered while visiting a marshland in northern England. Ah yes—water hemlock. Such a pretty little flower. The most wretched passenger on this ship had a fondness for parsnips and other root vegetables. One tasty mouthful is all it would take to exterminate the disgusting creature.

Last of all, there was a very special poison in the watcher's arsenal—the one that had been saved for the perfect occasion. It could be injected at any given moment with the dart gun the watcher had acquired in southern Africa. This remarkable concoction would induce a heart attack within minutes and leave the victim believing they'd been bitten by a mosquito, or perhaps they wouldn't feel it at all. But once the damage was done, the poison would vanish quickly in the bloodstream, leaving everyone believing the victim had died from natural causes.

Ah...decisions, decisions. Perhaps the best solution was to utilize all three, saving the best for last. Then there wouldn't be any chance of failing. The mere thought of fulfilling the long-awaited dream made the watcher smile and stand a bit taller.

Yet time was running out, and acquiring Vivian's assistance was paramount. There was a nice vegetable soup on the breakfast menu and a savory whitefish with potatoes. With Sara Lyons feeling sick, her dear friend could bring it up to her room as a show of support and encourage her to take nourishment. Of course, Dr. Hoffman would scarf down the fish in nothing flat, believing himself entitled to it all. The whole process would only involve a room service order and request that Vivian deliver the peace offerings to her bosom buddies at the captain's request. He already had five blemishes on his record for the deaths on this ship, so what would it matter if there were a few more?

34

TRAPPED

Devon tried to sit up, but his body wouldn't obey. He lifted one foot and was greeted by the rattle of a heavy chain holding it to the floor. After his captor tormented him with a leather whip and attempted to dispel his love for Akira, Devon couldn't imagine what she was planning next.

The sound of a door slamming came from the next room. Yuki entered the space where Devon was being held and walked past him dressed in a red bra and matching lace panties. At the sight of her bare skin, he caught his breath and gulped. Her body was covered in ink, from the massive butterfly on her lower abdomen to the lotus blossom, peonies, koi, and female pirate on her back and shoulders. A nasty looking dragon twisted around her waist, moving as she paced back and forth.

"Ah, sweet Devon," she said. "What am I going to do with you?" She halted her steps and looked down at him. "Wait, don't try to answer. I'm going to do something ridiculous and ask you to tell me something, but hear what I have to say first. I promise it will be worth your while."

Devon fought against the pain in his head before slowly opening his eyes again. Yuki's red lips and wicked cat eyes were a few feet in front of him. He tried to move, to get up, but the sound of the chains reaffirmed his predicament. He wanted to scream from the anger swelling up inside him, but something had been jammed in his mouth.

"I am very serious, Devon. You need to listen to me, or you'll die."

He shut his eyes again and concentrated on slowing his breathing. Despite Yuki's failed efforts to break him, she continued her relentless assault.

"Listen to me, Devon," she said quietly, kneeling down in front of him. "I don't want to hurt you. Not physically anyway. But I had to take some precautions. You understand, of course," she said, smiling. "By now, I'm sure you've realized that I'm keeping you on a chain while you're in this room. But rest assured, I put a lot of thought into keeping you secure. There's no point in struggling or screaming for help. By doing so, sweetheart, you'll only endanger yourself. And I know you'll agree with me that while we're on this ship, it's all about safety first."

Separate chains led from the cuffs on his ankles to the heavy links drilled into the floor, forcing his legs into an uncomfortable, splayed position. He tried to shift his body, but the pressure from the collar was too much, and he was forced to look straight ahead.

"Don't worry about that just yet," she said. "We have more important matters to discuss. Remember what I told you about Akira killing those three men in Kanto, Japan? Well, that was nothing compared to the Mikami massacre. She single-handedly took out six men in a communal bathhouse before they could get off a single round. Rather impressive for a sweet, adorable geisha, huh? Now does that sound like someone you'd want to spend the rest of your life with?"

Devon tried to reply, but his dry mouth, held open by yet more metal, produced only another groan.

"I'm sure that you think yourself capable of ripping those chains off; however, I wouldn't recommend trying it. The manacles around your neck, arms, and legs all have extremely sharp metal spikes built inside. You can probably feel them pricking against your skin even now. If you struggle too hard, those spikes will penetrate some of your major arteries, spilling your blood all over this beautiful room. I would imagine that your death will be quick though, if not painless." Yuki moved to mere inches from Devon's face and grinned, her white teeth gleaming in the light. "After all, my training has left me skilled in the most interesting forms of torture. It really is a true talent when you sit down and think about it."

Yuki stood up and grabbed Devon by his hair, yanking his head upward.

Devon twitched in his bonds.

"You see, puppy dog, I'm hoping you'll make the right choice by understanding your situation and delivering what I asked for." She smiled again. "By the way, I have to say that I didn't think I would be able to squeeze you into those tight leather pants. I have to give you credit there. You're pretty well endowed for a pup."

Devon began squirming, his frustration and rage building. He watched as the young woman approached with a glass of water in her hand, stopping at the side of the sadistic ma'am. He could tell there was something wrong with her, as her eyes appeared to be fixed with a blank, vacant stare. Was this a geisha too?

"Doesn't he look good—so natural sitting there, Tamayo?"

The young woman nodded obediently.

"By the looks of him, you would never know he's your half brother. But then you've never officially met, unlike Rachel Lyons and her husband, Chase Cohen. How sweet it must have been for the three of you in Japan, making plans for a wonderful life together. Unfortunately, I wasn't able to join in the celebration because I was excommunicated by my father-in-law and sent to Thailand for two years. Thanks to all of you, of course."

Tamayo kept her eyes low.

"*Kaesite!*" Yuki snapped, and Tamayo gave her the glass with both hands. Then she bowed her head and lowered herself into a kneeling position next to her mistress.

"Now let me recap for you, Devon," Yuki said, "just so you're perfectly clear. If you can manage to behave for five minutes, I might lighten up your restraints a bit. But for now, you're just going to have to deal with them until I'm ready to move on. You see, I only have one more hour to play with you, and I'd hate for both of us to be disappointed." She set the water down on a table before him. "I'm going to ask you once again, are you thirsty? If the answer is yes, then nod nicely for me."

Devon paused before nodding slowly, mindful of the spikes in the manacles.

"Good. Now, on your knees. I'm going to remove a chain, but I need you to put your hands behind your back first."

Devon furrowed his brow in concentration as Yuki leaned over him, her hands on his shoulders.

"Control, " she whispered seductively in his ear. "Close your eyes and bow your head."

Devon could feel beads of sweat collecting on his forehead and at the back of his neck as he shifted uncomfortably on his knees. His lips moved as he silently repeated Yuki's command to himself. She took the first short length of chain and wrapped it through a ring on each of Devon's wrist cuffs. Then she passed it through multiple times, ensuring that his hands were held tightly together. She repeated the process with his ankles and took the longest chain and attached one end to the ring in the back of his collar.

Devon's head was pulled back slightly by the pressure on his neck.

"Are you ready to obey? Because if you're not, this will come to an end—and so will you."

Devon nodded slowly.

Yuki moved behind him and waited a full minute before speaking again. "Tamayo, assist him."

The young geisha hurried to his side and lifted the glass to Devon's mouth. There was a tinge of blue in the water, but Devon chose to ignore it in light of his desperate thirst. He gulped down the water like a dying man, swallowing it as fast as it came. He coughed and could feel his throat constrict, leaving him gasping for air. His instinct was to breathe in, but the tingling in his body was a reminder to exhale. Eventually, the muscles in his throat loosened a bit to where he could get small amounts of air in and out of his lungs.

"*Da me!*" Yuki yelled, knocking the glass away. "*Ike.*"

Tamayo scampered into the next room like a wounded animal.

"I have to admit she's not the best servant I've ever had. But bringing your half sister here was an absolute necessity. I need to demonstrate to everyone that I've earned my right to rule—much like a queen in a castle. You see, challenging my authority has been Akira's greatest downfall. In spite of my father-in-law's claims, she needs to step down and disappear."

Yuki checked the time on her watch. Then she glanced at him and smiled. "Let's not waste time on idle conversation. Normally

I have three or four days for this sort of thing. But you've been so busy running around, and so have I—preparing everything just for you."

Devon had dozens of questions gathering in his brain, but this woman wasn't about to answer any of them. Not without getting something in return. Something he couldn't provide. He looked down, trying to remember. What was it? A box?

"Did you know this ship is a floating pharmacy?" she said. "It's amazing what you can find with so many doctors on board. You know there's even one that specializes in erectile dysfunction? Can you imagine *that*? Oh, but then I guess that isn't a problem for you. Especially right now—after all the pills you ingested."

Pills? Devon willed himself to remain calm, but his body had other ideas in mind—ideas that were beyond his mastery.

Yuki smiled. "I understand you have a reputation as a sex machine. You should be *real* proud of yourself for that." He watched as she moved behind him. She leaned down and whispered in his ear, "I've always loved virile men."

Her hands touched the chains on the back of his waist. He heard the clink of the lock as she removed it. The metal jockstrap between his legs fell away, releasing his engorged, throbbing member from its confinement.

"Looks like someone has a rather big problem," Yuki said playfully, assessing her new toy. She came back around and leaned down in front of him. "Would you like me to do something about this?"

Devon kept his eyes closed, his lips forming the word *control* over and over again. As much as he wanted to turn away from her, he couldn't. His mind was reeling as a burning need for release washed over him, drowning out his sense of helplessness.

"Devon, look at me," Yuki said softly. He slowly opened his eyes. She was kneeling before him with eyes as cold as a lioness.

"Don't forget who's in charge here. I can make this pleasant for both of us or as painful as hell. Believe me—it's all up to you."

He held his breath, wishing her dead.

"I'm waiting, puppy. Do you want this to be over or not?"

The chains were chafing his wrists. He heard the giant in the next room talking softly to Tamayo in Japanese, perhaps controlling her in a similar fashion.

"Are you going to answer me?" Yuki growled. She picked up a black crop and was threatening to use it again. "If you think I can't break you, you're sorely mistaken."

"Yes," he whispered.

"What was that?"

"Yes, mistress," he rasped, his voice hoarse.

"Much better."

Devon looked up at the ceiling, studying the streams of light cast from the chandelier. He thought about Akira and the anger he had invoked in her. While he was lying on her bed half unconscious, she had promised to come back—promised to look after him. By now, she had to know he was in trouble. Surely she wouldn't believe he'd leave her room without saying a word.

Yuki ran her finger lightly down his swollen penis. She smiled, enjoying his first groans of frustration as her fingertips rested lightly on the sensitive end of his erection. It appeared that she was in no hurry, as she casually examined his cock and balls, using both hands. "Hmm, very nice indeed. So shall we get started?"

With what? His mind was racing, and his body was aching.

Yuki laughed as his rock-hard cock twitched under her touch. She grinned up at him impishly and deliberately slid her thumb lightly across the tip. "I'm afraid you're going to be like this for a long, long time." She ignored his agonized moans and calmly curled her slender fingers around his rigid organ and squeezed it gently.

"Please, " he begged. "Don't do this."

"Do what?" She held his cock firmly and moved her hand up and down slowly. "You mean this? You did give permission, you know." She continued with a steady, relentless rhythm, adding to his angst. "My goodness, just look how big you are. Akira is such a lucky girl, isn't she?"

When his excitement mounted to the point where his body was shaking, she paused and slid her thumb teasingly across the tip. All the while, her eyes gazed calmly into his. She repositioned herself between his legs and took one nut in each hand. After rolling each of them between her fingers and thumb, she giggled. "My God, these are full. You really must need to let go by now. I can't imagine what kind of a load this is going to be—if I allow you to finish."

If? Devon thought. His reaction was immediate. He began thrashing around, pulling furiously at the chains that held him, but to no avail. She was obviously enjoying the control that she had over him. Very slowly and sadistically she teased him nearly to the point of tears for the next fifteen minutes using various techniques, including a makeup brush on his legs and thighs, balls, and shaft. Then she stopped when he was right on the brink of orgasm and just held him there, never really letting him calm down but never quite giving him enough stimulation to ejaculate.

Every inch of his body was helplessly exposed to her torturous maneuvers. His penis was so stiff it looked like it might burst any moment. He watched her through glazed eyes as she stroked feathers over his genitals, leaving him cringing. "This feather duster is my new favorite," she explained to him. His cock was twitching at the air, and his balls were beginning to suffer from an all-too-familiar dull ache. She looked at his face and giggled. "No, you won't be coming just yet." The tickle of the feather was the last thing he expected as she slowly ran the soft bristles lightly around his glans. "Doesn't that feel good?" she mocked.

His body shook. There was no erasing his thoughts.

"Does it? Tell me, Devon. Does it feel good?"

"Yes...it does," he mumbled.

"Yes, what? Don't you remember my name? Or do I need to remind you again?"

"Mistress."

Devon wanted to cry out—curse her for all eternity. But then what else would she do? Cut off his balls and serve them to him?

"Hmm...I wonder if this will do the trick." She resumed her assault with the feathers, swirling them round and round.

Devon realized the only way to end this was to tell her what she wanted to hear. "Yes. Please, please make me come," he begged. "I want to show you how happy you've made me." However, he was wrong on that account. While the feathers brought him maddeningly close to orgasm, there was not enough friction to put him over the edge. He was literally delirious at this point. As Yuki mocked his predicament, it seemed that hearing him beg only spurred her on to teasing and punishing him more.

She looked at her watch again and smiled. "Ah...it's almost time. I want this to be perfect. A wonderful, beautiful surprise."

Devon moaned, longing for it all to end. What was she hoping to accomplish by this? Ruin him for women? Or only Akira? The answer was suddenly clear.

"Do you know what they say in the book *Joy of Sex*?" she asked. "Dr. Comfort claims that a man can't stand more than ten minutes of slow masturbation, but I think it's more like thirty-five minutes. Don't you agree?"

He tried to focus on something else: scuba diving, race-car driving, parachuting. Anything other than Yuki's hands. But it was virtually impossible. She wouldn't stop touching him—wouldn't stop testing the level of his endurance. Then all of a sudden, she stopped all the stimulation. She left the room and waited for his erection to subside.

After a short while, she returned and used some ice water on a washcloth to reduce his swollen penis to its normal size. She immediately placed the chastity device back onto his now sore penis and told him that maybe another day he would get to come—or maybe never. Especially after Akira got wind of this.

"Just think about it," she said. "How can she love you knowing that you begged me over and over again to make you come? What kind of boyfriend does that?"

Devon remained silent, his head and eyes down toward the floor. Yuki was right. She had found his weakness and used it against him in the cruelest way possible. Akira would never understand. Would she?

"Now, behave yourself, my sweet puppy," Yuki said. "I will be back for you soon enough. I just need to make a few last-minute preparations before our special guest arrives."

Goddamn! Devon jerked at his chains. The thought of Akira rushing to her doom because of him was eating him up. After everything he'd been through, he couldn't imagine what kind of torture Yuki had planned for her.

"Akira." His heart ached from his inability to warn her—to keep her from harm. He leaned over and dropped onto his side. Then he closed his eyes and thought of all the ways he would kill Yuki…if given the chance.

35

THE PERFECT SHOT

The watcher stood in the hallway outside the Presidential Suite, puzzling over the cruise director's strange behavior. It had been rumored that a Chinese princess was residing at this address, although no one had seen her in days. One of his ears was pressed tight against the door like the pervert the watcher had taken him for, and a lewd smile was plastered on his face. It seemed he was enjoying every second eavesdropping on the room's inhabitants and had no qualms about being seen by any of the tourists in the neighboring suites.

This piece of shit loved the finer things in life and was not above lying, cheating, or stealing to get what he wanted. It was a known fact that he would threaten to have maids fired if they rejected his advances. One of the bartenders left expensive liquor in his room on a daily basis to avoid negative comments and write-ups and the possibility of dismissal. Even the jewelry shop clerk catered to his wishes, giving him huge discounts on anything he desired.

As he listened more intently, Donley sipped his wine, freezing only for a moment when he heard someone speak. It was a quick pause though, as he lifted his glass and continued drinking, amused by whatever was transpiring inside. A loud noise escaped the confines of the room—a smack and then a man's yelp. Donley palmed his cock, his excitement steadily growing. There was an explosion of activity: a woman's laugh and the sound of flesh smacking flesh. Donley took a deep breath and moved his hand from his groin to his thigh. He squeezed it hard, waiting for any hint of the sexual perversion that was apparently taking place inside.

The watcher reached into the deep, right-hand pocket of the uniform required for employment and withdrew the dart gun reserved for the right occasion, which seemed to have arrived. With one pull on the trigger, the tiny poison dart flew through the air, striking the imbecile on his left shoulder and serving up rightful justice.

Donley reached his hand around the back of his neck but found nothing. He looked down at his hand and shrugged, perhaps assuming he'd been bitten by a mosquito or any number of flying insects. His lack of discovery warmed the watcher's heart and set the timer in motion.

Everyone would immediately assume Donley had overexerted himself from the extra duties he had taken on to warrant his large salary. In addition, the women who had suffered at his hands and male crew members who had experienced his verbal abuse would be openly celebrating in the staff bar tomorrow. It was all just too much to hope for—the party of a lifetime and the death of a rodent no one would miss.

Within seconds, Donley grabbed his heart and rushed to the elevator, desperate for help. He stepped inside and fell back against the rear wall, staring out at the watcher's smiling face. He was sweating profusely and looking extremely anxious—like a two-legged dog. As the door was about to close, he reached out before collapsing on the floor. Unfortunately, his outstretched arm and hand had become an unexpected obstacle. The new elevators had been equipped with motion detectors and an unseen mechanism preventing operation should anything cover the threshold or obstruct the steel doorway. Both eliminated harmful injuries and had been a welcome safeguard for the last three months, but tonight they were proving to be a problem.

The watcher glanced up to confirm the security camera had been turned slightly to the right, recording the view at the end of the hallway. Before edging closer, a look down confirmed Donley's mouth was slightly open. Apparently he was still struggling to say a few words or maybe preparing to release a high-pitched scream with the hope that some sympathetic person would hear. Yet even if they had, there would be no saving this vermin, since the fast-acting poison had no antidote to serve as a cure.

Ah yes. Poor, unfortunate Michael Donley. Although the watcher preferred the benefits of self-inflicted wounds and pharmaceutical overkill, Donley's list of depraved acts had tipped the scale of justice to an all-time low. After a swift kick, his limb and moneygrubbing hand were returned to the inside of the elevator where they belonged, allowing the door to close properly and the watcher to get back to more important matters.

36

COMPLICATIONS

After studying the diagrammed map of each floor on the ship, Akira realized the enormity of her task. With over two thousand five hundred rooms spanning twelve decks, the *Starfish* was a miniature city in itself. These included not only passenger rooms but also crew member quarters, offices, and storage facilities. Finding Yuki would be virtually impossible. Up until now, she hadn't been seen by anyone other than Takashi—and possibly the captain. She was a master of illusion and could be hiding anywhere.

Then something came to mind.

Akira remembered Devon mentioning a Chinese princess vacationing on the ship with her full-time bodyguard. It was on the night they had first met in the Aquarian restaurant—a night filled with stolen looks and hopeful anticipation. She had been so taken with Devon's wit, good looks, and charm that she had dismissed the reference as idle chatter. Now she realized the foolishness of her oversight in not confirming the presence of a real princess.

During their shore excursions, there were plenty of opportunities for the mysterious woman and her trusted companion to venture out and explore the ship—opportunities when only the remaining crew members would see them. If Yuki had, indeed, stumbled onto the idea of killing the princess and assuming her identity, she was more conniving and clever than Akira had given her credit for being.

With the suite now to herself, Akira placed Keiko's black brooch into a small decorative box. Then she strapped her red katana sword to her shoulder, tucked a switchblade knife into her waistband, and pulled on the black raincoat she had found next door. It was a warm, balmy night, and a few brows lifted as she passed through the outside corridor on her way to the customer service desk. She suspected the two service clerks had seen strange things on this ship, and an unseasonal raincoat was hardly exceptional.

"Excuse me," Akira said, hoping to garner the attention of the short, curly-haired blonde. "I feel very silly asking this question, but I was supposed to drop off a package at the princess's room before we arrive in Florida. I don't remember the suite number and thought you might be able to help me."

"I'm afraid I can't give out that information," she said. "If you'd like to leave it with me, I'm sure I can have someone deliver it."

Akira feigned concern. "It's very special, and I wouldn't want it to get into the wrong hands. Are you sure you can't help me?"

The female clerk turned to the young man standing next to her. "Greg, she hosted a pirate party last week for the VIP club members. Can't we make an exception here?"

"No, I'm sorry," he said. "We have to abide by the rules. Princess Li Chen left specific instructions regarding her need for privacy. She asked not to be disturbed, unless it involved an urgent matter."

Akira looked down. "Oh dear. I know she'll be very disappointed. My employer was adamant about giving this to her."

A group of six people came into the room, followed by four more. They were all asking questions about their connecting flights and transfers, and Greg seemed extremely overwhelmed. He blew out a heavy sigh. "Let me try calling upstairs. If she's open to it, I'm sure the princess wouldn't mind you bringing it to her. I would myself, but as you can see, things are a little crazy right now." He offered a kind smile. "By the way, is the air-conditioning on too high? I've been complaining about it all day."

Akira smiled. "I was feeling a little chilled, but it's nothing to worry about." She waited as he verified the room number, holding the box in plain sight.

"Is it possible to tell me what's inside?" he asked.

"Just tell her it's a gift from the jewelry shop. A show of appreciation for her patronage. She'll know what it means."

"Are you sure?"

"Definitely. She's been supporting our business for years."

His attention shifted to the phone. "This is the customer service desk. I'm so sorry to disturb you, Your Majesty, but I have a gift from the jewelry shop that…umm…" He covered the phone with his hand and quietly asked, "What's your name?"

"Mira," Akira whispered. "From Headquarters."

Greg quirked a brow. "Mira from Headquarters would like to drop it off." He waited for an answer and followed up with, "She said it's to thank you for your patronage." He was quiet for a few more seconds, listening to her response. Then he added, "Thank you. I'll send her up right away." He set the phone down and pursed his lips. "She said she never expected to receive anything."

Akira smiled, unsure of how to answer.

Greg shrugged a shoulder. "I guess she'll be pleasantly surprised, won't she? It's the Presidential Suite: room 801."

"Thank you. And her bodyguard?"

"Oh, to tell you the truth, I don't know. But I assume he's nearby. You aren't planning to cause trouble, are you?"

The corners of her lips curled. "Do I look like a troublemaker to you?"

His forehead frowned, his eyes full of suspicion, and he kept looking at her without saying anything. Akira got the distinct impression that he was trying to find an ulterior motive in her request. Yet somehow she managed to smile.

He nodded, and she turned to leave. But then he suddenly called her back. "Wait a minute." He took a business card and scribbled a note. "Give this card to the security officer and tell him I said it's OK." Then he returned to his impatient customers, becoming instantly preoccupied.

Akira walked into the main foyer and spotted a uniformed officer standing next to the bank of elevators leading to the VIP areas and restricted floors. She was about to approach him when a familiar sound froze her in her tracks.

"Akira!" It was Paul Lyons, moving almost as fast as he spoke. "I've been trying to track down Devon for two hours but haven't had any luck." With a frustrated sigh, Akira turned toward him. "I thought maybe you'd have some ideas where to look."

Akira had hoped to sneak out unnoticed. All she needed was a few seconds to escape. But no such luck. "No, I'm sorry. I haven't seen him."

"I guess I misunderstood. For some reason, I thought he went looking for you and your father." His smile twisted. "Anyway, I wanted to let him know there was an accident on the sixth floor. An electrician was injured, and now one of the elevators is out of order."

Akira was stunned for a moment. "Really? I hadn't heard that." It seemed all rumors about Takashi's death had been buried in record time. The captain was better at hiding bodies than she was.

Paul touched her arm, pulling her mind back. "Well, have a good night now."

"Oh...right. You too."

Akira's hand was on the elevator call button when a voice behind him said, "And where are you off to at this time of night?" It was Sara, as obstinate as ever.

"For a walk." Cursing under her breath, Akira turned to see Devon's aunt standing next to the spa. She looked formidable in her white, tightly wrapped robe.

Sara snorted. "It's after eleven, and you're going for a walk?"

Akira nodded. "Pretty much."

"Well, I don't believe you. You're sneaking around. You don't sneak around to go for a walk." Sara's eyes widened. "Are you going to meet someone? You are, aren't you? Someone other than Devon," she said when Akira didn't immediately deny it. "Is it Captain Brice?"

"No, Sara," Akira said, desperate to prevent that train of thought. "Seriously, I can't sleep, so I'm going for a walk. OK?"

Sara looked doubtful, but she shrugged anyway. "Fine. Whatever. Just try to be back from your booty call before morning. I'm not covering for you with Devon." With that, she left. Paul threw his hands up in exasperation. Then he stood by, watching Akira as she passed the security guard the clerk's business card. She rang the call button, stepped through the open the elevator, and dismissed his presence as the doors closed.

Within seconds, she was transported to the eighth floor. Despite her best-laid plans, she didn't know what to expect after exiting the elevator and coming face-to-face with Yuki. Lost in thought, she wandered aimlessly, paying very little mind to where she was going. After passing six doors, she arrived in front of the Presidential Suite—a luxurious apartment reserved for diplomats and the wealthy elite. She was about to ring the doorbell when she spotted Bradley leaving a nearby room. He was the butler who had been looking after her suite, making all the arrangements for her excursions and meals, and not someone she would've expected to see at this hour—or on this floor.

"Good evening, Miss Hamada," he said. "Did you get turned around again?"

She had to think fast. "Actually, I was hoping to deliver a gift."

"To room 801? That's Princess Chen's room. Do you know her?"

"My boss knows her very well and was adamant about giving it to her tonight."

"Really? Well, I would assist you myself, but she left strict instructions not to be disturbed. Maybe you could leave it with her bodyguard instead?"

"Her bodyguard?"

"Yes. He's staying right down the hallway in room 806."

"Oh, of course. Thank you, Bradley." She smiled and waited until he turned the corner. Then she resolutely marched through the corridor to the last door on the right and rang the bell. She waited a few seconds, then rang again. Just as she was starting to believe no one would answer, a man's disgruntled voice emanated from the speaker beside the door.

"Who is stupid enough to wake me up at this hour?" he said. "What could you possibly want that couldn't wait until morning?"

Akira swallowed hard, struggling to maintain her brief spout of courage. "Um, hi. Uh, this is Mira. From...from the party?"

"I've been known to throw a few parties. To which are you referring?" The deep voice had a slight edge to it, as if the man inside were losing what little patience he had.

"It was about five days ago. The party everyone was raving about." Akira hadn't perfected the act of lying and most likely never would. But any information this guy might have in regard to Yuki could prove useful.

"Oh yeah," the voice replied, sounding slightly more awake but still cautious. "The one they had at the other end of the hallway—on the day we arrived. And which one are you? Not the mouthy bimbo with the big tits? Because if so..."

"No, no." Akira cut him off. "Not that girl. The other one. With the dark brown eyes."

"Ah." He sounded positively delighted as he purred, "Well, come in then. I have some leftovers in the dining room. We might as well make good use of them." From the sound of his voice, Akira ascertained that he was Asian. But his identity was disguised by his ability to speak English—almost as proficiently as Takashi had.

There was a buzz as the door unlocked. Akira reached out to the doorknob and froze, her hand hovering over the handle. What was she doing here? What was she thinking? Did she really want to go inside? What would happen if she did? She lifted the edge of her collar, confirming her sword was within reach. Then with the last of her courage, she wrapped her hand around the doorknob, opened the door, and began walking toward the living room. The door shut behind her.

Akira stepped forward, arriving in the center of the room. She was surprised to see how large and empty it appeared without suitcases, Japanese newspapers, and an inquisitive roommate filling the space. The suite was steeped in luxury with European furniture, dangling crystal chandeliers, a china cabinet, and a fully stocked bar. Still sitting on a nearby table was a half-empty bottle of Yamazaki Whisky, making Akira's lip curl up slightly in a smirk. She couldn't help wondering if Mitsui-san had been informed that his daughter-in-law was enjoying a life of equal extravagance.

"Hello, Akira."

She spun, her hand reaching reflexively for the handle of her weapon. Standing a little ways away, as tall and bulky as she remembered him, was Cujo, a Zakura-kai freelancer, confirming Yuki's presence on the ship. After watching a late-night thriller, her psychotic handler had given this guy the nasty nickname because of his immense size and unpredictability. It was a known fact that he had bitten off a man's ear for insulting him and had a penchant for howling like a wolf after every judo match he won.

She noticed he was barefoot and had on silk pajama bottoms, golden brown in color. The same color as his open bathrobe. Although he was in his early forties, his Samoan heritage had provided him with a youthful appearance and, unfortunately, equal vitality.

During the one and only occasion when she had met him, Cujo was wearing jeans and a white dress shirt. However, tonight he was proudly displaying his previously hidden patchwork of tribal designs on his torso, neck, and arms. Akira's vision moved upward and landed on his hair. She was surprised to see that his head wasn't topped by his black gelled spikes; instead, his hair hung loose and clean, topping his shoulders.

He shifted his body, and his dark almond eyes flashed in amusement at Akira's involuntary movement. "Jumpy tonight, aren't we?" He crossed his arms over his broad chest and leaned back against the wall. Despite his lack of couth and sophistication, he still managed to remain memorable. Perhaps it was the fact that he pulverized four men on Yuki's behalf following a strained business meeting simply because they had annoyed her. Or maybe it was his ability to emanate a presence that made her feel exposed, as if he were capable of seeing right through her.

"I hope you didn't bring a weapon with you," he said. "Not unless you intend to use it." He gestured toward the kitchen table a few feet away. "Do you mind? I like to think of this place as a sword-free zone."

Akira's gut instinct told her to hold on to her katana—not to surrender it at any cost. But at the moment, Cujo wasn't posing a threat, and his cavalier attitude made her feel surprisingly welcome. With slight hesitation, she pulled out her sword and laid it gingerly on the table, making sure the handle was within easy reach.

"There are only two reasons why you would be here," Cujo told her.

Akira relaxed her stance but kept her sword within eyeshot. "And what would those be?" She was surprised at how calm her voice sounded, in spite of her racing heart.

"You are either here to ask me for a favor," he said, leaning forward slightly, "or to ask for my assistance. Either way, they're the same to me." A smile played on his lips.

"No favors," Akira said, drawing on her courage.

"Oh, really?" Cujo slumped, visibly disappointed. "Then why are you here, Mariko?" Annoyance was evident in his voice.

She was amazed that he had remembered her real name, but then realized she'd been the source of Yuki's displeasure for some time now. "I'm looking for your employer, and since you're here, I can only assume she is too."

His lips twisted into an ugly smile. "After going on a killing spree, you would think she'd be all tuckered out. But not dear, sweet Yuki. How many is she up to now? Six? Counting Bradshaw and Keiko, of course. And then there was that little Chinese chick staying in her room and the guy who was taking up oxygen here. A real shame when you think about it. But as I'm sure you're aware, Yuki's never been into sharing."

Akira's patience was spent. "Where is she, Cujo?"

"To tell you the truth, I don't think she wants to be interrupted right now. You'll just have to wait until she's done with your boyfriend. Fifteen more minutes, and he's all yours. Whatever's left of him anyway."

Akira was too stunned to comprehend his words. "What did you say?"

"Devon Lyons is at the other end of the hallway. I'm sure he's having the time of his life. While it lasts."

Akira was fuming. Her hatred had never been so intense. She swung her fist at Cujo, knocking him in the jaw. Caught off guard, he stumbled backward, and she hit again, this time in the temple. He blinked for a moment as she flailed her arms around in a wild attempt to slug him, but he just laughed and side kicked her, sending her crashing to the floor.

"Yuki said you would be difficult," he said, yanking her up by her arm, only to throw her to the floor again. "I promised her that I was more than up for the challenge. The problem is you're not even providing one."

Akira stumbled to her feet, hoping the look she gave him was as sharp as she thought. "I think Yuki might have overestimated you." She threw an elbow in his direction, but he jumped out of the way. He swung a wild punch at her, but she ducked quickly and aimed a kick at his shin. He took a step back, calculating her moves.

Akira pulled the knife from her waistband and hid it in the palm of her hand. She took a quick breath, and before she knew it, he had her arms behind her back and a steak knife pressed against her throat.

"I'm really disappointed in you," he said. "I was expecting you to be tougher than this. Fighting gets old after a while. Especially if no one bothers to put up a fight."

He hadn't noticed the knife that was hidden in her fist the whole time. However, her arms were almost completely trapped between his body and hers. All she needed was to just...get...a little more...space.

"Trying to escape now? I'm afraid it's too late, Akira. Even if you could get away, there's no one here to help you. Not anymore." He stuck out his smug jaw and smiled. "No one on this ship gives a damn who you are or who you're destined to become."

She managed to turn her fist inward and brought it forward in a quick jab. Cujo yelped as her knife sliced his gut. His wound wasn't as deep as she had hoped, but blood was streaming down his front, covering his pajama bottoms and allowing her valuable time to get away.

While he was bent over holding his stomach, she shoved him as hard as she could into the wall. Then she grabbed her sword from the kitchen table and held it before her.

She backed onto the balcony, and he pushed himself up from the floor. She stepped onto the springy chaise lounge that was pushed tight against the railing. Then she prepared for his angry approach. "All right, you son of a bitch," she said, "bring it on!"

Cujo came at her in a stumbling run, the knife held before him like a wand. He leaped onto the lounge, and she dropped beneath him, spearing his thigh with her sword. He tumbled over the railing, slamming his head on the deck of level four and then a lifeboat on three before his battered body reached the ocean. It happened so fast that he didn't have a chance to scream or an opportunity to warn Yuki that Akira was pissed and headed her way.

Without a backward glance, Akira charged through the open glass door and through the living room with her bloody katana in hand. She turned the door handle and stepped into the hallway, thankful that no one was present. Then she dropped to her knees, still shaking.

Room 801 was waiting at the opposite end of the hallway, daring her to enter.

Akira reached into the raincoat's right-hand pocket and pulled her hand out—empty. She tried the left pocket, and it was empty as well. *Oh my God!* She had dropped the master key card in Cujo's suite. It was her only way to access Yuki's room without being detected. In a panic, she looked back at the door to 801, half expecting it to be shut, just as it had been when she'd arrived. But surprisingly, it remained slightly ajar, as if someone were holding it open, urging her to rescue Devon and destroy Yuki while there was still time.

37

THE CHALLENGE

After securing Devon's wrists and ankles to the bed, Yuki removed the metal jockstrap and stood before him in her red, lacy underwear, provocatively licking her lips. By all appearances, it seemed she now had something else in mind—something more sinister and depraved.

"My goodness, would you look at that?" she said. "Still standing at attention after all this time. It would be a shame to let that go to waste." With the knife in her hand once more, she climbed onto the bed and straddled his waist. She started grinding her hips into him until she was satisfied with the wetness between her legs. Then she pushed her silky underwear aside and sank down onto his cock, moaning at how it made her feel. She clamped her inner muscles tight and began moving up and down, driving him in and out of her in a forceful, steady rhythm. She gradually increased her speed until her breasts were bouncing along with her. "Ah, good...so good. Oh yes. Move with me, Devon. Come on...do it. Show me how much you want it. How much you need it."

Devon could feel himself losing control. She was making him crazy with her breathy words and constant moving. His reflexes took hold, and before he knew it, his body was bucking up against her again and again, desperate for release. He squeezed his eyes shut as his mind filled with thoughts of Akira and how he would never be able to face her again. Not after this.

Yuki braced her hands on his chest and continued her ardent stride. She pushed her body against him harder and faster, creating more friction. "Look at me, Devon," she demanded. "Don't come until I do. Understand?"

Devon was groaning with each thrust of her hips. He struggled with maintaining his self-control as she continued to pant and writhe, enjoying every inch of him. At one point, she was practically bouncing off the mattress and slamming back down onto him.

"Oh yes," Yuki moaned. "Oh yes, yes," she said again. "Oh, oh, oh, ahhh…" She closed her eyes and threw her head back. "Give it to me," she ordered and frantically rocked back and forth. "I want it, Devon. Come on…give it to me. All you've got. I want it now!"

Instinctively, he opened his eyes and was about to cut loose with the biggest load of his life when he spotted Yuki's knife in the air high above him. *Holy shit!* She was ready to plunge it into his heart the moment he came.

Then suddenly she stopped moving. The bed was still, and the only thing he could hear was her heavy breathing. He swallowed hard and leaned to his right to see around her. The tip of a katana sword was pressed into the middle of her back, and on the opposite end stood Akira, holding its long grip with two hands.

"Get the fuck off him!" she screamed. She used one hand to shove Yuki aside, slamming her into the nightstand and sending the knife flying. Then she tossed a gold pillow at Devon, landing it between his legs.

Yuki got back on her feet in seconds flat and made a move for the knife.

"Come on," Akira said. "Try it."

She stood in front of Devon, holding her sword in a protective stance, daring Yuki to move. While they both watched, Yuki turned and ran into the next room. She returned seconds later with a kodashi sword and sliced it through the air. "I wasn't expecting you for another ten minutes. What are you doing here?"

"I might ask you the same question."

"Look around. Isn't it obvious?"

Akira ignored her insinuation. "Cujo told me you've been rather busy."

"And I was close to finishing too," Yuki said with a devious smile.

Akira glanced at Devon. A look of relief crossed her face.

"Donley was supposed to announce your arrival. That idiot has terrible timing—in more ways than one."

Akira narrowed her eyes a fraction. "You killed Peter Bradshaw—an innocent man."

"We're all entitled to make mistakes. Don't you agree, Mariko?"

"Seems you've made more than your fair share. First Keiko, then Oka-san, and now Takashi." Akira shrugged a shoulder. "Why? Why did you do it? Was it all because of me? Because of Kenji's death?"

"Everyone keeps asking me that," Yuki said in a snarky, sarcastic tone. She looked down at the weapon in her hand and quirked a smile. "Let's just say it was...necessary."

"Really?" Akira snorted a short laugh. "Is that what you're telling yourself or just me?"

Anger fueled the heat in Yuki's eyes. "You said you never wanted to be a member of the Zakura-kai. That you would do anything—even kill Paul and Sara Lyons—if it meant your freedom."

Devon struggled to free himself until his eyes met Akira's and he realized Yuki was telling the truth. His body slumped, and his mouth sagged. The woman he loved was an assassin? A cold-blooded, manipulating murderer?

Akira mouthed the words "I can explain," but Devon didn't want to hear it. He didn't want any part of her. There was no difference between the bewitching pair. They were both cruel and heartless, filled with lies and deceit.

Yuki snarled. "The gold dragon belongs to the leader of the Zakura-kai. The one chosen to succeed Mitsui-san. Even if it's true and you are his bastard child like Keiko and Oka-san said, you haven't earned the right to rule. But I have, Mariko. Ten times over. It belongs to me, not you."

By the look on her face, Devon knew Akira was shaken. She lowered her voice and her sword halfway. "Mitsui-san is my father?"

"Get over it," Yuki snapped. "If you don't want me to kill your boyfriend, give me the dragon, and I'll let him walk."

Akira's eyes were blazing with hate. "After everything you've done, do you honestly think I'd ever trust you—that I'd give you anything?"

"Ahh!" Yuki yelled, thrusting her weapon at Akira. She dodged the attack and swung her sword hard. But Yuki ducked even faster, hitting Akira in the back with her elbow.

"Bring it on, geisha. I can do this all day."

Akira pushed herself up and stood on the foot of the bed. "You'll never control the Zakura-kai. Not ever."

"I hate you!" Yuki swung her sword at Akira's ankles, and she jumped in the nick of time, bounding off the bed. Yuki charged after her again with her single-edged blade raised high in the air. Akira spun around, landing a roundhouse kick to Yuki's chest. She flew across the room, slamming into a chair and knocking it over.

Akira placed her hand on her left arm and pulled it away. It was covered with blood. She'd been hit without even knowing it. "You're crazy!" Akira yelled.

Yuki pushed herself up from the ground. "At least I got to fuck your boyfriend before killing him." She leveled her weapon and came at him, defenseless on the bed.

With Yuki's back turned, Akira sprang at her, swinging her katana hard. It sliced through Yuki's shoulder, spinning her around. "Get away from him!" she yelled.

Yuki was bleeding hard from her shoulder, but still she managed to slice the air wildly with her sword. Akira danced about, dodging her attacks like a boxing pro. But her heavy breaths were a sign that her physical stamina was waning.

"Getting tired, geisha?" Yuki taunted.

"Not at all. I'm just warming up." Akira surged forward, and Yuki seemed strangely amused as their swords clashed before them. Akira swung wide, and Yuki ducked out of the way, coming up behind her.

"We'll see about that," Yuki challenged her. She swept her blade in a wide circle, and Akira backflipped out of the way, amazing Devon. Then she brought her sword down over Yuki's head, but Yuki blocked it with her blade. She kicked Akira in the stomach, knocking the wind out of her. But Akira recovered quickly and surged forward again, delivering a kick to Yuki's face.

Yuki stood motionless for a few seconds. She used her sword to hold herself up as she wiped traces of blood from her lips. Then she lunged at Akira again, knocking the sword out of her hand. She stepped closer, snarling, and pressed the tip of her blade against Akira's throat. "You lose."

Devon stared wide-eyed. He wanted to hate Akira, but he loved her with immense passion and feared she might be killed. "Yuki! No!" he screamed.

Something whizzed through the air and struck Yuki in the forehead, sending blood spraying across the wall behind her. Her body crumpled to the ground, like a puppet without strings. Someone had killed her with one shot. But who?

"Tamayo!" Akira yelled. "What are you doing here?"

The young girl stood in the open doorway with a gun in her hand. "I'm sorry I couldn't help you sooner, Devon-san. The drugs were so strong. I couldn't fight them off—no matter how much I wanted to."

"Oh shit," he said, breathing a sigh of relief. "I just thank God you were here."

38

THE AGREEMENT

Devon walked into the living room wrapped in one of the white robes from the closet. Based on the sad look in Akira's eyes, it was easy to assume she saw disappointment written on his face. She lowered her chin and stared down at the floor, perhaps knowing any explanation would be played off as another attempt to deceive him.

Meanwhile, Tamayo sat on the edge of the sofa with her head in her hands, traumatized from the shooting. The notion that she was responsible for Yuki's death overwhelmed her, leaving her sobbing uncontrollably.

Akira checked the cut on her left arm to make sure the bleeding had stopped before sitting down next to her. She put her other arm around Tamayo's shoulder, drawing her close. "Calm down, *Imouto*," she said. "It's going to be OK."

The young geisha swallowed hard, her bottom lip trembling. She bit it to stop it. "How can you say that? I'm going to spend the rest of my life in prison."

Akira handed her a tissue. "No, you won't. I'll make sure of it."

"But how? Someone's bound to find out what happened here."

"You're right," Devon told Tamayo, the tone in his voice an octave lower. "The worst is yet to come. I'm sure the neighbors are on to us. Probably already called security."

Akira rose from her seat and walked toward the window. "The gun had a silencer, and this ship is filled with old folks. It's after midnight, and no one's going to be awake at this hour."

Devon looked down, shaking his head. "You've got it all figured out, don't you? What the fuck do I know about anything?" His comment was rude, and it was pointless to attack her, but he was unable to stop himself. "So is it true? What Yuki said? You kill men for a living?"

Akira looked away, debating how to answer. "It's not what you think," she finally said. "In my world, it's kill or be killed. It's a matter of survival, not a livelihood."

Pain filled him. "I would never have pegged you for a murderer."

He watched her expression change from hurt and sorrow to growing anger. "You haven't got a clue, Devon," she spat out. "I would have chosen any life other than the one I have. I envy your naïveté. Your belief in the possibility of love. I know you don't understand any of this or who I am, but I was like you at one time. I only wanted to see the best in people. To believe this world was filled with hope and kindness." Her bitterness was apparent. "I thought compassion came with understanding— with seeing inside a person's heart and knowing their true mind. But I was wrong. Nothing in this world is what it seems."

Devon could feel her watching him. "Why did you come here, Akira?"

"I came here to find the person who killed Keiko Mitsui, and I did. It was my only way out—the only way to protect the woman who had been a mother to me most of my life. But now she's gone—murdered by Yuki—and my obligations are over."

Devon was quiet. His emotions vacillated among regret, unbearable anger, frustration, and heartache. He was desperate for hope, but his faith was fading fast. He wanted to believe that everything about him and Akira was real—the love, the passion, the future. But at the same time, accepting that it was all true was pure madness.

He stepped up behind her and asked, "Was I part of your scheme?"

Akira turned just enough to let him see her eyes close and her shoulders slightly hunch, as if she were fighting off the effort to break down and sob. After a long, heavy moment, her lips parted as if to defend herself. But then she simply closed her mouth.

He wasn't about to back down. Not now. "Did you use me to find out what you needed to know?"

"At first...I did," she admitted. Her voice wavered as she failed to suppress a tear, allowing it to slide down her cheek. "I didn't know you...or how I would feel after spending time together. Although it matters little now, I honestly care about you, Devon. I'm not saying it to lessen the hurt I've caused. It just happens to be the truth." She shifted a little and lifted her gaze to him fully. "If you're willing to help me, we can get out of here fast. Then you won't have to see me again. Not ever."

Devon watched her face, silently testing his endurance. Then he shrugged a shoulder. "All right," he finally said. "What do you want me to do?"

39

CLOSURE

Now was the hard part. Akira looked down at Yuki on the floor, and a wave of anxiety washed over her. It had been a long time since the sight of a dead body unsettled her, but familiarity was hard to ignore.

When she began working for the Zakura-kai, she had a horrible nightmare. A ghostly gangster appeared in the night and stood next to her bed. He glared down at her with such an intensity that it frightened her. "Why are you here?" he demanded to know. "What's your purpose for living?" She was struggling for an answer when he disintegrated into ash before her eyes.

In an odd way, Akira had found comfort in his presence. She came to believe that the dead didn't need anything from this earthly life. They certainly didn't need their broken bodies and sick, diseased minds. The afterlife was only a story men told themselves to stave off mortality and erase their sins.

"Akira?" Devon was at her side, looking more confused than ever.

"I'll be right back," she told him. After using the bathroom faucet to clean the splatter blood off her face and arms, she scrubbed down the sink to make sure all the blood had gone down the drain. She took off her black shirt and cleaned it too, squeezing out the pink water before laying it aside. Then she noticed a red ornate chopstick lying next to the sink—the one Yuki had made a habit of wearing. It was elegant looking but cheaply made—as deceptive as the woman herself. This was the perfect token to pass on to Mitsui-san. To add to his twisted collection.

Akira tucked it into her pocket and came back into the room. Then she assessed Yuki's body, crumpled on the floor. Her stomach churned. She didn't want to touch Yuki—didn't want to go anywhere near her. But she had to make some kind of move. She couldn't hang out here until someone came looking for the real princess. The one Yuki and Cujo had murdered. The woman's elegant clothes, fine jewelry, and cosmetics were still scattered about, representing her level of wealth and lack of assistance.

After opening the closet, Akira noticed an open black suitcase overflowing with tight pants, sheer tops, and lace thongs: the kind Yuki was known to wear. Apparently she had been living out of her bag, which made disposing of her far easier. Black corsets, strange metal implements, and leather gear were also piled in the corner, reminding Akira about Yuki's interest in sadomasochism and the cruelty Devon must have endured, all for Yuki's personal pleasure.

Akira pushed the thought aside and told Tamayo to pack all of Yuki's belongings—anything that would tie her to this place. Then her gaze shifted to Yuki's body and the blood surrounding it.

Devon stepped forward to offer his assistance, but she could feel his disapproval in the air. "What do you want me to do?"

"Can you grab the top bedsheet from the mattress?"

While he tore the bed apart, Akira wrapped Yuki's head in one of the pillowcases to try to contain the worst of the bleeding. Then with his help, they rolled her body over, covering it in the sheet. After wiping off the wood-paneled wall and cleaning the tile floor with bath towels, she bundled up the mess and stuffed it into the black garbage bag she'd found in the bar. There was bleach in the bathroom closet and a sponge under the counter. The carpet proved to be the hardest, but after a few minutes, she had managed to make it look reasonable.

Akira glanced down at Yuki's concealed body and breathed a sigh of relief. Surprisingly, the bedding was absorbent, and the floor was still clean. Yet she remained wary, looking around for anything they might have missed.

Devon left the room for a few seconds and returned with a vacuum from the supply closet. Akira nodded her thanks but remained silent, grateful that the suite was so well equipped.

"I figured we might as well do it all," he said. After using the vacuum to suck up every hair and skin cell the four of them might have left behind, Devon turned back to Akira. "Now what?"

"It's time to make Yuki disappear." It was almost as important as making herself disappear. After putting her damp shirt back on, Akira pulled another trash bag from the box. It was the last one, which seemed fitting. She called Devon over, and they set to work, cramming Yuki's folded body into the bag and adding the chains she'd used on Devon as ballast. After tying the bag shut, Akira walked across the room and opened the sliding glass door. She took a quick look around and noticed an empty metal bracket high overhead, where a camera had been previously mounted. It seemed Yuki had removed it after arriving, perhaps to avoid being detected.

"It's still dark outside," Akira told them. "No one will see us."

Devon met her eyes with a curious gaze. "See us do what?" he asked.

"The same thing she was going to do to you."

He hesitated before grabbing one end of the bag. Then he followed after Akira, carrying Yuki outside and setting her down.

Tamayo waited next to the railing, looking dazed and confused. By all appearances, she was mentally hyperventilating—debating what to do next. "What about the clothes?" she asked. "All the skirts and fancy dresses? We don't have any more bags—"

"Leave them where they are—exactly like we found them."

"But why?"

"They don't belong to Yuki." Akira was losing her patience.

"Then whose are they?"

"The woman who was staying here. The Chinese princess she murdered."

"Oh, that's horrible. How could she do that?"

"If given the chance, she would have killed all of us!" Akira glimpsed Devon. His eyes were down, revealing nothing but saying so much. "Let's finish this and go back to our rooms," she said. "Everyone will be off this ship in seventeen hours. No one will know what happened here unless we tell them."

Devon nodded and picked up Yuki's suitcase. He hurled it high into the air, clearing the railings. Akira pitched the bag filled with the soiled linen next, and then they worked together, swinging Yuki's body and throwing it as far away from them as possible. Akira held her breath. Seconds passed, and still there was nothing—not the sound of a thud or even a remote splash. With the balcony of the Presidential Suite situated on the top floor, facing their wide, trailing wake, the only thing she witnessed on her final morning with Devon was the moon's shimmering light on the ocean and a million stars covering the sky.

Then something caught Akira's eye, far off in the distance. It was the black bag holding Yuki Ota's body, making a last appearance on the surface of the ocean before sinking into oblivion. But it wasn't over yet.

Akira slipped her sword off her shoulder and looked down at it. Two years ago, the red katana had belonged to Kenji Ota. It failed to save him from a surprise attack. It had been her defense against Yuki after his death, but today it failed to save her once again. If not for Tamayo, she would be long gone—just another casualty on this godforsaken ship. She needed to let go of the past. To be strong.

Akira took a deep breath. Her very existence stemmed from the power within the sword's blade—from the multitude of spirits trapped inside. It was time to free them all and step away from her heinous life. From the past she longed to erase. She held her arm back in the air and took another deep breath. Then she threw the katana sword as hard as she could, hurling it into the ocean and strengthening her resolve. Tamayo came to her side, shocked by what she had done.

The weight of the world fell off Akira's shoulders—at least that's how it felt. She looked down at Tamayo and smiled. "My life in Japan is over. But yours is just beginning. I want you to lead the Zakura-kai in a new direction. Turn Mitsui-san's company into a legitimate business. Before you leave this ship, I have something I want you to have. Something to prove your legal right to take over as Mitsui-san's niece. Can you do that? Can you be the person I know you're capable of being? The person I can trust to be forthright and kind?"

Tamayo swallowed hard. "Akira…"

"I know you can do this, little sister. You're more intelligent and far stronger than you believe."

Tamayo dropped to her knees and bowed her head to the floor. "I'll do it for you."

"No," Akira said, pulling her up by the hand. "For once in your life, do it for yourself."

40

RECONCILIATION

Akira started back to her suite and heard Devon rush up behind her.

"It feels so…unreal," he said. "How do you get over it: all the blood and the dead body?"

What could she say? She could tell him the truth—about how you eventually become immune, but his hostility made it impossible to listen. "Actually, you don't. You just think of it less—until it becomes a bad dream." She angled a look and recognized the disapproval on his face. "Don't you have somewhere you need to be?"

He followed her into her suite, slamming the door behind him. "How can you turn off your feelings so easily?"

Akira's chest tightened as she turned to face him. "How do you think I've survived this long?"

"Is it so easy to forget what we had?"

Akira lowered her eyes and gnawed on the corner of her lip. This was impossible. He would never understand, not ever. "I still love you," she whispered.

Devon's hands clenched, and he thrust the raincoat she'd been wearing at her. Then he stormed out of the room, leaving Akira alone.

Tears welled up in her eyes, and her entire body trembled. She looked down at her hands and saw blood on them. Not knowing what else to do, she took off her clothes and stepped into the shower. She turned on the hot water and stood under it. No matter how hard she scrubbed, the stain remained—the guilt threatening her sanity.

She pressed her back against the wall of the tub, brushing away her tears. Begging for her life to be over. A sound alerted her to someone in the room. But this time, there was no sword to protect her. She took a deep breath, then she pulled the edge of the curtain back to peer into the steamy room. Devon took shape, and she jerked the curtain shut. "Christ, Devon, you scared me!" she exclaimed, gasping for air.

Apparently he had gone to his room to grab clothes, as he was now wearing jeans and a white T-shirt. "I'm sorry," he said. "I assumed you heard me come in."

She could hear him walking around in the small bathroom, turning the sink faucet on and off. "What are you doing here?" she asked. She watched his dark silhouette through the white opaque curtain as he ran his hand through his hair and looked away, still obviously frustrated and angry.

"After Hamada-san died, I made a promise to myself that I would never leave you alone again."

"Oh…I see." Akira pursed her lips, unsure of how she felt about his need to protect her. "I appreciate your offer, but it's really not necessary." In many ways, she was more dangerous than Devon, but she had to admire his tenacity and unwavering loyalty.

She pulled back the curtain and reached for her towel. Although he had already seen her naked, she felt extremely uncomfortable with him watching her towel off and pull his oversize T-shirt over her head. She'd gotten so used to wearing it to bed that it became a habit to keep it on the door hook within easy reach.

He moved aside, and she stepped out of the bathroom to brush her hair and to hang her damp clothes over the bar near the door so they would hopefully dry quickly. She finished using the brush and set it down. Finally, she turned to Devon, who was sitting at the small table in the corner of the room. He was watching her carefully, his expression forbidding. Akira felt like a small child who had misbehaved, and she tugged at the hem of the shirt. She looked down, not knowing what to say to him.

"You should sleep," he told her, looking away from her and out the window. "I expect you won't be getting much rest on the flight to Japan tomorrow."

Akira shook her head and climbed into her bed. She drew the covers over most of her face like a scolded child would do. Despite being called an old soul by Oka-san, despite having accomplished more than the average twenty-five-year-old, despite everything she'd endured, she was younger than her years. She was also terrified. She was terrified of the berating she was sure to receive after texting Mitsui-san and rejecting his request to assume his position in the Zakura-kai. She was terrified to start over in a strange, new place, not knowing anyone or what kind of life she might lead. But more than anything, she was terrified at the thought of not seeing Devon smile again. To know after all they'd been through, he could never forgive her deceit or allow himself to trust her again.

"Hey." Devon had moved next to the bed, and by the sound of his voice, he had knelt next to her.

Akira rolled over timidly, the covers still hiding the majority of her face. He gently pulled the covers away from her face, and his expression softened. "Baby, you truly are beautiful and not the villain you think you are. I came here because I wasn't about to let someone walk out of my life believing I don't care. Because I do." He ran his fingers along her jawline, and she tentatively nuzzled into his touch.

"I'm sorry," she murmured, closing her eyes and relishing his touch as he cupped her face in his hand. "I was stupid not to tell you the truth. I got drawn in by the money and the chance to be free for the first time in my life. I'm an idiot for misleading you, and for that…I'm sorry." She took a deep breath and opened her eyes to meet Devon's. "I love you," she whispered. "But I'll understand if you can never forgive me."

"I forget sometimes," he said. "I forget that you're young and capable of making bad choices. A couple of years ago, I was an idiot too, but for very different reasons."

Devon pushed back the covers and slipped out of his shoes and into bed with her. He wrapped his arms around her and pulled her close to his chest. He kissed the top of her head as she snuggled in next to him. "I love you too," he said. "Even if we go to jail."

41

PARANOIA

Six months ago, Paul hadn't been quite sure what he was supposed to feel after his banished daughter referred to Sara as batshit crazy before making her escape to London. Or even more recently, when his nephew, Devon, had recommended confining Sara to a mental ward as soon as possible. In Paul's opinion, Sara was too brilliant for that—far too sensitive for the degrading experience.

Yes, Sara Lyons had been many things over the span of many years and had visited over fifty countries around the world. She had controlled every aspect of her husband's life and had raved that she knew all the answers to any question, any given situation—except the fate of her own delirium. Her accusations of incompetence by everyone she encountered and bullish, superior attitude were enough to make anyone a little paranoid and willing to go to great extremes to make her happy. Yet in all truth, Sara was a broken pipe. A fixture that no one could repair. The special circumstances she was living under with Bradshaw's unconventional treatments had brought about her eventual downfall. There was no denying that. But she had always been a force to be reckoned with—a thorny rose impossible to ignore but painful to hold.

However, Sara also had a creative mind that could be hampered by her confinement, and that would be terribly unjust and extremely unfair for the woman he had agreed to marry more than ten years ago. The same woman who had rescued him— only to turn his life into a living hell.

Paul had to admit that Sara had looked damn scared when the woman from housekeeping arrived after breakfast to offer her assistance. It made absolutely no sense at all why Sara had chosen that exact moment to attack poor Felicia, the thoughtful maid who had looked after them throughout their trip. The sweet woman had nothing but kind words to say about everyone. And yet Sara had subjected her to rude, hurtful insinuations, claiming Felicia was trying to poison them and reducing the poor soul to tears.

My God, no one in their right mind could have predicted Dr. Hoffman's heart attack and imminent death. Or foreseen that Vivian Ward would be found in bed with Captain Brice at the worst possible moment. Just because Felicia had offered to search for her didn't make her a villain in the strange turn of events. In all truth, it was the captain who was responsible for all the mishaps. He was the one the FBI director and his ten field officers had led away in handcuffs. They were the men who had stepped on board, claiming they'd never encountered such a travesty at sea—so many deaths and disturbing activities and not a single report. Not even a summons for the Coast Guard until Bradshaw's body was positively identified. And even then, Paul had done everything within his power to keep his wife calm. He had gone so far as to adjust the dosages on her prescription medications in an effort to maintain her even keel. But her verbal attack on the maid had been the last straw, leaving his conscience snarling.

As Paul glanced around, it dawned on him that the doctor's room on the ship was hardly remarkable; the walls were bleak and painfully resembled tofu squares stacked one upon another. While discussing her hysteria, Sara claimed that she had once been to a dimension made entirely of softness—specious softness. As Paul listened, he realized there wasn't any reason or rhyme to anything she was saying.

"I had the best nap in the cool abyss on the top of the world. It's like heaven," she said, smiling. "Have you ever been there? It's really quite remarkable."

Paul tuned back into the real world, catching up with the nervous faces surrounding him and a paper being pushed under his nose. An ambulance would be waiting with several attendants once he signed his name. Transferring her to a facility in England, closer to their home, would take a few days. It would all be arranged after careful evaluation and a thorough investigation into all the murders she might have committed. Many of them in England.

"Sara. Sara!" Paul choked out, his eyes blurred with tears. He tried to focus on her and was telling the doctor how smart and creative she had always been. "I think it's been coming for years. Dr. Bradshaw had been looking after her before his unfortunate accident. He mentioned long-term care to me a number of times, but I never thought she would confess to all those murders. I never believed she was capable of anything so horrendous. All those people...dying so horribly. Obviously her mind has snapped. She can't be a killer. It's all Bradshaw's fault for putting crazy ideas in her head."

She zoned out again, asking about their absent granddaughter and why she wasn't there. Paul stared at her, amazed at how she morphed into the shadow of her problems, drifting in and out of her psychotic phases. She was so many types of high-strung it was hard to keep track.

"Mr. Lyons..." The paper was no longer in front of his face, but the pen was in his hand. His shaking hand. Why was he shaking? He couldn't recall. His mind was positively hazy. He was unsure whether it was the tranquilizer he had taken at 3:30 a.m. or the bourbon in his coffee—or possibly that little seed from Planet A-3789 that made their feet grow and everything smell like cotton candy, according to Sara anyway. Maybe it wasn't just her mind that had snapped. Perhaps it was alcoholism too. Sara loved her champagne cocktails, wine spritzers, whiskey shots, and vodka sodas. However, so did a great number of Paul's friends—even his nephew, Devon. At least before he met Akira. But where was she now?

Then Paul remembered what Devon had said while he was still in a fog. Akira had been personally escorted off the ship by executives from her father's company shortly after arriving in Florida. The president of the ship line had agreed to pay for the cost of having Takashi's remains transported directly to Japan in a sealed casket. Even though it was going to cost a pretty penny and involve greasing a few palms, the president agreed it would be peanuts compared to a nasty lawsuit.

"Mr. Lyons..." Sara was about to be led away by the doctor, and Paul needed to resume his role as the crushed, doting husband everyone expected him to be.

"Sara...oh, Sara," he whimpered. He made a weak attempt at pulling on the cotton fabric of her blue sweater. Somehow she knew she couldn't turn back, despite his grasping hand and mournful expression. Even Felicia was there crying. *Crying?* The word warped in Paul's mind. Her face was blotched and red, and she was foolishly shaming herself for all of it. But for what? For enduring Sara's obstinacy? For attending to her endless list of needs and never pleasing her? For not seeing the madwoman she'd become? The housekeeper was downright pitiful; however, her good intentions were duly noted and would not be forgotten by Paul.

Meanwhile, Devon stood back, watching Sara. Paul hated seeing the disappointment on his face, but there was no avoiding it. He was a caring young man after all and never deserved to be thrust into all of this—even though he had behaved poorly years ago. In spite of all the confusion he must have felt, Devon had managed to muster some kernel of maturity and wisdom. He stood still, like the rest of them, while the nurse's strong hands clasped Sara's shoulders in the hallway outside the doctor's office and ship's pharmacy. With forceful insistence, she directed Sara toward an isolated room, where she would be collected in a matter of hours. Although a small group of passengers had huddled nearby, discussing her condition and the drama unfolding, Devon remained solemn and aloof—as if shaken by the whole experience and incapable of reacting.

Paul said nothing when Sara changed her mind and came charging after him with her arms outstretched, claiming everyone on the ship was out to get her.

"Why are you letting this happen, Paul?" she tearfully asked. "Don't you love me anymore?" Her vulnerability made her seem small and fragile—almost childlike—weakening his fortitude. But like a switch on a railroad track, she changed the direction of her thoughts, reminding him of the extent of her illness. "It's really funny when you come to think about it," she said. "It's the silver lining I never expected to find. The prize for surviving this god-awful journey—and living with you." Then her words were reduced to blubbering and confused outbursts as she was led away.

Paul drew a long, deep breath and turned to the doctor. "It will only be a couple of nights, right? She could use a quiet place to relax until her calm returns."

"Oh, I would expect it to be much longer than that, Mr. Lyons," he said. "You should prepare yourself for long-term care, just as Dr. Bradshaw had indicated." He removed his spectacles, frowning. "It might even be years before she's well enough to return home."

Members of the security team and several FBI officers were standing a short distance away. Paul could have sworn someone got pepper-sprayed when they demanded to leave the ship after being told they were on lockdown for forty-eight hours. As Paul soon learned, the officers were in the midst of interviewing the crew and about two hundred passengers when it was discovered that Princess Li Chen was also missing. Several VIP guests had seen the shy, raven-haired beauty and her attentive companion when they first arrived on the ship. But they had up and disappeared five days into the cruise.

An outspoken gentleman on the same floor where she'd been staying spoke up, claiming an exotic Asian madam and her enormous bodyguard had hijacked their rooms. "They threatened everyone, demanding our silence," he said. But the story was deemed preposterous by his fellow travelers, and it seemed no one on the ship was willing to listen to or believe him. Not even the police.

42

LATERS

The space above the watcher was a vast thing, stretching out for infinity above the gangway. Glorious, heavenly light shone through the wispy clouds, signifying a new day. They parted, presenting a beautiful sky beneath. It was mesmerizing, how simple it looked, yet it seemed to hold every thought, every dream, every secret. The immensity of it all was terrifying and yet affectionate, seeming like it could swallow you up whole, and at the same time could hold you and whisper words of comfort. Yes, it was amazing, almost magical, anticipating the changes about to take place. If you kept your eyes on the celestial sphere for long enough, watching the clouds come and go and the sun set in a magnificent flourish, you would think maybe it was talking to you in an esoteric language. But ignorant people would undoubtedly say, "It's only the sky."

"Are you sure you won't change your mind?" Felicia asked, playing the part of a caring friend. "I'd be more than happy to share a ride to the airport."

The watcher smiled and rested a hand on her shoulder, silently assuring her that everything would be fine. There was no reason for her to worry—not any longer. The monsters from the past had got their just rewards. They were being carried off one after the other in black, zipped-up bags, along with a few extra unscrupulous souls.

Life was filled with wonderful opportunities now—more than the watcher had ever believed possible. The flight to England would be especially nice with the right person holding a hand, talking about the future and all the ways to make up for lost time. The lighthearted conversation would touch on all kinds of exciting things, including renovations for a new bedroom in the imposing 17th-century mansion. The one the watcher had only seen from a distance and never had the privilege of entering. It was going to be incredible being pampered at Cumberforge Manor, like the woman who had resided there for the past thirty years. As promised, Sara Lyons would be locked away forever in a straightjacket for her part in all the injustice she had caused, and divorce paper would be rightfully drawn up.

The watcher waved back as Felicia's taxi pulled away from the curb and disappeared around a corner. It would be sad not to see her pretty face and hear her stories about her children and their children and all the vacations they had taken together. The kind housekeeper would be joining them soon and enjoying her retirement benefits, now that the ship was permanently docked. No one in their right mind would ever step foot on the *Starfish* again, not with all the ghosts milling about in corridors, haunting the daylights out of the living.

A black limousine suddenly pulled up, and the watcher settled inside, taking up the glass of champagne from the center console. It had been a long time coming but definitely worth waiting for: the sweet taste of revenge. Especially when it came in large doses.

The driver turned around in his seat and smiled, adding a new layer of comfort to the day. "Are you ready to go? The ride to the hotel shouldn't take more than fifteen minutes, accounting for traffic, of course. Is it cool enough in here for you, ma'am?"

The watcher nodded and sat back in the seat, taking another sip of champagne. "It's perfect," she said, "but ma'am makes me feel old. I prefer Allison...Allison Lyons." It was the name she would be using from now on. The sound of it would take some getting used to after spending so many years away from Paul. Their wedding next year would come as an unexpected surprise for the residents living in Bellwood and her grown children, Devon and Rachel. And most especially for their youngest daughter, Ginny Elizabeth, or Sloan as Sara had called her.

Shortly after her birth, Dr. Bradshaw had stolen Ginny from the hospital, leaving Allison with Sara's stillborn granddaughter. It would take some time to become reacquainted with her family members after being wrongfully locked away in a sanitarium for ten years. But she was looking forward to catching up with everyone and being involved in their lives.

"Just let me know if you want anything," the driver said, reminding Allison of his presence.

"Oh, I think I have everything I need." Allison smiled at the eyes in the mirror. Then she sat back and took another sip from her glass, watching frightened passengers depart from the ship as the car slowly drove away.

EPILOGUE

With a sigh of relief, Devon sat down and stretched his legs out as far as the seat in front of him would allow. He had been one of the first in line to get on the airplane destined for Albuquerque, and even though he still had to wait for everyone else to board, at least he could do it sitting down. And his seat was near the front, which meant he could leave faster too. He tried to arrange his large frame more comfortably, scowling at the suffocating space. With any luck, the seat beside him would remain empty, and he would be able to take advantage of the extra room.

Resting his elbows on the armrests, he idly watched the other passengers boarding. Most of them looked tired and confused, trying to grapple with their carry-on luggage and still fit down the aisle. As the seats around him began to fill up, Devon started to feel confined. But in spite of the inconvenience of limited space, he preferred the anonymity of traveling coach. He would be surrounded by people too wrapped up in their own problems to notice his sullen mood, and even if they did, their curiosity would be a passing interest and nothing more.

As time ticked by and more people shoved luggage up in the tiny compartments, the air grew stuffy and warm. Devon pulled off his light-blue jacket and laid it on the open seat next to him. Hoping that takeoff would be soon, he closed his eyes and tried to relax. He was tense, annoyed by the frantic airport and now this plane, and sleep would be the best and only way to escape his surroundings and thoughts of Akira until they landed. More than forty-eight hours ago, he watched her climb into a stretch limousine with Tamayo and four members of her yakuza family. They drove to the airport and flew back to Japan—back to the life she had left behind. In spite of everything—in spite of her leaving without so much as a goodbye, he still loved her. God forbid he would ever love another woman as crazy and amazing as Akira.

A blond flight attendant stood in the aisle checking her clipboard and looked up, smiling. "Excuse me, Mr. Lyons. I see that you're a gold medallion member. We'd like to thank you for choosing to fly with us. Can I bring you a complimentary drink after we take off?"

Devon almost laughed. "No, thanks," he said, forcing a smile. Not so long ago, he wouldn't have hesitated to ask for a double Jack on the rocks, especially when it was offered for free. But that wasn't the case anymore. If he got nothing else out of his time with Akira, at least he'd been cured of his heavy drinking and reminded of the value of life.

Miraculously, he managed to doze for a few minutes. Then the same flight attendant began talking through the speakers. "Preparations for takeoff are being completed. Please take the next few minutes to power down your computers and switch your cell phones to airplane mode."

Satisfied that the open seat had remained empty, Devon began to relax more and glanced out his small window, watching the ground crew tool around in their rolling carts with oversize headphones and bright orange vests.

The plane was noisy, filled with children crying and tired parents trying to hush them, but Devon's ears perked up as a gentle voice floated from the front of the plane. "I'm so sorry," the voice said. "The traffic getting here was horrible."

"That's quite all right," the flight attendant answered. "Happens all the time. Please find your way to your seat."

Devon rolled his eyes at the conversation and glanced toward the aisle. A woman with shoulder-length ebony hair was making her way down the aisle, clutching her boarding pass and eyeing the numbers printed above the seats. She was wearing a cream dress that clung to her shapely frame in an appealing way and had a tense expression fixed on her face. A pair of oversize sunglasses concealed her eyes, and her cheeks were pink, either from the heat or running to catch the flight—probably both. She was carrying a black bag in her hand and a rolled-up magazine under her arm, looking like a typical tourist. She came closer, and Devon realized that she was destined for the empty seat next to him. He watched her, feeling increasingly uneasy as she halted her steps and bent down.

"I believe you're in my seat, sir."

His heart nearly stopped. He told himself it couldn't be her. It just couldn't. "Huh? I'm sorry. What did you say?"

The attendant returned. "Is there a problem?"

Devon's shock wore off, and he gave the attendant a quick smile. "Not at all." He picked up his coat and stood, moving into the aisle seat. The woman slid past him into the window seat, and he sat down next to her.

"Thank you," she said, stowing her bag under the seat. She buckled her seat belt and turned to him. "I'm Mariko Mitsui.

And you are..." Their faces were a foot apart, and she was looking him in the eye, showing no signs of recognition.

Devon's mouth played with a smile. He was thrilled to have her here but wasn't sure what to say. Was he expected to play along? To pretend they'd never met?

He tried to speak but ended up too choked up to get things out as clearly as he would have liked. "I...I thought you were on your way home...that I'd never see you again."

She tucked her *Vogue* magazine into the seat pocket ahead of her and continued her stoic act. "Actually, a kind gentleman offered to show me the sights in his favorite city. I understand they have wonderful places to shop and interesting tourist stops in New Mexico."

Devon couldn't resist the urge to glance at her. Akira had rested her head back and was staring at the front of the plane, her hands folded neatly in her lap.

"So might I ask," he prodded, "what you do for a living?" He enjoyed watching the slow smile form on her lips.

She took off her sunglasses and turned toward him. "Actually, I'm retired. But I'm interested in trying new things."

"I see. Well, I hope you find what you're looking for."

"Oh, I believe I already have." She looked into his eyes. "They have great diving spots off the coast. I've been dying to try out my new gear. Do you have any suggestions?"

Devon stared at her, mystified by this new reveal. "You actually scuba dive? I had no idea. I thought you only snorkeled." His eyes drifted down to her mouth. He let his own twitch at the sight of her pretty pink lips, begging to be kissed.

Akira contemplated him quietly for a moment, and then she said, "There's a lot you don't know about me, Mr. Lyons. But I'm planning to change that." She reached for Devon's left hand and twined their fingers together.

"You don't say." He looked down at the pink ring she was wearing and smiled. Then he squeezed her hand ever so gently, and she laughed. It was such an intoxicating sound: that laugh. A reminder of what he had found and almost lost. Devon watched her face as the corners of her eyes crinkled a little, her cheeks blushed, and her whole face came alive. He decided then and there that he would spend the rest of his life making her smile and protecting her heart—the way she had protected his.

ABOUT THE AUTHOR

Kaylin McFarren has received more than forty national literary awards, in addition to a prestigious Golden Heart Award nomination for *Flaherty's Crossing*—a book she and her oldest daughter, Kristina McMorris, coauthored in 2008. Prior to embarking on her writing journey and developing the popular Threads action/adventure romance series, she poured her passion for creativity into her work as the director of a fine art gallery in the Pearl District in Portland, Oregon; she also served as a governor-appointed member of the Oregon Arts Commission. When she's not traveling around the world or spoiling her pups and three grandsons, she enjoys giving back to her community through participation in and support of various charitable and educational organizations in the Pacific Northwest and is currently the president of the Soulful Giving Foundation—a nonprofit focused on cancer research, care, and treatment at hospitals throughout Oregon.

For more information about McFarren, her writing process, and her books, be sure to visit her website at www.kaylinmcfarren. com.

Inspiration behind the Story

For many years, Kaylin McFarren has been privileged to experience remarkable things and rare opportunities while traveling the globe. This includes many forms of transportation, ranging from private planes, helicopters, and hot air balloons to kayaks, submarines, and elegant cruise ships. Her journeys have allowed her to meet interesting people, discover fascinating cultures, forge lifelong friendships, and introduce dear friends to all parts of the world. Personal experiences, extensive research, and interesting tales shared by business associates have contributed to making this character-driven story possible. It is not the intention of this author to discredit or damage the reputation of travel agencies or cruise lines with the writing of this fictional account, but only to entertain the public with its reading.

Other Books by Kaylin McFarren

Award-winning inspirational suspense novel:
Flaherty's Crossing

Award-winning psychological thrillers in the Threads series:
Severed Threads
Buried Threads
Banished Threads
Twisted Threads

Available at Amazon.com, Barnes & Noble, Kobo,
and independent bookstores

www.kaylinmcfarren.com

Proof

Made in the USA
Columbia, SC
09 November 2017